RAVES FOR
JAMES PATTERSON

"Patterson knows where our deepest fears are buried...There's no stopping his imagination." —*New York Times Book Review*

"James Patterson writes his thrillers as if he were building roller coasters." —Associated Press

"No one gets this big without natural storytelling talent—which is what James Patterson has, in spades." —Lee Child, #1 *New York Times* bestselling author of the Jack Reacher series

"James Patterson knows how to sell thrills and suspense in clear, unwavering prose." —*People*

"Patterson boils a scene down to a single, telling detail, the element that defines a character or moves a plot along. It's what fires off the movie projector in the reader's mind." —Michael Connelly

"James Patterson is the boss. End of." —Ian Rankin, *New York Times* bestselling author of the Inspector Rebus series

23½ Lies

THRILLERS

JAMES PATTERSON

with Maxine Paetro, Andrew Bourelle,
and Loren D. Estleman

GRAND
CENTRAL

NEW YORK   BOSTON

For a complete list of books, visit JamesPatterson.com.

23½ Lies

Grand Central Publishing
Hachette Book Group
1290 Avenue of the Americas, New York, NY 10104

grandcentralpublishing.comtwitter.com/grandcentralpub

First Edition: September 2023

Grand Central Publishing is a division of Hachette Book Group, Inc. The Grand Central Publishing name and logo are trademarks of Hachette Book Group, Inc.

The publisher is not responsible for websites (or their content) that are not owned by the publisher.

The Hachette Speakers Bureau provides a wide range of authors for speaking events. To find out more, go to hachettespeakersbureau.com or call (866) 376- 6591.

ISBN 9781538752685 (trade paperback) / 9781538757055 (large-print trade paperback) / 9781538752708 (ebook)

LCCN is available at the Library of Congress

Printed in the United States of America

LSC-H

Printing 1, 2023

CONTENTS

23½ LIES

A Women's Murder Club Story

James Patterson
and Maxine Paetro

CHAPTER 1

OVER THE LAST three months, the SFPD homicide squad had been swamped by nightmarish murders of all types. Robbery-homicides, murder-suicides, and a kidnapping where the victim was locked in a car trunk and the drugged-up abductor, the victim's nephew, turned himself in. But he had no idea where he'd parked the car. The car was found, but too late for Uncle Dave.

I punched out of work at six on Friday and drove home to my family. Mercifully, the horrible week had been overwritten by a weekend of eat, play, love, and sleep.

Now, it was Monday morning.

My closet was the most organized part of my life. I opened the doors, ran my eyes across the neat row of blue trousers, button-down shirts in white, beige, pink, and blue-striped and at the end of the rod, five blue gabardine blazers hung in dry cleaner's plastic bags. It was very satisfying to just grab and go.

I was dressing, listening to my husband, Joe, and our daughter, Julie, laughing in the large, open, loft-type room outside the bedroom door. I was also thinking of breakfast—a big bowl of granola, say, with strawberries—when I heard a loud crash followed by my daughter's shrill screams and the barking of our elderly dog, Martha.

What the hell?

I cleared our bedroom in a second and, once inside the main room, focused on the chaos in the kitchen. Julie Ann Molinari, our nearly five-year-old, had her hands to her cheeks, eyes to the floor, screaming, screaming, taking a breath and screaming some more. Joe was admonishing our border collie.

"No, Martha, *no*. Stop that. Now."

As Joe made a grab for Martha's collar, Julie wailed, "Noooo, noooo, nooooo! Mommeeee, hellpppp!"

I hurried into the eye of the storm, shouting, "What's happening, what?"

"Lindsay, don't come over here in your bare feet."

I braked and saw what had gone wrong. A glass globe that had held water, gravel, and two orange goldfish had somehow sailed from its place on the kitchen counter, dropped to the floor, and shattered. Mr. Bubbles and Fanny flopped among the shards and colored bits of fishbowl decor.

"They're going to be fine," I said to my daughter. "Don't worry, but we have to work fast. Joe, can you take Julie?"

"You bet. Lift your arms, Bug. Hang on to me."

There was a pitcher of distilled water near the sink that I used to top up the fishbowl. I picked up each of the flip-floppers by the tail, slipped them into the pitcher, and dropped in the aerator. Joe tossed a towel onto the floor and said, "Good job, Blondie. I'll take it from here."

He handed off our red-faced kiddo and I carried Julie to the couch in the living room. She was still crying as I checked her toes and soles, then mine, and then Martha's paws. There were no injuries, but the tears continued.

I asked, "What happened, Jules? No, don't cry. The fishes are fine. I just want to know."

She gulped down a sob, then said, "I moved the bowl close so I could make fish mouths at them and I slipped..."

"And you grabbed the bowl. Okay. I understand, Julie. I'll order an aquarium today. It'll be bigger."

"You're not mad?"

"Accidents happen," I said. I hugged Julie and ruffled Martha's ears, then finished dressing for work. I planted kisses all around, geared up in the foyer with gun and badge and shouted, "See you all tonight!"

Then I was out the door and down the stairs into a beautiful San Francisco morning. My car was waiting on 12th Street where I'd parked it Friday night. I started her up, then turned my Explorer out onto Lake Street. I was anticipating a smooth fifteen-minute drive to work, an oasis between two points of chaos.

I couldn't know that in a half hour, I would be faced with a murder that would change my life.

CHAPTER 2

AT QUARTER TO eight, I pushed open the gate on the fourth floor of the Hall of Justice. Homicide's day shift was logging in, hitting the break room for a stiff mug of leftover night-shift coffee and one of Cappy McNeil's fresh peanut butter cookies before dropping into their desk chairs. Phones rang, tweetled, and tinkled out music. Cops shouted to each other across the small, gray squad room.

My partners, Rich Conklin and Sonia Alvarez, and I have arranged our desks in a square horseshoe at the front of the bullpen. My desk is in the center, my back to the wall, giving me a clear view of the entire squad room including Lieutenant Jackson Brady's glassed-in office at the far opposite end of the room. He wasn't in.

Conklin, my ride-or-die partner of many years, greeted me, as did Alvarez, our new teammate. She joked, "What time is it? I haven't been home yet."

I knew the feeling. "Can I top up your mug?"

"Thanks, no, Lindsay. I'm good to fly to the moon."

I got myself a mug of highly sugared coffee and, passing on the cookies, returned to my desk.

"So, what'd I miss? Where's Brady?"

As if summoned, the lieutenant burst through the gate—and he looked worried.

"Boxer. Conklin. I need you downstairs."

Leaving Alvarez, we followed Brady down the fire stairs. Brady is six two, muscular, with white-blond hair banded in a short ponytail, wears denim everything. But more to the point, he's a great leader. We three exited the building through the lobby's back door, took the breezeway out to Harriet Street, which is where a lot of Hall of Justice workers take advantage of free parking under the overpass.

This morning, squad cars had formed a barrier that cordoned off the street to traffic. Sergeant Bob Nardone, was standing at the intersection of Harriet and our breezeway. Another couple of uniforms blocked my view.

Nardone broke from the huddle and approached us.

He said to Brady, "The victim is white, male, sixties to seventies. I was about to get into my car when I saw him lying facedown next to my vehicle. Bullet in the back of his head, looks like it was fired at close range. Lieutenant," he said to Brady. "Will you take a look before the swarm moves in?"

It was too late to avoid that. Hall of Justice workers and passersby were crowding in for a look. There was no room for all of us, so Brady and Conklin joined Nardone while I called my closest friend, Dr. Claire Washburn.

"I'll be there in a minute," she said. And she meant that literally.

Claire is San Francisco's chief ME. Her office is a hundred yards from where we stood on Harriet Street.

While I waited for Claire, I called the crime lab and got director Eugene Hallows on the phone. I said, "Gene, first homicide of the week is right here on Harriet Street between Bryant and Harrison Streets. You'll see the cruisers."

"I'll send the van, ASAP."

We clicked off and I went over to the squad car barricade hoping to get a closer look at the scene, but Conklin put his hand at my back and headed me away from it. No question about it, my cool-under-fire partner looked very troubled.

CHAPTER 3

TIRES SQUEALED AS the coroner's van rounded the corner of Bryant to Harriet. It came to a hard stop when the driver rolled up on the barricade that was now hemmed in by a gathering and restless crowd. Al Bunker, the ME tech at the wheel, climbed down from the van and began loudly "negotiating" with Officer Kieran Laughton to make room for the ME as was required.

But there was little Laughton could do.

Harriet is a side street; narrow, industrial, bounded by high chain-link fencing. Vehicles were parked on both sides of the fences and pedestrians used the gates in the chain link.

Nardone shouted to Bunker, "Al, back up. I'll spit on the fender for ya', awright?"

The van was in reverse when I heard Claire Washburn calling my name. I swung around to see her step off the curb, her expression a cross between *Glad to see you, girlfriend*, and *what's the holdup here?*

"Suggest you bark at the uniforms until they make room for you," I said to my BFF. "This is as close as I've gotten."

"Follow me," she said.

Claire is a big woman, but she squeezed between two cop cars and I followed. I nearly caught up with her as she closed in on the dead body and the uniforms barring the way. I took a seat on the hood of a cruiser. I only had a view of her back and the deep ring of surrounding uniforms as Claire stooped down and did a preliminary assessment of the victim in situ.

When she stood up, Claire called out to me over the heads of the uniforms, "From what I can see, he was shot execution style, one round through the back of his skull, no facial injury. He's coming out of rigor. I'm saying he's been here for ten to twelve hours. Make it eight to ten o'clock last night. Call me later for updates."

Then she picked Conklin out of the crowd.

"Richie. Help me roll him."

From my seat on the cruiser, I could just see that the body was lying between an SUV and a panel van and that it would be hard to flip the DB onto his back. The sum of what else I could see of him was a gray tweed jacket, dyed black hair, and blood at the back of his neck.

I'd had enough.

"Let me through," I said to the uniforms in front of me. "I'm not kidding."

I'd hopped off the car hood and was shoving the uniforms ineffectually when Conklin called out to me.

"Hang on, Lindsay. I'll come to you."

"What? Why?"

He edged through the thick blue line, and when he got to me I saw him holding a man's bulging leather wallet. The victim hadn't been robbed.

"Cash and cards in there?"

Conklin said, "Yes, and I gotta show you something. Meet you on the curb."

I couldn't go forward so I backed up and made my way to the sidelines as Conklin suggested. And the look on his face was scaring me.

CHAPTER 4

I THINK OF Rich Conklin as the brother I never had.

I love him because he's smart, honest, reliable, a great investigator, and literally, he has my back—and I have his.

In the years of riding together, we'd worked innumerable homicides. A few flashed through my mind. A firefight in a dark alley, with no cover, nowhere to hide. A shootout in a hotel corridor with a killer who'd already taken out an FBI agent standing beside me. A mass murderer who was aiming his semiauto at me when Rich came up from behind him and disarmed him like the pro he was.

We'd learned to pick up on each other's cues during all-night interrogations and had taken turns giving mouth-to-mouth resuscitation to dying citizens. That we're both alive speaks to our connection and that we can almost read each other's minds.

But on this Monday morning, in the thick of a chaotic crime scene, I looked into Conklin's eyes and couldn't read him at all.

"Don't make me beg, Rich."

He put his arm around my shoulder and steered me away from the crowd. We kept walking until we found an empty patch of asphalt between the street and the chain-link fence.

"You're scaring me, bud."

He said, "Lindsay, you have to prepare yourself. This wallet was on the dead man. It belonged to a Marty Boxer."

"What did you say?"

I reached for the billfold, but Rich snatched it away.

"Hold on," he said.

"Jesus."

I took a breath and Rich opened the wallet and pulled the driver's license out from behind the yellowed glassine window inside the billfold. He held the license by the edges for me to see. I gripped Richie's wrist and brought the picture closer. I focused on it.

My father's eyes stared back at me from the DMV photo. My heart cartwheeled.

I said, "That's my dad."

A moment ago, morning rush traffic had been churning up exhaust fumes as it rumbled east and west on Bryant. There had been sirens and the crackle of static coming from squad car radios. But now, all the sound in the world faded. Snapshots of my father flickered through my mind and took me far away from Harriet Street.

But there was one problem: As far as I knew, Martin Boxer had passed away years ago. Heart attack, I'd been told.

So who was the man lying dead on Harriet Street?

Had someone been impersonating my father?

"Lindsay. Lindsay."

I turned back to my partner. "Did you get his phone?"

"I did." Conklin patted his jacket pocket. "And I took a picture of the DB with mine," he said. "It's cruddy. Shadows falling across his face. I know this is a strange thing to ask, but does this...? Does the DB look like your dad?"

"Hold it still," I said, drilling in on the phone.

Was the face pictured on the screen really my father? The more

I stared at the image on Richie's phone, the more the dead man's features, captured in profile, came together.

It was impossible, but...

I looked up.

Conklin said, "See this? It was right behind the license."

He showed me a torn scrap of paper. Numbers had been written between the fold lines. The paper shifted in the breeze but I could read the handwriting. It was a phone number, mine, from my landline in the Potrero Hill house before I married and moved to Lake Street with Joe. I looked back at the just-snapped image of the dead man's face.

My knees buckled. Richie caught me before I dropped and called out to a uni standing beside his marked car a few yards away.

"Thompstett. Open your back door for me, now."

Officer Thompstett opened the car's rear door and Rich led me to the seat. Instead of sitting, I steadied myself against the door frame. I took a few deep breaths and looked into Richie's eyes.

I said, "I want to see him."

"You sure?"

I nodded and my partner stepped back and got a bead on the crowd. He guided me past the edge of the cordon, ordering people to make way until I was through the break in the fencing, standing next to Claire, both of us staring down at the lifeless body lying face-up on the street.

CHAPTER 5

MY FATHER TOOK off when I was thirteen and my sister, Cat, was seven. He left a note for Mom and booked, leaving his job and family behind, not even reappearing when my mom was dying of breast cancer a decade later. We weren't shocked. Cancer was too heavy for Marty.

Marty was small comfort when he was around, and later, I'd decided that he was some sort of sociopath. I'd turned my back on him. He came to my mother's funeral, but never stood up to speak a word for his wife of twenty years. He attended the ceremony the day I was sworn in as a cop, but we didn't speak. Not too long before I met Joe, Marty had slid back into my life, full of regrets and promises that he wanted to make up for lost time—but then ran off to Mexico when his past started catching up to him and had barely been in touch since. He promised Cat he'd walk me down the aisle at my wedding, then ghosted me.

Later, my old boss, Warren Jacobi, told me that Marty hadn't abandoned me—he'd died of a heart attack months earlier. Jacobi had gotten the news through some kind of administrative notification regarding my father's police pension.

There was no body, no funeral, no nothing.

Now I stood looking down at the homicide victim on Harriet Street, confronted by yet another reality.

This was unquestionably my father.

Marty looked smaller in death than I remembered him, the vehicles flanking his body like the steep sides of an open grave. Police cleared onlookers from the scene as CSI moved in, set up lights to take pictures of my dead father where he'd been dropped. After a moment, I too was shooed off so CSI could work. After telling Rich that I was okay, I headed to the medical examiner's office a block away.

I opened the door to the waiting room and took a seat at the end of an attached row of blue plastic chairs. "I'm waiting for Dr. Washburn," I said to the receptionist.

"She's out of the office. Do you want to wait?"

Realizing Claire must still be at the scene, I said yes and stretched out my legs, leaned back, and stared at the ceiling. Alone, under that plain white surface, I saw images of my father, mother, sister, and me.

My father had once also been a homicide cop. When I was young, he'd take me to cop bars, hoist me onto a barstool, buy me a Coke—and forget I was there. I heard many stories from my perch: of the ponies that brought in the money, of bars Marty "protected," of bets made while a cuffed perp was in the back seat. I saw my father take rolls of cash from his trouser pocket and heard jokes that the dough came from crime scenes, from the pockets of the dead. I knew he was dirty before I knew what dirty was.

I had to wonder—had he faked his death years ago, or had Jacobi passed along bad information? What I knew for sure was that I hadn't heard a word from or about him since before he missed my wedding...until about two months ago.

That day, two months ago, a group of my coworkers and I had gotten together for lunch at MacBain's, the bar and grill a block from the Hall of Justice. After gorging on burgers and fries, we'd split the check and headed toward the exit. We were passing the bar that was banked with standing-room-only customers when I heard the name "Marty Boxer," or thought I did. But who'd spoken it? And why here?

I'd looked around but saw only the backs of HOJ workers laughing and drinking beer. Our group was swept out the door along with an exiting crowd, but once outside, I'd looked back into the bar through the front windows. I didn't see my dirty dog of a father, but I glimpsed a man in the crowd with big hair and a prominent nose, who looked a little like Bruce "Goose" Cavanaugh. Goose was a private investigator and reputed to be a high-level but unindicted contract killer.

Had I really seen the Goose at MacBain's? Had he been the one who mentioned Marty Boxer's name? He'd had a well-known dislike for my father, dating back to a number of clashes between them when Marty was on the force.

As a homicide cop, I'd caught more than one case where Goose Cavanaugh had been the number one suspect. He'd slipped the noose. Last I heard, Cavanaugh lived in Reno, Nevada.

My phone rang. Richie.

"The boss is asking for you," he said.

"I'll be right up."

CHAPTER 6

BRADY STOOD UP and opened his office door for me.

"Sit, Lindsay. You must be...How are you doing?"

I didn't know. I said, "Too soon to tell, but I'm glad you were there this morning."

He said, "If you need anything...You want some time off?"

"No, thanks. I have to work this case."

He shook his head vigorously. No.

"You're too close to this one. You can't be neutral about your father's murder, Lindsay. I don't have to tell you that."

I dug in. "I'm already working it."

"Wait a minute. That's my call, right? Make sense."

The Cavanaugh connection had unlocked recollections I had about an old unsolved case with a similar MO. The pieces were still crystallizing in my head, but I stood up and opened the door, calling Cappy McNeil in to join us. He'd been lead on that unsolved case.

When Cappy made his way over, I told them about the day I'd heard my father's name. "I was walking out of MacBain's about two months ago and I heard someone say the name 'Marty Boxer.' I looked around and within the crowd at the bar, I swear I saw Goose Cavanaugh."

"Who?" asked Brady.

"Bruce Cavanaugh," said Cappy. "Also goes by Goose. He's a PI, but a shady one."

"Tell Brady about the Joanna Lake case," I told Cappy.

Cappy didn't need more encouragement. "Back in the day, Cavanaugh and his wife were going through a messy divorce, one Goose in no way wanted. He even threatened to kill his wife's attorney, Joanna Lake, if she didn't drop the case. Lake said Goose appeared out of nowhere one night as she was leaving work and told her, 'Drop Jodi Cavanaugh's case if you want to see forty.' Joanna Lake wasn't the type to back off. She filed the papers anyway.

"Not too much later, Lake leaves her office for the day. Next thing we know, she's dead. Shot in the back of the head on Harriet Street. She was thirty-nine when she was shot. Nobody saw the shooter. No witnesses. No surveillance footage."

Brady's phone rang. He picked up and said, "I'll get back to you in a few." To Cappy, he said, "Go on."

Cappy continued, "So, Joanna Lake's death happened two blocks from here. Warren Jacobi and I were partners on it, and we worked the case hard. Our only real suspect was Cavanaugh. All we had were his threats against Lake, but we couldn't place him at the scene. He had an alibi. The bullet didn't match his gun. The DA said we couldn't indict let alone convict. So the case went cold."

Brady moved some objects on his desk. He'd already made up his mind, and I wasn't going to accept "No."

"Cold, but not dead," I said. "My father's murder reopens the Lake case."

"Because?"

"The connection between Cavanaugh, Lake, and Marty Boxer. Both Marty and Lake were killed a block apart, same means and manner of death. I have to check it out."

Brady was scrutinizing me and Cappy, who nodded. No doubt asking himself if I was even stable enough to have this conversation. He stopped staring at me and looked through his window at traffic on Interstate 80.

He said, "That's all you've got?"

I pushed on. "Brady, I've got to do this. Maybe I'll solve both cases."

Brady's expression had changed from doubt to sympathy.

"I'll give you two weeks," he said, "to make me a believer. Don't make me regret this, Lindsay. You, Cappy, Conklin, and Alvarez work Marty Boxer's murder. Don't get hurt."

"Thanks, boss. We're on it."

I got out of there before he changed his mind.

CHAPTER 7

I RETURNED TO my desk to brief my team, but my phone kept ringing. I couldn't chase down a single thought without interruption.

I said to my partners, "Let's move."

Interview Two was empty. I turned off all the mics and we three took seats at the table. By now, Marty's clothes and gun were at the lab, but Rich put my father's phone and wallet on the table.

He opened the wallet and spread out the contents. Alvarez made notes. I felt uncomfortable about invading my dead father's privacy—which underscored Brady's concerns that I couldn't be neutral—but I got past it.

Rich snapped credit cards down on the table like playing cards, read the numbers to Alvarez, and I counted the cash. Marty hadn't been killed for his money. There was seven hundred thirty dollars in large bills on his person when he died and an old betting slip on a horse that had lost weeks before.

Rich put a short stack of business cards in front of me. I dealt them out. There was one card each for JR's Aces High Dry Cleaners, Sasha's Hair Salon, Center BMW, and Bay Street 24/7 pharmacy, plus a dozen business cards for Spinogatti Private Investigations with my father's name listed as partner.

I grabbed my phone and googled Spinogatti Private Investigations, then read the reviews. They averaged 4.2 stars. Not too bad. I opened our internal PI database. Yes, they were licensed and there were no black marks on their record.

I dialed the number, got Leo Spinogatti on the line, introduced myself. His voice was raspy and heartsick. He said he'd been expecting my call.

Told me he was sorry. That he and Marty were close. My dad had been following my career, Spinogatti said. I thanked him, without letting it soften me. I had no idea how Marty had felt about his business partner.

"I'd like to stop over," I said.

"How about tomorrow afternoon?"

"Gotta move fast on this," I said. "We'd need to come over now."

After hanging up, I asked Alvarez, "Are you up for this?"

"Yes to the max, Sarge."

Before the meeting broke up, I assigned Conklin to finding Marty's car, getting it to the lab. I asked Alvarez to check in with the ME before we took off, to find out when Claire would have Marty's autopsy report.

Now that my phone was on, I scrolled through the calls I had dodged during our meeting. One stood out like a blinking neon sign. My sister, Cat, had called. I pressed redial, listened to the ring tone and the *please leave a message*. I didn't know what kind of message to leave. So I simply said, "Cat, please call me when you get this."

I thought about calling Joe but didn't know what to tell him, either. I texted him instead, letting him know I had a new case and would probably miss dinner.

Minutes later, I met up with Alvarez at the carpool in front of the Hall.

"Claire says she'll call you at the end of the day. Do you want to drive?"

"Not really. You?"

She jingled the keys and we got into the unmarked car.

CHAPTER 8

SPINOGATTI PRIVATE INVESTIGATIONS was located at 802 23rd Street in San Francisco's Dogpatch neighborhood. The two-story, dun-colored stucco building was wedged between a shoe repair shop and a house that had survived the 1906 earthquake. I pressed the bell. An answering buzz sounded, and I said my name.

"Ground floor, rear," said a woman's voice. The door lock clicked open, and Alvarez and I entered a dim hallway that led to my late father's place of business.

The waiting room at the end of the corridor was dark and empty except for the gooseneck lamp throwing a circle of light over the red-haired receptionist at her computer. Across from her, the few pieces of furniture were Art Deco, reminiscent of *Twin Peaks* and *Casablanca*. A pair of torchère lamps bracketed a red velvet sofa and matching armchair. On the walls hung framed movie posters of famous actors in PI roles: Bogart, Falk, Penn, Eastwood, Dunaway.

The receptionist looked up at me and said, "I'm Marge Spinogatti, Leo's wife. You're Lindsay, aren't you? This news about Marty comes as such a shock. I'm so sorry."

I thanked her before I tuned her out. My feelings were rocketing back and forth between inexplicable sorrow, numbness, and an urgent need to cut past the niceties and get down to business.

Marty Boxer had been alive when I thought he was dead. But now he'd been murdered. Why? By whom?

Marge buzzed Spinogatti on an old intercom and a gravelly voice came through both a door and the intercom speaker.

"Yes, yes, ask them to come in. Did you cancel Schneider? Good."

Marge said, "Go right in," and pointed to Leo Spinogatti's door. A gray-haired man of about seventy in a black suit opened the door from inside and said "hello" in a voice ravaged by burning cigarettes.

Spinogatti had hooded eyes, large ears, and an expression weighed down by grief.

"Condolences, Lindsay. What happened to Marty is horrific."

He shook my hand with both of his, said hello to Alvarez, then ushered us into his office. The room was bright, with traditional furniture and a wedding photo of Leo and Marge on his desk.

Alvarez and I took the two side chairs and Leo lowered himself behind his desk. Pressing the intercom button he said, "No calls, Margie."

Then he asked, "How can I help?"

I had many questions but started by asking when and where Leo last saw my father.

"Around seven or eight yesterday evening. Marty and I had pulled a long day, especially for a Sunday. We got together at Briny's for drinks. Marty was in good spirits," he told us. "It's unimaginable. Unthinkable, that in a few hours, he'd be dead."

CHAPTER 9

SPINOGATTI REACHED FOR a pack of Camels in front of him, tapped the package, reviewed his inventory of smokes, and put the pack down beside what looked to be a solid gold lighter. He saw me looking and said, "A gift from Marty."

Alvarez asked, "Mr. Spinogatti?"

"Leo, please."

"Leo," she said. "Did Mr. Boxer say where he was going after drinks with you?"

"You know, I didn't ask. I thought he was going home. I walked him out. Said 'See you tomorrow,' and went back here to the shop. Marge worked for another hour, then we shut out the lights and drove home."

I asked my father's former partner, "Do you have any idea who may have wanted Marty dead? Was he on anyone's radar?"

Spinogatti said, "Lindsay, Marty has been my friend for decades. I loved him. Brought him in as a partner a few years back. And for the record, I had no reason to kill him. We both have wills. Marty made provisions and his lawyer will give you that information."

The big gray man punched the button on the intercom, leaned over and spoke into the mic. "Marge, Lindsay's going to need Mitcham's contact info."

"I've got it right here, love," Marge replied.

I asked my father's old friend, "So, to your knowledge, no one threatened my father? He had no enemies?"

Leo swiveled in his chair, then turned back to us.

He said, "He'd mellowed some, but...Marty said I was an idiot to worry."

I waited for him to go on.

He asked, "You ever hear of a guy named Goose Cavanaugh?"

I went on alert. "I have."

"He's a real SOB," Spinogatti sighed. "I once had a client named Joanna Lake, a divorce lawyer, who wanted to hire me as protection because she was repping Cavanaugh's wife and this bastard was on her case. Next thing I knew, she was already dead."

"Tell me whatever you've got on Cavanaugh. The Goose is shaping up to be a person of interest."

CHAPTER 10

FOR THE NEXT ten minutes we shared what we each knew about Goose Cavanaugh.

Spinogatti said, "Lemme get you the Lake file."

He left his seat and opened a connecting door to another room, probably Marty's office, and closed it behind him.

I waited three long minutes for Leo to open the door again, and then I got up and opened it myself. Alvarez was beside me when I found Spinogatti bent over Marty's desk stubbing out a butt in an ashtray. Looked like a kid caught with his hand in his mother's handbag.

"Aw damn. Don't tell Marge."

I said, "The Lake file would be great, but I'd like to see all of Marty's current files."

"We've scanned most of them. Margie will send them to you. But hang on a second. Let me see what I can give you now . . ."

Leo opened a file cabinet.

"These are all from this year. Mostly cheating-husband files. I'll put them in a box for you."

I looked around my dad's office and saw him everywhere but here. There were photos on the walls of famous racehorses, Sea Biscuit, Secretariat, Native Dancer. Marty standing with a snappy-looking bay and the jockey in the winner's circle. He looked very happy. I opened his closet. A number of three-quarter-length dark-blue coats hung on the rod, and the top shelf held a collection of old cameras: a Leica, a couple of Nikons, the Minolta he'd always loved.

I became aware of Leo herding us back to his own office with a box of files in his arms, saying to me that after the reading of the will, he would hold any personal objects for me that Darla didn't want.

Darla?

Spinogatti said, "And you'll want this. Marty kept it in his top drawer."

Leo handed me a small, framed photo of my mom standing on our patch of lawn, one arm around my sister, the other around me, the two little girls grinning at the camera. Tears came. Marty had taken that picture on Cat's seventh birthday. It had been a good day.

Our *last* good day. He'd walked out shortly after.

Misunderstanding the tears that caught me unexpectedly, Leo handed me a tissue and said, "I miss him already, Lindsay. If you need anything else, call me. If I learn anything, I'll call you. And if you want to go into private investigations, Sergeant Boxer, let me know. We won't even have to change the name on the files."

CHAPTER 11

I HELD THE bankers box filled with my father's case files and Alvarez took the wheel. As we headed back to the Hall, Alvarez said, "Talk to me, Lindsay."

"Okay. Personally, that was total immersion therapy that almost cracked me open like an egg. I didn't expect that. But no wallowing on the job. At least not while the sun's up."

Alvarez said, "Okay, then. Let's rough out an action plan."

"Right. We've got three tasks right now. Go through Marty's files on a hunt for red flags. I'll talk to his lawyer. We'll follow the facts."

"And Goose Cavanaugh?"

"Maybe there'll be something in the files or the book. We have to find something recent connecting Goose to my dad before we get the Reno police to bring him in."

"Marty mentioned to Leo that Goose was around."

My phone rang. It was Conklin.

"Got the car. Baby blue Beemer with some wear on it. Traffic ticket on the windshield from 6:10 this morning. CSI just got here with the truck."

"Where are you?"

"Jeff Adachi Way, about three car-lengths off Bryant."

I knew that street well. There was a bail bond office on Bryant, and Jeff Adachi Way was around the corner. It was only a few blocks from where my father had been shot.

"We're ten minutes out from your location. We'll meet you there."

Alvarez stopped for a light on 7th Street and said, "Here's what I think of Spinogatti. He's either a sociopath or he had nothing to do with the hit on your dad. He seems authentic; loyal to your father and to you, too."

"Good to hear, Sonia."

But the opposite scenario was playing out in my mind. I could see Leo having a motive to take Marty out. He knew about Marty's gambling and maybe he no longer trusted him with half the business. Instead of walking Marty out the bar's door last night, he could have followed him on cat's feet and fired the kill shot. Duplicating the Joanna Lake murder may have well been intentional. A smart way to throw suspicion onto the Goose.

"Brace for landing," Sonia said.

Conklin didn't have to wave us down. A blue BMW was parked at the middle of the block and a CSI flatbed truck was pulling up just ahead of Marty's car. I braked next to the BMW and Conklin stepped out into the street.

I buzzed down my window.

He said, "I've been thinking that maybe Marty was meeting someone on Harriet Street. Say, his killer lured him out. Marty parks his car off the main drag and goes for a short walk in the dark. Whoever he was going to meet is in hiding, waiting for him to walk past, and once he did . . ."

Conklin made his hand into a gun. "Bang."

I nodded. I could see it happening, but I couldn't see the doer. Not yet.

"That's all I've got," Conklin said.

"We need to see what the car turns up," I said. "And take a good look through his phone."

Rich crossed his fingers and turned back to help CSI.

CHAPTER 12

OFFICER GRABO CLIMBED out of the flatbed truck with a slim tool in her hand. She exchanged words with Conklin, high-fived Alvarez, and said, "Very sorry, Boxer," to me.

I nodded my thanks, and watched Grabo slip the jimmy into the BMW's passenger-side door, then unlock the driver's side for her coworker, Ben Stukas.

Stukas got behind the wheel and jumped the engine. Conklin spoke with Grabo, who opened the glove box, reached in, riffled through flyers and manuals and receipts. Then she pulled out a small four-by-six-inch spiral notebook and held it up.

Conklin said, "Grabo, can I see that?" I watched as Conklin flipped through the small notebook.

He called out to me, "Mileage and fuel records."

I called back, "Rich. Check the driver's side visor."

Conklin reached in and folded it down. Another notebook, the same size as the first, fell into his hand. Conklin held it up so I could see the betting slip taped inside the front cover.

After a quick look, Conklin said, "Personal notebook. Notes, observations, horses, bets, phone numbers."

"Bingo."

I told Rich to bring both books and we'd see him back at the

Hall. Fifteen minutes later, while Alvarez and I were leafing through Marty's surveillance files, Conklin came through the gate with the two small notebooks, bagged and processed at the scene.

He gave the books to me, then went to talk with Cappy. Alvarez and I gloved up, and I took the notebook with the betting slip out of an evidence bag. I was looking for his most recent notes. A name. A date. A clue.

I turned pages carefully and Alvarez took photos. Marty had been meticulous with his betting records. They were organized by date, track conditions, the names of the horses and the jockeys, the odds and amounts of the bets, wins and losses. It didn't take higher math to see that financially, my dad was in deep. His bookie's name wasn't listed, but in places I found the initials "JR" beside a dollar amount and the word "paid." And in some places, I saw entries crossed out and marked with the letters "FSR."

There were a few pages of phone numbers attached by a bulldog clip to the inside of the betting book's back cover. While Alvarez snapped photos of the mileage book, I unclipped the phone numbers from the betting book and checked them against my dad's phone log.

Several names and numbers were in both places. Jack Robbie, Brad Mitcham, Darla, no last name. There were multiple daily calls to and from Darla. Today's call log registered dozens of missed calls from her. Darla had to be Marty's girlfriend. No number for Goose.

Conklin returned from speaking with Cappy, edged around his desk and took his seat. He tapped the desk next to the notebook Alvarez was photographing.

"Before I bagged that, I did some quick math. Looks like Marty owes his bookie two hundred thirty grand. The bookie kept taking his bets."

"Bookie's name could be Jack Robbie," I said. I showed my

partner the notations beside the initials "JR." "Then there's these initials, 'FSR.' Maybe he had some kind of patron?"

Conklin reached over the small pile of phone numbers that had been clipped to the betting book.

"What's this?"

He moved a restaurant matchbook cover to me and after I read it, I passed it to Alvarez. There was small handwriting on the two square inches of cardboard written in two different hands. Both were cryptic.

"Marty wrote that," I said of the first line that read: *"Bet I get you."*

I didn't know the handwriting on the second line, but I got the message.

"All bets are off, Marty."

Dueling threats—yet Marty kept the matchbook cover with him. Why? Was this the bet he'd lost last night?

CHAPTER 13

ALVAREZ AND I got back in the car. She drove, dodging the drug-addled, mentally challenged, and ordinary working pedestrians meandering across Mission Street. A man with a sign that read "Kick me for a buck" danced to street music. Horns honked.

I said, "That's it. Right there."

Alvarez jerked the wheel, parked at the curb beside JR's Aces High Dry Cleaners. Behind us, Cappy and Conklin peeled off and drove to the gas station across the street. To our left was a row of blocky stucco apartment buildings, interrupted every hundred yards or so by a grungy storefront like JR's, an illegal gambling shack.

Alvarez, an experienced undercover cop, had dressed in street clothes: leggings, short boots, and a long pullover. She went into JR's first, her cowl-neck sweater hiding her shoulder mic. When she called me with an all clear, I pushed open the door.

The place reeked of sweat and weed and echoed with electronic dings from the slots and shouts from the craps table at the far end of the room. On a TV over the bar, an announcer narrated the last seconds of a too-close-to-call sixth race at Santa Anita. I pictured my father on a stool, hunched over that bar. I pictured him putting down money for the horse of the moment. I pictured a loss written into his book.

I met Alvarez at the row of slots she was studying. She used her chin to indicate the man behind the Plexiglas cash-register cage across from us and near the entrance.

"That's Jack Robbie," she said.

She showed me JR's photo on her phone and scrolled down to his record; multiple arrests for petty crimes, two years for bookmaking. When his business at 2300 Mission closed down three years ago, he'd reopened here, a few blocks away.

I looked up. The man in the cage was on the phone. His thin hair was slicked back, his jowls were unshaven, and he was in his undershirt, a checkered dishcloth tucked into the neck. A bowl of pasta sat in front of him. He noticed me, made me as a cop, turned his eyes away, and finished his phone call.

As I moved toward the booth, I heard Robbie say into the phone, "Lady. I don't know your husband. You talk to him. Anyway, my linguini's getting cold so let's, no, no, don't call here. Talk to your husband."

He clicked off and I stepped forward. I slid my badge through the cash slot and said, "Mr. Robbie, this isn't a bust."

"You got the wrong guy. Robbie is outta town."

"I'm Sergeant Lindsay Boxer, homicide. This is my partner, Inspector Sonia Alvarez."

"Your name is Boxer?"

"Yes. Martin Boxer's my father."

"You must be very proud. He's almost put me out of business. More than once."

"He was shot last night," I said.

"Shot *dead*?"

"That's right. We're not busting you, Mr. Robbie. We have some questions about Marty and I need you to come down to the station with us."

CHAPTER 14

ROBBIE TWIRLED HIS fork inside the bowl of linguine. Lifted a roll of pasta to his mouth. Chewed. Swallowed. Dropped the fork back into the bowl. He looked disgusted and resigned.

He said, "I need a lawyer?"

"No. We have some questions about Marty Boxer," I said again.

"This is a bad time for me. How about tomorrow morning?"

Cappy and Conklin came through the front door. Cappy is big, bald, and streetwise. The badge he wore on a chain around his neck was visible once he opened his jacket.

Jack Robbie said, "Damn it. Give me a second. Stay here, okay? Don't scare the pigeons."

I pictured Robbie making a break for the rear exit. I didn't want to chase him, pile on, cause a riot instead of avoiding one. But I was prepared to do all of that and make an arrest if I needed to when Robbie stopped at the craps table.

"Tony," he called out. He bent, put his mouth to the croupier's ear. Whispers ensued. The croupier made an announcement.

"That's it, gents. Table is closed due to circumstances beyond our control."

Tony pushed chips across the table, pocketed the dice, and put down the arguments. He checked out our crew as he walked forward and took Robbie's seat in the cage.

I frisked Robbie and removed a 9mm Glock tucked into his waistband.

"I got a license for that," said Robbie.

I sniffed the muzzle. It hadn't been recently fired.

"Have any other guns?"

"I live here. Second floor, front. I've got a .45 inside the drawer next to the bed. Don't mess with the girls up there, okay? And I got a shirt hanging on the back of the chair. If you don't mind."

Of course JR had working prostitutes on the second floor where he lived. Probably sold drugs while he was at it. Conklin took the stairs and ten minutes later he came down with the bedside .45 and a shirt.

Robbie said of the gun, "Like I said. It's licensed."

"Fine, Mr. Robbie. Is this everything or do I need a search warrant?"

"I didn't shoot your father," he said. "I haven't left this place for a month and about twenty people here can attest to that."

I said, "We'll send your guns out to the lab and get them back to you in a day or two."

"You want me to thank you?"

Robbie ditched the checkered napkin, put on the shirt, and told Tony to stay put until he heard from him. Then the four of us walked the proprietor of JR's Aces High Dry Cleaners out to Mission Street and helped him into the back seat of Conklin's unmarked car.

CHAPTER 15

BACK AT THE Hall, we brought Jack Robbie to an interrogation room. Alvarez settled our person of interest at the table, bought him a vending machine ham-and-cheese on a roll and a can of Sprite.

I checked that the video camera in the corner of the ceiling was recording. Cappy and Conklin were behind the one-way mirror between the observation room and the box.

Alvarez is not just smart, she's beguiling. Robbie was asking Alvarez why she became a cop, flirting as if he'd ever have a chance. She hooked her hair behind her ears and put Marty's PI license on the table facing Robbie.

She asked Robbie, "Is this a photo of Marty Boxer?"

I was thinking Robbie had plenty of reason to kill my father. True, you can't squeeze money from cold dead hands, but Marty owing Robbie a six-figure debt could only encourage other clients to bet above their means. Robbie was the bank and carrying debt was bad for his business.

Robbie said, "I didn't *know* him *know* him, you get me? We didn't socialize."

"Just looking for a positive ID on your customer," Alvarez said.

"That's him," said Robbie. "Okay?"

He put his hands flat on the table, preparing to get to his feet.

I said, "Hang on, Mr. Robbie. We have a few more questions. Mr. Boxer's records show that he's into you pretty deep."

"Sure, two hundred k," said Robbie. "Nobody owed me more. But I cut him slack because he was a cop once. He could watch the store for me. Find other deadbeats. I made allowances."

"So he was your enforcer?"

"Whoa, whoa. That's too much, too far. He was a part-time bouncer. That's all. I wasn't losing as much as you seem to think. Are we done now?"

I said, "This is important, Mr. Robbie. Do you know anyone who'd have liked to get Marty out of the way?"

He shrugged. "No insult intended, but he wasn't diplomatic. I'm sure there were plenty of people who didn't like the sight of him. Dozens."

Oh, brother. Unnamed dozens of people who wanted my father dead. I could imagine that some of them had gotten a beating from Marty on behalf of Jack Robbie.

Alvarez said, "Does this look right?" She showed Robbie a picture of the JR tab page from Marty's betting book.

Robbie looked at it.

"That looks right."

"And what does 'FSR' stand for? Here. Next to a dollar amount, a line drawn through an amount."

Robbie shrugged. "Taking a wild guess. 'For services rendered'?"

Okay. A fair exchange. His debt was shaved for services rendered. I jumped back into the interview. "Mr. Robbie, where were you last night?"

"To repeat. Where I always am. In the shop. I live there. I didn't go out. I ordered from the Chinese at the mall at around seven something. I used my double cash card."

"Good. And the last time you saw Marty?"

"Gee, I don't know. I only see him on payday. So sometime last week."

I asked, "What can you tell me about that meeting?"

"What do I remember? That he busted into the shop two seconds before the pistol went off at the track. He wanted to double down on what he just lost. Another two grand. See, the rich guys bet twenty-five bucks. The bums bet the bank. Your dad bet beyond his means. I said, 'What about what you already owe me?'

"He was persuasive in the stand-up comic way that he has. Needed to make a mortgage payment first. Said, 'Please.' That I shouldn't worry. He would pay me back no matter what. Hadn't he always come through? Like that.

"This time I rolled over so I could close the book. I placed his two thou on Pretty Baby in the seventh to win. She stumbled in the stretch and...and she's in horse heaven now. I expected Marty to call this morning."

I thought of my father lying on the street between two vehicles. I excused myself and went next door to the observation room.

I asked Cappy and Conklin what they thought.

Conklin said, "He's a gifted storyteller. Want us to give him a lift back to his shack?"

"Yes and stop off at the Chinese restaurant. Get the receipt for Jack's dinner, if there is one."

I didn't know if Jack Robbie was the doer, if he'd hired someone to shoot my father, or if he was just a slob running a gambling joint, making his car payments like the rest of us. Jack Robbie had given us nothing but dozens of unnamed possible suspects Marty may have threatened or shaken down or pistol whipped.

I doubted we would ever know the name of even one of them.

CHAPTER 16

I WAS LATE for my appointment with Marty's attorney, Brad Mitcham. He practiced law at Sayles, Mitcham and Lalhezar at 450 Sutter, an imposing building in Union Square. It was quarter to five when I stepped into an open elevator, hoping that despite the hour, Mitcham would still be waiting for me. I tapped in the floor number and watched the numerals above the doors light up as the car climbed steadily to the twenty-first floor.

Those ascending lights lifted my mood until I felt almost optimistic. Mitcham could help me make sense of my father's life and death. I was sure of it.

The receptionist was straightening her desk when I came through the door. She looked up at me and said, "Detective Boxer? Brad said to send you right in."

I was about to knock when the door swung open and a man about my age with streaked blond hair and blue-framed glasses, dressed in khaki and blue, stretched out his hand.

"I'm Brad," he said.

"Lindsay Boxer," I said.

"Good to finally meet you, Lindsay."

Mitcham's office was lined with bookshelves and had a seating area with a wonderful city view. I sat down on the sofa, and the lawyer took a chair with a coffee table between us. I couldn't wait another minute before telling him why I was there.

"Finding my father's killer is my number one priority," I told him. "My father and I hadn't spoken in years. Not since he ran off to Mexico close to a decade ago. I was under the impression that he died several years back. So I know very little about his recent life. I'm hoping you have some ideas about who may have benefited from his death."

Brad Mitcham went over to his desk, picked up a folder and a small box, and brought them back to his chair in the seating area. He sat down, and of course I tried to gauge his expression, his posture, and the items he'd set down on the table. All I picked up was that he had something big to tell me.

Mitcham cleared his throat.

"Lindsay, I have good news and bad. Which do you want first?"

The optimism I'd drawn from the rising numbers above the elevator doors begin to drop. I clenched my hands together and looked at my lap. I wanted a shot of good news on the rocks, but what I said was, "Hit me with the bad news."

Brad said, "Bad news first?"

I nodded my head.

Brad cleared his throat and said, "Martin Boxer was not your biological father."

CHAPTER 17

HAD BRAD MITCHAM just told me that Marty wasn't my father? How could this be true?

Images of our home in Berkeley flashed like an old video montage. *Daddy's home.* Tom Brokaw on the news. Dad cooking hot dogs on the grill. Mom in her bathrobe chanting, "Where is Daddy?" Cat and I replying in unison, "Out of town."

I said, "You're absolutely sure?"

"You never suspected?" he asked.

"No. Not a clue. Is that the bad news?"

"Isn't it?" said Brad Mitcham.

I wasn't sure of that. I'd been told as a young girl that I had Marty's eyes, but the idea that I wasn't the child of a dirty cop, a neglectful father, and a despicable husband gave me a jolt. Something like a zap of adrenaline. Not good or bad, just electric. But was it true?

I said, "How do you know?"

"I have papers including your birth certificate. Marty told me that you didn't know that your mother was pregnant when they got married. He wasn't the father, though he agreed to put his name on your birth certificate. And I have a letter for you written by your mother, given to Marty while she was ill. Marty only gave it to me recently."

"You've read the letter?"

"No. But Marty thought he knew the salient points."

I scoffed.

Brad said, "Lindsay, I've spent many hours with Marty. He told me the whole story." He shook his head. "Anyway. He's too smart to lie to his lawyer."

I was still rocked. Not entirely getting it, but I was trying to take it in.

I said, "And what about my sister? What about Catherine?"

"Martin and Helen Boxer are Catherine's biological parents."

My mind was seeking balance and some things were making sense. This blast from the past was confirming my long-held feelings that Marty hadn't loved me.

I threw a long sigh and dropped my face into my hands.

Mitcham asked, "Can you tell me what you're thinking?"

"Something like, who am I now?"

Marty's lawyer said he was sorry a few times. Handed me a box of Kleenex. After I wiped my eyes, I looked up.

"What's the good news?" I asked.

"The good news is that you're not responsible for his debts and I'm going to do my best for Catherine. I'll have to call her. And Darla."

Darla. That was the name I'd seen in Marty's phone, the multiple daily calls.

"Girlfriend?" I guessed.

"Wife," Mitcham said. "They live in Ingleside Heights. He's left her his car, and the furnishings included."

"He remarried again? Does she know he's dead?"

"I don't know. I have Darla's phone and email," Mitcham said. "I'll get in touch with her."

I nodded. I knew I'd have to speak with her eventually, but I'd let Mitcham prep the news.

"Marty also had some savings bonds from the nineties," Mitcham continued. "I'm in touch with his broker. He left the bonds to Catherine. Marty told me that he owes his bookmaker, Jack Robbie, like, two hundred thousand dollars. Could be more or less right now. Robbie can't sue without being charged with having an illegal gambling parlor."

"I just met Robbie. I wouldn't mind arresting him."

Mitcham smiled. Then he went on. "Marty left his share of the PI business to Leo Spinogatti. If you want, I can handle the transfer of ownership."

I nodded again.

He said, "Very good, Lindsay. I do have something else for you."

There was only so much more I could take. Mitcham slid a small square box and a card-sized envelope over to me.

"This is for you," he said.

"This" was a box and an envelope both addressed to "Lindsay"—my mother's handwriting, not Marty's. I put the envelope in my inside breast pocket. I couldn't take any more emotional battering until I'd processed what I'd just learned. But Brad Mitcham was looking at me expectantly. I knew without opening the box that there was a small blue velvet-covered box inside. Out of simple respect for my poor dead mother, I felt I should do it.

I held the small box, opened the lid, and saw my grandma Frances's engagement ring winking up at me. The stone was a large diamond solitaire, crudely cut given its age, but my mother had loved this ring. I knew my mom must have left it in the safe deposit box before she died, to give to me. Someday.

This was the good news.

My grandmother's ring that my mother had worn every day.

But the bad news wouldn't be quiet. I left Brad Mitcham's office and went downstairs to my car. I closed the door. Fought my anger and sadness and sense of loss. I needed to do something and I knew what it was.

First, I called Cat.

CHAPTER 18

I WAS DRIVING along Highway 1 toward my sister's house in Half Moon Bay at quarter after six that evening. I was consumed with all things Marty, furious at him for more reasons than I could count and it didn't matter that he was dead. I visualized him alive, cuffed to a chair while I grilled him, shouting all the things I'd never said.

It would have felt good to mash down the gas pedal and find out just how fast my car could go. But good sense reminded me that I didn't need any accidents or incidents, not one more crap thing today. Right now, I had to be a rock for Cat.

My phone buzzed and Joe's name came up on the dash. I pressed the Bluetooth connection and his voice filled the car. He asked how I was doing and I said, "Just fine," which was an outrageous lie, and he knew it.

He said, "Hey, Linds. This is me. Where are you and what's going on?"

I told him I was fifteen minutes out from Cat's.

He said, "Do you understand that I'm worried? Can you give me the headlines maybe? Boil it down?"

I said, "Okay," but I didn't know if I could. My mind was scrambled; my anger, volcanic. I didn't want to relive this horrible, mind-altering day and I couldn't avoid it. I pictured standing over Marty's body at the feet of the crowd this morning—and then I was stuck, staring down at the criminal who had faked being my father for my whole life. I felt the crowd blocking me in on all sides. I saw the anguish on Richie's face as he held up Marty Boxer's driver's ID.

Joe was saying my name, repeating it. I said, "Hang on a sec." I followed the wide curve in the road and when I hit the straightaway, I said, "I want to tell you everything, but I should wait until I get home."

"When will that be?"

"Could be hours."

I buzzed down the window and let the breeze dry the sweat from my brow. "It's about my . . . I learned some things about Marty Boxer today. Things I really need to talk to Cat about in person. I need to pull myself together for her."

Joe said, "Got it. I wish I were with you. I'll wait up."

I wished he could be with me, too, but I needed to speak with Cat alone.

"I'm not going anywhere," he said. "Call if you need me."

"I will, Joe. Can you . . . ? Go to Pet World, and bring Julie. Buy an aquarium."

"I will. Now keep your eyes on the road," he said.

I promised and we clicked off.

I drove on. Light faded as the sun melted at the horizon. The highway dropped off to my right where the ocean rolled slowly in, pulled away, came back to shore. When I saw the sign in the twin beams of my headlights, I turned right off Highway 1 toward Sea View Road.

I arrived in Cat's driveway still trying on versions of the best way to tell her about Marty's life and death. I turned off the engine, leaving my car in the dark, the better to see the lighted rooms in her sweet-looking, beachy clapboard house on a dead-end street. It was backlit by sunset and animated by the sound of waves.

I'd just pocketed my keys when Cat's kitchen door flew open and she ran down the short flight of steps, opening my car door while I was still releasing my seatbelt.

She stood impatiently like a racehorse stamping at the gate and then I was free and Cat pulled me out of the front seat, flung her arms around me, and sobbed into my shoulder.

"He wasn't supposed to die, not yet," she cried out.

She'd known he was still alive?

I hugged her and rubbed her back and let her cry.

I was furious and Cat's heart was broken. How could both things be true?

CHAPTER 19

WE WERE ON Cat's bed with the bedroom door closed. The volume of the TV on the dresser was high enough to prevent Cat's daughters, Meredith and Brigid, from hearing us talking, crying, and occasionally laughing. Cat twisted her long blond hair into a knot, shook it out, cried into her pillow, and let it all out. When she caught her breath, she had questions and commentary.

How had this happened? Dad was too smart for someone to get him from behind. Do you have any suspects? This is killing me, Lindsay.

I said, "I thought he was already dead."

She nodded miserably. "I know you did. And I'm so sorry I never told you, but the way things ended last time..."

"How long have you known?"

"For a few years now. There were so many times I wanted to tell you," Cat said. "He did have a heart attack, you know, and that *is* why he missed your wedding...but he recovered. I guess I figured it was up to him to reach out to you after that, and when he didn't...I'm really sorry, Linds."

"Do you understand how crazy mad I am?" I said. "I feel betrayed. Left out. Treated like an idiot. Am I mad at you? No. A little, maybe. Mom? Same thing. Marty? I've hated him for so long, this is just another layer of knowing what a shit he was and I'll tell you, Cat, we didn't know the half of it. He was not just a dirty cop and a terrible father, he was a criminal."

Cat said, "I'll be right back," and she went to put the girls to bed. Exhaustion took me right there on her soft bed.

When I woke up, Cat had opened a shoebox filled with letters and photos from Marty to her daughters, letters to her from Mom, and letters from me.

I rolled over and looked at the box, said, "Let me see the pictures."

My sister lifted out a few, including one of Joe and I had getting married in a gazebo at the water's edge at the outskirts of a small town. Marty had stood me up as father of the bride, no explanation from him.

I put my hands on her shoulders and shook her gently until she begged me to stop.

"Okay, okay," she said. "I'm sorry. Please calm down."

I'd come here to be Cat's rock. Now she was being mine.

I collapsed into the pillows and said, "It would be better for me if you hated him, too."

"I get it," she said. "I don't expect you to forgive me but try to understand. He had his reasons, I guess. Probably didn't want you to think badly of him."

"Marty left me Grandma Frances's engagement ring, and the lawyer gave me a letter from Mom."

"Wonderful ring, sis. What did Mom say in her letter?"

"I'm not ready to read it yet. Do you have any ideas?" I was feeling her out. Did Cat already know Marty wasn't my biological father?

"No, and I didn't ask. She was so out of it by the end, Linds," Cat said. "Tea?"

"With a side of Scotch."

"No way you're having booze and driving. That would make me an accessory. Besides, you're not that crazy."

"What are you going to tell the girls?" I asked.

"I guess I could go in there and say Aunt Lindsay has something to tell you. Or I could do it your way: 'Your rotten grandfather was murdered.' What do you suggest?"

"I suggest you find the right words and you should start thinking. Marty's death is already in the news."

My phone buzzed. It was my dear friend Cindy Thomas, chief crime reporter for the *San Francisco Chronicle,* a true-crime book author, and Rich Conklin's live-in love. While I was telling Cindy that I wasn't authorized to tell her about a case in progress, she interrupted to twist my arm anyway.

"But Lindsay. There was a big crowd. People know. I just need a quote."

"Here it is, Cindy. 'No Comment.' Sorry and I love you dearly."

When I hung up there was a tray on the bed with two mugs of coffee. With cream for Cat. Black with sugar for me. Homemade cookies.

Cat said, "Are you okay to drive or not, because I'd love, love, love for you to spend the night."

"I can't. I need to be up early. But before I go, I have to ask, do you have any ideas about who killed him?"

She shook her head no almost violently.

"I don't. He sent cards to the kids. He stopped over about once a year around my birthday, or on Christmas. He never told me much about himself. Just the basics. Oh. Speaking of which, you should talk to Darla."

"The new wife."

"You heard?"

"Lawyer told me."

"She has a son, Austin. He's seven or eight, something like that."

"Is he—"

"Dad's? No, at least I'm pretty sure he's not. Darla's pretty young—younger than you and me—but she already had Austin when she and Dad got together."

I nodded my head.

"You have Darla's number? Because I have to ask her the usual questions. She's likely our last best hope."

My sister said, "Take it easy on her, Lindsay. She's a single mom and now also a freshly minted widow."

"What if she killed him?"

"Shhhh. You'll figure it out. Thanks for going after Dad's killer. I love you, sis. Cookies to go?"

CHAPTER 20

AN HOUR AFTER leaving Cat, I parked around the corner from our Lake Street apartment building. I turned off the engine and sat for a while, looking at the quiet street. My thoughts still churned, even more so for having spent half the night with Cat speaking about what would have been unthinkable a day ago.

My feelings were unresolved and I realized that no one could calm my roiling emotions but me. Only working hard, well, and fast would put the Marty Boxer case to bed.

When I opened our front door, Joe leapt up from his recliner and hugged me until I yelped.

"Sorry."

"It's okay," I said. "Do that again."

This time, I hugged him back, and we rocked together in the foyer until Joe said "ouch." He stepped back, unhooked my shoulder holster that had been digging into his side, and hung it in the gun safe. I took a moment to peek into Julie's room. Both she and Martha were sleeping soundly.

Joe toasted bread, dished up chicken soup but I couldn't fake it. I had no appetite at all. I put the spoon back in the saucer. I admired the new aquarium on the counter and finally spoke my mind. "Joe? We have any wine?"

Joe went to the fridge, then held up an opened bottle of Chardonnay for my approval.

"Yes, yes, yes."

I sipped cold fermented juice of the grape, set down the glass, and looked across the table into my husband's steady blue eyes. Telling him about the longest day of my life wasn't going to be easy, but I put my elbows on the table, leaned in, and grabbed Joe's hands. Then I started to talk.

I began with ID'ing Marty's dead body—and my confusion over how a man I'd long considered dead already had been shot last night. Then I took Joe through the meeting with Leo Spinogatti. I showed him the photo Leo had given me of my mom, Cat, and myself and got bogged down in the weeds again.

Joe knew I was lost in thought and asked me to raise my hand if I could hear his voice.

I shook off my meeting with Spinogatti and virtually walked Joe through the door of JR's Aces High Dry Cleaners, Jack Robbie's weed-reeking, electronic-beeping gambling shack.

I said, "I'm thinking about a gambling joint in the Mission."

I described the place in a few concise sentences, telling Joe that Marty Boxer, former homicide dick, had been in deep arrears to his bookie to the tune of a quarter million bucks or so.

"The bookie's name is Jack Robbie," I said. "He's the bank, and clearly not a fan of Marty Boxer." I described Robbie, "the bank," and that in order to zero out some of his own debt, Marty had become Robbie's freelance enforcer.

"Marty kept weapons in his car, Joe, and also a ledger of his debts and his collections, crossing off his debts to his bookie, 'FSR'—'for services rendered.'"

"Very low," said Joe. "You like the bookie for killing Marty?"

I said, "Motive is obvious. Robbie has an iffy alibi for the time Marty was shot. We're not done with him yet."

Joe said, "I wonder how many enemies Marty made with his side hustle. What did his lawyer say?"

I pictured myself with Brad Mitcham asking me, *"Which do you want first? The good news or the bad?"*

The good and bad had been one and the same.

Joe said, "Linds. The lawyer. What did he say?"

"He said that Marty wasn't my biological father."

"Oh my God." Joe tightened his grip on my hands. "You believe that?"

I nodded. "It explains a lot, Joe. How he treated me."

"Did Cat know?"

"Which part? Actually, it doesn't matter. She for sure knew he was alive, they'd been keeping in touch, but chose not to tell me. Her intentions may have been good, but seriously. It was a time bomb."

"Brad Mitcham also gave me these."

I fumbled in my jacket pocket, brought out the ring I'd seen on Mom's ring finger for so many years and the letter she'd written to me just before she died.

"This was my grandmother's engagement ring. It's a family heirloom. I'm going to wear it as a pendant for a while, I think. And she left me this letter. I haven't read it yet. I want to be in a cooler mood."

Joe nodded.

I was starting to slur my words, not from the half tumbler of wine but from the stress of the day. But I still had more to say. So, I tried.

"Also, Marty had a new wife. Darla. And a stepson named Austin. Cat gave me the wife's number. I need...to...interview..."

I heard Joe as if from a distance. A long way away.

"Conklin. You want Conklin."

I didn't understand.

CHAPTER 21

I WOKE UP at the table where Joe caught me before I fell off my chair. He walked me to the bedroom, helped me undress, and had his hand at my elbow as I stepped into the shower. It had to be midnight. I didn't care. I was done.

Joe had given me his arm and I'd climbed out of the tub and stood on a sodden bathmat as he toweled me off. Five minutes later, I was in our big bed, tucked under Joe's arm, holding him tight. I fell asleep with my head on his shoulder.

It was still black outside our windows when something shocked me awake. Joe was sleeping. I may have had a dream. And then, I heard it again. It was the crack of gunfire. One shot.

I shook Joe's shoulder and he started awake.

"What? What's wrong?"

"I think I heard a gunshot."

And then there was another. Joe swung his legs out of the bed, asking me questions as he got to his feet. *How many shots? Had I heard voices? A speeding car?* He kept the lights off as he went to the window and looked down on the street. Then he dressed, stuck his gun in his waistband, put on a Kevlar vest and a windbreaker.

"Joe. Don't go out. I'm calling for backup."

"I'll be careful. Be right back," he said.

I scrambled out of bed. I found my phone in my jacket pocket and called dispatch, gave my name and badge number to the night supervisor.

"What do you need, Sergeant?"

"Shots heard, near 1023 Lake Street between 11th and 12th. Three minutes ago. Request backup, forthwith."

I told dispatch that my husband was an off-duty FBI agent, armed, looking for the shooter and described his clothing.

"Plainclothes operative on the street. Copy that, Sergeant."

I watched from the window as Joe, looking like a shadow, stepped out from the alcove surrounding the front door. He stood still for several minutes then got into his black Mercedes, parked only yards away.

I heard sirens coming up Lake. Joe flashed his lights, and after the squads parked in front of the building, he had a few words with the uniforms. Minutes later he was again inside our apartment, throwing the lock, stowing his gun.

"I saw nothing," he said.

"Good," I said. "Am I getting paranoid?"

"I heard shots, too. Really. Come here," he said.

Sunlight woke me up, I felt rested because it was half-past nine. I threw on a robe and did some apartment surveillance. Julie's lunch box, backpack, and her cute little girl self were gone. So was Joe. From Martha's absence I knew she'd been walked and must be with Mrs. Rose across the hall.

I looked down on Lake Street and saw a patrol car idling outside the building, my watchdog. Everything else looked completely normal. And I felt normal too. The good sleep had cleansed away much of yesterday's trauma. My anger had cooled and my thoughts were clear.

Marty Boxer was dead and he'd left plenty of evidence that he was just as bad as I'd thought he was. Actually worse. Cat had loved him and would handle the funeral arrangements with Darla. Finding out who killed Marty was my job, and as soon as I got to work, I'd be on it.

I put myself together, then called the squad room to let Brenda know that I'd be at my desk by ten-thirty, latest.

Brenda said, "Brady wants to see you."

"He's my first stop when I get in."

Downstairs, I greeted Officers Dench and Ementhaler and released the patrolmen back to their regular assignments. My car was where I'd parked it on 12th Street last night. Since then, one car had parked in front of it and another had parked behind. It took me a moment to see that something was off.

My heart jumped without knowing why, then my brain caught up. The car was on an odd slant. There were a couple of shiny shell casings on the street beside it, and all four tires were flat. Then I noticed something under the windshield wipers. It was a paper napkin, a note penciled in block letters: "Let Marty RIP. Or yr next."

No signature.

The killer was writing to me? Warning me off? There were evidence bags and latex gloves in my glove box. I opened the passenger-side door with my key, extracted a glassine envelope and a pair of gloves, and secured the casings and the note.

The traffic light was red on Lake and the squad car was waiting for it to change. With the bagged shell casings and note inside my pocket, I dashed to the cruiser, knocked on the window, and hitched a ride with Dench and Ementhaler to the Hall.

I hadn't charged my phone last night, but if I worked fast, the battery would last. I called Joe. I called Brady. And I called Claire.

CHAPTER 22

THE CRUISER LET me out on Harriet Street where Claire was waiting for me in scrubs and tennis shoes.

"Where's your car?"

I said, "On the way to the crime lab."

"What? Why?"

I told her the little I knew, but her shocked expression told me that she'd seen through my casual description of the holes in my tires, the death threat on the windshield.

"How are you doing?" she asked me.

"Much better than yesterday. It could only be better."

Claire drew me into a hug, then stepped back and said, "I've got the autopsy report."

"I'm guessing cause of death is a bullet to the back of the skull."

"Yes, Sergeant smarty-pants. The .38 slug is mushroomed but it's on its way to the lab. But that's not all. Marty had liver cancer."

"Awww, geez."

Claire said, "He wouldn't have made it to Christmas. Other non-fatal disease and injury will be in my report."

"Thanks, girlfriend."

"You call me as much as you want."

"Is the report ready now?"

"Being typed."

"Okay. I'll call you later." I kissed her cheek and was walking away when Claire called out.

"Wait," she said. "What are we doing with my patient?"

"Cat will be in touch."

I waved goodbye and headed down the breezeway to the Hall's back door. It was just over thirty-six hours since Marty Boxer had been shot in classic execution style. I wanted to see Yuki Castellano. Yuki is an ADA, a rising star in the DA's office. She's also Brady's wife and my very good friend.

CHAPTER 23

I CALLED YUKI from the street and she picked up on the first ring. I asked if she had a minute to meet me outside HOJ's main entrance so we could walk and talk.

"Be right there," she said.

It was a short trip from Yuki's second-floor office to the building's entrance, and two minutes after I called her, Yuki was there, dressed in a fine blue suit, four-inch heels, and a navy-blue streak in her hair.

"Oh my God. Linds, I'm at a loss for words. Brady told me about your father," she said. "How are you? Are you okay?"

Yuki is so sharp sparks fly off her and I knew all I could tell her was the bare truth.

"Yesterday almost made me crazy. Too many thoughts. Well, you know how I felt about Marty. I woke up this morning thinking that his death doesn't materially affect my life. But it affects Cat and her girls. I have to find his killer for them."

Yuki was following me. "What's your plan?"

"I'm working on it."

"How can I help?"

I said, "I've gotta give you the short version now, okay? I have a meeting with Brady in ten minutes."

"Do the best you can."

I told Yuki what little I knew about Marty's second wife and that I needed to see Darla Boxer, pronto. "She may know who did this—or she may have done it herself."

"Call me if you need a warrant."

"Let's just say I need a search warrant for Darla Witt Boxer's house and car."

"Done," she said.

Yuki and I hugged outside the main door to the Hall. And once I was inside an elevator, I understood what I'd half-heard Joe say as I was falling asleep in my soup last night. Something about wanting Conklin, and want him I did.

Conklin has a gift. Women just trust him.

I'd never seen him fail.

CHAPTER 24

I REPORTED ON yesterday's operations to Brady and he took notes.

"There's a term for all this."

"Harrowing," I said. "Mind-splitting."

"I call it Boxer's idea of a good time."

"I'll have a typed report for you on Friday."

"Good job, Lindsay. Keep going."

Before he shooed me out, I said, "There's more."

His look said, *Not possible.*

I took out the sealed bags holding two .38 shell casings and a paper napkin. I showed him the note on one side. "Let Marty RIP. Or yr next."

"Where did these come from?"

"Gunshots into my tires at about 3 a.m. and the note was stuck under my windshield wipers. Whoever shot Marty knows I've been on the case, knows where I live, and is trying to intimidate me. Gotta tell you, Brady. This scares me."

"Scares me, too. Will you listen to me, Boxer? Take time off. Go out of town with your family. You lookin' to die with your boots on?"

"Brady, you know what I'm going to say. This is my case. I've got to see it through. I want to. I have to."

He shook his head like "What's the point?" and signed off on a 24/7 patrol unit for my family's protection. Then he filled out a voucher for a car to use while my Explorer was being given a complete workup at the lab.

Back at my desk, with Conklin to my left, Alvarez to my right, my back to the wall, the local news was coming over the TV hanging overhead. FORMER SFPD COP MURDERED NEAR THE HALL OF JUSTICE was the headline. I picked up the remote and muted the sound. I ignored complaints from the bullpen. I had coffee, keys to a loaner car from the repo depot, and a partial plan.

I said, "Sonia, please keep working the files we took from Marty's office. Make a copy of this paper-napkin note for us and send the original to the lab with these shell casings. They're number one priority. Rich, let's saddle up."

We took an unmarked Chevy and made good time. The house where Marty had lived with Darla and her son, Austin, was on Arch Street in Ingleside Heights. Arch was a steep road running down from north to south, near Garfield. A family neighborhood, it was populated with a double row of 1940s bungalows, each with peaked, red-tiled roofs and round, gated entranceways mostly unchanged since World War II. Marty's house was in the middle of the block.

I pulled up to the small stucco house and blocked the driveway so that the car parked there was hemmed in. I had a feeling that Darla Boxer was going to resist coming in for questioning.

I said to Conklin, "You give her the flowers and I'll slam her against a wall, cuff her, and call her names until she tells us what we want to know. Okay?"

Conklin laughed as we marched up the walk together.

"I'm happy to be your front man," he said.

"We'll see. Meanwhile, take the back door."

I rang the doorbell and a moment later, I heard a door slam from inside the house. Damn it. I sighed and met Conklin coming around the side yard with Darla. She was late thirties, dressed in black, streaked hair neatly brushed, minimal makeup. Rich had a good grip on her arm.

"Let go of me," she said. "You have no right."

Conklin said, "Please be nice, Mrs. Boxer. We're all on the same side here."

"I've heard about *her*," she said, shooting sharp looks at me.

"You might want to consider the source," said Conklin.

"What does that mean?"

I stepped closer and said, "I'm sorry for what happened to Marty. We didn't get along, as you know, but it was a family matter and I have never wished him any harm. I'm the primary investigator on Marty's case and my team is going to work hard to find out who killed him."

Darla relaxed a little, dropped her gaze, and Conklin unhanded her.

I said, "Inspector Conklin here is a great investigator and we're totally committed to bringing in Marty's killer."

"How would you like to be called?" Rich asked her.

"Mrs. Boxer."

"Mrs. Boxer, you can call me Rich if I can call you Darla."

Darla shrugged, said "Fine."

"And you can call me Lindsay," I said.

"I guess I should call you that. I am kinda your stepmother, right?"

I didn't blink. I just listened.

Conklin went on. "Do you have any weapons in the house, Darla?"

"Like guns?"

"Right," Rich said.

"I didn't allow it. We—I have an eight-year-old."

"I assume he's at school now?"

Darla nodded.

"Mind if we take a look just so we can cross it off our list?"

Darla shrugged again. I had the warrant from Yuki but it looked like we wouldn't need it. Darla gave Conklin a tour of the closets and drawers while I poked around in Marty's home office. When we were satisfied that there were no guns in the house, we three got into the patrol car and Conklin drove us back to the Hall. Twenty-five minutes later, Conklin, Darla, and I were in Interview One at the station. Alvarez was observing behind the glass and the camera was rolling.

"May I have some water?" Darla asked.

Conklin got up and returned with three varieties of bottled water and a cup of ice.

"Thanks," she said. "What do you want to know?"

CHAPTER 25

WE WERE AT the scarred gray table in the interview room. I sat beside Rich and he sat across from Darla. Rich had established rapport with our subject and for the most part, I just listened as Rich asked and Darla answered his softball questions.

"Darla, how long have you and Marty been together?"

"About seven years. We met in Mexico, but we're both from California. After Marty had his heart attack, we decided to come back to be closer to family."

Darla didn't look me in the face as she told this story, and I wondered how many holes she was covering up.

"Darla, where were you on Sunday night?"

"Home."

"Who can verify that?"

"My neighbor, Angela, and my *little boy*, Austin. We watched a movie on TV."

"When did you last speak with Marty?"

"When he was leaving Briny's after having drinks with Leo. Eight something. Sunday night."

"Was anything troubling Marty?"

"There was always something, but nothing stands out."

"If there was something wrong, would he tell you?"

Darla shrugged. "Probably. *And, then again,* maybe not."

"Had anyone threatened him? Do you know of anyone who wanted to harm him? Had either of you gotten strange phone calls, seen any strangers or unfamiliar vehicles?"

According to her, he was a good husband with bad habits. He stayed out "working late," sometimes didn't come home until morning.

I thought, *He's out gambling, or worse.*

Rich said, "I hate to ask, Darla, but it's standard operating procedure. Do you think Marty may have been seeing someone else?"

Darla said, "An affair? Marty? At his age?"

"What about you?" Richie asked. "Let's say you were seeing someone who wanted you for himself, see what I mean? A jealous man who thought you deserved better?"

"No, and marriage is a holy sacrament. Marty was faithful. He talked about horses. He talked about his bookie, Jack Robbie. He liked Jack. He talked about food, and Austin and Leo and cash in the bank; spending money so he could get lunch or have his shoes resoled. I'd give our marriage a B+ and I'm proud of that.

"I already miss him so much." Darla sniffled, then looked up. "You think I could use the washroom?"

Brenda brought Darla to and from the ladies' room and once Darla was settled in again, we got into round two of the interrogation.

CHAPTER 26

I JUMPED INTO the conversation and asked Darla if Marty had enemies from his work as a PI or if anyone from the bookmaking business had a score to settle.

Darla said, "He didn't have enemies, Lindsay. He never came home looking beat-up from a fight. No lipstick on his shirt. Not once. There were no angry calls." She paused. "Oh. There was one call a few years ago that sticks out in my mind. Marty was swearing into the kitchen phone. When he hung up, I asked him. 'What was that about?'

"He said something like, 'Oh, that was Billy Tomato. Called me out of the blue. I think he was working up to borrowing some money.'

"I asked for more of the story," Darla said, "but that's all he gave me. Billy Tomato. I swear. Can I get a ride home now? I have to be home for my son."

CHAPTER 27

THE NAME "BILLY Tomato" did sound ridiculous, but it rang a distant bell. I looked around for Cappy McNeil, who had encyclopedic knowledge of all things SFPD. I found him making fresh coffee in the break room and put it to him.

"Does the name 'Billy Tomato' mean anything to you?"

"Coffee, dear?"

"I'm caffeinated to the eyeballs, but thanks anyway."

"Really. Are you doing okay, Lindsay?"

"It only hurts when I laugh."

"I gotta be careful, then. You say Tomato, I say D'Amato."

"D'Amato?"

"You got it. Bill D'Amato was Marty's partner for a while, maybe thirty years back."

"Marty's wife says there was a heated phone call some six or seven years ago between Marty and this Tomato D'Amato. Cappy. Can we talk for a moment?"

We took seats in a pair of rickety folding chairs.

I said, "So, what was the Bill and Marty story?"

"Pretty short story," Cappy said. "I thought D'Amato was a good cop. Marty thought otherwise."

"Don't stop now," I said.

"I'm stirring up my memory. Okay. Marty told the boss that D'Amato was dirty. Something about looting a crime scene. Billy was pretty by-the-book, maybe a year or so out of the academy on the job, tops. Marty had friends in medium-high places."

"So, what happened to D'Amato?"

"Well," said Cappy. "He wasn't going to fight the decision or join up another PD with 'looting a crime scene' in his file. I'm really reaching for an actual memory, Lindsay, but I think he moved to LA and got a job as a consultant to a cops-and-robbers TV series. But Marty really did hate the guy. If I had to guess, I'd bet that D'Amato ratted Marty out for looting. And Marty punished him for it by flipping the story."

"You know, Cappy. There's no shortage of people who hated Marty. If I'm going to nail his killer, I don't need to tell you, we need a witness. A murder weapon. Evidence. This case is all needles, no haystack."

"I didn't hate Marty, kiddo. But I wouldn't have trusted him with a stick of gum."

"Thanks, Cappy."

I returned to the bullpen. Conklin and Alvarez were both at their desks. I told them about my conversation with Cappy and said, "Let's find out where D'Amato lives, what he does now, and any other bit of information that could add up to a hit on Marty Boxer."

Alvarez is a wiz at technology. I'd put her up against any computer pro. We didn't have loads of time but Alvarez typed, refused to be drawn into any conversation until she was done.

"I'm still working my way through Los Angeles," she read, "but I've got this: 'William A. D'Amato, creative consultant on *The Crack of Dawn,* an HBO production, also worked with Randy Wilson on a film called *The Beat.*'"

"When was that?" I asked.

"Uh. Date on this article is five years ago. Just over."

"Anything else?" Conklin asked.

"I'll keep looking," said Alvarez. "Oh. I've got a cell phone number. LA area code."

"See if you can get him on the phone."

Alvarez punched in a number, said her name, and why she was calling.

Then she handed me the phone.

CHAPTER 28

"HELLO, MR. D'AMATO? This is Sergeant Lindsay Boxer."

He said, "Lindsay, Lindsay, it's Billy D'Amato. Great of you to call. I just heard the news about your dad on TV. I'm actually in San Francisco with my wife, Beverly, for the week. She remembers you as a kid. My God, I've been thinking about you. My condolences. Do you remember me?"

"I'm sorry to say I don't. But I'd love to talk with you."

"Your wish is granted," D'Amato said.

Beverly. Beverly, Bill's wife came into my mind. I'd gone to the D'Amatos' dinner party at what I thought of then as a grown-up restaurant.

Bill was speaking, "Lindsay, I can be at the Hall in half an hour. Is that good for you?"

"It sure is. You remember Cappy McNeil? He's still here. I know he'd like to see you, too."

I joined Alvarez in a digital file search but switched from General to Specific. I opened the SFPD personnel files and found Marty Boxer and Billy D'Amato. There was more in there than I'd expected. Three commendations for bravery and three reports to the commissioner's office.

I was glad to see that Sergeant Marty Boxer had been cited for bravery under fire, but of course more interested in the reports.

"Alvarez. Look at this. Cappy was right."

She scooted her chair next to me and we looked at D'Amato's complaints. Marty had been cleared of two charges, and the third was unresolved. He was damned lucky he didn't go to jail.

"See here?" I said to Alvarez.

The first complaint was an accusation of theft of a solid gold cigarette lighter from a Mrs. Reva Bolo's house in Russian Hill. Mrs. Bolo called the police to report a possible stalker. Marty Boxer and Billy D'Amato had caught the call. A day after the police came to Mrs. Bolo's home, she reported that a gold lighter that had once belonged to Vincent Lombardi was missing. It wasn't discovered missing until after the police had left Mrs. Bolo's home. The stalker was never found. Neither was the lighter.

The second was D'Amato's response to a dispute resolution over the same issue. Marty accused D'Amato of stealing Mrs. Bolo's lighter. D'Amato said he hadn't done it. He was quoted saying that when he left the complainant's bedroom, the lighter was on her night table. He later added a note to the file, an official notice that he was leaving the department. He added that this was a cautionary attachment for the file that Marty Boxer was known to take personal effects from victims. In one case, the object was medication and the victim had later died. A note from the captain confirmed the victim's death.

"I have no intention of going to war over this," D'Amato's note concluded. "Just be apprised that as Martin Boxer's onetime partner I saw evidence of multiple petty and major crimes."

Alvarez said, "Oh, my God. If Marty was questioned about this—"

"—there would be no 'all is forgiven' handshake with D'Amato," I said. "And here's D'Amato's letter of resignation."

Alvarez said, "I wonder what that lighter was worth."

An image of a gold lighter came to me. It was on Leo Spinogatti's desk. Had Marty pocketed it, given it to Leo?

Pushing the thought out of my mind, I scrolled digital pages until I found D'Amato's third complaint to the commissioner.

I read that it involved dereliction of duty. Their lieutenant had assigned Marty and D'Amato a new partner, Dillon Kennedy, to stake out a payday-loan check-cashing shop.

There was an armed robbery at that shop while Kennedy and Boxer were on the job. Kennedy was shot dead inside the store and so were the two shopkeepers. The safe was empty. Marty was nowhere around.

According to the notes and transcript of the board review, Marty reported he had a kidney infection, and that claim was backed up by a note from his doctor. He told the board that he'd left the stake-out and his partners to find a place to relieve himself. He went to the Fillmore Hotel a few blocks away, got to talking with a hotel clerk, and when he returned to his post, he saw that bloody hell had broken up the payday-loan storefront. And that Kennedy, his new partner, had been killed.

The money, calculated to be in the tens of thousands, was never recovered. Nor were the surveillance camera's hard drives. They had been pulled by the robber or robbers and also not recovered. The only witness was a frightened teenage kid who'd been smoking weed on the other side of the street.

The kid, Rocco Baldacci, said that masked men robbed the store, that two cops went in, only one cop came out and from a lineup, he identified Marty as the survivor.

I kept reading. Marty's response to the holy-hell screwup was when he returned from his break, he went into the shop to check the damages, and then he had called in the robbery and homicides.

There was no proof that Marty had been involved. His gun hadn't been fired, there was no money on him or in the car, the hotel clerk who had let him use the bathroom confirmed his alibi. But to D'Amato this charge was strike three.

As Alvarez and I knew, Marty quit the force not too long after, then headed down to Mexico before coming back to join up with Leo Spinogatti.

I said to Alvarez, "Here's how it sounds to me. He was either innocent. Or he made his last big score and was in on the theft. I swear it's a fifty-fifty guess."

Alvarez looked up and said, "Do you know that man?"

I followed her gaze. At the reception desk manned by Bobby Nussbaum on Brenda's days off stood a white man in his sixties, round of face, a port wine birthmark on the left side of his neck, of medium build, wearing a canvas jacket, jeans, loafers, no socks, and an LA Lakers baseball cap.

That's all I got by the time Bobby called my phone, and even though we were thirty feet away, when I picked up, I heard Bobby's voice in stereo.

"Sergeant, a Mr. Bill D'Amato is here. He says you're expecting him."

CHAPTER 29

I BROUGHT BILL D'Amato to the break room, where he stowed his jacket. We poured coffee for ourselves, then took a short walk to the interview room.

I asked D'Amato, "How does it feel being back in this place?"

He said, "Mixed. Let's talk in the box."

Interview One was the bigger of the two interrogation rooms, and a little homier. There was a padded desk chair in the corner and a small fridge. Pads and pens were on the table, and I knew that the videotape would be rolling.

We sat at the table and D'Amato said to me, "Can you please turn off the tape?"

"Why is that necessary?"

"Because I don't want to go to court for anything that might throw a bad light on anyone, even me."

I got up and, with regret, shut off the switch by the door.

"Turn off the mic to the observation room, too, okay, Lindsay?"

Damn it.

"Go ahead," he said. "Please."

I went into the next room, said to Cappy and Alvarez, "If he goes nuts, break in. I'm going to record what is said on my phone."

Cappy said, "Tell him you turned off the mic and don't do it. He's not going to know."

Alvarez said, "I'll record with my phone. You just talk."

"Good."

I walked back into Interview One and said, "We're all alone, Bill. I've got a few questions, and then anything you want to say, I'm here and I care."

I took a notepad and pen from the center of the table and headed the top page with our names and the date and time.

Then, "Bill, when was the last time you saw Marty?"

"When I quit, because of him, all those years ago. I wanted to be a cop since I was about ten and resigning broke my fuckin' heart. That and I had to explain it in job interviews. Still, everything worked out okay. Working on cop films. Being the authority. Having a gig where you go home on time and no one shoots at you."

"I'm guessing the pay's better."

"You'd be half right. The cost of living in LA is higher. But Beverly and I have a house with a pool. You met my wife a couple of times when I brought her to the station. Do you remember Beverly?"

"I think I do. Blond hair. She was very nice to the kid I was back then. So you haven't seen Marty in what, twenty or thirty years?"

"Something like that."

I nodded, and casually asked, "And where were you this past Sunday, from 6 p.m. through about midnight?"

"You think *I* killed him?" D'Amato said in a loud, querulous voice.

"Hell no, Bill. Just account for your time and we can move on. You know how this goes."

He scoffed, shook his head. I was watching his hands, ready to draw down on him if he reached for a weapon. Knowing backup was four feet away on the other side of the mirror was comforting.

CHAPTER 30

D'AMATO GLARED AT me, then decided to tell me his whereabouts at the time Marty was murdered.

He said, "Okay. So yesterday Beverly and I got into SFO at four o'clock. We got to the place we're staying on 39th Avenue. I showered, changed my clothes. Bev watched some liberal news crap on the tube. I did not think of Marty. I didn't call him. I had no idea where he was and I sure didn't cap him, Lindsay. I can show you my boarding pass from the flight. I have a printout in my jacket pocket back in the break room.

"I spent the whole day and night with my beautiful bride and we watched Cop TV until we woke up in the morning. Beverly will testify to this."

I dotted an i, crossed a t on the pad in front of me.

"Good, Bill. Now that we've got your movements down, who do *you* think killed Marty?"

"I know thirty guys and more than a couple women who'd kill him for free."

"And?"

"I've got to say, Lindsay, I'm surprised that I'm being treated as a suspect. Feels like the worst of times. I came here, don't forget, on my own time, my own dime."

"Bill, you know you would be asking anyone who knew Marty the same questions."

"Okay. Point, Boxer. Here's something you might want to know."

What he told me made my poor aching head reel. After that, I walked Bill to the break room, accepted his boarding pass from LA to San Francisco, and his business card. I thanked him and walked him to the elevator.

CHAPTER 31

ALVAREZ AND CAPPY were waiting for me in the pod.

I asked, "Sonia, did you get all of that?"

"Absolutely, and the tape quality is totally clear."

I brought out D'Amato's boarding pass and showed it around.

"Looks real enough to me," Conklin said. "Arrival Monday at 4 p.m., the day after Marty was shot on Sunday."

I said, "D'Amato's wife will vouch for him, for what that's worth."

Cappy said, "Thinking out loud."

"Please do," I said.

"It's a six-hour drive from LA to San Francisco. D'Amato could have driven here anytime during the week. Say he makes a date with Marty to maybe, who knows, bury the hatchet. D'Amato stoops to tie a shoelace, shoots Marty in the head on Sunday night. Then he drives home to LA. Little less than a day later, he flies back and arrives at 4:00."

I said, "Rich, can you see if there was a call or two between Bill and Marty on or before Sunday?"

While Conklin was getting Marty's phone from the property, I said, "The major dispute between Marty and Billy happened over a theft from this woman..."

"Bolo," said Alvarez. "Reva Bolo."

"Right. Mrs. Bolo calls the police about a possible stalker. Why did her call get shifted to homicide?"

Cappy said, "Slow night."

"Okay. So the two of them go to check if the lady's fear is something actual, and after they've left, Mrs. Bolo was missing a pricey keepsake. Billy says Marty took it. Marty says it was Billy. Marty had more weight and Billy is out of a job. This changes Billy's life plan to be a cop. That's motive."

Conklin came back scrolling through Marty's phone.

He said, "Three calls to and from Darla on Sunday, nothing from D'Amato. We found no gun on Darla but we didn't check out Darla's alibi with the neighbor Angela. I'll get on that."

I nodded. And I was having thoughts about Darla. Had she had enough of her husband's "bad behavior"... I was trying it on when movement down at the end of the aisle caught my eye.

Brady was leaving his office, heading toward us in a hurry. When he reached our pod, Brady said, "We've got a confession. A dying declaration."

CHAPTER 32

ALVAREZ SAID, "A confession to Marty's murder? By whom?"

Brady said, "Jack Robbie. Tried to shoot himself in the head but his girlfriend pushed the gun away. He still took a head shot and he's not expected to make it, but he can speak a few words. You'll want to talk to the girlfriend."

I said, "Robbie's at Metro Emergency?"

"Girlfriend is there, too. Only one of you can see him," Brady said. "Boxer, you're up. Record what he says. Fly."

Conklin said he'd drive. Alvarez said she'd man the desk and relay messages.

If there was ever a time for Code Three, this was it. Deathbed confession during noon rush. Rich shot off the mark with lights flashing and sirens screaming. We had to get to the hospital while Robbie lived and breathed.

Traffic on 101 South was fair. We took Cesar Chavez Street to Valencia, dodging, weaving, taking tight corners. We pulled into Metro's parking lot, and Conklin let me out at the ER entrance.

Conklin said, "Go for it. Run."

"You can come to the waiting room."

"Boxer. Run," he said again.

I patted my jacket pocket, felt my phone, then ran toward the revolving door. I badged all human impediments including the charge nurse at the entrance to the ER.

The attending physician said, "Sergeant, the patient comes in and out of consciousness. I can only give you five minutes with him and if he lights up the board, you've got to leave."

"Okay. Thanks. That should be enough time," I said, thinking, *as long as his memory was present and he could speak I was going to stay with him.*

CHAPTER 33

JACK ROBBIE WAS cocooned inside a curtained stall, one of twelve in the emergency room. I badged his nurse and told her that this was official police business.

She let me pass.

Robbie was a bloodless version of the man I'd met just yesterday afternoon. He wore a white cotton hospital robe. There was a cannula in his nose, an IV pole with a drip bag, tubes transporting fluids to and from his body, and a stent draining the bandaged gunshot wound at the back of his skull. His eyes were closed and his vital signs blinked on the bedside monitor.

We were not alone. Along with the nurse who came in to check on him, there was a pretty woman in her twenties wearing a short pink dress, her brown hair loose around her shoulders. This was Pearl Joy, Robbie's massage girl, sitting by his side.

I introduced myself to Pearl, told her who I was and why I was there, that since I was only permitted a very little time with Jack, would she answer some questions about the shooting incident?

Pearl said, "Let's go outside."

We stood in the wide corridor, close enough to Jack's stall to hear the beeps of his vital signs monitor.

Pearl was very ready to talk.

"Here's what set Jack off," she said. "He was going over the weekly book and he was grumbling. He was coming up short and that's when Mr. Boxer called with another bet. That was way after lunch on Sunday, like, we're pretty much closed. Mr. Boxer kept doubling down on his losing bets, working some of them off and I have an idea how, but it's guesswork. So like, I shouldn't tell you."

"I know about that, so please go on."

"Okay, so Jack warned Mr. Boxer that he didn't want to see him again without being paid back half of what was owed. That he wasn't taking any more of Mr. Boxer's bets until that happened. I heard all of that," said Pearl.

To my great relief, she kept talking.

"Mr. Boxer stopped by with a down payment that was way less than Jack had said he had to have. So Mr. Boxer left and Jack just got very mad. Like Mr. Boxer thought he was a sucker and it had been going on too long."

Pearl stopped talking as the nurse went into the stall the size of a department store dressing room, apparently checked Robbie's vitals and came out. When she saw me, she wagged her forefinger, a warning that my time was almost up. Then she left.

"I tried to calm him down," Pearl said. "You know I really love Jack and he doesn't take care of himself. He has high blood pressure. But, so, he keeps like talking and getting madder. And then he makes a phone call. And I hear him say something about a wire transfer. Then he calls Mr. Boxer and says, 'Marty. Sorry I yelled. Where are you?' And it seems like Mr. Boxer told him where he was. And Jack says, 'Why don't you stop by here when you finish up over there.'"

"This is all helpful, Pearl," I said. "Jack knew where Marty was having drinks?"

"Yes, and he told me. 'The son of a b. is at Briny's.'"

I said, "So Jack went there?"

I was trying to imagine this soft hulk of a man lying in wait for Marty as he walked from his shop to his car.

Pearl said, "No, no. He waited for Marty."

I said, "The wire transfer. It was payment for the hit on Marty?"

Pearl didn't hesitate.

"Right. Exactly. And as soon as Jack hung up with Marty, he knew he couldn't change his mind. He was kind of crying and from what I could make out, he said he was so sick with himself, he couldn't go on. How broken he was, financially and physically and morally. But the train had left the station."

CHAPTER 34

PEARL WAS SAYING that Jack had commissioned Marty's killer. It was an admission to a crime but was it enough to charge Robbie with murder? It was all reported speech. Hearsay. Pearl had to tell me who Jack had hired to do the job.

Just then, we heard Robbie moan. Two nurses sped past us, yanked open the curtains to Robbie's stall, and rushed to his bedside. I had my phone on Record. I followed them in, nudged them aside, and would not let anyone get in front of me. I'm not sure if that was a crime of some sort, but I was beside myself. I leaned over Robbie.

"Jack. Lindsay Boxer. We met yesterday."

He opened his eyes.

I showed him my badge and moved closer with my phone still recording. "Jack. You hired someone to shoot Marty Boxer?"

"I was going to hell anyway."

"Who did you hire?"

He closed his eyes.

"I need his name. Jack?"

He'd just muttered a name when an alarm went off on the bedside monitor where a green line was diving. Two more people crowded into the stall. One of those people was an orderly.

He said, "You. You have to get out."

I hesitated. Had I gotten the shooter's name on tape? The orderly put a hand on each of my upper arms and half-lifted me off my feet and removed me from the stall.

I stood in the hallway, my own blood pressure soaring, but my head was working.

When Pearl and I were standing together again, I said, "Pearl. I'm sorry to interfere when you're going through this. I want to confirm what Jack just told me. Were you with Jack when he hired the shooter?"

"I *know* him. I was with Jack when he called him and wired the money. The deal was made and Jack paid him in advance to do the job."

Pearl covered her eyes with her hands. Her shoulders shook as she cried. I waited out the long thirty to forty seconds it took for Pearl to take her hands from her eyes and stop crying, but she did and she picked up where she'd left off.

"The shooter called me later and asked me to book him on a first-class flight to Morocco. His flight leaves today. The details are on the computer back at the store, but you can look it up. It's on Qatar Airways. They only have a few flights.

"I made the call and when I went back to Jack, he'd already taken his gun out of the nightstand. He put his arms around me, told me I was a good girl and that he loved me. And he said he'd left money for me under the mattress with a note saying it was for me.

"I started to argue with him—but it was too late. He'd made up his mind and was pointing the gun—like this—at his head. I pushed his hand away hard but...he had his hand on the trigger and the shot...that shot." Pearl looked up at me. "I think he's going to live. Don't you?"

I said, "I hope Jack makes it. Pearl, this is so important. I may need you to testify."

She nodded.

"Please speak." I put my phone up to her face.

"Yes. I'll do it. I'll testify. For Marty."

I gave her my card. And as I left the ER, I phoned Richie.

"See you in two minutes," I said.

CHAPTER 35

RICH FLIPPED ON all the flashing lights: cherry, grille, and dash. Then did the same with the sound, using horn and sirens. He jammed on the gas and took Cesar Chavez to 101 South and from there, a clear shot to SFO.

Qatar Airways' flight to Morocco boarded in fifty-three minutes. Now, fifty-two. If Brady was able to get the flight delayed, if we didn't run into a traffic jam at the airport, if we had the help of the airport police, if we made it to the gate on time, if the man who shot Marty hadn't changed his flight, we had a good chance of grabbing him up and putting this nightmare into the very capable hands of the district attorney's office.

Given every lucky break, there was plenty of room for disaster starting with the word "if." If our subject saw us coming, if he grabbed a hostage . . . or if he fled from the gate and buried himself in the crowd, he could leave the gate and the concourse and melt back into traffic. He might even buy a new ticket and catch a plane to anywhere.

And Marty Boxer, for better or worse, would never get justice. On the other hand, if we pulled this off with no plan or prep, we could dance the merengue in the streets.

As if I had manifested it, a traffic snarl filled all lanes in the circular airport access road and all the horns and sirens in the world wouldn't move the solid clot of traffic between us and the Qatar Airways' boarding gate.

Brady called, checked in over our dedicated radio channel.

"I left your name and Conklin's with the airport police and airport security. The flight has been delayed for a few minutes. It was made to sound like they were still cleaning out the plane. God willing, Alvarez and I will meet you at the gate."

I said, "Brady, I've got the girlfriend's story on tape. It's good. Robbie mumbled the shooter's name into my phone but Pearl will be a witness regardless. We're stuck in traffic. I don't know if we'll make it in time but we'll keep you posted."

We moved slowly through the traffic jam. The volume of our sirens caused drivers ahead of us to pull over when possible. We spent a full twenty minutes on that traffic circle, then another ten minutes working our way through the miles of drop-off points where airline and taxicab passengers were unloaded.

It was now ten minutes to takeoff. Rich parked in a No Parking Anytime zone. Inside the building, I glanced at the flight board and saw Qatar 1020 would be leaving in eight minutes.

Rich badged an airport cop whose name tag read FLYNN. Flynn was sharp and fast. He commandeered a motorized luggage cart and we all boarded it. With Flynn driving, we sped along the international concourse, slowed when we saw that it was backed up with passengers in the wide center aisle, thicker around the gates.

I wanted to yell, "Come onnnnn!" as passengers shuffled to the news and food kiosks and little screaming kids raced around, going wild. It should have been an easy run to the gate, but it was a freaking steeplechase.

The airport cop said, "Let's go."

He braked, abandoned the cart, and ran with us to the gate just as the boarding announcement began. The PA squealed, then a voice ordered first-class passengers to join the queue. I saw him first.

"Rich. The guy with the hair."

"And the nose?"

"Yes. For sure."

Our airport cop didn't know what we were talking about, so I filled in a few adjectives. "Over six feet. Gray hair. Prominent nose. That's our guy."

The three of us crept along both sides of the line of passengers waiting to board. The flight attendant who was at the head of the queue looked up, saw us—but she'd not been clued in. Her face took on a number of sequential expressions: confused, PO'd, questioning, adamant. If our subject had been watching her, he would be alerted.

Flynn walked up to our person of interest and said, "Excuse me, sir. I need to see your passport again."

Bruce Cavanaugh muttered, "For God's sake," and reached into his jacket's inside breast pocket. Conklin and I sprang, and I do mean literally sprang, right up to Cavanaugh, me on the left, Conklin on the right, and we shoved him out of line.

Flynn held a gun on Cavanaugh while Conklin cuffed him and dropped him to his knees. While Conklin frisked him thoroughly, I said, "Bruce Cavanaugh, you're under arrest for the murder of Martin Boxer."

Cavanaugh interrupted my reading of his rights with protests and arguments, but I pushed on. I saw a tall, well-built blond-haired man heading our way with a sprightly brunette who was new to Homicide. They sprinted toward us.

Cavanaugh wasn't having it. He struggled and shouted, and although I thought Rich and I could've wrangled him out to the patrol car, it was better to have Lieutenant Jackson Brady to supply the muscle.

Out at the curb, I thanked Flynn, and Brady said to all of us, "God, we're good. Not a shot fired."

I checked my pocket to make sure I hadn't lost my phone, and I pulled it out to show Brady.

"It's all here, Brady. The Goose is cooked."

CHAPTER 36

THE REST OF the day went as smoothly as if we'd planned it.

Brady and Alvarez had a grille partition between the front and back seats of their car, and after stuffing a cuffed Goose Cavanaugh into the back seat, they drove him to the Hall for booking. Conklin and I got into our unmarked car, and I called Metro's emergency room to check on Jack Robbie.

I was told he was still in the ER but that his condition had stabiiized. I knew he would have to be arrested for felony murder and Brady was busy, so I said to Rich, "We have to go back to Metro."

Once inside the ER, Rich and I both cleared the succession of nurses and orderlies and went directly to Robbie's stall, where I arrested him for the felony murder of Martin Boxer, and I read him his rights. Either he understood me or just knew the drill by heart, since he grunted every time I asked him, "Do you understand?"

Conklin cuffed Robbie to the side bars of his bed and called dispatch for a uniform to guard his ER stall.

Pearl's visiting time had long expired and she had left the hospital, so Rich and I headed downtown to the Mission District. We picked Pearl up at JR's Aces High Dry Cleaners and brought her back to the Southern Station to make a statement.

Which she did.

By then, it was after five.

I phoned the lab and spoke to the director, Eugene Hallows.

"Got anything for me, Gene?"

"Plenty."

He told me that Marty's car was still being processed, that I had new tires on my Explorer, and that he would have my car delivered to the Hall in the morning. As for the shell casings I'd found next to it, there were no prints on them or on the damaged lead retrieved from the old tires.

"And the napkin note?"

"Nothing to compare it with," he said.

"Gotcha. Thanks, Gene."

Well, we *did* have something to compare it with.

Alvarez, Rich, and I were back in our pod and it was very quiet. Rich was filling out paperwork three feet to my left. Alvarez was writing up the airport arrest and I was answering email. And I was having a fantasy that confetti was going to drop from the ceiling or the chief of police was going to come downstairs, shake our hands, and give us field bonuses.

Barring that, I still had a feeling that we weren't done until the shooter who'd blown out my tires was no longer driving around with a loaded .38 looking for me.

"Rich?"

"Yup."

"You still have that matchbook cover? The one with the writing on the back?"

"Christ. I meant to turn it in to the evidence room." He opened his desk drawer, took out the glassine envelope with the matchbook reading *"Bet I get you"*—and the reply—*"All bets are off, Marty."*

I had a copy of the paper-napkin threat, printed in pencil in block letters. Of course the letters were larger on the napkin than on the matchbook cover, but I saw a distinct similarity in the lower loops of the letters and the shape of the *a*'s in the second line.

Rich said, "We're going to need an expert to compare them."

"I may have a connection," I said.

CHAPTER 37

CONKLIN, ALVAREZ, AND I were at our desks, the pod crowded with extra chairs, when Alvarez said, "While we were out . . ."

What now?

"I found something in the Joanna Lake files we got from Leo Spinogatti."

"I'm ready for it," I said.

Alvarez smiled and said, "The last time Cavanaugh was in lockup pending arraignment, his gun was in the property room. When he didn't claim it, it was archived. I checked. We still have Goose's old gun."

Alvarez said, "For laughs, I sent it out to the lab. Asked Gene to have it taken apart. To look at every part of that gun, swab everything. Spare nothing. I told him that we had the gun's owner in custody."

"CSU found something?"

She nodded, wearing a huge grin. And then she told me. "They found something. Has to be processed but the results should be in in a day or two."

"Good police work, Sonia. Mind if I give you a hug?"

She didn't mind. She did blush, though. Which made me smile. I downloaded the audio files with the recordings from the hospital, and emailed them downstairs to be transcribed. Before I left for the day in my loaner car, I called Joe.

"I'm on my way home. I should be inside the living room in seventeen and a half minutes."

And I was. Julie was all over me with stories to tell, songs to sing, and requests to "Please, please go see Mr. Bubbles and Fanny in their new home, pleeease."

My husband asked, "Have a good day, Blondie?"

"Sure did."

"It's all over your face."

Julie had me by the hand and was pulling me to the kitchen. I saw what she saw. If fish can be happy, these two were. I sat down in my lounge chair and Martha jumped up on my legs and licked my chin and honest to everything, this was better than confetti. Better than a handshake and a bonus. Better than all of it.

I could tell from the look in Joe's eyes, we were going to have a good time tonight...

I admit, some part of my mind was listening for another shoe to drop. But I didn't hear the thunk of a falling shoe. Joe and I played Princess with Julie and wrestled with Martha and her rag toy. Finally, Joe and I went to bed.

As anticipated, we had a real good time.

I woke up once that night. Not by a gunshot, or any kind of threat. I thought about my mom's letter, still unopened. Still unread.

CHAPTER 38

THE CHAPEL WAS small and sparsely filled. Marty's widow, Darla Boxer, and her young son, Austin, sat in the left-hand front pew. Cat and her daughters, Meredith and Brigid, sat beside me and Joe across the aisle. Julie stayed at home with Mrs. Rose. In the pews behind us, Cappy McNeil, Pearl Joy, and Marge and Leo Spinogatti made up the complement of mourners who'd come to say goodbye to Marty Boxer.

Marty's coffin rested on a stand in front of the altar, and Pearl Joy had sent flowers. Darla had sent a large vase of lilies and a color enlargement of Marty looking young and happy in his police officer's blues. The photo was set up on an easel behind the casket.

The priest hadn't known Marty, but he had kind words for him, saying that he was in a warm and loving place, under the care of God, and that he could hear our prayers.

He asked if anyone would like to say a few words and I had nothing—but my lovely sister, Catherine, got to her feet. Wearing a buttery-yellow suit and our mother's crucifix, her blond hair held back from her face with combs, she stepped up to the podium.

I was sitting next to my niece Meredith and she grabbed my hand. I put my arm around her shoulders and she leaned against me, her aunt Lindsay.

Cat said, "Thank you, everyone, for coming. I know we all loved Marty in different ways, and will also miss him in our own ways. I've been thinking of both my parents, what hard lives they lived. Mom raised two rambunctious little girls largely alone. Dad was gone much of the time, taking cases up and down the state, doing dangerous work so that his family would have a roof, and food, and school. And then, Mom got cancer and was lost to us too soon.

"But right now, I remember one particularly ordinary summer day that Dad turned into an unforgettable memory. He made it a surprise, too, and we loaded up into his roomy old Pontiac, rolled down the windows to take in the breeze. Destination unknown became the ferry terminal.

"We had a wonderful lunch in a real restaurant, and it was the first time I'd had roast beef on a roll with horseradish. I was still little. About six or seven, and Lindsay was almost thirteen, but she was as pleased as I was—and there was more to come.

"After lunch, we got ice cream cones and took them aboard a beautiful white ferry. There were rows of seats both inside and on the top deck. We went on top, of course. Ran up and down the center aisle and made friends with another girl who had a white fluffy dog. And we hung over the railing before Mom told us not to do that. We watched the beautiful blue water, stirred by the breeze, taking on a miraculous quilted appearance.

"All around us were sailboats.

"There were so many that it seemed like everyone with a boat in the Bay area had decided to use it that day. And from the top deck, this was a wonderful sight.

"I know now that this was only a one-hour cruise, but it seemed so much longer. Dad put me on one knee and had his arm around Lindsay and we cruised under the soaring Bay Bridge with all the sails, like flags, flying around us.

"There were other moments, other times when Dad would stop by to see my own girls, to put delicious treats in their Christmas stockings. One year he brought a kitten who'd been abandoned— and that little cat turned out to be a blessing. The girls named her Chrissy, and she is still with us.

"Marty Boxer had a hard life but good came from it.

"And I see him now, in a blue sky with clouds sailing past him, looking down on his family and friends, thinking of us."

The chapel emptied. Darla introduced herself to Cappy and to Joe. Cat was in the center of a circle of admirers, and I waited until she was free.

I reached out to her and told her, "That was beautiful."

"Do you remember that day?"

"Now I do."

Like Cat, I had good memories of my dad. There. I said it. Memories of my dad that were sweet. And I remembered times when I challenged him and told him that he didn't care about me. And that I didn't care about him. And a time when he'd said I would make a good cop.

And right then and there, tears I didn't know I still had for my father spilled over. Cat put her arms around me and I got makeup on her suit jacket.

"Oh, no, Cat. Your jacket..."

"It's nothing. Nothing."

Joe complimented Cat on her eulogy. He met Darla and Austin, said sweet things to his nieces, shook hands with Cappy and the Spinogattis. Then he swept me into his big black car. Before we pulled out onto Ashton Avenue, I was sobbing into my hands.

CHAPTER 39

THE WOMEN'S MURDER Club met the next evening at what we referred to as our clubhouse. Susie's Café is a Caribbean-style restaurant at the edge of the Financial District, close to the Hall where Yuki, Claire, and I worked. Cindy was a cab ride away.

As usual, Yuki, Claire, and I arrived first. We walked through the front door and we were home. The room welcomed us with delicious aromas, the sounds of the steel drum band warming up, boisterous laughter coming from the regulars at the bar where everyone knew the *Cheers* song backward and upside down.

We greeted Susie and the bartender who calls himself "Fireman" and a bunch of guys we've known and had laughs with for years. Then we continued through the ochre, sponge-painted main room, down a corridor that took us past the kitchen into the back room, which was smaller, quieter, and cozier. The booths provided perfect privacy for four best friends to speak freely, to share secrets, and we'd worked out a few knotty cases here, never to be forgotten.

But tonight, the occasion was just to unwind. Our waitress—the wry, red-headed Lorraine O'Dea—waved in our direction and said, "Take your pick."

There were six red leatherette upholstered booths and five of them were taken. It almost seemed that Lorraine had saved one for us. She brought us chips and dips and a pitcher of beer from the tap and set a place for Cindy.

Claire said to me, "Cindy has headlines this big," holding up thumb and forefinger opened wide. "I hope you're the one who gave them to her."

"Some came from me. Some from Rich. We both had the go-ahead from Brady—and here she comes."

Our friend Cindy Thomas, who covers crime like she was born to do it, is petite, five four, with curly blond hair that she holds off her face with a headband. She wore jeans, a pastel-blue pull-over, and a cream-colored scarf—soft, harmonious colors that are a form of camouflage. Wrongdoers and criminals don't make her as the pit-bull reporter she is until she's gotten her story.

As she crossed to our booth, Cindy looked particularly happy. She was waving the print edition of today's paper with the head-line, SFPD HAVE SUSPECT IN CUSTODY.

Cindy slid into the booth next to Claire, across from me, and gave hugs and fist bumps depending on how close or far we were from her.

"You're an ace," she said to me. "And I've got a scoop for you."

I said, "Tell me."

"Your man Jack Robbie is out of the ER and in 'observation.' He's alive."

"Wow, thanks, Cindy. Please tell me you didn't print our sus-pect's name."

"Trust me a little, would ya? NO. I didn't mention his name or even allude to it."

"Whew," I said. "Tonight, I'm buying."

Lorraine came over, said, "Good going, Lindsay, and you, too, Cindy." And then she read the specials.

We gave Lorraine our orders, including a new pitcher of brew. And Yuki said, "Wait. What's that hanging around your neck?"

"It's my Grandma Frances's ring. I'm going to wear it as a pendant for a while, then lock it up before I lose it."

Yuki leaned over to lift the ring.

"Four carats," Yuki said of the solitaire. "Rose cut. White gold. An antique, Linds. Very, very nice."

I had to laugh, then said, "Girlfriends, something a little different tonight."

I took the card-sized envelope out of my jacket pocket and showed it around.

I said, "Cindy, what am I going to say now?"

"No idea," she said, cocking her head like a baby chick.

Claire and Yuki chimed in in unison. "It's off the record."

"Right. Okay, Cindy?"

"Yes ma'am. You betcha."

I blew her a kiss, then said, "My mother left me a letter before she died. She actually left it with Marty, and he left it with his attorney who gave it to me on Monday."

"The letter," Claire said. "You haven't read it?"

"Nope, and I have no idea what it says. Wanted to share it with you guys, whatever Mom wanted to tell me."

Three pairs of eyes were pinned on me. Beer mugs were set down. I used a knife to slit the flap and pulled out a stiff folded piece of blue stationery. Mom must've written this close to the end. Her handwriting was very shaky, and she'd only filled half of the card.

I squinted, read it fast, then said, "My mother wrote:

Dearest Lindsay,

I'll always be your mother. And Marty will always be your father... In name only. It was never the right time to tell you that he wasn't your biological father. That was someone else. Someone who was a brief but important presence in my life. Because he gave you yours.

Time is short, but we all must move forward. I advise you to dismiss the past. If you spend too much time there, it can bring you down. Just keep moving forward. Know that I love you, that you've already made me so very proud. I see great things ahead for you and when you think of me, please remember my love.

Forever, Mom

Inside the card was another surprise. A photo I'd never seen before, showing Mom holding newborn me.

We all got a little teary. Of the four of us, only Cindy had a mother who was still alive, and she never discussed her. I thought my mother's advice was good—up to a point. But sharing secrets and remembering tough things was how you learned. My opinion.

Lorraine brought our meals, we ate like we'd never seen food before, and because we were all driving, we switched to club soda.

The key lime pie was on the table when I saw Sonia Alvarez coming through the narrow corridor.

She said, "Okay to come outside for a second, Lindsay? I have something to tell you."

I said "pardon me" to my girlfriends, all of whom had met Alvarez before, and went outdoors with my newest pard.

"I'd invite you to join us, but we just asked for the check," I said.

She waved my noninvitation away.

"I've got news."

"Good or bad?"

"Good. Only."

"Oh, man. Am I ready."

Alvarez said, "Like I already said, I asked Hallows to strip Cavanaugh's gun down to the pieces and parts. He did it. He found a fleck of blood. Hallows rushed the DNA test."

"Whose blood?"

"You're not going to guess? Spoil all my fun?"

"Tell me. Please."

"Joanna Lake."

It took two or three seconds to get it, and then I said, "Oh, my God."

"Yes," said Alvarez. "When the Goose shot her at close range, a minuscule droplet of blood flashed back and got lodged under a screw on the grip."

"We've got him for sure."

"We do."

"You want to know the other thing?" Alvarez asked rhetorically. "It's this. Joe Molinari, your excellent husband, got an FBI handwriting analyst to read the death threat on the napkin and the note on the matchbook—and compare it with some of Goose's handwriting samples I found in the Lake files."

"You're saying that they *are* all a match."

"It was Goose. The threat left on your car. The writing on the matchbook saying, 'All bets are off, Marty.'"

"Goose will make some kind of deal," I said. "But no. The DA won't make him an offer."

I gave Alvarez another hug. And as we said good night I thought about how much I loved all of the women in my life. In the back room, the Women's Murder Club had polished off the pie and buttoned their jackets. I took the check from Lorraine and added an extra-big tip.

I followed my friends out into the perfect night and we all hugged, wished each other good night. I found my Explorer with its new tires, got in and fired up the engine. I called Joe to say I was on my way.

And that I couldn't wait to get home.

FALLEN RANGER

James Patterson
and Andrew Bourelle

No man in the wrong can stand up against a fellow that's in the right and keeps on a-comin'.

—Texas Ranger maxim first attributed to
Captain Bill McDonald (1852–1918)

PROLOGUE

ONE

DELIA MARQUEZ RIDES shotgun in the armored truck, staring out the window as the scenery of Central Texas rolls by. The roadway runs parallel to the Brazos River as the wide waterway meanders through a rocky canyon with mesquite trees choking the shores. The truck rides high on one side of the canyon, separated from the scree-covered bankside by a steel guardrail. Up ahead, at a bend in the river, there's a lone fishing boat floating on the surface, a little aluminum thing with a single figure kicked back, watching the line for signs of a bite. Otherwise, there isn't a soul around—not a car, not a person, not even a hawk flying overhead—except for the armored truck and its three occupants.

Delia, new to the job.

David Green, a fifty-year-old former trucker from Louisiana, behind the wheel.

And Seth Frederickson, a tall kid only two years out of high school, in the back with the money.

David and Seth have both been with the First Lonestar Credit Union for more than a year now and seem to know what they're doing, but Delia doesn't have too much respect for them. They're soft. She's done two tours in Afghanistan, where she fired her weapon on more than one occasion and witnessed friends injured and killed. These guys, Dave and Seth, wear Kevlar vests and carry semiautomatic pistols on their hips, but they go about their business with a casualness that makes Delia uncomfortable. They wouldn't hack it in the Army.

But this ain't Afghanistan and she tries to cut them some slack.

The armored truck has bulletproof windows, puncture-resistant tires, and gun ports in the doors, but the three of them aren't exactly riding in a convoy through enemy territory in danger of running over IEDs or being besieged by rocket launchers.

It's not her coworkers who need to be more alert—it's Delia who needs to relax.

This is just a job.

It's not life and death.

She lets out a deep breath and tries to enjoy the drive. The view sure beats the desert landscape she's used to.

As the truck approaches the bend in the river where the fishing boat is floating, there is less vegetation crowding the bank, just a rocky slope down to the water. Delia's eyes drift to the person in the boat. She squints, unsure if what she's seeing is correct. She would have expected a guy wearing cargo pants and a fishing vest, maybe a hat to keep the sun out of his eyes. A beer in one hand and a rod in the other. Instead, this person is dressed in a black wetsuit and is wearing snorkel goggles and swim fins. A scuba tank sits inside the boat.

The Brazos is deep in this stretch, maybe fifteen or twenty feet, but she certainly wouldn't have expected someone to go scuba diving here. A muddy Texas river is a far cry from the Great Barrier Reef.

"That's weird," Delia says, sitting up for a closer look at the diver.

"What?" David says from the driver's seat.

Delia doesn't get a chance to answer.

An ear-splitting explosion causes Delia and David to recoil in shock. Ten yards in front of the truck, the roadway erupts in a geyser of flame and debris. Chunks of asphalt rain down on the windshield. Both lanes of the road crumble and begin sliding down the steep slope toward the water. The guardrail tears away like it's made of aluminum foil.

David slams on the brakes, but the armored truck weighs fifty tons—as much as a blue whale—and he can't stop in time. The vehicle skids into the massive hole in the road and tumbles sideways in the landslide. Delia's body is thrown against the restraints of her seatbelt as the truck rolls over and she's turned upside down. She feels like she's strapped inside a clothes dryer.

The truck crashes to a stop, lying on its passenger side. Delia experiences a brief moment of relief but then realizes that they haven't landed on solid ground. The truck is sinking into the river, and the cab is beginning to fill with water.

Delia unclips her seatbelt and splashes into the cold liquid. She gasps from the shock, then rights herself. Kneeling against her door, up to her waist in water, she reaches for David's seatbelt. He has a panicked look in his eyes, paralyzed with indecision.

Delia's seen it before.

She's going to have to do the thinking for both of them.

She gets his belt undone, and he falls on top of her, submerging them both in water. The water is halfway up the cab now. She pulls David's head above the surface and shouts, "We've got to get out of here!"

David has the same panicked look, and Delia elbows him out of her way, grabs ahold of the steering wheel with one hand, and clutches the handle of the driver's door with the other. The door is heavy, not meant to open from below like a submarine hatch. David, finally getting his wits together, helps her, and the two of them wedge the door open. Delia lets David scramble up first, and then she follows, finding it surprisingly hard to climb up and out the door. Vehicles just aren't built to be exited this way.

They stand for a moment on the side of the truck like it's the deck of a sinking ship. Only a foot or two more and the whole truck will be underwater.

Delia hears pounding from below and realizes that Seth is still in the back.

TWO

DELIA TAKES A deep breath and leaps into the water.

She swims down to the door lock and fumbles with the keys, which are attached to her belt by a retractable lanyard. She can hear muffled metallic pounding from inside. Seth could open the door, if he wanted to, but he must be panicked.

Or injured.

Getting the key into the lock is more difficult than she ever would have imagined. The truck continues sinking, yet her own buoyancy keeps pulling her toward the surface. She kicks her legs, squints her eyes in the green murk. Pressure in her ears is building, squeezing her head like a vise.

She needs to take a breath.

She refuses to surface.

Seth has gone quiet inside.

Finally, she slides the key in the slot. Putting one foot on the bumper, she pries open the door, a herculean effort with the weight of the water fighting against her. Seth squirms through the opening and pushes toward the surface.

She joins him and they both gasp for air as they tread water.

Delia is faintly aware of two motorcycles zooming up the highway toward the explosion site. She hopes they stop before they crash into the hole, but she doesn't have time to give the bikers any more thought. She and Seth swim toward shore. It's not easy to do, weighed down by boots and bulletproof vests, but she reaches the bank. Out of breath, she crawls on her hands and knees in the gravel. Liquid pours out of her waterlogged clothes. David, who got to dry ground first, helps her to her feet. Then the two of them help Seth, who has a bloody patch on his wet scalp, where he must have hit his head as he was tumbling around inside the truck.

Delia, standing with her hands on her knees, trying to get her breathing under control, turns her head toward the truck. A cluster of bubbles rises to the surface. Otherwise, there's no sign of the vehicle they were just riding in.

Out on the lake, the diver, now wearing the oxygen tank, leaps from the boat into the water.

"What the hell?" Seth says.

From behind them, Delia hears the familiar metal-on-metal sliding sound of someone racking the cocking handle of a firearm.

She turns slowly.

Two men sit astride motorcycles on the roadway at the top of the scree slope, holding compact submachine guns aimed at Delia and her dripping-wet colleagues. Both riders are covered in black leather clothes and helmets hiding their faces. The air around them is clouded with dust and smoke from the explosion.

"Don't do anything stupid," one of them says, his voice muffled from the helmet. "We've got armor-piercing rounds that'll turn your Kevlar into Swiss cheese."

The rider instructs them to take their handguns—very slowly—and toss them into the river.

Delia considers snatching her sidearm and firing at the men. If she's lucky, she could squeeze off a few shots before they let loose a barrage of bullets. But she has no cover, and the range is in their favor, not hers.

Going for her gun would be suicide.

And, worse, she'd get David and Seth killed.

Moving slowly, she takes her gun and tosses it into the water with a *plop*. Her partners follow her lead and do the same.

"Now your cell phones and radios," the guy says.

They do it.

"Okay, Mr. Y," says the motorcyclist, giving his partner a nod.

The other motorcyclist—Mr. Y, presumably—scrambles down the scree slope, keeping his gun pointed at the men. Within a minute, the three security guards' hands are zip-tied behind them.

"All secure, Mr. X," the robber calls up to his partner on the road.

Delia gets the impression Mr. X is in charge.

The diver emerges from the water with two duffel bags loaded with what Delia can only assume is money. Mr. Y hauls one bag, heavier still with the weight of the water dripping off of it, back up the slope. The diver, whom the others refer to as Mr. Z, removes the flippers and tosses them into the water, then does the same with the oxygen tank, which makes a large splash before sinking. Mr. Z runs up the slope with the second duffel bag.

The three mount their cycles, with Mr. Z riding behind Mr. Y. It's a lot for one bike to hold—two riders and a bag of money and a gun—but the driver zips away skillfully. Before leaving, Mr. X, also with a bag of money slung over his shoulder, turns to Delia and her partners.

"I'm sorry you got caught in the middle of this," he says matter-of-factly.

Then he revs the engine and the bike bursts away like a shot from a gun. Delia is struck dumb by how fast everything happened. In a daze, with the whine of the motorcycles fading, she turns with her hands still restrained behind her back and looks out at the river. The little fishing boat, abandoned and unmoored, drifts toward the other side of the bank. Closer to her, hundred-dollar bills have begun floating to the surface. As she watches the money she was hired to protect drift away with the current, she has two thoughts.

She regrets ever thinking this job was boring.

And she feels lucky to be alive.

PART 1

CHAPTER 1

WILLOW AND I are sitting in the back of a pickup truck over-looking a pretty pond lined with cattails. The night air is filled with the chorus of bullfrogs serenading us. The sky is packed with more stars than either of us have ever seen.

"Rory," Willow says, sliding her hand into mine, "does life get any better than this?"

"I don't see how it can," I say, and we lean in to kiss each other.

Our tongues dance. We hold each other tight, like we're afraid of what might happen if we let go. Willow untucks my T-shirt and strips it off of me. Then she sits back and slowly begins to unbutton her blouse, her face alight with a coy grin. She knows she's driving me wild. I want nothing more than to be with her, skin to skin, our bodies melting together.

She crawls on top of me, putting her lips close to my ear as her golden hair falls around my face.

"Tell me you love me," she says in the slightly raspy voice I fell in love with the first time I heard it. "Tell me you'll be mine forever."

I open my mouth to declare my love to her. I want to tell her she's the only woman in the world for me. That I'll love her, and only her, for the rest of my life.

But I hesitate.

Sensing my reluctance, she props herself on her arms and stares down at me, her expression hurt and confused.

"You still love me, don't you?" she says.

Of course I do.

Don't I?

Something about this doesn't feel right. The sky is no longer black and filled with stars. It's bright with morning light, harsh and blinding. I squint into the glare as Willow pulls away from me.

I reach for her, but she's gone, and so is the truck and the lake and the croak of bullfrogs in the night. I sit up in bed, shirtless and covered in a sheen of sweat, the sheets tangled around me. Warm morning light pours in through the window.

I was only dreaming.

In my grogginess, I become aware of Willow lying in bed next to me. She's facing away from me, the covers pulled back just enough to show the flawless skin of her shoulders and back. Still half asleep, I lean to kiss the nape of her neck and put my arm around her. We can snuggle for a while and maybe when she wakes up we can pick up where the dream left off.

But I stop.

This woman is a brunette—Willow's hair is golden blond.

Then it hits me like a bucket of water. Willow isn't the woman sleeping next to me. She and I broke up a long time ago. The woman in my bed is named Megan.

My girlfriend.

CHAPTER 2

WEARING ATHLETIC SHORTS and nothing else, I pad around the kitchen in my bare feet, filling the coffee percolator and putting it on the stove. Before it's ready, Megan strolls into the kitchen wearing nothing but one of my shirts, which hangs down only low enough to cover the tops of her long lithe legs. She gives me a long kiss and hugs me. With her hair a mess and not a lick of makeup on, she's a knockout.

I'm a lucky guy.

But I feel guilty as hell after the dream. I had my chance with Willow, and no matter how many times I've told myself I'm over her, I guess maybe I'm not.

It doesn't feel fair to Megan.

I haven't cheated on her. I'm a one-woman man, no doubt about it. But I haven't given Megan my whole heart yet. I don't know what the hell my problem is because any man would be blessed to be with her.

"Good morning, Ranger Yates," she says in a jokey tone.

"Good morning, Professor Casewick," I say.

This has become the way we greet each other when we're in a humorous mood. Megan is an assistant professor at Baylor. She's just finished up her first school year on the job and plans to spend the summer doing research to make headway toward tenure.

As for me: I'm a Texas Ranger and plan to spend the summer catching bad guys.

We make breakfast together and talk and joke. It's Sunday morning and, for a change, neither of us has anywhere to run off to. But we don't quite have a morning ritual down, and our interactions aren't as comfortable as I would like. With Willow, we'd had a routine—coffee (she'd make it), breakfast (I'd make it), then sitting on the porch with our guitars (making music together).

But Megan and I don't live together—we haven't even talked about it—and most of our time together is squeezed into brief windows in our busy schedules. On the rare nights one of us does get to sleep over, it's usually me staying at her apartment in Waco, which isn't far from the Texas Rangers Company F headquarters. And I'm always rushing off in the morning, often before she's even out of bed. But she stayed over at my place in Redbud last night, and life always feels just a little bit off when she's here. Probably because Willow and I used to share this house. I've lived in it alone longer than I ever lived in it with Willow, but still I often think of it as *our* home.

The uncomfortableness might also be because Megan and I had a fight last night. Not really a fight. Just a little argument. I'm supposed to go with her to a brunch at one of her colleagues' houses this morning, and I made the mistake of whining like a fourteen-year-old boy and saying, "Do I have to go?" All of her coworkers are nice enough, but I just don't fit in when I'm at their get-togethers. They talk about student retention, curriculum changes, and the latest agenda items coming up before the faculty senate. I've got nothing to add. In fact, it's like they're speaking a language I don't even understand.

But Megan made the point that I've dragged her to plenty of cookouts hosted by cops, where she's been forced to make small talk with people she has nothing in common with. I agreed she was right—if I ask it from her, she should expect it from me—but the damage had already been done. She said she didn't want me to do anything I didn't want, but I could tell she was hurt.

Now I'm going to try to make up for it.

"I've decided I'm going to go with you today," I tell her.

She sets down her cup of coffee and gives me a discerning look.

"Only if you want to," she says.

"Of course I don't *want* to," I say. "I'm doing it for you."

Shit.

Wrong thing to say.

"I mean I *want* to spend time with you," I say. "I'd prefer if it was sitting on the porch, drinking sweet tea, or spending the day in bed with no clothes on, but I'll take what I can get."

This gets a smile out of her.

"Well, we need to get going soon," she says. "I need to stop at my apartment and change before we go."

I rise and set my coffee cup in the sink, resigning myself to a fate of uncomfortable small talk with people I hardly know. Out the window, I see a familiar Ford F-150 coming up the drive.

"What the heck?" I mutter.

Fellow Texas Ranger Carlos Castillo steps out of the truck. Carlos and I worked together on a couple of big cases about a year ago and he has become my closest friend in the Ranger organization. He's since been promoted to lieutenant and has been working in Company C, headquartered in Lubbock. He's got a droll sense of humor, and I usually get caught by his jokes hook, line, and sinker.

I open the door, and his expression tells me that what brings him here today is no laughing matter.

"Sorry to interrupt your Sunday," he says, "but I need to talk to you. It's important."

I look at Megan and she lets out a soft, exasperated breath.

"Looks like you're off the hook for brunch," she says with good humor.

"Sorry," I say.

But secretly I'm relieved.

CHAPTER 3

CARLOS AND I stand on the porch and wave goodbye to Megan as she drives off. Her Dodge Dakota curves around my parents' ranch house, only about two hundred yards from my little two-bedroom place, and then hits the paved road and disappears among the fields of wheat and sorghum.

"How are things going with you and Dr. Casewick?" Carlos asks, giving me a sideways look.

"Great," I say. "She's amazing."

"But?" Carlos asks, sensing that there's more.

I take a deep breath, not knowing how I should answer. Another car, a little blue subcompact thing, is making its way up my parents' driveway. I don't recognize it, but that's no surprise. My parents have lots of friends.

"You didn't come here to talk about my love life," I tell Carlos, turning toward my door. "Want some coffee?"

"Does the pope shit in the woods?" he says, showing a little of his usual humor.

I throw on a T-shirt and get us each a fresh cup. Lubbock's a good five hours from Redbud, so if Carlos is here this early, that means he either woke up in the wee hours of the morning or never went to bed at all. I don't ask which. I just hand him the coffee and settle down in a chair next to him on the porch.

Whoever came to visit my parents must be inside now. The subcompact is parked by the front porch.

The day is already getting warm. Butterflies flitter in the tall grass in front of my house. There's just a hint of a breeze and it brings with it an earthy aroma I've always associated with the smell of my parents' ranch.

The smell of home.

"How are things going in Lubbock?" I ask.

"The city's not bad," Carlos says.

"But?"

He smiles. "I wouldn't have driven through the night to come see you in secret if things were going well."

"So we're not having this conversation?" I ask.

"Nope," he says. "I'm not sitting here drinking your coffee."

Carlos is in his early forties, with a rangy build, long sinewy muscles, and not an ounce of fat on his frame. Usually when I see him, he's wearing the typical Texas Rangers attire of dress pants, shirt, tie, boots, and hat, with a Colt 1911 on his hip, which he prefers over the standard-issue SIG Sauer I carry. But today he's unarmed and dressed casually in jeans, a Spurs ball cap, and a gray T-shirt with big red and white letters that say REZ BALL, a nod to his Native American Kickapoo and Comanche heritage.

"You hear about the armored truck robbery on the Brazos?" Carlos asks.

"Of course," I say.

Everyone in Texas has heard about the robbery. Company C, where Carlos works, has been collaborating on the investigation with the FBI and local police. I know Carlos is still learning the ropes in his new job, so I wasn't sure if he'd been assigned to work on the case.

Apparently so.

"I've got a suspicion about who might be responsible," Carlos says, giving me a look that, rare for him, has absolutely no humor in it.

"I don't work in Company C," I say. "Why tell me?"

"Because you're the only Ranger I trust."

I frown. There are a hundred and sixty-six Texas Rangers in the state, and I trust just about all of them. There are several I don't know well and a few I don't particularly get along with, but I'd trust every one of them to do the right thing in a tough situation.

"There's a chance the person behind the robbery is a former Ranger," Carlos says. "That makes me think other Rangers might be involved. Or at least compromised."

Goose bumps rise on my skin. I can't quite believe what he's saying.

Carlos explains that he mentioned his theory to his captain and was told, in no uncertain terms, not to pursue that line of investigation.

"Maybe he thought I was just barking up the wrong tree," Carlos says. "But there might be more to it. I don't trust anyone to help me figure this out but you."

"Who do you think it is?" I say.

When he tells me, I can't believe my ears.

CHAPTER 4

CARLOS SAYS HIS suspect is Parker Longbaugh, who was a mentor to me when I first joined the Rangers. He was one of the most upstanding, moral men I've ever worked with—in my company, or any law enforcement around the state. If someone asked me to make a list of all the possible ex-Rangers who might turn into criminals, Parker's name sure as hell wouldn't be on it.

"No way," I say. "It can't be him. I'd stake my badge on it."

The expression on Carlos's face tells me that he'd gotten that kind of reaction from his captain and had expected better of me.

"I'll listen to what you have to say," I tell him, holding my hands up in surrender. "But I can see why this was a hard pill for your captain to swallow."

Carlos explains that the Rangers and FBI believe a group of thieves known as the XYZ Bandits hit the armored truck. There've been previous robberies over the past year conducted with similar modus operandi.

Three men on motorcycles.

Carrying submachine guns.

Referring to each other as Mr. X, Mr. Y, and Mr. Z.

They robbed a shipping facility on the coast outside of Galveston last year. They hit a warehouse in Nacogdoches last fall. And all spring, banks throughout West Texas and the Panhandle were robbed by a group that fit the description. The armored truck was by far the most high-profile—and most complicated—but the bandits had been at it for a while.

The robbers are fast.

They're professional.

They stay away from the big cities.

And, as far as anyone can tell, they only work in Texas.

"We think they carry MPXs," Carlos says, referring to a gas-operated submachine gun manufactured by SIG, the same company that makes the Sauer I carry. "But they've never fired a shot. They've never had to. They're efficient enough they get the drop on every type of security they've faced. The armored truck on the Brazos was the only time anyone got hurt, and it was just the guards getting banged up in the crash."

"What makes you think Parker's involved?" I ask.

Carlos explains that after the recent armored-truck robbery, he started poring through evidence on all the cases of the XYZ Bandits. He scrutinized the bank footage prior to all the robberies and recognized Parker Longbaugh going into one of the banks to meet with someone. Last Carlos had heard, Parker was still living in Snakebite, Texas, in Hamilton County, only about ninety minutes from Redbud. But Parker was in a bank another two hours north in Stephens County—a week before it was robbed.

"I showed the image to the bank manager and asked if he could remember why the guy came in," Carlos says. "He had to check his calendar, but once he did, he said Parker had come in inquiring about a loan to buy some land. But Parker didn't follow up. The guy never heard from him again."

"That's a pretty flimsy reason to think the guy robbed the bank," I say.

Carlos nods. "Yeah, but I found him in the footage of two other banks. Both of them were also robbed."

"Has it occurred to you that maybe he's just looking to buy some property?" I say. "Maybe he wants to build a hunting cabin somewhere. Maybe he wants to get his family the hell out of Snakebite. Did you ask him?"

"I can't show my cards yet," Carlos says. "I need more information. If he gets any idea that I'm onto him, he'll disappear."

One thing Carlos did do was look into Parker's credit report.

"When you apply for loans, that stuff shows up in your records," Carlos says. "He hasn't looked into getting a loan from any other banks. No other banks in Texas. No national banks. No credit unions."

I shrug. "Could be a coincidence."

"You've been a Texas Ranger long enough to know there's no such thing as coincidence."

I feel flustered. Part of me is frustrated with Carlos for pushing this theory with so little to go on. But the other part of me knows that if he were talking about any other suspect—besides a man I know to be upstanding and lawful—I'd say the whole thing was suspicious enough that it should at least be pursued. As an investigator, I believe in following every lead. Everyone's a suspect until you can rule them out.

"Suppose I agree to help you," I say, "what is it you want me to do?"

Carlos gives me a look that suggests if I didn't like what he's had to say so far, I'm not going to like what's coming next.

CHAPTER 5

"I NEED YOU to get close to him," Carlos says. "Pretend to be his friend."

"I *am* his friend."

"All the better," Carlos says. "Don't let on like you're looking into him as a suspect but see what you can learn. I'd call it undercover, but you're not lying about who you are."

"I'm just lying about my motivations," I say.

I don't like the sound of this at all. I remember when I was a rookie in the Rangers, fresh off my stint with the Texas Highway Patrol. Some Rangers have the attitude that new guys are either going to sink or swim and making it in the job is something they need to do on their own. Other Rangers think they should lend a hand and make sure the new guys succeed. Parker was the latter.

In fact, I might not have made it through that first year without him. If I was confused about procedure, I knew I could call Parker. If I had a question about dealing with red tape or state government bureaucracy, I called Parker. When I was feeling stressed out by the emotional weight of the job, what did I do?

You guessed it.

Called Parker.

And now Carlos wants me to spy on him.

"What am I supposed to do?" I say. "Just show up and say, 'Hey, long time no see'? 'You happen to have a motorcycle and a submachine gun lying around?'"

"I've got a plan," Carlos says. "Remember why he quit the Rangers?"

I do.

There'd been a suspected serial killer preying on migrant workers throughout Central Texas. The press dubbed the guy the "Cereal Killer" because the crops the victims worked on were all grains like wheat, oats, and millet. Parker, the lead Ranger working the case with local jurisdictions, thought the flippant moniker trivialized the seriousness of the crimes and was disrespectful to the victims. After a few months on the case, he figured out who was responsible: a guy named Jackson Clarke who happened to operate a grain elevator right in the town of Snakebite, where Parker lived. But there was debate among other agencies over whether they had enough evidence to arrest the guy. Parker couldn't stand the idea that the killer might strike again, so he went ahead and made the arrest. It turned out the DA in Hamilton County wouldn't prosecute and they dropped the charges.

Jackson Clarke went into hiding, never to be captured.

Parker was livid. He resigned immediately. He said he just couldn't do the job anymore knowing that justice wasn't served and a murderer was free to continue preying on victims in some other part of the country.

"What's that have to do with the robbery?" I ask Carlos.

"That's your in," he explains. "Tell your supervisors you want to reopen the Cereal Killer case. It was never solved."

"When Jackson Clarke disappeared, there were never any other victims," I say. "It's a cold case, but we all know who did it."

Carlos shakes his head. "You're not really going to try to solve the Cereal Killer case. You're using that as an excuse—for him and for your supervisors. But between you and me, it's just a reason for you to go to Snakebite. Knock on Parker Longbaugh's door and say, 'Hey, buddy. I'm looking into your old case. Can you help me out?' Then you keep your eyes open for anything suspicious."

I hate the idea of going there under false pretenses. I haven't seen Parker in years, but I still consider him a good friend. Hell, if he called me in the middle of the night asking for help, I'd be there in a New York minute.

As if Carlos were reading my mind, he says, "Look, Rory, if you believe this guy's actually innocent, then you'll be doing him a favor."

"Doing *him* a favor?" I say, incredulous. "You're my friend. Would you think I was doing you a favor if this was the other way around and I was spying on you?"

"You're damn right," he says. "If someone out there thought I was committing felonies, I'd want someone I can trust to be the one handling it. Help me cross him off the suspect list. You'll be helping me *and* helping him."

I stare out at the ranch while Carlos lets me think through the problem he's placed before me. A good cop knows when to shut up, and Carlos is as good as they come.

The breeze is picking up and I watch a line of magnolia trees by my parents' house sway in the breeze. Mom is out in her vegetable garden, and Dad's headed out to one of his apple trees with a ladder tucked under his arm. It looks like whoever was visiting my folks left without me noticing.

"Look," Carlos says finally, sensing that I need a little nudge. "I want it to turn out that Parker is innocent as much as you. I'm not looking to railroad the guy. You're the best person for this job. You're going to make sure everything's done right."

I take a deep breath. I hate myself for what I'm about to say.

"All right. As long as I can get my lieutenant to give me the green light, I'll head up there."

Carlos smacks his hands together, and I realize that he wasn't sure I was going to go through with it.

"You're a good man, Rory," he says, clapping me on the back.

I grimace and say thanks, but I doubt my friend Parker Longbaugh would describe me in those terms right now.

CHAPTER 6

THE NEXT EVENING, I'm packing a bag for my trip to Snakebite. I'm not sure how long I'll be gone, but I've got the essentials laid out on my bed: a few changes of clothes, a toothbrush, a paperback novel to read at night, and—something I never leave home without—my guitar.

Part of a Texas Ranger's job is to *range* across the state, so leaving home like this is nothing new to me. But my nerves are going haywire. I can feel my blood pressure rising. There's no use telling myself that this job is like any other.

I've never spied on a friend before.

I keep telling myself that I'm also doing this job for Carlos, one of my closest friends, but I just can't feel good about it. I met with my lieutenant, Ty Abrams, this morning and told him I was interested in reopening the Cereal Killer case. A tough sixty-year-old Ranger who grew up working long hours on a farm in Killeen and now works long hours in law enforcement, he's always been an advocate of not letting cold cases stay cold for long. He was all about the idea.

"You go to Snakebite and see what you can find out," he said. "I'll do some digging on my end and see if I can turn anything up."

Ty is the kind of guy who never married, never had kids. He

puts in sixteen-hour days, works weekends, scrutinizes cases and makes sure no stone is left unturned. It feels wrong to mislead him like this, so I tell myself I'm going to have to put in some actual time on the Cereal Killer case, even though that feels like a waste. Wherever Jackson Clarke is now, it sure isn't Texas.

Once my bag is packed up and I'm ready for tomorrow's trip, I leave my little house and head down the hill toward my parents'. Mom invited me to dinner, said she'd make my favorite, country-fried steak. Sometimes when I have to go on long trips, she'll invite my brothers and their wives and kids for a big sendoff, but Snakebite's only an hour and a half away, and I'm hoping this won't take more than a couple of days.

When I get to the house, the home I grew up in, I find my mom in the kitchen finishing up dinner and my dad in the living room watching the Rangers play the Blue Jays. Dad wants me to sit down and watch the game with him, but I offer to help Mom instead.

She's got everything under control—as always—but I keep her company.

"Have you talked to Willow yet?" Mom asks.

I furrow my brow.

"She's in town," Mom says. "She stopped by the other day to borrow a recipe book I told her about. She was going to walk up and say hi to you, but we saw another Ranger's truck up there and figured you were talking business."

"Oh," I say, remembering the blue compact car from yesterday morning. "So that's who that was."

"I know you two broke up," Mom says. "But your dad and I still like her. You should look her up while she's in town."

"I've got a girlfriend," I say. "I thought you liked Megan."

"I *adore* Megan," Mom says, handing me a big bowl of mashed potatoes to put on the table. "You can still be friends with Willow, can't you?"

After the dream I had the other night, I'm not so sure.

I don't want to say it to my mom, but I think the best thing for me is probably to stay away from her. If I want to give my relationship with Megan any chance at surviving, that is.

Mom says that Willow's in town taking a break before her big summer tour starts. This will be her first year as headliner and she's got some hot new artist, Riley Chandler, opening for her.

"He's the one with that song that was big last year, 'Sundown in Whiskey Town.'"

"I think I've heard it," I say.

The truth is most songs on country radio seem to blend together for me these days. I prefer old Tim McGraw or George Strait to most of what I hear being played.

I try to move the conversation away from Willow and ask about my brothers' kids. If there's one thing my parents like to talk about more than my love life, it's their grandchildren.

Dinner is delicious, as always. You can't go wrong with country-fried steak, mashed potatoes, green beans, and, for dessert, apple pie made with fruit my dad picked with his own hands. Afterward, I thank my mom and give her a big hug. I embrace Dad, too. He wasn't a big hugger when I was growing up, but we almost lost him to cancer a while back, and ever since we've been better about expressing our emotions.

I could be killed any day on the job—I want the people I love to know how I feel.

On the walk back up to my house, the sun has just finished setting and the yard is starting to light up with fireflies. The sky is filling with stars. I feel strangely lonely. I don't want to end up like my lieutenant, approaching retirement and married to the job. I want to be like my parents, married forty years and still in love.

My phone buzzes.

It's Willow.

I want to answer, but I've got a strong feeling I shouldn't. Instead, I send it straight to voicemail. Then I dial Megan to let her know I'll be out of town for a few days.

As she picks up, enthusiastic to hear from me, I try to convince myself she, not Willow, is the one I really want to talk to.

CHAPTER 7

ON THE ROAD the next morning, I feel so nervous about what I'm doing that I almost call Carlos and tell him the deal is off. But I've already gotten the go-ahead from my lieutenant to look into the Cereal Killer case. I have to go.

Out the window, the scenery blurs by, with farms and windmills and the occasional armadillo hobbling along the side of the road. I have the radio on, but I'm lost in thought and don't pay attention to the music until Willow's most famous song, "Don't Date a Texas Ranger," comes on and grabs my attention. She made the song as a joke back when we were dating, but it turned out to be a hit—and prophetic.

"I should write my own song," I mutter. "Don't date a country singer. You'll never get over her."

I pull into Snakebite by midmorning. With about three thousand residents, the town lies close to the border of Hamilton and Comanche Counties, right on the very edge of Company F's jurisdiction. If the town were any farther north, it would be in another county and I would have had a lot more difficulty convincing my lieutenant to let me go.

Snakebite is a nice enough place. There's a tributary of the Lampasas River running perpendicular to Main Street, with a bike path alongside it and a scenic walking bridge overlooking the creek. A water tower stands on the north edge with SNAKEBITE PROUD painted on the side.

In no particular hurry, I check into my motel room, eat an early lunch in a restaurant called the Snakebite Sizzler, and then stop by the local police station to let them know I'm here and what I'm doing. I spend a good two hours looking at old files and talking to a detective who worked on the Cereal Killer case. All of this feels like such a waste of time, for me and for everyone I talk to, but I go through the motions so I have something to report back to Ty.

Finally, in late afternoon, I tell myself I can't put it off any longer. I climb into my truck and head over to Parker Longbaugh's house.

He actually lives a good thirty minutes out of town, and I drive below the speed limit the whole way, delaying the inevitable. On the way, I pass by the grain elevator where Jackson Clarke used to work. It looks like it's been closed ever since he ran off. The parking lot is overgrown with weeds and the doors and windows are boarded shut.

Finally, I approach the address. Even though Parker lived here back when he worked for the Rangers, I've never seen his house. He always told me that he liked it because it was secluded, and that's the truth.

As I pull into the driveway, I spot two kids playing out front with superhero figures. The boy, maybe about eight or nine, and the girl, four or five, stop battling Captain America against Thor and Spider-Man, and eye me suspiciously. I saw the boy as a toddler, but I haven't seen Parker in years and didn't know he had a daughter. I climb slowly out of the truck, not wanting to scare the kids. I doubt many Texas Rangers with guns on their hips show up to their house, even though their dad used to be one.

I tip my hat to the kids and head up the walk toward the front porch. I can hear the static buzz of grasshoppers out in the field.

Parker and his family live in an old two-story farmhouse on a spacious corner lot, with a large wooded area on one side and a cornfield on the other. The corn stalks are still short this early in the summer. A cluster of fruit trees sits at the back of the property, and several tall red oaks shade the house and the lawn. One oak has fallen down close to the woods, where it looks like Parker has started cutting it into firewood. There's a barn and a large vegetable garden, along with a jungle gym, a horseshoe pit, and a fire ring of blackened cement blocks. When Parker bought the place, I remember him saying the house had belonged to a family that owned the adjoining fields, but the farmlands had been sold off to bigger operations that had no need for the home.

"Dad," the boy calls from the front yard. "There's somebody here to see you."

I step up onto the porch and raise my hand to knock. Through the screen door, I can see the foyer and kitchen. But no one's inside.

"As I live and breathe," a voice says from behind me, causing me to jump. "Look who it is."

I turn around to see my old friend, Parker, standing in the grass next to the porch, wiping his hands with a rag. He must have come around the side of the house, as silent as a cat. Whether he'd meant to sneak up on me or not, if he'd been a criminal, he would have gotten the drop on me.

I try to act like he didn't startle me. I can't tell by his expression if he's suspicious of me turning up like this or just pleasantly surprised.

"Hey, old buddy," I say, sounding more chipper than I mean to.

"What brings you here, Rory?" Parker says, and I can't help but detect a trace of unfriendliness in his voice.

CHAPTER 8

PARKER WALKS AROUND to the porch steps and starts up, tucking the rag into his back pocket. He's wearing jeans and a sleeveless T-shirt, showing off muscular arms. He was always a fitness buff, and even though he's in his early fifties now, he looks like he's in better shape than most men half his age. He's my height, but he's got at least fifteen pounds on me, all muscle. He always had an intimidating glower that he could turn on and off like it was on a switch. I've seen many criminals squirm under that stare, but this is the first time I've seen anything but approachable friendliness leveled on me.

"I was in the neighborhood," I say, trying not to let his intense gaze get to me. "Thought I'd stop by for a visit."

"Really?" Parker says, not hiding the disbelief in his voice.

"No," I say, forcing a laugh. I gesture to the cornfields and woods that abut his property. "There's nothing in your neighborhood."

He chuckles, and I'm pleased to see his tough exterior begin to soften.

"I'd shake your hand," he says, "but I was fixing the lawnmower out back. Might be a little greasy."

"I'll take my chances," I say, and give his hand a firm shake.

I still sense a feeling of confusion about my visit. He's got his guard up.

"I'm sorry I haven't kept in touch," I say. "And I wish I was just stopping by for a visit. But I am here on some business."

Now his expression darkens again.

"Lieutenant Abrams has me looking into one of your old cases, the murders that happened around here." I make sure not to use the name Cereal Killer—and I don't mention it was my idea to revisit the case. "You know how Lieutenant Abrams always was about cold cases."

Parker nods seriously.

"I don't think I can be of any help to you, Rory," he says. "I haven't stayed connected with law enforcement in any way. I don't even think like a cop anymore."

"Still, you'd be doing me a favor if we could talk for a few minutes," I say.

He takes a deep breath, and his body stiffens. Just then, I hear footsteps coming from inside the house and look up to see Josie, Parker's wife, strolling down the hallway. The screen door opens with a screech from the hinges.

"Rory!" she says, showing more enthusiasm than Parker did. "So great to see you."

Josie wears jeans and a tank top, showing off arms that are svelte and strong. Probably in her mid-forties now, she's stopped dying her hair since I last saw her, but the varying shades of silver pulled back in a loose ponytail suit her more than any artificial color could. Her skin is tan from outdoor work, and despite some wrinkles, she looks like she could pass for ten years younger.

I always figured Parker got lucky when he found her. They always had the kind of relationship I wanted but could never quite find. They had kids later in life than most people do, but that's because they hadn't met when they were younger. I'm still in my thirties, but if a family is in my future, I better get to work on it soon. Either that or I'm going to end up like Lieutenant Ty Abrams—no bride except the badge.

Josie gives me a tight hug, which I return, feeling guilty for not keeping in touch. These are good people. I hate being here under false pretenses.

When she breaks the embrace, she asks, "Can you stay for supper?"

"He's here on Ranger business," Parker says with a tone of disapproval.

"So what?" Josie says, shrugging. "You two can chat work stuff and then we'll all catch up." She looks at me. "We've got some friends coming over for a cookout tonight. We'd love it if you'd stay."

I turn my gaze to Parker to make sure he's okay with it.

"Actually, I'll be in town for a few days," I say. "I was hoping I'd get to catch up with y'all a little bit. Make the trip business *and* pleasure."

"That would be fantastic," Josie says, squeezing my arm.

Parker nods, and for the first time he seems more at ease with my presence. I decide he doesn't like the idea of talking about anything related to law enforcement. But catching up with an old friend? He's more than okay with that.

The kids have wandered up from the yard to the porch, and Parker introduces me. Their names are Leroy—they call him Leo, for short—and Etta.

"This is an old friend of mine," Parker says to them.

"Are you a Texas Ranger?" Leo asks.

He looks a lot like his dad, and I know he'll grow up to be just as tough and just as moral. The girl is as cute as could be, a younger version of Josie.

"I am," I say, tapping the star pinned to my shirt.

"My daddy used to be a Texas Ranger," Leo says.

"I know," I say. "He was as good as they come."

"Daddy," says Etta, "why aren't you a Texas Ranger anymore?"

All our eyes turn to Parker, who has an expression like he's just been asked a question he doesn't want to answer.

"Don't ask," he jokes. Then he adds, "Come on, Rory, let's get this over with."

CHAPTER 9

PARKER LEADS ME through the house. It's a nice home, with wood-plank floors and a variety of pastel walls a different color in each room. I look for extravagantly expensive items, such as huge TVs or fancy decorations, but everything seems modest. There are some amazing watercolor landscapes hanging here and there in frames, but the initials of the artist are JL.

"Josie paint these?" I ask.

"Sure did," he says. "These are the ones I couldn't let her sell."

I remember Josie sold paintings on the side. She was a dispatcher for the county police years ago, but I heard she quit when Parker did.

"What do y'all do for work these days, if you don't mind me asking?"

Parker says he's been building furniture and sells it on commission in various stores and markets throughout the state. He's got a shop set up in the barn with everything he needs.

"There were a few lean years after I quit the Rangers," he says. "But things have picked up and I make more now than I ever did as a cop. Josie still paints some, but mostly she can focus on home-schooling the kids."

The house is big, with more rooms than a family of four probably needs, but I don't see that as evidence that Parker's been swimming in extra money. House prices in Middle of Nowhere, Texas, aren't exactly sky high. He bought this place back when he was a Ranger.

Finally, he leads me to a little office near the back of the house. There's a small wooden desk—maybe Parker made it?—with some invoices and furniture drawings scattered on top of it. He picks up a stack of books off a chair and invites me to sit. Then he plops next to me in his own rolling chair.

He takes a deep breath, like a man resigned to a fate he doesn't want—not unlike my reaction when I thought I had to go to brunch with Megan's colleagues.

"Okay," he says. "Ask me whatever you want. But once we leave this room, no more talking about the case. We're just old friends catching up."

"Fair enough," I say.

I ask him to summarize the case and his findings, and he does so with a certain amount of discomfort. Clearly, I'm asking him to dig through a part of his past that he doesn't like to think about.

"Sometimes I feel like I really screwed up," he says. "Like I was too quick to arrest that son of a bitch. Maybe if I'd been patient we could have come up with more evidence over time. But then I think about those people he killed, their bodies left out in the fields with their throats slit, and I know I wouldn't have been able to live with myself if he'd killed another person while we were sitting on our hands not making an arrest."

He clears his throat, shaken by the memories.

"That's the thing about law enforcement," he says. "Sometimes your hands are tied. All you have is bad options. I realized I couldn't do it anymore. I blamed the system, said I was quitting in protest. But the truth is I just couldn't hack it anymore. I couldn't face those impossible choices."

I feel sorry for asking him these questions and putting him through this, but as we're wrapping things up, he actually seems relieved to have gotten all of this off his chest. Maybe me coming here will end up being a good thing for him after all.

There is a gentle knock on the door and Josie pokes her head in.

"Y'all about ready to knock off for the night?" she says. "Our guests are going to arrive soon."

"We're all done," I say. "Thanks, Parker, for taking the time."

"For you, Rory," he says with a heartfelt smile, "anything."

All the tension created from my impromptu visit seems to have abated.

Parker and I rise to our feet, and I'm just about to thank him again for his help, but then Josie pokes her head back into the room.

"Rory," she says, "you didn't happen to bring your guitar, did you?"

I can't help but grin.

"I did, actually."

"After supper, we're going to light a bonfire," she says. "You mind playing us a few songs? The kids will dance to just about anything."

"That would be nice," I say and, for a moment, mean it.

But then I realize why I'm here and I feel ashamed for the way they've welcomed me—a spy—into their home.

CHAPTER 10

I HEAD OUT to my truck, where I take off my badge and lock up my gun. I remove my tie, loosen the top buttons of my shirt, and roll up my sleeves. I toss my hat in on the passenger seat and tell myself to just enjoy the evening.

Forget the espionage.

These are good people, and in my head, I'm already preparing my speech to Carlos saying I couldn't find anything suspicious.

I carry my guitar case back and set it near the fire pit halfway between the garden and the orchard. The heat of the day is starting to break. The whole lawn is lush, but there's a swath that's particularly green and bushy, no doubt from the leach line running underground. The orchard's peach and fig trees are starting to bear fruit.

I help Parker and Josie get ready, unfolding a couple of portable tables, covering them with checkered tablecloths, and setting out paper plates, plastic cups, and utensils. Parker carries an armload of lawn chairs from the barn, and I offer to help but he waves me off as he goes back for more.

Another family arrives, with three kids roughly the same age range as Parker and Josie's children. The little ones run around in the grass and play on the fallen oak at the back of the property. They use the extra green strip of grass from the leach line as a running track and take turns racing each other.

Josie introduces me to the couple, Harvey and Angie Curry. Harvey, short but fit, with a thick goatee and a toothpick between his teeth, looks at me askance when Josie tells him what I do for a living. People often react differently when they learn you're a Texas Ranger. Some people treat you with a certain reverence and awe—and they're filled with questions about what the job is like. Others put their guard up right away, not sure quite how to act. It's not necessarily that they're hiding something.

But it could be.

That's the way Harvey reacts, squinting at me and taking a step back before trying to act normal and shake my hand.

"You come to take me away?" he says, a joke that lands flatly because he can't quite deliver it.

I shake his hand and try my own joke.

"Not yet," I say. "We're still compiling evidence."

Angie, a short woman with a round cute face and curly black hair, laughs loudly, which works to deflate the tension. We talk for a few minutes and Harvey seems to loosen up.

Another couple arrives, Ellis and Candace Kilpatrick. They're younger than the rest of us, maybe not yet thirty, and have only one child in tow, a toddler who looks like he hasn't been walking long. The child is wearing a shirt that says FUTURE DIVER, with an illustration of an old copper dive helmet.

When Josie introduces us, Ellis looks me up and down and says, with much better delivery than Harvey, "You come to take me away?"

Everyone bursts out laughing, and Ellis looks around in surprise that his joke got that big of a reaction.

"I said the same thing," Harvey explains, and Ellis and Candace join the laughter.

Over dinner, Josie sits next to me and I talk mostly to her. The others are busy feeding their children and doing their best to eat their own food in between cutting up hot dogs and getting refills of Kool-Aid. Afterward, as the sky darkens and the children occupy themselves chasing lightning bugs, Josie and the other wives are cleaning up and Parker brings over a wheelbarrow full of wood from the back of the lot to build a fire. I see this as my chance to talk to Harvey and Ellis, and I ask them what they do. I don't want to question them too hard, but I figure I need at least something to report to Carlos.

"I work at an auto shop in town," says Ellis.

I notice he's wearing a blue T-shirt with NAVY in big bold letters. Remembering his son's FUTURE DIVER shirt, I ask him if he was a diver in the Navy.

He nods like he's got nothing to hide.

"I did some commercial diving for a while," he says. "Underwater welding on oil rigs in the Gulf. But I botched an ascent once and got the bends. Did some permanent damage to my lungs. I had to give it up."

"I'm sorry," I say. "So you can't dive anymore?"

"Not deep," he says. "Candace convinced me to move inland and find a new career."

Over by the newly lit fire, Parker and Josie are helping the kids spear marshmallows so they can roast them over the fire and make s'mores.

"What about you?" I ask Harvey, meaning to inquire about his career, not old injuries, but he gives me an answer to both.

"Worked in aggregate mining for a while," he says, "but then I went and blew myself up."

He holds up his left hand, which is missing the ring finger and littlest finger. The tissue around the missing digits is white and bulbous, like melted wax.

"Now I'm a landscaper," he says, grinning with the toothpick sticking from his teeth.

The hairs are standing up on the backs of my arms.

CHAPTER 11

AS MUCH AS I was ready to write off this investigation as a fool's errand, I can't help but think there might be something here. Ellis was a diver and Harvey—judging by his injury—used explosives when he worked in mining. The armored-truck robbery required accomplices with experience in both.

Can it be a coincidence?

I want to continue this conversation with Ellis and Harvey, see what else I can find out about them, but before I can say anything else, Parker calls out to me.

"Hey, Rory," he says. "These kids just ate about a pound of sugar each." He gestures to my guitar case sitting in the grass. "How about you play a song or two so they can dance and burn off some of that energy?"

I excuse myself from Ellis and Harvey and pick up my guitar case. I pull out the guitar—a gift from Willow a while back—and sit down on a stump. I strum the pick across the strings and take a deep breath.

In my experience, kids don't care much what you play as long as it's upbeat. They want something fast-paced and fun to dance to, so I hit them with songs like John Denver's "Thank God I'm a Country Boy," the Nitty Gritty Dirt Band's "Fishin' in the Dark," and Mel McDaniels' "Louisiana Saturday Night." The kids dance around outside the circle of the bonfire, and a lot of the parents join in, too. Everyone's laughing and clapping and singing along. I believe in quitting while you're ahead, so I play a quick rendition of Tanya Tucker's "Texas When I Die" and call it a night.

I set my guitar down to a round of applause. Then I finish my last swallow of beer and excuse myself to use the restroom.

"I think Candace is in there changing a diaper," Josie tells me, out of breath and glowing from dancing with her two kids. "There's another bathroom in the basement."

Parker and Harvey share a look—like maybe they don't want me to go down there—but I can't be sure if it's just a trick of the firelight or maybe my overactive imagination. As I walk toward the house, I tell myself to get my head back in the game.

I worked up a sweat playing and singing for the kids, so the night air feels cool away from the fire.

I'm not really going in to use the bathroom.

I want to snoop around.

I can't believe one minute I'm having a blast playing for people who seem like friends, the next I'm switching to detective mode looking for clues.

The bathroom door is closed, and I hear Candace in there talking to the toddler. Otherwise, the house is as silent as a cemetery. I move as quietly as I can—which isn't easy with cowboy boots on a hardwood floor—and find the stairs to the basement. I descend and grope in the dark for a light switch.

I'm not sure what I'm expecting to find, but it isn't this.

In the center of the room, propped up by sawhorses and a large sheet of plywood, is an elaborate model train set. The terrain is unfinished, but the tracks are laid out over papier-mâché hills and it's easy to see the potential of what it could look like when it's completed. Parker's children are too young to do this themselves, so it must be something Josie or Parker, or both of them, do with the kids.

I pull my eyes away from the train set and keep searching.

The rest of the room is in various stages of remodeling and cluttered with storage. The cinderblock walls are partially concealed by sheetrock, spackled but not painted. A shag rug lies across part of the floor, but otherwise rough concrete is exposed. One wall is hidden by rusted metal shelving full of glass jars of food—beans and pickles and spaghetti sauce—presumably made from food grown in the Longbaughs' garden. A water heater stands in one corner near an open door, revealing a tiny bathroom inside.

I spot a pile of storage containers—plastic bins, cardboard file boxes, wooden crates—and one in particular catches my eyes. It's wooden and stenciled with the faded words DANGER EXPLOSIVES, like an old box that dynamite could have been stored in.

I step quietly over to the wooden crate and—slowly, carefully—lift the lid.

CHAPTER 12

I LET OUT a sigh of relief when I see what's inside.

Comic books.

I fan through the stack quickly—*Wolverine, Avengers, Ghost Rider*—and put the lid back on the crate. When Parker's kids asked if Daddy had anywhere they could store their comics, they must have had a good laugh when he handed over an old dynamite crate.

Maybe there's something else here. I reach for the top of a file box when I hear the creak of footsteps coming down the stairs. I bolt upright and pretend like I'm studying the model train display, the way the tracks cross rivers and roadways.

Josie comes down, sees what I'm looking at, and smiles.

"Parker acts like he does this for the kids, but they're not really interested," she says. "Who would have thought a tough-as-nails Texas Ranger would find joy in making dioramas?"

"Seems like he's changed a bit."

"Only for the better," Josie says, and her face lights up with a smile.

"I wish I'd stayed in touch," I say.

Josie offers her forgiveness with a shrug.

"Communication is a two-way street," she says. "Parker couldn't care less about some of his old colleagues, but he has a real fondness for some. You're one of them. When he quit the Rangers, it was so hard on him that I think he just needed to make a clean break. He didn't keep in contact with anyone."

She reaches over and takes my arm and we start up the stairs together.

"I think it's been really good for him to see you tonight," she says. "I hope you'll come back while you're in town."

Once again, I feel guilty for treating Parker as a crime suspect. But once Josie and I step outside together, I find Parker walking out of the barn with Ellis and Harvey. From the far-off glow of the firelight, they seem to glance my way and pick up their pace, a little too quick to put some distance between themselves and where they've just been. Are they hiding something in the barn?

I tell myself my mind might just be playing tricks on me. A detective needs to be careful of confirmation bias. Sometimes you want to believe something so bad that you interpret the clues to give you the outcome you want. But, in this case, I actually don't want Parker to be involved. So you'd think I'd brush off anything suspicious. Instead, even simple glances between these men seem to be setting off alarm bells in my brain.

One thing's for certain: I need more information.

Unfortunately, I'm not going to get it tonight.

The party is winding down and it's time to go home. Candace holds her sleeping boy in her arms. Angie is ushering her three children toward the car. I tell the Currys and the Kilpatricks that it was nice meeting them. Then I wait for both families to leave before I give Josie a hug. When I offer my hand to Parker to shake, he ignores it and throws his arms around me for a hug. Stunned for a moment, I embrace him back.

"I missed you, brother," he says.

He's had a little bit too much to drink—I can smell it on his breath and in the sweat on his skin—but the sentiment pulls at my heartstrings.

"Missed you, too."

As I climb into my truck, Josie and Parker wave goodbye and I toot my horn in a final farewell. Not in any hurry to get back to my hotel, I slow down as I pass the grain elevator. Lit only by moonlight and surrounded by cornfields, the building looks ominous, abandoned and monolithic out here where there isn't anything else but field after field. The main building is a good three stories tall, with a steeply slanted roof on the second level and a trio of wide, squat silos attached. Checking to make sure there aren't any cars behind me, I pull into the driveway, circle behind the building, and kill the lights. Hidden from view from the road, I step out.

The corn whispers in the breeze.

I get a chill thinking about how the guy who used to run the grain elevator turned out to be a serial killer. There's no way he'd be here now—clearly no one's been here for a while—but the fact that Jackson Clarke was never caught is enough to give me the creeps when I'm standing next to his old stomping grounds.

There is a dirt road—barely more than two wheel ruts cutting through a lane of weeds—that leads into the fields between two fence lines. I walk down one of the gravel grooves. If it was broad daylight, the corn wouldn't be high enough to hide me from any cars driving on the main road. But in the darkness, with no light except what's coming from the moon and stars, there's no one to see what I'm doing.

I walk for a good mile or two and find that the road leads into a wooded area.

The same wooded area that abuts Parker's property.

I step into the trees, and what little light I had from the stars and moon diminishes to almost zero visibility. I pull out my pocket flashlight and move on, only to find that the road ends in a small clearing at the edge of a ravine. A cluster of rusted-out old cars— barely more than husks now—are parked here, sunken into the weeds. The ravine looks to be filled with junk: discarded washing machines and other appliances, stained mattresses with stuffing sprouting from holes, old box TVs with shattered screens, porcelain toilets broken into pieces, paint buckets and beer cans riddled with bullet holes.

It's clearly a place people use to dump things they no longer want.

But as I turn and head back to my truck, I've got an idea.

If need be, I can park my truck here, out of sight, and sneak through the woods to the edge of Parker's property. I hate the idea of spying on my old friend like that, but I've come this far.

There's no turning back now.

CHAPTER 13

THE NEXT MORNING, as I steel myself for another day of duplicitousness, I fix myself a cup of crappy hotel coffee and flip through the TV channels trying to find something worth watching. As I skip through the endless stream of infomercials, B movies, and depressing morning news shows, I catch a glimpse of—could it be?—Willow.

I stop scrolling and realize it's one of the country-music channels doing an interview with Willow and the guy she's going on tour with, Riley Chandler, about a duet they're recording.

Christ, I think. *I can't escape her.*

I've seen Willow on TV before, but it's always a surreal feeling. I've held that woman in my arms. Once upon a time, we would say *I love you* to each other.

Apparently the song they're recording is called "Sincerely, My Broken Heart," and it's going to be the first single on Willow's new album. They show some clips of the two of them in the studio and filming the music video. In the studio, Willow's wearing distressed jeans with dozens of rips in them, along with a tight tank top. Her hair is pulled back in a ponytail. In the video, she's got on a leather skirt and boots that go up past her knees. Her gorgeous blond locks are spread over her shoulders in all their glory.

God, she's beautiful.

Riley Chandler has tattoos up and down his arms, a hip haircut I could never pull off, facial hair that looks like it's been sculpted by a professional. I know it's just a song, and it's not like they're boyfriend and girlfriend, but seeing Willow perform with someone else—especially a young, handsome, *cool* musician—makes my stomach churn. Carrie Underwood and Brad Paisley were happily married to other people when they recorded "Remind Me," but it must have been hell for their spouses to watch the music video.

At the end of the program, the reporter, a bubbly blond woman with a permanent smile, says to Willow, "You've had a lot of songs about broken hearts. And you've had a couple of high-profile breakups. Is there anyone special in your life right now?"

"I'm just focusing on my career and my music," Willow says with a laugh. "My life's full with or without a man."

I should be happy for her. Besides, I've got a good woman waiting for me back home. But the whole interview manages to make my bad mood worse.

The news program switches to a story about Garth Brooks narrating a documentary series about the national parks. I switch off the TV and pour what's left of my coffee down the drain. Just then my cell phone beeps with a text.

Lo and behold, it's a message from Willow.

Hey, it says, *I'm in town for a few days. I'd love to get together and catch up. R U available?*

I take a deep breath. I think about ignoring it. But I figure there's no harm in telling her I'm out of town for work.

She replies with a frowning-face emoji and says, *When will you be back?*

Don't know. Soon, I hope. Then—because what could be the harm in it?—I add, *Would love to see you.*

Me too, she texts back immediately. *Let's make it happen.*

CHAPTER 14

I SPEND THE morning going through the motions on the Cereal Killer case. I conduct a few interviews with people who used to know Jackson Clarke, and I spend a good hour talking to Lieutenant Abrams on the phone. He's been doing all kinds of legwork on his end, checking leads where Clarke might have ended up, finding known associates elsewhere in the country, talking with police in other jurisdictions with similar murder cases.

Once again, I feel guilty that the Cereal Killer case isn't my real priority.

My real priority is Parker: finding out if my suspicions about his friends are unfounded or—God forbid—merited. So, after a quick lunch, I hit the road and head toward Parker's place. I call Carlos on the way.

"Lubbock morgue," he says upon answering. "You stab 'em, we slab 'em."

"That isn't very funny," I say, not particularly in the mood for gallows humor.

"You know what else isn't funny?" Carlos asks.

"What?"

"You."

I can't help it—this brings a smile to my face.

When I got back to the hotel last night, I called Carlos to fill him in about Ellis and Harvey—and their previous occupations. He said he'd look into their backgrounds to see what he could find.

"Nothing yet," he reports. "Neither has a criminal record. Started looking into their financials and can't find anything suspicious yet. No big expenditures of money. Nothing on paper anyway."

"Neither of them walked into a bank in the last year scoping it out?" I ask.

"Not that I can find," he says. "Looks like that's Parker's job."

"*If* it's them," I say.

"*If*," he agrees. "We sure as hell don't have anything solid yet."

In the warm light of day, I'm starting to feel like my suspicions last night were unfounded. The idea of Parker and his drinking buddies turning out to be the XYZ Bandits now seems silly.

"It would be nice to know if any of them have alibis for the dates of the robberies," I say.

"Let me probe around a little bit more," he tells me. "I might not be able to find that out, but maybe I can find something useful."

I hang up as I'm passing the grain elevator. It doesn't look quite so spooky in the bright sunlight. Just a run-down old building, like you see in lots of Texas farm country.

When I pull into Parker's driveway, I find Josie on the porch, snapping off the ends of green beans and separating the pieces into paper sacks. Today, she's wearing a pretty yellow sundress, and she hits me with one of her smiles that can put anyone in a good mood. I spot the kids in the back of the yard, climbing around the fallen oak and the woodpile next to it.

No sign of Parker.

"Howdy, stranger," she says.

I tip the brim of my hat. "Parker around?"

"He's in the barn," she says, rising to her feet. "I was just about to bring him a glass of lemonade. Come in for a minute and I'll send you out there with two."

I follow her into the kitchen, where she pulls a pitcher out of the fridge.

"So," she says, giving me a sidelong glance, "what's this I hear about you dating a country-music singer?"

"We broke up a while back," I say. "I've got a new girlfriend now. A college professor."

She raises her eyes, impressed.

"What subject?"

"English."

She grins. "Does she correct your grammar?"

I laugh. "Luckily, no."

She hands me a glass, with ice cubes and lemon pulp floating in the cloudy liquid. One swallow makes my lips pucker.

I tell her it's delicious, then add, "I must say, I'm a bit envious of you and Parker. You seem to have it all. Beautiful family. Perfect marriage."

"I picked a good man," she says. "The best."

I can't argue with that.

At least not until I have more evidence, I think with a pang of guilt.

I say, "Megan's great and all . . ."

Josie says, "But?"

Just like Carlos, she can sense a *but*.

"We don't have what you two have," I say.

"Being married to a Texas Ranger isn't easy," she says. "Trust me: I know. But if it made Parker happy to stay a Ranger, I would have stuck with him. If you're with the right person, you figure it out."

As much as I wouldn't mind sitting down with Josie and talking through the woes of my love life, I'm here for another reason. And

I'm anxious to see what's out in the barn. I take the second glass of lemonade from Josie and head through the back door.

Halfway to the barn, I hear a shriek coming from the back of the yard. Kids can make all kinds of racket when they're fooling around, but there's a distinct difference between shrieks of play and screams of pain or terror.

These are the latter.

Parker bursts out of the barn, looking around. He glances at me and doesn't so much as register an ounce of surprise that I'm there. I point toward the back of the yard, where the kids were playing by the fallen tree, and he takes off in a sprint.

I drop both glasses of lemonade in the grass and run after him.

CHAPTER 15

IT TAKES US only a second or two to sprint to the back of the property where the fallen oak lies. Parker sawed many of the branches off and split them into logs, but the main trunk—a good three feet in diameter—is still intact. Parker leaps it like an Olympic hurdler, and I place one hand against the bark and vault over.

On the other side of the tree, we find Parker's two kids, tears streaming down their cheeks and looks of fright on their faces.

"What happened?" Parker says, keeping his voice steady—instilling calm rather than panic.

"A snake bit Leo," the girl wails.

Parker kneels to examine his son's leg, as Josie comes running up and lifts Etta into her arms. From where I'm standing, I can see nothing more than a small red welt on Leo's leg, no bigger than a dime. I lean forward and spot the bite marks, just small punctures like two bee stings.

It doesn't look bad.

Probably scared the kid more than hurt him.

"You okay?" Parker asks his son.

The boy nods, trying to put on a brave face, but his mouth is turned down in a frown. At any moment, he's going to burst back into tears.

"Where did the snake go?" I ask, keeping my voice calm so I don't spook the kids any more than they already are.

Leo points into the woods, and I start walking that way, eyeing the grass at my feet.

Parker follows me, leaving Josie to comfort the children. We step from the grass into the woods where the vegetation is thick with weeds growing up through a layer of leaves and fallen branches.

Parker says, "There's no way we're going to find that sn—"

About ten feet away, a slithering rope of red, black, and yellow slides underneath a log and disappears. I run to the log and spot the snake on the other side, about to disappear in a cluster of tall grass.

I pull my pistol in a flash.

Fire leaps from the barrel.

The snake jerks, as if zapped by an electric shock, and falls still on the ground. Birds take flight from nearby trees, startled by the sound of the gunshot. Back in the yard, we can hear the children squeal with surprise.

"They're not going to hurt the snake, are they?" Etta asks her mom.

"Shh," Josie says reassuringly. "Everything's going to be okay."

Parker and I step closer to get a good look at the snake. Blood spills out of the bullet wound, which nearly blew it in half. Only a sliver of scaly skin keeps the body in one piece.

The snake, what's left of it, is small and slender, only about a foot and a half long, no thicker around than one of my fingers. The head is tiny, hard to distinguish at first glance from the tail. Along the length of the body, there is a pattern of large bands of red and black bisected by thin rings of yellow.

"Just a milk snake," Parker says, relieved. "Thank God it wasn't a rattlesnake."

I try to remember the saying I was taught as a kid.

Red touch black
Safe for Jack
Red touch yellow
Kills a fellow

If it were a harmless milk snake, the red bands would touch the black bands. But on this one, the yellow touches the red. Which means...

"It's not a milk snake," I say. "That's a coral snake."

Parker stares at me with a look of confusion. He either doesn't know what that means or is hoping that what he's thinking is wrong.

"The venom is more toxic than a rattler's," I say. "That's one of the deadliest snakes in the world."

CHAPTER 16

PARKER LIFTS LEO into his arms.

"Hey, bud," he says, his voice shaky, trying to keep the boy calm even though Parker isn't. "We're going to take you to the hospital and get you checked out. Just to make sure everything's okay."

The kid wraps his arms around his father as Josie stares at us with confused, terrified eyes.

"I'll drive," I say, picking up the dead snake by its tail, just in case the doctors want to see it. "We'll get there faster."

With his son in his arms, Parker jogs around the tree and heads through the yard. Before I follow—now that Parker's son is out of earshot—I explain to Josie what kind of snake it was and that Leo needs medical attention ASAP.

"You take Etta and meet us at the hospital," I say. "Don't drive recklessly. Everything will be okay."

Without waiting for her to respond, I sprint after Parker and get to the truck at the same time he does. I open the passenger door for him, then I hurry around the hood, jump in, and fire up the engine.

"Hey, Leo," I say, trying to sound nonchalant. "Ever ridden in a police vehicle while the siren was going?"

He gives me his best brave smile. I turn the lights on—blue and red flashes that come out of the grille and from underneath the passenger sunshade—and I let the siren wail. As soon as I hit the roadway, I push the truck up to a hundred miles an hour. I zoom past cars puttering down the two-lane.

I grab the police radio, identify myself, and ask to be patched through to the hospital in Snakebite.

"This is Rory Yates from the Texas Ranger Division," I say when someone answers. "I'm bringing in an eight-year-old boy with a bite from a coral snake."

"Are you sure it was a coral snake?" the female nurse asks, surprise in her voice.

"Positive," I say into the radio mic. "Do you carry antivenom?"

"I know we have it for rattlers and cottonmouths," she says. "This town doesn't get its name for no reason. But we don't get many coral snake bites. I'll have to check."

I glance over at Parker and whisper, "She's checking."

He closes his eyes, as if in silent prayer.

I roar past a tractor driving down the road by the grain elevator. Parker is holding his son tight, whispering to him that everything is going to be okay.

What I remember about coral snakes is their venom contains a neurotoxin that's more dangerous than almost any other snake's. But they don't have retractable fangs, like a rattlesnake, so they can't deliver the venom with quite the same punch. They can't bite through boots and maybe not even denim. But for a little boy in a pair of shorts, his exposed legs would have been an easy target. And Leo probably doesn't weigh much more than fifty pounds. Whether it was a big dose or a little one, it won't much matter. Whatever poison got in will take its toll.

"Daddy," Leo says, his words slurred, "I don't feel so good."

Parker's eyes well with tears, and his arms are trembling as he holds his boy. I've never seen my old friend like this before.

"You're being very brave," I say to Leo, and add, as much for Parker's benefit as Leo's, "You're going to be okay."

The boy's breathing is becoming labored, each inhalation wheezing more than the one before it.

"Don't talk," Parker says, but the boy keeps uttering sounds, mostly unintelligible.

"Can't...feel...my fingers," the boy whispers in a hoarse, wheezy voice. "Can't...feel...legs."

"Oh, God," Parker groans as the boy turns limp in his arms. "What's happening?"

I don't answer. The last thing Parker needs to hear right now is that the neurotoxin is paralyzing his son's muscles. If it stops his lungs or his heart, Leo will die before we get to the hospital.

"Make sure he keeps breathing," I say, and Parker lowers his head to listen to the weak rasping sounds of his son's labored breaths.

I blast into town and speed the F-150 through a red light, honking my horn along the way. Up ahead, I see the hospital.

The voice comes back on my radio: "You there, Ranger?"

"Yeah," I say.

"We've got the antivenom."

"Thank God," Parker mutters next to me.

"Get it ready," I say into the radio. "We're here."

There are a couple of cars ahead of me waiting to turn into the hospital parking lot. A car exiting the lot from the wrong lane has everything jammed up.

I yank the wheel and the truck lurches over the curb, racing through a patch of grass. The truck tires kick up hunks of sod. I hit the pavement, the tires chirping, and head toward the ER entrance. I honk my horn over and over as I pull up, and a trio of doctors or nurses in scrubs run out.

Parker is out the door before I even get the gearshift into park.

CHAPTER 17

AN HOUR LATER, I'm sitting in the waiting room with Etta, while Parker and Josie are inside the hospital with Leo. Not knowing how to keep a five-year-old busy, I put buds in Etta's ears and let her listen to a playlist of Willow's songs.

That seems to do the trick. She nods her head and dances in her seat, her worries about her brother forgotten.

My worries aren't, though.

I pace up and down the floor, my boots loud against the tile. I feel like we got here in time, but until you get word from the doctors, you just never know. Maybe the antivenom might not be working. Maybe the poison had spread too much throughout his body.

I'm also racked with guilt.

I keep thinking about Parker. The man I saw today, holding his ailing son in his arms, is a good man. He can't be a criminal.

A door opens and Parker comes out. His eyes are red from crying.

Oh, hell, I think. *We were too late.*

He makes eye contact, opens his mouth, but can hardly get the words out.

"He's going to be okay," he finally gasps. "The antivenom seems to be doing the trick."

Tears spring to my eyes and I blink them away. I try not to show how worried I was.

Parker lifts off the earbuds and tells Etta her brother's going to be okay, hugs her tight, then he stands before me, looking emotionally spent. I've been on grisly crime scenes with this man, and he was always unflappable—a closed book. But today Parker's emotions are on full display. He looks like he's had the fright of his life.

And maybe he has—he came face-to-face with every parent's worst nightmare.

"I can't thank you enough, Rory."

"It was nothing," I say.

"No," he says, his voice choked. "It was a hell of a lot more than nothing. I didn't realize that snake was poisonous. I wouldn't have brought Leo to the hospital until he started showing symptoms. And you were able to get us here in record time. I can't even imagine what would have happened."

"It all worked out," I say, trying to downplay my role. "He's going to be okay."

Parker clears his throat. "You saved my son's life, Rory. I'm indebted to you."

I open my mouth to tell him he owes me nothing. He would have done the same if my loved one was in jeopardy. He would have done it for a stranger. He saved dozens of lives while he was a Ranger, maybe more. But before I can speak, Josie rushes out into the lobby and throws her arms around me.

"Thank you, thank you, thank you," she says. "You're a blessing from God, Rory Yates. We hadn't seen you in years and suddenly you show up on our doorstep. I know *He* had a hand in you coming to visit."

I feel a pang of shame knowing what really brought me to their doorstep.

Josie explains that the doctors are going to hold Leo for a few hours for observation. But he should be able to go home tonight. Josie's mom lives in town, and they ask me to give Etta a ride over there. When Leo is released, Josie and the kids will spend the night with the kids' grandmother.

"We don't know what time he'll be released," she says. "Could be six o'clock, could be twelve. Etta might already be asleep, and I don't want to wake her just to drive back home. Besides," she adds, clearly as emotionally exhausted as Parker, "I think I'd feel safer keeping Leo close to the hospital for the night."

I nod, thinking everything she's said sounds reasonable enough.

"That means we need one more favor from you," Parker says, with a look in his eyes suggesting that he hopes he's not asking too much.

"Anything," I say.

"Can you give me a ride back home in a few hours?"

"Of course."

He explains that the kids' grandmother's house is quite small. Josie, Leo, and Etta can stay over without too much trouble, but Parker will make the space too crowded.

We make plans for me to return around dinnertime.

"I've got a bottle of bourbon waiting to be opened," Parker says. "You ought to plan on sleeping on the couch. My nerves are shot and I could use a drinking buddy."

I start to object but remember what I'm really here for. If Parker wants to get drunk, this might be my opportunity to ask him questions or snoop around and see if I can find anything that will get

Carlos off his back. I know I'm not going to find anything incrim-inating. But I also know Carlos won't be satisfied until I've found something to exonerate Parker.

"I'll bring my toothbrush," I tell him, "in case I have one too many."

I just want to get this over with, so I can stop lying and go back home.

CHAPTER 18

AT SUNSET, I'M back at Parker's, sitting in a lawn chair and looking at the short stalks of the cornfield. I've changed out of my work clothes and am wearing a plain white T-shirt and jeans. My gun's locked up in my truck. The kids and Josie are at her mother's house, and Parker and I have the whole property to ourselves.

Parker and I carried lawn chairs out into the yard, and then he left me to go fetch the bourbon. Before leaving, he tossed his cell on his seat, and now it buzzes with an incoming message.

I glance at it and see that it's from Harvey.

Still on for tomorrow?

A moment later, another comes in.

Be there at 11 unless you cancel.

The back door of the house opens, and I settle back into my seat. Parker walks up with two tumblers and a fifth of Garrison Brothers Cowboy Bourbon. When I see the bottle, I raise my eyebrows. I'm pretty sure this stuff goes for two hundred dollars a bottle.

"That's some high-dollar liquid gold right there," I say.

"I've been saving it for a special occasion," Parker says, settling into the seat next to me. "Today, my family is safe and healthy, and a good friend is visiting—what could be more special than that?"

This is the first extravagant item I've seen that suggests Parker might be living beyond the means he declares each year to the IRS. Or maybe he's telling the truth—buying the bottle was a rare indulgence and he's been waiting for the right moment to crack it open.

He pours three fingers and hands the glass to me. He pours the same for himself. I hold the glass close to my face and inhale. The bourbon smells like freshly cut cedar—I can feel my sinuses clearing from just the heat of the aroma.

"To family and friends," he says, holding up his glass for a toast.

He clinks his against mine, then downs his whiskey in one swallow. I take a healthy sip, savoring the sweet caramel and coffee flavor. Instantly, my tongue feels numb and my belly warm.

Parker offers me the bottle for a refill, but I wave him off. I still have half of my original pour. He fills his and settles back. The sun is an orange blob disappearing into the cornstalks.

It will be dark soon.

"You've got a really nice life here," I say. "I'm envious."

He nods, takes another drink. "This is my oasis," he says, gesturing to the property. "My safe place from the horrors of the world."

I say nothing, hoping he'll continue.

He does.

"Out there," he says, gesturing to the world beyond the cornfield and the woods, "society is immoral and sick, and the bad people sure as hell outnumber the good. Drug dealers. Human traffickers. Pedophiles. Sociopaths in business suits pulling the strings. Corrupt politicians enabling crime and profiting by it. Nothing changes. People who actually want to do good can't. Their hands are tied by a broken system. Only way to raise a family in this world is to shelter them from all that evil."

While I understand the sentiment, I'm shocked by the vehemence of his words.

"This country has a sickness of greed that keeps good people down," he says. "We working folk have to tithe to the rich. These billionaires get tax breaks while the poor and working class can't get ahead no matter how hard they try. The system's rigged against the little guy."

He refills his glass again and continues in this vein, talking about how he couldn't stand to be a Ranger anymore because the system doesn't work. His eyes are growing glassy as he continues to drink. I can feel the power of the one-hundred-thirty-proof alcohol in my bloodstream, but Parker's matching my drinks three to one. And the more he drinks, the looser his tongue gets.

"How can you stand it, Rory?" he says. "You're a good person, yet your hands are tied by a flawed and corrupt system."

"I just try to do what little I can to make the world a better place," I say. "I'd rather do what I can than not do anything at all."

I realize too late that this might have sounded like an accusation.

"Is that a dig at me?" he says, his eyes fiery in the last glow of twilight. "Are you saying I should be doing something to make the world a better place? Trust me—I do my part."

"I'm sure you do," I say. "I wasn't suggesting you weren't. The way I see it, as long as you're not hurting anyone else, living a good life, you're doing what you're supposed to." I add, pointedly, "As long as you're not breaking laws—as long as you're not a criminal."

"What if breaking laws is the only way to do good?" he says.

"What if that's the only way to keep your family safe in this immoral world?"

I feel a cold chill creep up my spine.

"What if," he adds, "the system is so broken that the only way to do good in this world is to break the law?"

CHAPTER 19

"WHAT ARE YOU talking about?" I ask, trying to sound nonchalant—just a buddy chatting over a drink—but I get the sense that Parker just remembered he's talking to a Texas Ranger. We stare at each other, but the darkness has descended enough that I can't quite make out his expression. He's just a shape in the gray light.

"Nothing," he says finally. "I'm a little drunk. I've hardly eaten all day. This alcohol's going straight to my head."

He's quiet for a minute, and I sense he wants to say something. Sometimes, as a police officer, you have to know when to shut up and let someone talk, but this time it doesn't work. Parker rises to his feet and says, "Look, Rory, I'm bushed. I think I'm going to head for bed. You okay to drive?"

He says this in such a way it's clear that he doesn't want me to stay. So much for sleeping on the couch. I tell him that I'll sit and enjoy the night for a little while and sober up.

"Thanks again for what you did today," he says. "And come visit again before you head out of town, okay? Don't mind me. I'm a little drunk."

"No problem," I say. "It's been a hard day."

"Forget what I said, will you? Strike it from your brain."

"Sure," I say.

But as he walks away, I know that I can't. What the hell was he getting at with all that talk about breaking the law?

I wait a few minutes until he's inside, and I think hard about snooping around. I could walk over to the barn and take a look inside. Or, if he passes out, I might even be able to sneak inside the house.

But all of that seems risky.

If Parker really is an XYZ Bandit—and that's a big if—he could be inside his house watching me right now. He was inebriated, but he didn't seem *that* far gone—not yet on the verge of passing out. From my vantage point in the yard, all the windows are black. There's no way of knowing if he's on the other side.

He could be holding a high-powered rifle on me for all I know.

I can't let on that I'm spying on Parker. If he is one of the bandits, I gain nothing by showing what I'm up to. And if he isn't, what would he think if he happened to look out the window and saw his friend snooping around?

I rise from my seat and stroll through the grass. I don't allow myself to turn my head to look at the house.

Act normal.

As I climb into my truck and fire up the engine, I can't shake the feeling that I'm being watched.

CHAPTER 20

THE NEXT MORNING, I call Carlos from my hotel room. I've got the morning news on, and I mute the sound before he picks up. I was tempted to put the channel on CMT or GAC but decided it would be too distracting if one of Willow's videos came on.

"Lubbock morgue," Carlos answers. "You kill 'em, we chill 'em."

"Jesus, this again," I say. "Do you answer the phone like that when your captain calls?"

"Nah," Carlos says. "When he calls, I say, 'Go ahead, caller, you're on the air!'"

This makes me laugh.

"That's nothing," he says. "You should hear what I say when my mom calls. 'Lubbock sperm bank—you squeeze it, we freeze it.'"

I burst out laughing.

"You do *not* say that to your mother," I say. "Do you?"

"No," he says. "My mother's dead actually."

"Oh," I say. I hadn't known about his mother. "I'm sorry."

"Not really," he says. "She's retired and living on South Padre Island."

"Shit, Carlos. Knock it off. I called for a reason."

He quiets, all business for real this time, and I tell him about yesterday's events, including Parker's radical rant last night about the ills of society and the broken system governing it. Earlier that day, I'd been ready to exonerate Parker, thinking no one who loved his son like he did could be an armed robber. But after last night, I was more convinced than ever that Parker *could* be our guy.

"What he said is interesting," Carlos says, "but it's far from conclusive. If every Texan who has a little too much to drink and starts spouting off against the government and big corporations might be one of the XYZ Bandits, our suspect list would be longer than Highway 83."

"I feel like I'm on a roller coaster," I say. "One minute, I'm sure it can't be him. The next, I think, *Hell, maybe it could just be.*"

"Well, I've got a little news that won't help your uncertainty any," Carlos says.

"What's that?"

He tells me that he looked into the auto shop where Parker's friend Ellis works.

"They specialize in motorcycles," he says. "They've got rows of bikes in inventory. You go to their website, there are a dozen or more that fit the descriptions we've gotten from the XYZ scenes."

"Christ," I say, and flop down onto the corner of the bed. We're no closer to tying Parker to the crimes, but we're sure as hell not any closer to crossing him off the list. "Well, we know they have access to bikes. But what about guns, explosives, diving equipment, everything else they'd need?"

"They seem like the type of people who could get all that," Carlos says. "But we need some proof that they actually have it."

I run my hand through my hair as I listen to Carlos talk about what he wants to do next. On the TV, the muted news reporter is talking to some children showcasing their goats at a county fair. The caption at the bottom of the screen says, KIDS WITH KIDS!

"I think it might be time for me to come to Snakebite and help out," Carlos says.

"How are you going to square that with your captain?"

"I don't know yet," he says. "Maybe I'll tell him my mom died. You believed me."

"Very funny," I say. "Just give me more time."

"Okay," he says, "I guess if you're not in any hurry to get back to your girlfriend..."

He says it like he's about to make a joke about my relationship, but I stop him.

"Don't start about that," I say. "I'm not in the..."

"Sorry," he says earnestly.

But I'm not listening. On the TV, the news coverage has changed. Now a different reporter is featured interviewing someone next to a pile of cash bundles stacked into a cube roughly the size of a coffee table. The caption along the bottom states, ANONYMOUS DONATION TO STATE CHARITY FOUNDATION.

I jump to my feet and unmute the volume.

"Turn on the TV," I shout to Carlos. "I know what they're doing with the money."

"Who?" Carlos says.

"Parker," I say. "It all makes sense now."

CHAPTER 21

THE SEGMENT IS over before Carlos can get to a TV, but we both find the report on KCBD's website and an article in the *Austin American-Statesman*. Apparently, last week a highly reputable charitable foundation in the capital received an anonymous donation of two million dollars. The cash literally showed up on their doorstep, left overnight in garbage bags. The first employee in the door that morning almost threw the bags in the dumpster, but she decided to take a peek inside first.

The mission of the foundation, we discover, is to provide grants to nonprofits, specializing in programs that help Texas communities: food banks, homeless shelters, literacy programs.

"You think Parker is robbing from the rich to give to the poor?" Carlos asks.

"Yes," I say, surprised that I'm saying the words aloud. "Nothing made sense before. Parker isn't the type of guy who would rob a bank or armored car out of selfish interests. *But* he is the type of guy who would commit a crime if he thought he was actually helping society.

"Think about it," I add. "The bandits have never fired their weapons. He doesn't want to hurt anyone. He's trying to redistribute wealth to those who need it the most."

Carlos says that he'll contact the foundation and see about checking the serial numbers against what was stolen during the XYZ Bandits' crime spree.

"It's probably a long shot," I say. "Wouldn't they launder the money first?"

"Maybe they can't," he says. "Maybe they don't know how. If these guys are what you say, they're not your typical criminals. They don't have contacts in the criminal world. The way you describe Parker, I can't see him doing business with criminals even if he did have the contacts. Maybe they can launder a little bit through their work, but none of them owns a major business. Ellis is just an employee at the bike shop."

"Parker sure as hell can't declare millions in earnings for his one-man furniture factory," I say.

"Oh, man," Carlos says, as if he's just realized the difficulty of what he might have to do. "That foundation's going to be pissed if I have to impound all that money as evidence."

I can't help but think that that is precisely the kind of red-tape rule-following Parker would hate. The foundation could do a lot of good with that money, a lot more than a huge corporate bank. I find myself having weirdly conflicting emotions. I wouldn't condone robbery for any reason, but his intentions aren't selfish and immoral—he's trying to do good, even if his methods are misguided.

Carlos says he'll do some digging and see if there have been any other unusual charitable donations over the past year.

"If that money came from the XYZ Bandits," he says, "they've stolen a hell of a lot more than two million dollars. There's got to be more out there."

He asks what I'm going to do today.

I think for a moment, remembering Harvey's text. I could make another visit to Parker's house, but I won't get any closer to the truth by wearing out my welcome with Parker and Josie.

I need to take a different approach.

CHAPTER 22

I PARK IN the wooded clearing where the old cars and other junk have been discarded into the ravine. As I step out of the truck into the shadows of the canopy, the woods are quiet except for the buzz of insects and the whispers of tree limbs swaying gently in a barely perceptible breeze.

Today I'm not wearing my typical shirt, tie, and Stetson. I'm wearing camouflage BDUs and a boonie hat, more like a soldier from Vietnam than a Texas Ranger. Except for my footwear, that is. I've got on my cowboy boots. And my gun is on my hip, as usual.

I turn my phone on silent and hang a pair of binoculars around my neck. As I walk through the woods in the direction of Parker's property, the ravine levels out to a dry streambed, overgrown with thorny brush. I pass deer tracks in the dried mud, but the only wildlife I spot is a squirrel skittering from tree to tree.

After about a half mile, I spot cornstalks where the wood abuts the field. Over the short crop, I see Parker's house and adjust my trajectory, careful of my footing after yesterday's encounter with the coral snake. There's no telling what might be crawling—or slithering—through the underbrush.

As I pass by the fallen oak, I notice that more of it has been sliced into rounds, and a chainsaw sits atop a large stump. The air has the distinct smell of freshly sawed wood.

The back door of the barn swings open, and Parker steps out. He's wearing jeans, running shoes, a sleeveless muscle shirt, and plastic safety goggles. There's a long-handled tool slung over his shoulders. A maul. With one side of the head shaped like a sledge-hammer, the other a dull V-bladed axe, the unwieldy tool looks lightweight in Parker's muscular arms.

He heads toward the tree. If not for my camouflage clothes, he could probably spot me easily. But I hope that I blend in well enough, lost among the tree branches and shadows.

Parker begins splitting logs. He has perfect form for a wood-cutter, holding his hands apart at the start of his swing and draw-ing them together as he brings the sledge down. The oak sections don't stand a chance, exploding apart with each swing. Parker works steadily. Sweat glistens on his brow, but he doesn't slow down.

I'm not sure what I was hoping to see today, but this isn't it. I thought perhaps I might finally get a look inside the barn. Also, if he's meeting with Harvey, I hoped the meeting might happen here.

Josie exits the back of the house with a load of laundry. She heads to a clothesline by the garden. Parker stops and looks over his shoulders.

"How's Leo?" he asks, hardly out of breath despite the mountain of firewood he just chopped.

"Just a little tired," she says. "I'm letting them watch *DC Super Hero Girls*."

Parker nods. "Recovering from a poisonous snakebite seems like a good reason to get a little extra screen time."

Josie laughs and starts hanging wet children's clothes.

I really like these people. It will break my heart if it turns out

Parker is involved in the XYZ Bandits. I was almost sure of it earlier this morning, but now I hope with all my heart that I'm wrong.

There's a moment of silence as Parker prepares to resume work.

I hear a phone buzz.

Parker hears it, too, looking around for the noise. I wonder why he doesn't answer it, then I realize the phone is mine. Out here, with nothing to hear but the breeze and birdsong, the vibration is loud. I inch my hand to my pocket to silence the phone. But I freeze when Parker turns his gaze my way.

Parker seems to be staring right at me, but I still don't move. There's plenty of cover—branches, leaves, shadows—and I try to have faith that the camouflage is doing its job.

"Weren't you supposed to meet Harvey and Ellis in town?" Josie calls out to Parker.

"Oh, crap," Parker says, turning away from the noise in the woods and checking his watch. "I've gotta get going."

I feel relieved as he lays the maul down and heads toward the house. I check my phone and find a missed call from Lieutenant Abrams. As I look at the screen, a text comes through from him.

Need you to come back to Waco tonight, he says. *Want to interview a guy in County. Lawyer's setting it up for tomorrow.*

Which means I need to drive back to Redbud tonight.

I let out a silent sigh and take this news as my cue to leave the woods. I move quietly through the trees, keeping one eye out to make sure neither Parker nor Josie hears me. Parker goes inside, and it looks like Josie has the line almost filled. I can barely see her through the branches. I'm far enough away now that I don't need to worry about being spotted.

As I push through a cluster of branches into a clearing, I freeze when I see three mule deer standing in front of me, their big ears erect, their bodies rigid. One is a buck, its short antlers fuzzy with summer velvet. The other two are does, one full grown and the other barely more than a fawn.

I hold my breath, not wanting to spook them.

But it's too late.

The buck vaults away, springing through the air. The others follow, and I watch them crashing through the brush. Deer can move through the forest as silent as ninjas, but when they're bounding like this, they make a hell of a racket.

The deer run into Parker's yard, circle around Josie, and disappear into the cornfield.

I can't quite see Parker, but I hear the back door swing open and shut.

"That was cool," Parker says with a laugh. "What was that all about?"

"I don't know," I hear Josie say. "Something spooked them."

I lift my binoculars and try to get a better look through the branches. I spot Parker, seeing his expression change from curiosity to concern. He walks slowly through the yard, looking toward the wood. At the back of the property, where the remains of the old oak lay, he stops and considers the chainsaw and the maul.

He reaches for the chainsaw, hesitates, then moves his hand to the maul.

He carries the heavy instrument two-handed into the woods toward me like a knight heading into combat with a battle axe.

CHAPTER 23

CROUCHED AMONG THE foliage, I turn myself into a statue, moving only to lower the binoculars. I don't want Parker to see a glint of sunlight on the lenses.

A gnat buzzes around my ear, and I control the impulse to swat it away. Another buzzes in the corner of my eye, and it's all I can do to not squish it with my fingers. Through my twitching eye, I watch my former colleague about fifty feet from me, obscured by leafy branches. I debate about whether I should stay in place.

Or try to move.

Either option is risky. If I move, he might hear me. If I don't, he could swing back this direction any second and spot me. He seems to be looking the other way, and I try backing away. I'm in a small clearing, without many branches or leaves, and I'm able to travel stealthily. I move when he moves, so the sound he makes will cover mine.

But when I get to the other side of the barren patch of earth, I find myself at the edge of the dry creek bed I followed earlier. The ditch is thick with thorn bushes, so dense it's hard to see into them.

Parker shifts back toward my direction. He steps forward. If he keeps heading this way, it's just a matter of time before he finds me. When his eyes are diverted elsewhere, I slowly kneel to the forest floor. Moving as quietly as I can, I crawl into the thicket. The thorns tear at my clothes. Their needlepoints stab into my skin. On my belly, I low-crawl deeper into the tangled brush.

I ignore the pain of the thorns and find the rocky bottom of the ditch. I crane my head to see Parker and can barely make him out through the brambles. He might be only fifteen feet away, but—camouflaged and buried in the thicket—I'll be hard to spot.

He pauses his pursuit and kneels. I can hardly make out his face, but I swear I sense a grin come over his features. He holds that expression for a moment, then takes a deep breath, as if resigning himself.

Abruptly, he rises to his feet and heads back the way he came.

I let out a sigh of relief but I don't move. When he gets back to his yard, I hear him call out to Josie, "Nothing there. I'm going to head out now, okay?"

"Okay," she says. "Love you."

Through the quiet of the forest, I hear the engine of his Ford Bronco come to life, and then the sound of it driving away.

I decide my best way out of this bramble is the way I came, so I crawl back to the clearing. I'm as careful as possible, but the thorns snag my clothes and tear my skin. When I finally get free of the thorns, I rise to my feet, brushing the dirt and leaves off my chest. My BDUs have several tears, and I'm sure there are plenty of small cuts and scrapes on my skin underneath. But it beats facing Parker and explaining what the hell I was doing dressed in camouflage behind his house.

I approach where I think Parker stopped. I kneel down the way he did. In a barren patch of dirt, there's the distinct mark of cowboy boot prints.

They're mine. I'm sure. Parker was wearing a pair of running shoes, and I spot his prints, easily distinguishable from mine. And, worse, I'm sure that Parker knows—or at least suspects—that the boot prints are mine.

That was what the smile was all about.

Thinking of it now, I consider what that grin might have meant. To me, there's no doubt. It was the kind of grin that said, *The game is afoot.*

May the best man—Ranger or former Ranger—win.

CHAPTER 24

I HEAD OUT of town immediately, leaving my clothes and guitar behind in my hotel room until I can come back to town to get them. Josie had said to Parker, *Weren't you supposed to meet Harvey and Ellis in town?* That tells me he's headed to Snakebite. So I take backroads away from town to make sure I'm not spotted. It takes longer, but that's the least of my worries. I'm planning to call Parker and tell him I headed out of town early this morning, but I've got to make sure no one sees me to contradict my alibi.

Just as I'm about to pick up my phone, it buzzes with an incoming call from—speak of the devil—Parker.

I take a deep breath, steady my voice, and answer.

"I was just about to call you," I say. "How's our little patient doing?"

He tells me Leo's fine—which I already know, of course—and then changes tack.

"Harvey and Ellis and I were just headed out to do some target shooting," he says. "Want to come along?"

My brain gives me the quick image of going out to some remote location with the three of them and being ambushed. Even as the thought occurs to me, I recognize how surreal it feels to think of my old friend this way.

Do I really think he's part of this?

Would he really ambush me with his accomplices?

"Sorry," I say. "I'm headed back home for a day or two."

"It won't take long," he says. "Come on. I've told these guys how good you are with a gun—the best I've ever seen. They want to see the legend in action."

I tell him I left Snakebite earlier in the morning.

"I'm driving through Gatesville right now," I say. I'm not even close. But I have to lie to throw him off my scent. Make it seem impossible that I could have been in the woods thirty minutes earlier.

Only silence on the other end.

"You been through here lately?" I ask. "They've got the road all torn up. Orange barrels as far as the eye can see and not a single worker in sight."

In reality, I'm seeing nothing but fields, but I remember the roadwork from two days ago when I made the drive in reverse.

He seems to ignore what I've got to say, as if he's lost in thought, or distracted.

"You still there?" I ask.

"Yeah," he says finally. "You're not leaving Snakebite for good, are you?"

"No," I say. "I've just got some things to take care of back at head-quarters. Not sure how long it will take, but I'll be back. Maybe not for long, though," I add. "If we're going to find Jackson Clarke, it's not going to be in Snakebite."

When he hangs up, I let out a relieved breath. I try to call Carlos but don't reach him. Then I call Lieutenant Abrams and leave a message to let him know I'm heading back. I'm wondering if I need to come clean with him about my real motives for heading to

Snakebite. Carlos faced resistance from his captain, but maybe it's time we brought someone else in on this.

I decide to sleep on it.

When it comes time that I really am driving through Gatesville, stuck in road-construction traffic, I remember Willow's text message about wanting to meet.

I pick up my phone.

I think about it.

Then I take a deep breath and call my girlfriend instead.

CHAPTER 25

"WHAT'S TROUBLING YOU, Rory? You seem distant."

"Sorry," I say, setting my fork down. "I was staring off into space, wasn't I?"

Megan nods, giving me a polite smile.

When I called her on my drive back to Redbud and told her I was going to be in town, but maybe for only one night, she was excited about the chance to see me. She came right over, looking stunning in a floral summer dress and matching yellow heels. We made dinner together: brisket, corn pudding, and grilled potato skins—and a bottle of red wine to go with it. Working in tandem in the kitchen kept my mind busy, but once we were at the dinner table, with nothing to do but eat or talk, I felt my thoughts drifting toward Parker and his buddies.

"You've got a lot on your mind, don't you?" she says, staring at me sympathetically. "Would you rather be alone?"

"No," I say. "Absolutely not."

Megan has the most gorgeous ocean-blue eyes, and tonight she looks especially amazing, with her dress showing off the perfect amount of sun-kissed skin and her hair pulled back except for a few strands hanging down artfully against her cheeks. All I want to do is dive into those blue eyes and get lost for the night in their depths. I tell myself there's not a damn thing I can do about the Parker investigation right now anyway.

"Is it Willow?" Megan says, and I can see she's nervous to ask this question.

"No," I say.

It's true: I have *not* been thinking about Willow. Not tonight. Here with Megan, staring into her arresting eyes, so close I can smell her perfume, I know I'm just about as lucky as a guy can be. She's an amazing woman—smart, sexy, fun. She has a great personality. She cares about other people.

On a scale of one to ten, she's an eleven.

In this moment, I want nothing more than to make this work with her.

"Sometimes I feel like I'm competing with her memory," Megan says.

It breaks me inside to hear this. Partly because it's true. And partly because she deserves so much better.

"You have nothing to worry about," I say, and I lean over in my seat, and put my lips against hers.

"Don't fool with my heart, Rory," she says through kisses. "I want a man who's all in."

"I'm all in," I say.

We kiss for several seconds, then Megan rises from her seat and throws her leg over me, straddling me in my kitchen chair with her back to the table. She nibbles on one of my ears and I run my hands up her smooth legs. She pulls the tie out of her hair and shakes her locks out.

"Careful," I say, grinning. "Don't get your hair in the brisket."

We scoot the chair away from the table but stay seated.

She reaches down, grabs her dress in both fists, and, in one smooth motion, pulls it over her head. She tosses it into a puddle on the kitchen floor and settles back onto my lap, kissing me while wearing nothing but a bra, thong underwear, and her yellow heels.

"Ranger Yates," she whispers seductively, "is that a gun in your pocket or are you happy to see me?"

I answer by stripping off my T-shirt. Unfortunately, this gives her pause. My arms and shoulders are covered in scratches from the thorn bush I crawled through this morning. I showered and cleaned myself up before she came over, but there was nothing I could do about the scrapes scoring my skin like a map of red roads.

"It looks worse than it feels," I say, leaning to kiss her again.

We get back to making out, and I'm ready to pick her up and carry her to bed when I hear a phone buzzing. I break my lips away from Megan's and look around. My cell is on the counter, five feet away, vibrating.

"Don't check it," Megan urges.

I want to do as she asks, but I've been burned by not answering the phone before. When you're a Texas Ranger, the next phone call could mean life or death for someone.

Including you.

And, in this case, it might be Carlos with news about the investigation that's preoccupied my mind all evening.

"Hang on just a sec," I say, squeezing out from under Megan.

She has a put-out expression on her face, and I don't blame her. But it doesn't stop me. I grab my phone and see it's a message from my mom.

Can you come to the house and help your dad with something?

I huff in frustration and explain to Megan what the message is about.

"It can wait," I say, setting the phone down.

But Megan is already tugging her dress back on, easing it down her body, her cheeks flushed with embarrassment. There's nothing worse than seeing a woman getting dressed *before* you've made love.

"I'm not in the mood to have a quickie so you can run off to other priorities," she says, obviously irritated.

"I'm sorry," I say. "I should have ignored it. I tell you what. Let me go help my dad with whatever he needs. Then I'll come back. We'll turn my phone off. Hell, I'll lock it up in my truck so it won't distract us again. Whatever you want. I'm all yours for the rest of the night."

She lifts her eyelids and the tiniest hint of a smile curves up her pursed lips.

"All right," she says. "But don't be long. I'm going to climb into your bed and wait. You better be back while I'm still in the mood."

CHAPTER 26

I STEP OUT onto the porch, tugging my T-shirt back on.

I shake my head, cursing myself for answering the phone. I usually like living within a couple hundred yards of my parents' house, happy to be close to them and help out whenever I can, but I'm irritated with them at the moment. Didn't they see that I had company?

I trudge through the tall grass toward their home. The sun is setting, with the sky to the east already dark and the western horizon barely lit from the sun's last dying ember. Fireflies start to light up around me. Out in the pasture, a couple of Mom and Dad's horses whinny and snort like something's got them irritated, but I'm lost in thought, trying to get my head straight about how I'm going to make this up to Megan.

As I approach the ranch house, I notice there's an old pickup sitting in their driveway that I don't recognize. I wonder what my parents could need my help with that their guests couldn't do. Considering who's back in my bed right now, I hope this is important.

And quick.

I open the back door by the kitchen. No need to knock. They're expecting me.

"Mom?" I call, not seeing them anywhere. "Dad?"

"In here," I hear someone call from Dad's office.

It's a man, but not Dad. I wonder for a moment what's going on. Do they really need my help or is this some kind of surprise? Has an old friend come to visit? I don't want this to take longer than necessary—I've got a woman waiting for me.

The door to the study is closed, and I open it and step through without hesitation. What I see freezes me to the bone.

Mom and Dad are seated in chairs, secured there with nylon ropes wrapped around their bodies and duct tape covering their mouths. Behind them stands a man dressed in black, with a ski mask hiding his face.

He holds a six-inch knife to Dad's throat.

"Hold it right there, Ranger," says another voice.

This voice comes from behind the door, as another masked man steps out and aims a small revolver directly at my face.

I put my hands in the air. There's no point in reaching for my belt. My pistol's locked up back at my house.

The gunman to my side tells me to step into the room, and I do so.

"It's going to be okay," I tell my parents.

Dad is putting on a strong face, but Mom is crying. I hate seeing her like this. I face dangerous situations all the time. But my family shouldn't have to. I don't know what these men want, but I can't help but feel this isn't some random home invasion. My job has followed me home.

"On your knees, Ranger," the man behind me says.

"Let's talk about this," I say. "Y'all don't want to do anything you'll regret."

"I said get on your goddamn knees!" the man yells.

He kicks me hard in the back of my leg, and I pitch forward

onto the hardwood floor. Mom lets out a moan. Dad grunts some-thing, but it's indiscernible with the tape over his mouth.

"It's okay," I tell my parents, rising to my hands and knees on the floor.

I crane my neck to look at my assailant. He's tucked his pistol into his waistband and is reaching for something leaning against the wall. It's the length of a two-by-four, about three feet long.

"Wait," I say, as he lifts it like a club.

The other man pockets the knife and picks up his own two-by-four, which he had tucked behind Dad's desk. It stands next to a bookshelf filled with framed pictures and schoolboy knickknacks of my brothers and mine: football trophies, crafts, even some out-grown toys Dad kept for sentimental reasons.

The guy takes his two-by-four and smashes it into the shelves, shattering glass and sending an avalanche of memories onto the floor. The other guy smashes a framed picture on the wall, then shatters a ceramic pot my brother Chris made in high school art class.

Mom lets out a wail. Dad glares at the guys as they continue their destructive rampage. Then suddenly they stop and turn their attention to me.

Both men cock their weapons back, ready to attack.

"I don't know what you guys want," I say, rising to my feet, "but this isn't..."

I don't get a chance to finish.

CHAPTER 27

THEY BOTH LUNGE at me and I duck and throw my arms up like a boxer in a defensive stance. One board hammers my shoulder. Another slaps against my ribs. I back away but quickly find myself in the corner. The narrow side of one of the boards lands against my thigh, shooting pain through my leg, and I drop to my knees.

I throw my hands over my head and curl into a ball, as the boards smack against my body. I kick and twist and try to avoid the worst of the blows, but they're coming fast and furious. Each strike brings a jolt of pain to my muscles or ribs, but my adrenaline is pumping too hard to feel the worst of it. One board skids across my scalp—a glancing blow but still a hit to the head—and I hardly notice.

"Take it easy," one of the men says to the other. "Don't kill him."

The barrage lets up for a moment.

"I remember," the other says, breathing heavy and irritated. "Two rules: Don't kill him. And make sure to break his fingers."

"The fingers on his *right* hand," the other clarifies.

My shooting hand.

"I just figured we'd do both hands. For good measure."

Instinctively, I ball my hands into fists and tuck them under my body because things are happening so fast that I don't have time to really focus. I don't recognize either man's voice. Parker is definitely *not* one of them. But Ellis or Harvey? Could be.

I try to get to my feet, ignoring the pain.

Dad keeps a pistol in a safe in their bedroom.

If I can just get there.

"Looks like he wants some more," one of them says.

I lurch toward the door, dodging a two-by-four and stumbling into the hallway. I take off running to the corridor, a space too tight for the men to have much room to swing their boards. I stagger into my parents' bedroom and lunge across the bed and onto the carpeted floor. The room is dark, but the hallway is lit by the last rays of the setting sun.

I reach for the small gun safe tucked under Dad's bedside table, but the door hangs ajar.

The gun is gone.

"Looking for this?" one of the men says, coming around the bed. He pulls Dad's .38 from his pocket and aims it at me.

"Now stop fucking around," he says. "It's time to take your medicine like a man. The only way you're leaving this house tonight is in an ambulance. But it's up to you whether your parents join you or not."

The other one stands on the other side of the bed, holding the two-by-four over his shoulder like a baseball player in the box waiting for his chance at bat.

"Yeah," he says. "We ain't supposed to kill you, but no one said nothing about not killing your mom and dad."

That's it. I've had enough. I rise to my feet. My muscles throb from where they've hit me already.

But I ignore the pain.

"Well, come on then," I growl, raising my fists.

The guy with the .38 tucks the gun into his belt and chokes up on the two-by-four. The one on the other side of the bed seems unsure how to proceed. As he hesitates, headlight beams flash through the window, and we can hear the sound of a car pulling into my parents' driveway.

"Hang on a sec," the guy says, and he approaches the window, which is cracked about six inches to let in the evening breeze. The guy peeks through the open window as the other one and I stand ready to fight. We hear a car door open.

"I'll be damned," the guy looking out the window says, his voice registering surprise.

"What is it?" his partner asks.

"I'll be damned if that ain't Willow Dawes," the guy says.

"The country singer?" the other asks.

"Looks like her."

We hear boot heels on the sidewalk as Willow approaches the house.

I take a deep breath and open my mouth to shout.

"Willow!" I roar. *"Run!"*

CHAPTER 28

"GO GET HER!" the man closest to me shouts at the other, who takes off out the bedroom door.

"Call 911!" I shout to Willow.

The man grunts in frustration and swings his board at me. I lean my head back just in time. I feel the wind off the two-by-four as it passes next to my nose.

So much for this guy's instructions to be careful and not to hurt me too badly.

Seems like he's not holding back anymore.

I'm not going to, either.

As he's getting ready for his next swing, I dive onto him, throwing my shoulder into his body like an offensive tackle sacking a quarterback. I drive him into the wall, shaking it so hard a framed picture of the family crashes to the floor. I keep the guy pinned to the wall and drive my fist into his gut. Air whooshes out of his mouth, and I hit him again.

He drops the two-by-four. At close quarters like this, he has no leverage to use it. Instead, he reaches for Dad's .38 tucked into his pants. I grab the barrel and chamber in my fist, and jerk down on the gun while pulling up on the barrel. It's surprisingly easy to rip a gun right out of someone's grasp with this technique. He doesn't even get a shot off. I aim the revolver at the center of his mask-covered skull, and he freezes.

Outside, I hear Willow's tires kicking up gravel, followed by the *pop pop* sound of the other guy shooting at her. The bullets *thunk* into the metal of the car and it continues to speed away.

The guy in front of me starts to speak through his mask, but I don't have time to waste on him. I drive my elbow into his jaw as hard as I can and watch him slump to the floor. Then I dart out the door and through the house. Just as I get to the kitchen, the guy who ran outside runs back in. His eyes—the only part of his face I can see behind the mask—widen in surprise when he almost collides into me.

I drive my left fist into his mask and feel his nose crunch underneath. He falls back on his butt, putting his hands down to catch himself, the revolver still in one hand.

I aim Dad's .38 at the wet stain in his mask from where his nose is leaking blood.

"Drop that gun," I say. "You have one second or you're dead."

He tosses the gun away like it's a piece of coal burning his hand.

"Did you hurt her?" I ask.

"No, man," he says, blinking back tears, his voice nasally from the bloody nose. "Not even close. She's heading to that house up on the hill."

My house.

Keeping my gun on him, I shift my feet so I can see out the window. There's just enough light left in the sky for me to see Willow slam the brakes outside my little cottage and run inside. That will be an awkward meeting between Willow and Megan, especially if Megan is actually in bed waiting for me—and depending on what she's still wearing.

But at least Willow's okay.

"You're lucky," I say to the guy.

There's no telling what I'd do right now if he'd shot Willow. I'm so full of rage. Bad guys can come after me all they want, but when they involve the people I love, that's unforgivable.

Keeping my gun on the guy, I reach over with my left hand and tear off his ski mask. He has short red hair, a peppering of freckles, and a gap between his front teeth. His lips and teeth are red with blood at the moment, but one thing's for sure.

I've never seen him before in my life.

"Who sent you?" I ask.

He hesitates.

"Did Parker Longbaugh send you?" I shout.

"Parker who?" the guy says, and I've interviewed enough suspects over the years to recognize genuine confusion when I see it.

CHAPTER 29

AN HOUR LATER, I'm standing out in front of my parents' house, holding an ice pack to my scalp, where one of the two-by-fours thumped me harder than I had realized in the moment, and directing law enforcement traffic. Local cops as well as Texas Rangers need to be told where to go and what to do. The night is pitch black, but the ranch is awash with flashing lights from police cars and ambulances. It breaks my heart to see my parents' property roped off with crime-scene tape.

Before anyone got here, I managed to untie my parents, give them each a hug, then use the same ropes to tie up the two intruders. I ran up to my house to make sure Willow was okay. She was shaken up but not injured. Lucky for all of us that she came by to return Mom's cookbook. The night probably would have turned out a lot differently if she hadn't.

Since the police arrived, Willow and Megan and my parents have all taken turns giving statements. Now they're outside, leaning against the split rail fence next to Mom's garden. I can see Megan and Willow both doing their best to comfort my parents, talking to them, placing consoling hands on their backs, offering hugs when my mom is about to burst into tears again. Whatever awkwardness there might have been when Willow burst into my house to find Megan seems to be gone.

The two women make a good team.

As for the intruders, they are being tended to by paramedics under the watchful eye of police. One's got a dislocated jaw, the other a broken nose, but considering what they did to my parents, they got off easy. I overheard one of the local cops say to them, "Y'all are lucky to be alive. Not many people draw a gun on Rory Yates and live to tell about it."

Both intruders have been cooperative, but not very helpful. They don't know who hired them. They were contacted by an anonymous phone number. A cash deposit was left for them behind a tree in Cameron Park in Waco. One of the guys is from Odessa, the other from Abilene. In time, we might find some connection between them and Parker, but it will take some digging. And for that to happen, it's going to take more than just Carlos and me doing this on our own.

I'll need to come clean with my lieutenant.

Ty Abrams is on the scene, chatting with a local detective, DeAndre Purvis. I approach them and say, "Lieutenant, you got a sec?"

DeAndre, a man I used to butt heads with but have since come to think of as a friend, recognizes his cue and takes a walk. Lieutenant Abrams studies me with a discerning stare. He's a big guy with a thick gray mustache and a head as bald as a cue ball.

"You ought to let one of these paramedics check you out," he says to me.

"I'm okay," I say. "Some bruises. No broken bones."

Lieutenant Abrams eyes me with a mix of sympathy, confusion, and disapproval.

"The perp over there says you asked him about Parker Longbaugh?" he says, his eyebrows raised. "You want to tell me what the hell's going on, Ranger?"

I take a deep breath.

Here it is—the moment of truth.

I confess, telling him everything about my real motivations for going to Snakebite, as well as my growing suspicions that Parker is involved. I downplay Carlos's role, saying that he confided in me but that it was my idea to go to Snakebite and lie about why I was there.

If we end up busting Parker and his buddies—I mean *when* we bust Parker and his buddies—I'll be happy to shift all the credit back to Carlos. But if things don't go well, I'll shoulder the blame.

"So you think Parker hired these guys to come take you out?" he asks.

"It doesn't seem like a coincidence," I say. "I'm sure he made me this morning. And then these guys show up with orders to break the fingers on my shooting hand but not kill me? There's got to be a correlation."

Lieutenant Abrams thinks long and hard about what I'm saying. The blue and red lights reflect off his bald scalp. His expression is unreadable.

"You and Carlos think someone in the Rangers might be involved?" he asks again, making sure he understands.

"Carlos's captain shut him down pretty fast when he mentioned Parker," I say. "But it's more likely he just figured he was barking up the wrong tree. We've got three suspects. I don't think it's as if a current Ranger is out there robbing banks with these guys. It's just that Rangers might protect their own."

He takes a deep breath, then—to my surprise—says, "Okay, let's keep this a secret for now."

He lets me off the hook for the interview he wanted to conduct tomorrow and says that he thinks Carlos should join me in Snake-bite. The two of us need to put all our time and resources into the case.

"You guys report to me, you got it?" he says. "I'll find a way to get the big bosses involved when the time comes."

Technically, Carlos and Ty are the same rank, but Ty's been in this position for years. He was probably a lieutenant back when Parker was a rookie. He'll know better than anyone how to talk to the higher-ups.

"Let's not involve anyone until we have enough for a search warrant," he says.

In this moment, angry as hell about two armed men coming into my parents' home, putting them and Willow in danger, I want some answers. I'm hungry to catch the men responsible—probably like Parker was to catch the Cereal Killer.

"Down in Parker's basement," I say, "I spotted a box labeled EXPLOSIVES."

His eyes widen.

I know it was only comic books inside the box, but I figure all we need is an excuse to get in the house. We need some goddamn answers, and this is the best way I can think to get them.

"That should be enough for a warrant," Ty says. "I'll get moving on it right away." Then he looks at me sharply. "You didn't see what was inside the box, did you?"

"No," I lie.

PART 2

CHAPTER 30

SUNRISE IN SAN Antonio.

Officer Luisa Ramirez is just finishing her shift for the city's River Walk Patrol Division. All the stores and restaurants have been closed for hours, and the night was quiet.

Just the way Luisa likes it.

The River Walk area is Texas's version of a mini-Venice. A series of canals shaded by seventy-foot-tall cypress trees and crisscrossed by walkways and bridges accessing a commercial district of two- and three-story buildings housing stores and restaurants. During the day and into the night, the paths are crowded with tourists eating on outdoor patios or meandering in and out of shops. Tour boats drift up and down the waterways. Music and conversation fill the air.

But during Luisa's shift—11 p.m. to 7 a.m.—the crowds clear out and the businesses close. The sticky heat cools off to a reasonable temperature. The air becomes quiet and peaceful. As morning approaches, she can hear the muffled traffic of the city and the melody of birdsong.

But Luisa's shift isn't a time to relax. She's vigilant about her job. She keeps an eye out for burglars and vandals. Anyone up to no good. She mixes up her routine, never repeating the same route through the pathways. She prides herself on upholding her motto: when the River Walk area is empty, it's vulnerable. That's when she keeps it safe.

Luisa leans over the railing, looking down at the canal. A leaf drifts by on the current. She yawns. She's got thirty more minutes until her replacements come and she can go home, pull the blackout curtains in her bedroom, and go to sleep as the rest of the city is waking up.

She hears the whine of a motor and looks down the canal to see a motorcycle riding on the paved pathway. He's not going fast, just creeping along, but day or night no motorized vehicles are allowed. The River Walk is strictly for pedestrians.

The biker stops and parks the bike, putting the kickstand down and dismounting. Helmet on, visor down, he faces a storefront—Gardiner's Gems and Jewels—standing completely still.

As the crow flies, the biker's location on the other side of the canal is only about twenty-five feet distant, but to get to him, she'd have to run down the path, cross a bridge a good twenty yards away, then run back.

"Excuse me!" she calls out to him across the water. "You can't have that motorcycle up here."

The man turns and looks at her. He's dressed head to toe in black motorcycle gear. His face is obscured by the visor of his helmet. There's a duffel bag strap slung across his body, from his waist to the opposite shoulder. The bag hangs with the weight of a compact but heavy object. Could be a tool, like a power drill. Could be a gun—larger than a pistol, smaller than a shotgun or rifle.

She tells herself to be careful.

"Sir, can you acknowledge that I'm speaking to you?" Luisa calls. He doesn't.

The bike is some kind of crotch rocket, black and sleek and

probably fast as hell once it's out on the open road. Why anyone would want to drive it on the River Walk is beyond her.

"Wait there," Luisa says, losing her patience. "I'm coming over."

The man doesn't move as Luisa heads down toward the bridge. She keeps turning her head to watch the man as she walks away. Then she notices something else. One of the tour boats is floating down the canal. Only the tours don't start for at least another hour.

And, besides, this boat is empty.

No passengers.

No pilot.

The motor is idling, just enough to keep the little skiff crawling down the waterway. Luisa climbs up on the bridge. From the vantage point at the top of the arched structure, she looks up and down the canals and along the tributaries she can see other boats drifting.

What the heck is going on? she thinks.

Suddenly, an explosion splits the quiet, as quick and as loud as a clap of thunder. Her body tenses and she whirls around to discover a cloud of smoke drifting up from the next bend in the waterway. She takes off running in the direction of the smoke, which is already dissipating. With one hand, she draws her service weapon. With the other, she shouts into her police radio. Somewhere in the area, an alarm is going off.

As she sprints, she passes by another tour boat floating riderless in the canal. She glances down. Lying on one of the floorboards is a reddish tube, spraying sparks. She thinks for an instant that maybe it's a flare but there aren't quite enough sparks. It looks more like a big firecracker.

Or a stick of dynamite.

And the wick has burned down almost to nothing.

CHAPTER 31

LUISA DUCKS AWAY from the edge of the canal just as the dynamite detonates.

She feels a concussive pressure in her chest, like the thump of a bass drum in a rock concert, but the force isn't enough to knock her over. Chunks of wood and droplets of water rain down around her, and a pillar of smoke pours into the air.

Her ears are ringing, and Luisa can hardly hear her own voice as she shouts into the radio.

She steps back over to the edge, waving her hand through the smoke, and sees water rising through a basketball-sized hole in the floor of the boat. The depth is only a few feet, so it won't take long for the boat to rest on the bottom. Luckily, it's not on fire.

Luisa shakes her head, tries to clear her mind. Too much is happening at once. Through the ringing in her ears, she can make out more alarms and the whine of a motorcycle.

She looks down the canal, in the direction of the first explosion, and sees another person identically dressed in black motorcycle gear and helmet. This person stands at the boat launch and holds a stick of dynamite in one hand, a lighter in the other.

Luisa opens her mouth to shout *Freeze!* but hesitates. She remembers the first motorcycle rider. She jumps up onto a stone planter in front of a restaurant for a better view. She can make out the bike but not the man.

Then the man runs out of the jewelry store, the duffel bag—now stuffed—slung over his shoulder. He mounts the bike and kicks it to life.

Luisa understands.

It's a robbery.

The dynamited boats were a distraction in case any police were patrolling the area. But the real objective was to rob the jewelry store.

Behind her, a good fifteen or twenty yards away, there's another explosion of dynamite, but Luisa ignores it. She races toward the site of the robbery. No one knows the labyrinth of the River Walk like she does, and she calculates where the rider might be going. If he's on a bike, he'll most likely avoid stairs. He might be able to go down them, but not up. He's going to have to follow a certain way to get out.

Luisa knows a shortcut.

She turns down a passageway between two buildings, heading to a long stairway going up and out of the River Walk. She sprints up the stairs, her lungs heaving, her heart pounding. When she arrives at the top, she doesn't slow down. She banks left onto the sidewalk and races along the empty storefronts at street level. Just ahead of her, on the other side of the four-lane roadway, is the world-famous Alamo, the familiar facade pale in the early morning light.

She rounds a corner, and just as she suspected, the motorcycle comes zipping out of a passageway from the River Walk. What she isn't expecting is another motorcycle rider there waiting. They don't see her yet, and the two bikes pull alongside each other, stopping for a moment.

The biker with the dynamite couldn't have gotten here that fast, so it must be that they're waiting for their third accomplice.

There's nothing she can do about that right now.

"Freeze!" Luisa shouts, aiming her gun at them with both hands.

She's out of breath and dripping with sweat, but her hands are steady.

Neither rider makes a move as she approaches. They simply stare at her through the black visors of their helmets.

She notices one of them has a submachine gun slung over his shoulders, but he makes no move to reach for it.

"Get off the bikes!" she shouts to them, but neither moves. "Get on the ground!"

Her ears are still ringing, but she makes out the sound of an approaching motorcycle, coming up behind her. She doesn't dare turn around, so she shifts her position, stepping out into the street, with the Alamo at her back, where she can keep her gun on the two bikers while the other approaches.

The new bike skids to a halt, and the rider, straddling it, pulls up a submachine gun. Luisa jerks her gun toward the newcomer.

But she isn't fast enough.

Flame spits from the barrel of the submachine gun, and a burst of bullets thump into Luisa, slamming her onto her back in the street. She's wearing her vest, but at this range, she knows it wasn't enough. She can feel the wet warmth of her own blood soaking her clothes and pooling on the blacktop. She feels the hot, searing pain of multiple bullets lodged inside her. She coughs out blood, and when she tries to inhale, her airway is clogged and wet.

She turns her head and watches as the three motorcyclists race by the Alamo and disappear around the corner. She has the strange thought that it's appropriate she, a lifelong Texan, made her last stand next to the old mission where so many Texans lost their lives. She feels guilty and disappointed for not being able to stop the robbers. She always prided herself on keeping her little piece of Texas safe. But she doesn't dwell on her failure. She did her best.

The pain is gone. Now she's just tired. So unbelievably tired. She thinks of the blackout curtains back at her apartment, how, when they're drawn, she can sleep through anything.

As the darkness comes, she imagines she's just pulling the curtains to take a nap.

CHAPTER 32

MEGAN, WILLOW, AND I spend the early hours of the morning helping my parents clean the house so my mom can feel okay about life getting back to normal. We clean up Dad's study, salvaging what we can from the wreckage, but don't stop there. We go ahead and sweep and mop the other rooms—then, after the sun's been up for about an hour, we decide we ought to have a good meal together as the last step toward putting the events of the night behind us.

Megan and Willow help Mom make a big spread of breakfast tacos, French toast casserole, and cinnamon rolls with honey butter. Dad and I offer to help, but we're pretty much just in the way. So while the women are cooking, he takes me outside into the warm glow of morning and says, "Rory, you've got a hell of a problem on your hands."

"I know," I say, thinking he's talking about the home invasion and what I must be embroiled in at work.

If only.

"As far as I can tell," he says, "you've got two good women here who both love you very much. I think what you've got to decide is, which one do *you* love?"

I have no idea what to say in response, so I'm relieved when my phone buzzes with an incoming call from Carlos. I tell Dad I've got to get it and he goes back in the house.

"The XYZ Bandits struck again," Carlos says when I answer. "About an hour ago."

"You're kidding."

"They hit two stores in San Antonio. A jewelry store and a pawn shop. They used dynamite as a distraction."

"Same MO?" I ask. "Three suspects? Motorcycles?"

"Yep," he says, and his tone takes a turn toward solemnity. "But there is something different: they shot a cop."

My blood goes cold.

"Name was Luisa Ramirez," he continues. "Apparently she was the only officer patrolling the area at the time. One of the bandits opened fire on her with a submachine gun."

I notice he said her name *was* Luisa Ramirez, not *is*, but I hope that was just a slip of the tongue.

"How bad?" I ask.

"Died on the scene before any help arrived," he says. "The XYZ Bandits have graduated from robbery to murder."

Not just murderers, I think. *Cop killers.*

"I'll call Lieutenant Abrams," I say. "Maybe this will get things moving faster."

"Good," Carlos says. "Let's get that son of a bitch."

There's no doubt that when he says *son of a bitch,* he means Parker. I surprise myself by not questioning his assumption. It looks like I'm finally on the same page as Carlos. We both believe Parker Longbaugh and his buddies are the bandits.

"I'm heading to Snakebite right now," he says.

"I'll leave in five minutes," I say.

When I go back to the kitchen, everyone else has started eating without me. Mom is at the counter, covering a plate in aluminum foil. I break it to them that I can't stay for breakfast.

"I had a feeling you'd say that," Mom says, handing me the plate.

I give Megan a big hug and kiss, trying to pretend that Willow isn't there watching, and I head for the door. Willow says she'll walk up the hill to my place with me since her car is still there. I feel awkward spending time alone with her while Megan helps my mom do the dishes, but there's nothing I can do about it—I can't stop her from walking with me.

It's a lovely morning, peaceful and quiet. The grass is wet with dew. Willow looks radiant in the early morning light. She smiles at me and I'm reminded all over again why I was—why I *am*—so crazy about this girl.

"I know now isn't a good time," she says, "but there is something I'd like to talk to you about before I leave town."

"Once I get through all this that I'm dealing with," I say, "I'll be ready to talk. I promise."

I give her a tight hug at her car, and for a moment, my racing mind clears. All I focus on is the smell of her hair and the way her body feels against mine. How many times have we said goodbye like this? Back when we were dating, I'd end our goodbyes by kissing her, long and hard, and then telling her I loved her.

It feels strange to end our goodbye with only a hug.

She climbs into her rental—still drivable with a couple of bullet holes in the bumper—and zooms away. Once I see her taillights hit the road, I walk into my house to get ready. I take off my shirt and examine the fresh welts from the two-by-fours, crisscrossing my body with the cuts and scrapes from the thorns.

It's been a rough twenty-four hours, but there's no rest for a Texas Ranger.

I pull on a shirt and button it up. I wrap a tie around my collar and knot it. I pin the tin star on my shirt, then, still looking at myself in the mirror, position my Stetson atop my head.

Almost ready.

Finally, I add the last piece of my uniform.

I strap on my gun belt.

Time to go to work.

CHAPTER 33

TEN HOURS LATER, I'm riding shotgun in Carlos's F-150, leading a caravan of local, state, and federal authorities down the highway toward Parker Longbaugh's residence. We've got everything—a K9 unit, explosives experts, you name it. Even my lieutenant, Ty Abrams, and Carlos's captain, Roger Lightwood, have come along.

A similar team is heading toward Ellis Kilpatrick's and Harvey Curry's houses.

It's amazing how quickly things moved once we got Lieutenant Abrams involved. He locked up search warrants while the team already working on the XYZ case shifted their focus based on the information we gave them.

"Nervous?" Carlos asks, as he drives past the grain elevator down the road from Parker's.

"Hell, yes," I say.

Serving a search warrant is always a high-anxiety time. You usually know who did the crime. You just need to find the evidence to prove it. In Parker's case, I feel more nervous than usual.

"However this goes," Carlos says, all business for the moment, "I want you to know I appreciate you going along with me on this. I came to you for help, and you had my back."

We roll in, followed by the rest of the caravan. The Longbaughs' driveway overflows with police vehicles, and most of them have to park on the grass.

Josie comes out on the porch, utterly confused. The little girl, Etta, hides behind her mom's legs, looking terrified.

I wish I didn't have to do this myself, but I approach Josie with the warrant in my hand.

"Where's Parker?" I ask.

She ignores my question and asks her own. "What's this about, Rory?"

"We have a warrant to search your property," I say, holding out the paper. "We're going to confiscate any evidence we find."

"Evidence of what?"

Before I get a chance to answer, I hear a commotion behind me. Over the heads of the agents and officers crowding the yard, I see Parker's Bronco circling around the other cars to find a place to park in the yard. Leo is in the back seat, Parker in the front.

My old friend bursts out of the door and storms into the crowd.

"What in the hell is going on?"

When he sees me, he stomps over and glares at me with burning eyes. I want to wilt under the glare, but I make myself hold his gaze.

"We have a warrant to search your property," I say.

"What for?"

My throat constricts, and I can't answer. Suddenly, this doesn't seem like a good idea at all.

"We have reason to believe," I say, but then I hesitate. "I mean, we need to check and make sure you're not one of the XYZ Bandits."

"The XY-what?"

"Robbers responsible for a number of crimes in Texas," I explain.

Parker lets out a breath and takes a step back, coming upon a realization. He looks stunned.

And hurt.

"You were spying on me?" he says, his voice full of injury. "That's why you came to my house? You think I committed some kind of crime?"

Seeing his reaction, I want to rewind the clock and take back what I said to Lieutenant Abrams. I wish we weren't here right now.

Instead, I ask, "Where were you at 6 a.m. this morning?"

He huffs. "Sleeping in a tent with my son."

"Any witnesses who can corroborate that?"

He laughs. "Yeah, every parent and child in Troop 395."

He points to his son, who is approaching us with a skeptical look on his face. The boy is wearing a blue Cub Scout uniform. Parker explains that, because Leo was still recovering from his snakebite, they considered skipping the long-planned Cub Scout camping trip. But Leo didn't want to miss it.

"We'll need the contact information of the other parents," Carlos says, saving me because I've lost the ability to speak, wilting in the glare of my old friend. "And we need to know your whereabouts for a handful of other dates over the past year."

Parker ignores him and goes to Josie, wrapping her in a tight hug. The two of them embrace the children, who look ready to burst into tears from all the commotion they don't understand. Both parents tell the kids everything will be all right.

"We'd also like to ask you some questions," Carlos tells Parker.

"Go to hell," Parker snaps. "I'll give you the name of the scout-master, and I'll stand by while you tear our home apart." He gestures to the warrant still in my hand, hanging limply at my side. "Because that's what that stupid piece of paper says you can do. But I know how this works. I don't have to say a goddamn thing until I talk to a lawyer."

"If you're innocent," Carlos says, "then you have nothing to hide."

"That line might work on the average perp you pull in off the street," Parker says. "I said it myself a hundred times. But this ain't my first rodeo, boys."

He looks back and forth between Carlos and me.

"If you guys are examples of what Texas Rangers are like these days," he says, "then the organization is more lost now than it ever was in my day."

"We just want to find out the truth," I tell Parker.

He smirks.

"You want the truth, Rory?" he says. "Here it is: I'm guilty of only one thing—thinking you were my friend."

CHAPTER 34

BY NIGHTFALL, I'M beginning to get a hell of a bad feeling about the prospects for our search.

The Longbaughs, Josie crying and the kids upset, have left the scene to stay at Josie's mom's house, where a patrol officer is keeping an eye on their door. Free from the family's watchful eye, our team's been scouring every inch of the property.

The barn, where I had high hopes we'd find something, holds only Parker's woodworking tools. And the paperwork in Parker's office documents his business and at first glance all seems in legal order. The bins in the basement haven't been helpful, either. They're mostly full of the kids' old toys or dioramas that Parker built and disassembled for the model train set.

We had to go through a whole rigmarole before opening the EXPLOSIVES box. While the bomb squad made sure it was safe, guilt washed over me like a wave, knowing I'd lied.

When Lieutenant Abrams discovered what I already knew—that there were only comics inside—and flipped through the issues of *X-Men* and *Aquaman* and *Wonder Woman,* he looked up at me, his expression unreadable.

"Keep looking," he told the team.

When law enforcement personnel search a home, they really

tear it apart. The cupboards have been emptied, desk drawers ransacked, furniture moved, mattresses overturned. Nothing is safe. Even the kids' rooms, where toys are scattered everywhere, some stepped on, some broken.

Walking around, seeing the wreckage of the Longbaughs' house, I feel sickened by guilt. I step out onto the porch, where I find Carlos alone.

We give each other a nod that seems to communicate everything we're thinking—this search isn't going like we thought it would.

"You think somebody tipped him off?" Carlos asks. "Abrams called in a big team here—could be somebody gave Parker a call."

I sigh. "There's always the other possibility."

"What's that?"

"Parker's innocent."

As I say this, Captain Lightwood and Lieutenant Abrams come around the house, talking low. I only catch the tail end of what Lightwood says—something about dishonoring the Ranger name—before Abrams spots us and hushes the lieutenant.

"Find anything?" Carlos asks them.

The two men climb onto the porch. Abrams is hard to read, but Captain Lightwood's mood is obvious from his furrowed brow and fiery eyes.

"What we've got," he says, practically growling, "is a big pile of jack shit."

Roger Lightwood is shorter than average, as lean as a welterweight boxer, with a scrappy demeanor that would deter most men, even much bigger guys, from messing with him. He has rough leathery skin and short black hair that's barely started to go gray even though he's well into his fifties.

He's always reminded me of a pit bull—not the biggest dog in any given fight but still the one you'd probably put your money on.

We've never worked closely together, which I've always been glad about. He's known for being tough on his Rangers, and I never wanted his scrutiny leveled on me.

Looks like that was a bullet I was only able to dodge so long.

"Yates," he says, "by your reputation, I sure expected better from you. And, you, Castillo, you really screwed the pooch on this one."

Carlos and I say nothing.

Sometimes you've just got to take your punishment.

Lieutenant Abrams, using a much more amenable tone, explains that thus far none of the searches—here or at Ellis's or Harvey's—have borne any results. They've found some motorbikes at Ellis's workplace, but that was expected. And we don't know enough yet to conclude if any of them match with the crimes. It will take some time to compare blurry street camera footage with the bikes themselves.

Otherwise, there's nothing—no money, no explosives, and no weapons.

The only gun anyone found was Parker's old SIG Sauer from his days as a Ranger. It was on a high shelf in his closet, unloaded and covered in a layer of dust.

"What about alibis?" Carlos asks.

"That's the best part," Captain Lightwood says sarcastically. "We've got half a dozen parents ready to swear on a stack of bibles that Parker was camping all night with his son's Cub Scout troop. And before you go thinking he snuck out of his tent and drove three hours to San Antonio, shot a cop, and drove back, he and his son shared a tent with the scoutmaster, who's an early riser and verified that Parker was fast asleep at the precise time of the robbery."

"What about Ellis and Harvey?" Carlos asks.

Lieutenant Abrams explains that neither of the friends have

alibis besides their wives. However, they've checked alibis for all three men for all the XYZ crimes over the past year. For nearly all the robberies, at least one of the men has a solid alibi.

"When the armored-truck robbery happened," he says, "Ellis was in Vermont at his wife's family reunion. He's got plane ticket receipts, not to mention two dozen photos from various family members' phones.

"And the robbery before that," he adds, "Harvey was at a bachelor party in Las Vegas. Might take a little time to get our hands on security footage verifying what his buddies have had to say, but I'm betting it checks out."

"And that robbery in Galveston," Captain Lightwood says gruffly, "that was the same weekend Parker took his kids to Six Flags in Dallas with a couple other families. They've got a hundred date-stamped photos and videos to prove it."

"The bottom line," Lieutenant Abrams says with equanimity, "is there's no way these guys are the XYZ Bandits."

CHAPTER 35

CARLOS SAYS, "JUST because we haven't found anything—"

"Save it," Captain Lightwood snaps, waving his hand like he's swatting away an annoying fly. "You two have done enough damage. You've hurt Parker Longbaugh and his family. You've hurt the reputation of the Texas Rangers. And you've hurt your own careers. If I have anything to say about it, you'll be busted back down to Ranger," he says to Carlos. "And you," he adds, looking at me disdainfully, "you'll be sitting behind a desk for the rest of your career, filing paperwork for the real Rangers who know how to do their jobs."

"It wasn't all their fault," Lieutenant Abrams says. "I'm the one who pushed for the warrants."

"I'm not happy with you either," Lightwood snaps. "But at least you didn't go behind anyone's backs. These two, as far as I'm concerned, they're not fit to wear those badges."

With that, he turns on the heel of his boot and storms through the front door. The screen door slams behind him.

Lieutenant Abrams looks us up and down. Normally hard to read, his expression is easy to interpret now. He's disappointed in us.

"I'm sorry, Ty," I say.

He takes a deep breath. "There's something else."

"What?"

"That interview I'd wanted you to do with me today," he says.

I'd completely forgotten about it. He'd let me off the hook for it—I remember that much—but I don't even know who we were going to interview or why.

He tells me he questioned a guy in county jail who once did a stint in the Huntsville Unit for armed robbery. His cellmate at the time, a guy named Chase Germaine, was there for selling stolen goods.

"They got to talking one night," Lieutenant Abrams says, "and started chatting about the worst stuff they'd ever done, trying to one-up each other about their criminal careers. Apparently this guy Chase started laughing and said he'd done the worst things a human could do. He murdered people."

I don't understand where he's headed with this, but then he says, "He claimed these murders all occurred in these parts. He cut their throats and left their bodies in the fields. All the victims were migrant workers."

My mouth suddenly goes dry.

"This guy in county ain't the most reliable witness," he says, "but he knew enough details—stuff never released to the public—to indicate he was telling the truth. Clothes the victims were wearing. Belongings that went missing. Chase Germaine is now our number one suspect in the Cereal Killer case."

"So . . . ?" I say, but I can't finish my thought.

Abrams doesn't need me to.

"That's right," he says. "Parker Longbaugh was after the wrong guy."

I ask if this guy, Chase Germaine, is still in prison.

"Nope." He shakes his head sadly. "Released last spring. Jumped his parole. No one knows where he is. Not only is the real Cereal

Killer still out there—God knows where—but it's not the guy we've been looking for. It looks like Jackson Clarke is on the run for a crime he didn't commit."

Up until now, Lieutenant Abrams has been using his normal all-business tone, but now his emotions break through. He's every bit as pissed as Captain Lightwood.

"You lied to me about what you were doing here," he says. "You made up some excuse about the Cereal Killer case. Well, guess what? That case could have actually used some extra attention, instead of this fantasy theory that one of the most decorated Texas Rangers in modern history was secretly a bank robber. I went out on a limb for you, boys. I shouldn't have."

Without waiting for a response, he turns and walks through the same door Captain Lightwood did a few minutes ago. Carlos and I are left standing alone on the porch.

"That went well," Carlos says casually.

After receiving back-to-back lectures from my superiors, I'm in no mood for his sense of humor.

"You think this is funny?" I snap. "I wouldn't be in this god-damn mess if you hadn't roped me into this wild goose chase."

Carlos glowers at me.

"I just got my ass handed to me by *two* of my superiors," I say. "Thanks a fucking lot, Carlos."

He's simmering with anger but he keeps his voice calm when he says, "You think *I* let you down?"

"Hell, yes," I spit.

"Let me ask you one question, Rory."

"What?"

He steps closer, staring me in the eyes, so close the brims of our hats almost touch.

"Did you know there were comic books in that box?"

All of my anger rushes out of me like air from an untied balloon. He's right. I'm the one who created this mess. I was so hot after those thugs showed up at my parents' house—so sure that it must have been Parker who sent them—that I wanted this investigation over as soon as possible.

I open my mouth to answer, but Carlos doesn't need me to say the words. He can see it on my face.

"That's what I thought," he says, and he walks through the front door, just like Abrams and Lightwood, leaving me on the porch, alone and admonished by not one, not two, but three of my superiors.

It's the disappointment of Carlos, my good friend, that hurts the most.

CHAPTER 36

SHORTLY AFTER MIDNIGHT, I'm sitting awake in my hotel, stewing in my thoughts. I feel about as low as I've ever felt as a Texas Ranger. I've made mistakes before, but never quite this bad.

I brought a six-pack of beer to my room and figured I'd drink about half of it and then sleep a few hours before heading back to Redbud in the morning. But I haven't been able to sleep a wink. Now the beer is warm and I'm flipping through the channels, trying to find something—anything—to take my mind off the mess I've made of things. There's a replay of a baseball game on ESPN and an old Western on Turner Classic Movies, but neither holds my attention. There are music videos playing on CMT, but the songs are mostly ones I don't know and don't much like. I don't even think about picking up my book—no way I'll be able to concentrate on the words.

I need someone to talk to.

I think about calling Megan, but shortly before I got back to the hotel, I got a goodnight text telling me she missed me and would talk to me tomorrow. I don't want to wake her. Dad's someone I've always gone to for advice, but I don't want to wake him, either. Besides, I'm not sure I really want to confide in him. He'll be as disappointed as my fellow Rangers if I tell him what I did.

That leaves one person I can think of.

Willow.

She works crazy hours—concerts that keep her out late, studio sessions that go deep into the night, hectic travel schedules that keep her on the go, no matter the time of day. I know she's in Redbud, visiting family, but she still might be awake.

I pick up my phone and send a text.

Any chance you're up?

A few seconds later, my phone rings with an incoming call from her.

"I didn't wake you, did I?" I ask.

"Nah," she says, sounding cheerful as always. "I played a show at the Pale Horse tonight for old times' sake."

That's the local bar where she and I first met, where I used to watch her perform before she made it big in Nashville. I can't help but feel a powerful nostalgia for those times.

"I'm sorry I missed that," I say.

"What's up?" she says. "You okay?"

"I've had a shit day," I say. "I needed someone to talk to." Then I add, "The person I most wanted to talk to was you."

"I'm here for you," she says happily. "Willow Dawes Therapy Inc. is open twenty-four seven and free for Texas Rangers and ex-boyfriends."

I don't go into details, but I tell her I screwed up royally at work. I've got two lieutenants and a captain who are all disappointed with me. Worse, one of those lieutenants is one of my best friends. Worse still, I've betrayed the trust of another friend—a former Ranger who didn't do anything to warrant the mess I've made of his life.

Willow listens sympathetically, then says, "You didn't go into this line of work because it was easy. Or even because you liked it.

Being a Texas Ranger is a lot of weight to bear. But you took the job because you've got the shoulders to bear that weight."

I think of Parker, who quit the Rangers because it was too much for him. The hard decisions, the gray areas, the rules put in place to keep you from making mistakes.

"Maybe I can't bear the weight," I say. "Maybe I'm not cut out for this. Maybe the Rangers are better off without me."

"Now you're just feeling sorry for yourself," she says.

She doesn't say this in an unfriendly way, but still it's hard to hear.

"Look," she adds, "as far as I can tell, the answer to your problem is simple."

"What's that?" I say skeptically.

"You have to try to make things right."

It sounds so simple but hearing her say it resonates deep within me.

"Maybe you won't succeed," she says. "Maybe all these guys will stay pissed at you forever. But you have to try. It's the only way you can move on."

She asks if I know what I could do to make things right.

I think about it for a minute. "Yes," I say, but I don't elaborate.

There are two things.

First: I need to apologize to the people I've let down.

Second: I need to solve the case I screwed up on.

That means catching the real XYZ Bandits.

That's a tall order, but Willow's right—I didn't join the Texas Rangers because I thought the job would be easy.

"Thanks, Willow," I say, feeling re-energized. "You've told me just what I needed to hear."

She says that I'm welcome, and then there's an awkward silence between us.

"I know there was something you wanted to talk to me about," I say. "But can we wait a few days? There's some stuff I need to take care of."

I can't imagine getting into a heart-to-heart about what we mean to each other right now. That emotional conversation deserves my full attention. I've got a case to solve first.

"Of course," Willow says. "I'm here when you're ready."

CHAPTER 37

I PULL MY F-150 into the driveway at Parker Longbaugh's house. Parker's Bronco is there, the back hatch open and packed with a few boxes and suitcases.

There's no sign of Parker or his family, though.

They must be inside cleaning up.

The yard is torn up with tire ruts from all the vehicles packed onto the property last night. I'm sure the inside of the house looks ten times worse. The morning light is bright and blinding, and I squint my eyes as I approach the door. When there's no answer, I peer through the screen door and see the house is in complete disarray. It's as if someone just moved in, only instead of everything they own being contained in boxes, it's been dumped out without any trace of organization.

"Anyone home?" I call through the screen.

I hear voices somewhere in the bowels of the house. I call again, louder, and this time I hear footsteps coming my way. I can tell from the sound that it's Josie, not Parker. She comes into the kitchen, dragging a large suitcase. She sees me and she inhales sharply, an unmistakable expression of anger coming over her face. She collects herself and walks to the door with purpose. Her graying hair frames her face in unkempt tangles.

"Go away," she says, her voice tired and hoarse.

"I came to apologize," I say.

"I don't want to hear it," she says.

"I'll handle this, Josie."

The voice doesn't come from inside the house. It comes from my right. Like before, Parker snuck up on me from around the back of the house.

"Get this Judas out of here, Parker!" Josie hisses, and she turns back into the house, where I can faintly hear one of the children crying.

Parker doesn't step up on the porch this time. He waits for me to come down into the grass.

"I wanted to say I'm sorry," I tell him.

I'm tempted to point out that he made mistakes as a Ranger, too—bring up the latest in the Cereal Killer investigation—but I don't want to use his past to manipulate his emotions. This is about my screwup, not his.

"You've said it," he tells me. "Now please go."

He doesn't seem angry, just tired—a man who's had a rough night and wants nothing more than for me to leave him alone.

I nod toward the back of the Bronco, packed with belongings.

"Y'all going somewhere?" I ask.

"You interrogating me, Ranger?" he says, his voice taking on a stern tone. "You think I'm making a run for it?"

"Just asking as a friend."

He huffs at my use of "friend," but he answers.

"We're moving," he says. "Josie's been wanting to get out of Snakebite for a long time. We've been looking at properties, trying to qualify for loans. As fate would have it, we just got approved yesterday. Timing's perfect since Josie doesn't want to live here anymore. Not after last night. She feels like our privacy has been violated—all the memories we've made in this house ruined."

I think of what started all of this—Carlos spotting Parker going into a bank. But, with the exception of the one bank where Parker was spotted, Carlos hadn't found any evidence that Parker had applied for other loans.

As if reading my mind—he probably knows we looked into this—Parker says, "The loan's in Josie's mom's name. She's got a better credit rating than we do. When I quit the Rangers, we fell behind on some payments before we got back on our feet."

I'm embarrassed by the stupid assumptions Carlos and I made to get us into this mess. We're supposed to be professionals.

"We're going to stay with her mom until the sale goes through escrow and all that," Parker adds.

"I thought there wasn't room at her mom's for all of you?"

"I'll probably still sleep here." He nods toward the house. "There's a hell of a lot of work that needs to be done before we can put this place on the market."

He looks at his house sadly.

"I thought you loved this place," I say.

"I did," he says. "I do. But marriage is all about compromise. You do what's best for the family, not just yourself."

Hearing him say this, I'm reminded about how much I admired—and still admire—his and Josie's relationship. They seem to have everything I want.

And I hate myself for how I came into their lives and interfered.

I wasn't welcome when I showed up this morning, but it's clear by Parker's demeanor that I've overstayed what little tolerance he had for me.

"I just want to say again how sorry I am," I tell him. "I'm going to make it right."

"There's no making this right, Rory," he says, losing his patience with me. "This isn't the kind of mistake that can just be easily forgiven. I wish you the best. I hope you find your Alphabet Bandits or whatever you're calling them. But I don't ever want to see you again."

He turns away, and—stinging from his words—I climb into my truck. I take a deep breath and put the truck in Drive. I remind myself what Willow told me.

It's possible Parker will never forgive me.

But I have to *try*.

CHAPTER 38

FOUR HOURS LATER, I park my truck across the street from the Alamo. I look at the old mission-turned-fort, with its sun-bleached limestone exterior and pole flying the flag of Texas.

When you see the Alamo in person, it looks a lot smaller than you'd expect.

It's hard to imagine a garrison holding the fort for any amount of time, let alone for as long as they did. I've been inside before, and the grounds and facilities are gorgeous, but I'm not here as a tourist today.

I've got work to do.

I step out of my truck and walk along the sidewalk. One lane is roped off, and I can see the dirty smudge where the crime-scene cleanup folks tried to wash away the blood. I take off my hat, hold it to my chest, and say a few words of prayer for Luisa Ramirez.

Then I take a passageway down into the River Walk and consult one of the maps on display. Mariachi music is playing to tourists navigating the walkways and riding the tour boats floating on the canals. A major robbery happened here just yesterday. Everyone around me seems to have forgotten it.

"Is that a Texas Ranger?" I hear someone ask their friend.

I ignore the attention and wend my way toward the crime

scene. The front of the jewelry store is roped off with police tape.
I think, *Now it's obvious a robbery happened here.* I approach the
uniformed officer posted outside the door, tell him who I am and
why I'm here, and he lifts the tape and lets me duck under.

Inside, I'm greeted by a woman in her late thirties or early forties, with a sharp blue suit and a shock of ink-black hair pulled
back in a ponytail.

"Rory Yates?" she says, extending her hand. "Sandra Post, chief
of detectives."

"Thanks for seeing me," I say.

She nods curtly.

"We've already been working with the local Rangers," she says,
not unprofessional but also clearly not excited to have to tell me
the exact same thing my colleagues probably already know.

I don't want to tell her that I'm not exactly in good graces with
the rest of the Texas Ranger Division at the moment.

"If you don't mind," I say, "I'd like to hear it from the source."

We walk outside and stroll down the paved walkway. She
points out where the boats exploded and where the other robbery
occurred in the pawn shop, which is also roped off with yellow
police tape.

"Very coordinated," I say of the robbers. "Professional."

"I haven't told you the most interesting part yet," she says.

She stops walking atop a bridge arching over the opaque waterway. Her previously pursed lips curve into a smile she can't quite
hide.

"What's that?" I ask.

"The River Walk area is full of potential targets. It didn't make
much sense to us that they would hit these two particular stores
and no others. So we've done some digging into the businesses
that were robbed."

"And?"

"Turns out both of these businesses were crooked," she says. "The pawn shop bought and sold stolen goods. The jewelry store laundered money for drug dealers. I don't know how the robbers knew, but they chose these places for a reason."

She explains that plenty of valuables were left behind. In the jewelry store, for example, no diamonds were taken. No gold. No silver. Same story in the pawn shop. Lots of expensive heirlooms were left untouched.

The robbers were after only one thing.

Cash.

Dirty cash.

CHAPTER 39

ON THE ROAD back to Redbud, as I'm debating whether to call Carlos, my phone buzzes with an incoming call from him.

"Lubbock morgue," I say. "You slice 'em, we dice 'em."

He laughs, a sound that warms my soul. Without discussing it, we're back where we were. All may not be forgotten—but it's forgiven.

"I've got news," I say.

"So do I."

"You first."

He tells me that the serial numbers on the cash donated to the trust match money taken from at least two of the robberies.

"And," he adds, "I've been looking into some other anonymous donations over the past year at other charities. I'm waiting on verification of numbers, but I think we're going to find this has been a trend."

What we suspected is now fact—the XYZ Bandits donated at least some of their spoils for good causes.

I tell him what I learned from the San Antonio Police.

"Our theory about robbing from the rich and giving to the poor has a new wrinkle," I say. "What if the XYZ Bandits are not just robbing from the rich, but robbing from criminals?"

He gives it some thought, then says, "Where are you?"

"Driving back from San Antonio," I say. "I'm about two hours from home. Where are you?"

"Still in Snakebite," he says. "I can't show my face in Lubbock right now. I'm a persona non grata in Company C."

"I'm a persona non grata in the whole division," I say.

"I'll meet you at your house," he says. "We'll work from there."

I put my foot on the gas and end up beating Carlos to my house by only a few minutes. The two of us spend the afternoon on the phone and on our laptops, working furiously.

It feels good.

Partners again.

Around dinnertime, we're both starving and decide to order Carlos's favorite food—pizza. While we wait, we go over what we've learned in the last few hours.

After a long conversation with the FBI, Carlos discovered that the armored truck that was robbed was actually carrying funds from a crooked bank laundering money for drug cartels. The FBI is still confirming solid proof, but, as far as they could tell, the robbers didn't take half of what they could have—just the dirty money. The guards transporting the money had no idea that some of what they were protecting actually belonged to criminals.

It also turns out the DEA has been looking at the shipping facility outside of Galveston that the XYZ Bandits hit, suspecting that they're a major distribution site for drugs that come in from South America. Again, the feds don't have enough evidence to start making arrests. But the XYZ Bandits don't operate within the boundaries of the law anyway.

"Whoever is doing this *is* trying to be Robin Hood," Carlos says. "They're not just giving money to the poor. They're taking it from the *criminally rich*. The more we look, the more it feels like this is someone in law enforcement. Or used to be."

I take a deep breath. I don't even want to say aloud what I'm thinking, but I can't help myself.

"Now that we know what their motives are," I say, "more than before, I can actually see Parker doing this."

It feels like a betrayal to even say the words aloud.

"But he's the one person we know didn't," I add.

"Do we?" he asks.

I raise my eyebrows.

"Just because we didn't find anything in the search doesn't mean they didn't do it," he says.

"What about the alibis?" I say. "We haven't found one lick of evidence. Not a shred."

I tell him that we can't keep going on hunches. Parker's last act as a Ranger was to arrest a man who it turns out was probably innocent. He wanted so badly for Jackson Clarke to be the killer that he ignored the fact that there wasn't enough evidence.

"We can't make the same kinds of mistakes," I say.

"You trying to convince me?" he says. "Or are you trying to convince yourself?"

Carlos stares at me, and it's clear we're both thinking the same thing. Can we really go down this road again? If we keep looking into Parker, we absolutely cannot ask for any help from the Texas Ranger Division. And we better not be wrong.

Before either of us speaks, two things happen at once.

Carlos's phone rings.

And there's a knock on the door.

"I'll get the pizza," I say, and turn toward the door as Carlos answers.

I grab my wallet off the counter and pull open my front door, expecting a teenager delivering pizza.

But I'm wrong.

Willow—looking like she stepped out of a music video—is standing on my front porch with the same coy smile on her face that always melted my heart.

CHAPTER 40

"GOT A MINUTE?" she says, blushing. "I've got to head back to Nashville earlier than expected."

"Sure," I say, although now seems like the worst possible time to have a heart-to-heart with her.

"A spot opened up at the Grand Ole Opry tomorrow night," she says. "When will I ever get another chance to share billing with Vince Gill and Crystal Gayle?"

"That's amazing," I say, awed by her success. "You've got to do it."

"I'm flying out early tomorrow," she says. "Rehearsal's in the afternoon."

What she doesn't say—but what's implied—is if we're going to have our conversation, it's got to be now. This feels like the typical problem Willow and I always had. We were great together, but our jobs always got in the way.

Behind me, I hear Carlos on the phone—surprise in his voice—but I try not to focus on what he's saying.

"All right," I say, stepping out onto the porch and closing the door behind me. "I'm all yours."

The sun is on the verge of setting, and Willow looks luminous in the glow of twilight. Her hair is pulled back in a loose braid, and she's wearing jeans and sandals and a faded blue T-shirt with the words MAGNOLIA FARMS underneath a picture of the silos owned by the famous Waco residents Chip and Joanna Gaines. Willow and I used to watch their show *Fixer Upper* together—just one of the many little things we shared.

We step out into the grass and meander slowly toward the pasture where Mom and Dad's horses are grazing.

I think of Megan and feel like I'm cheating.

But it's not cheating if all you're doing is talking, right?

"We've been through a lot together, Rory," Willow says. "Even though we broke up a while ago, you've always been special to me. We've stayed good friends."

My heart starts to speed up.

"I know it sounds corny," she says, "but I always kind of thought of us like Ross and Rachel from *Friends,* you know? It wasn't *if* we were going to get back together, but *when.*"

I feel a lump in my throat. As she says this, I realize that's how I always felt.

Like we were meant to be.

"But real life isn't like a TV show," Willow says. "A girl can't wait around forever."

As she says this, she stops and turns to face me. Her eyes are moist, as if she's on the verge of tears.

I never stopped loving her, I realize.

She opens her mouth to speak, but before she can get a word out, my front door bursts open and Carlos calls out to me.

"We've got to go," he shouts. *"Now."*

"What do you mean?" I say. "Where?"

"Back to Snakebite," he says, hopping off the porch and approaching us. "There might still be time."

So much for the moment Willow and I were sharing.

"What the hell are you talking about?" I ask.

He holds up his phone.

"Ty Abrams just called," Carlos says. "He said, *'You didn't get this information from me.'*"

"What information?" I say, irritated.

Spit it out, Carlos!

"Apparently Abrams talked to Ellis Kilpatrick's boss last night when they were checking alibis," Carlos says. "He called today to let Abrams know Ellis didn't show up for work. The boss was worried about him, and he went over to Ellis's apartment. His truck was gone, his stuff was packed up, and—the kicker—he made off with three of the shop's motorcycles."

I take a deep breath. "You think...?"

Carlos nods his head.

"I think they're making a run for it," Carlos says. "All three of them."

I turn to Willow.

"I've got to go," I say. "Whatever you were going to tell me, just hold onto it. A few more days. I'll call you in Nashville."

She nods with a sad expression on her face.

But this is a conversation I can't have right now.

"I understand," Willow says, reaching up and straightening my tie. "Go get 'em, Ranger."

CHAPTER 41

PARKER, ELLIS, AND Harvey circle around the house to the expansive yard at the back of the Longbaughs' property. Parker wears his pistol on his hip and carries a cordless drill in one hand and a paper grocery bag in the other. Ellis holds a four-foot-long gaff, the kind deep-sea fishers use to snag big fish. Harvey is carrying a flat-bladed shovel.

The sun has just set beneath the cornfield, and besides a faint orange glow coming up from the horizon, the night is dark. Josie and the kids are gone. They've got the place to themselves.

The men stop walking, and Parker points to a place in the lawn that looks like it's recently been patched with a two-foot-by-two-foot square of sod. The spot is hard to see in the long grass. There's only a faint outline of a square, like a trapdoor in the middle of the lawn, right at the edge of the long strip of extra lush grass where the leach line extends.

Harvey uses the shovel to pry up the sod, turning it upside down. Worms wiggle in the exposed soil. Parker kneels to wipe the dark dirt away from a plastic green saucer the size of a manhole cover embedded into the ground.

The lid to the septic tank.

"I hate this part," Harvey mutters, a toothpick wedged in the corner of his mouth.

Parker sets the drill down and opens the bag. He pulls out long rubber gloves and distributes them to his partners. Then he gives each of them a medical mask from the bag, and the three of them put them over their mouths and noses. Harvey spits out his toothpick to fit his mask over his face. The white masks stand out in the fading gray light.

Parker kneels and uses the drill, equipped with a Phillips-head screwdriver, to loosen the screws on the edge of the plastic lid.

"You sure was right," Ellis says. "You knew just where them Rangers wouldn't look."

Without answering, Parker pries the lid off the tank. Hundreds of drain flies spill out into the night air, followed by the overpowering stink of raw sewage.

The masks offer little protection. The stench is wretched, enough that the men fight back gagging.

Inside the tank is a pool of shit- and piss-filled water—what looks like a pond of diarrhea four feet deep.

Still kneeling, Parker takes the gaff and leans down. He dips the instrument into the muddy black porridge. He roots around with the gaff for a moment, then pulls with both hands, hoisting up a net containing a plastic bag. He sets it in the grass, and the other two men work to loosen the net and open the bag beneath.

Inside are three submachine guns.

Parker reaches back into the pool of sewage and pulls up another net, and another and another, each containing a plastic-wrapped square about the size of a cinder block. Inside each of these are cash—hundreds of bills wrapped into cubes.

"At least we get to keep some of it," Harvey utters, grinning beneath his mask.

"Before you take your share," Parker says, rising to his feet and facing Harvey, "I want to talk about something."

Parker bores into him with his glare, which, even in the starlit darkness, is intimidating.

"You talking about the cop?" Harvey says, his voice noticeably nervous even muffled by the mask.

Parker rips off his own mask and tosses it into the septic tank. "We vowed never to hurt or kill anyone," he says.

Harvey's eyes move to Ellis's, who looks away and shifts his feet uncomfortably, then back to Parker.

"Look," Harvey says. "What were we supposed to do? Get arrested?"

"And what about sending people to go after Rory?" Parker says. "You did that without consulting me."

Harvey shrugs. "I know you and that Ranger go way back," he says, "but he was getting all up in our business and needed to be taken care of. They were never going to kill him. Just hurt him a bit."

"When we started this," Parker growls, "we vowed to do this to help people. Not hurt them."

Harvey huffs. "In this line of work," he says, "things get messy. Sometimes you gotta make hard choices. I was just making the hard choices you weren't willing to."

"You think I can't make hard choices?" Parker snarls. "You might be right—because this is an easy choice."

With that, Parker's hand flashes to his holster, and he draws his pistol and aims it at Harvey's face.

Harvey puts his hands up in surprise.

"Hey, wait a minute, bud. Let's talk about—"

"I told you when we started this," Parker snarls, "if you ever hurt an innocent person, I'd kill you myself."

Without another word, he squeezes the trigger.

The bullet punches a dime-sized hole through Harvey's mask, and he slumps to the ground like a marionette with its strings cut. A dark stain spreads through the mask, turning the white fabric a dark crimson.

Parker turns his attention to Ellis.

"You got a problem with what just happened?" he says, holding his gun at his side.

"No, man," Ellis says, his voice trembling. "You said from the start—no hurting anyone innocent."

"Good," Parker says. "Give me a hand."

They lean down and shove and pull Harvey's corpse until his upper body is next to the septic tank hole. Parker pushes him over the edge, and Harvey's head sinks into the muck.

The rest of his body follows, disappearing inch by inch until it's gone.

CHAPTER 42

CARLOS AND I race into Parker's driveway, skidding to a halt in the gravel.

Parker's Bronco is gone. The house is completely dark. The front screen door is open and hanging ajar. The whole property has an air of abandonment.

Carlos runs around the house to go in through the back door, and I open the screen door, gun in hand. We sweep through the ground floor, then Carlos searches the upstairs while I go down into the basement. It looks like it was when the search team left it. Open boxes scattered around the room. Parker's model train set sits on the sheet of plywood, a sad reminder that even if Parker is a robber, he's still an ordinary guy with hobbies and interests.

I meet up with Carlos in the backyard.

"Goddamn it," Carlos says. "We missed them."

The night air is quiet except for the corn whispering in the breeze. The stars are bright, illuminating the backyard just enough that I can make out the last remnants of the tree that Parker was cutting into firewood.

It seems like so long ago that Parker and I rushed out there to find Leo bitten by the snake. So much had happened since then.

"What do we do?" I ask, my voice quiet with a sense of defeat.

If Parker and his buddies were actually suspects according to the Texas Rangers, we could call in an APB, get every law enforcement officer in the whole state looking for them. The problem is no one believes they're suspects but us. If we call it in, we'll get another ass-chewing from our superiors.

"Let's search the property again," Carlos says. "We need to find some evidence. Some indication of where they've gone."

"Talk about a needle in a haystack," I say. "Only we don't even know what the needle looks like."

I take a deep breath, glancing around the property. A whole army of investigators was here yesterday and they didn't find a damn thing. What can the two of us possibly do?

"Let's check the barn," Carlos says, and even though I know it's useless, I go along with him.

We strike out through the property, our boots swishing through the deep grass.

"Did you fart?" Carlos asks.

"What?" I say, irritated and in no mood for his humor right now.

"It smells like shit out here," he adds.

I stop in my tracks. He's right. There is a faint odor in the air. It doesn't smell quite like feces—not dog poop or livestock manure or the human smell left behind in a bathroom. This smell is a mixture of the rancid odor of ammonia and a sulfurous rotten-egg stench—like a porta potty that is overdue for cleaning.

I pull out my flashlight and shine it around, not knowing what I'm looking for. Carlos does the same.

"What's that?" he says.

I look to where his light is pointing and see, about ten feet away, a small object in the grass catching the light. It's tiny, whatever it is. A twig or a branch or a piece of straw.

We approach, both of our beams leveled on the object, and it's not until we're within a few feet that we realize what it is.

A toothpick.

"Harvey liked to chew on toothpicks," I say, knowing we're on to something but not sure what.

"Maybe this is our needle in the haystack," Carlos says.

CHAPTER 43

THE SMELL IS worse here where the toothpick is lying, and we shine our lights around and see that some of the grass is matted down and wet with a thick, muddy liquid. I make out a square of sod in the otherwise lush lawn, the outline practically invisible unless you're right on top of it.

I kneel down, work my fingers in the seam between the wedges of grass, and pull up. The sod square comes up easily, revealing a manhole-sized circular cap embedded in the ground.

I know what it is as soon as I see it.

I tell Carlos to go to his truck to get latex gloves and a screwdriver, and I run to the barn to find something we can stick down into the tank. I bring back a rake and a hoe. It takes a few minutes to remove the lid using the screwdriver, but once we do, a foul stench pours out into the air, a hundred times stronger than the stink that was already lingering.

I shine my light inside to find a pond of black water, floating with what looks like muddy chunks but that I know are globs of human feces. Sewage flies dance around the tank opening.

"That's some disgusting shit," Carlos comments. "Literally."

I take the hoe and submerge it into the filth. I root around, trying to find something solid. I keep my breathing shallow—inhaling through my mouth instead of my nose—but no matter what, the stench seems to pour inside me. I try to keep myself from throwing up.

"I hit something," I grunt.

I pull whatever it is—a branch, a log—toward the surface. A human hand bobs up out of the muck, connected to an arm that slants back down into the grossness.

"It's a dead body," Carlos says, stating the obvious.

"Not just any body," I say, pointing to the hand.

There are two fingers missing.

"That's Harvey Curry," I say.

Carlos reaches down, takes the slickened wrist in his gloved hands, and pulls. Once he manages to get more of the arm out, I join him. It takes a lot of pulling and navigating—and our clothes don't survive without getting sewage splattered on them—but we finally heave Harvey's body out and into the grass.

Every surface of his body is coated in slime, the clothes soggy, the hair matted and muddy. But there's no doubt, behind the black glop oozing down the skin and the muddy mask partly covering his face, this man is—was—Harvey Curry.

I stick the hoe back into the sewage and push it farther into the filth. Deep underground, as far as I can reach, the hoe snags something. I strain to drag the thing—whatever it is—closer.

Carlos joins me, submerging the rake into the muck. It's difficult work, the two of us struggling shoulder-to-shoulder, but we finally get the object lifted toward the surface.

While most of it's still submerged, the topmost part comes out of the muck. It looks like a volleyball at first—its white surface visible through dripping sewage—but the object shifts and empty eye sockets become discernible, along with a triangular hole where the nose once was and a gaping toothy mouth.

"It's another body," Carlos says.

"And this one's been down there a lot longer," I grunt.

"Yeah," he says. "So who the hell is it?"

CHAPTER 44

WITH CARLOS'S RAKE snagged in the ribcage and my hoe tangled in a belt around the corpse's waist, we manage to pull the fetid body up and out of the hole. It slumps down next to Harvey. Some skin remains, clinging to the bones like parchment paper, but most of what's left is a skeleton in muddy clothes.

I wedge my gloved fingers into the rear pocket of the dead person's threadbare jeans and find a wallet. It's a careless mistake to leave the wallet with the victim, but maybe Parker was overconfident that the body would never be found.

I flip it open, spilling credit cards onto the grass. I stare at the driver's license in disbelief.

Jackson Clarke.

Carlos and I stagger farther into the yard to try to escape the stench. I fling off my gloves, put my hands on my knees, and take a deep breath. The air is clearer here but only a little—the stink has followed me. It's on my clothes and in my hair.

"Parker killed Jackson Clarke," I manage to say between deep breaths. "He's a murderer."

Carlos thinks for a moment and then says, "It makes sense now."

Yes, it does. When Jackson Clarke was released, he didn't make a run for it like everyone assumed. He was innocent. We know that now. But Parker was convinced he was the Cereal Killer.

So Parker killed him.

He probably snuck over to the grain elevator from his house—taking the same route I did, only in reverse—and killed Clarke. Then Parker hid the body in his septic tank and resigned from the Rangers, claiming he was upset that Clarke had gotten away. But that was just an act. The whole time he knew that Jackson Clarke wasn't on the run. He was rotting in a sewage-filled grave under the grass where Parker's children played and where he and his wife hosted family cookouts.

"I'm going to call this in," I say, straightening my back and taking a deep breath through my nose.

"Wait," Carlos says.

His skin looks pasty in the moonlight, clammy with sweat.

"What do you mean?" I say. "We've got two dead bodies here. We have to call this in."

"We don't know who we can trust," he says.

He explains that if someone from the Rangers did, in fact, tip off Parker the other day, they could do the same again. If we have any chance of catching him, we need to keep this to ourselves.

At least for now.

But I don't like the sound of that.

"He's probably crossing the Mexico border right now," I snap. "What if there is no one tipping him off? What if he's just outsmarted us? Maybe our only chance of stopping him is calling this in right now. Alert agents at every border crossing. Get the FBI to track his phone.

"We can't do this alone," I say, exasperated.

"What if we have to?" he says.

Carlos and I stare at each other. Finally, he slumps his shoulders and relents.

"You're right," he says. "We have to call it in. He's gone one way or the other. We'll never catch him. At least now we'll be back in the good graces of the Texas Rangers. No one can say we were barking up the wrong goddamn tree now."

I stare at the bodies, feeling utterly defeated.

Maybe it's a small vindication that we can prove Parker is a criminal. But we can't catch him before he escapes.

It's over.

Parker wins.

I hang my head, staring at the ground.

"Okay," I say, and I pull out the phone to make the call.

Then my phone starts buzzing in my hand.

"It's Parker," I breathe when I see the caller ID. "He's calling me."

CHAPTER 45

I PRESS THE answer button and put the phone to my ear, but I don't say anything.

I don't know what *to* say.

"Rory?" Parker says.

"I thought you never wanted to talk to me again," I say, my voice low.

He laughs, a good-hearted chuckle.

"I had to say that," he says. "I had to keep up pretenses until we were safely away."

Maybe he'll confess now—try to explain away what he's done— but it's obvious he wouldn't be doing this unless he felt in the clear.

Carlos watches me, leaning close so he can hear both ends of the conversation.

"I wasn't really upset with you," he says. "You were just doing your job. And doing it pretty well, actually. Game well played, Rory. You *almost* got me."

"Are you calling to gloat?" I say.

"No," he says earnestly. "I'm calling to say thank you."

I frown but don't say anything.

"For saving Leo," he says. "I owe you. Honestly. My boy might be dead right now if it wasn't for you."

"I know a way you can pay me back," I say. "Turn yourself in."

He laughs again. It's clear he's enjoying this.

"That's the one thing I can't do, my friend," he says. "My children need me. My family."

"You'll be on the run for the rest of your lives," I say. "Is that any way to raise a family?"

"We'll be okay," he says. "I gave away most of the money—I'm sure you know that by now—but I saved enough that we could run when the time came. My kids will have a good life. A normal life."

"How does Josie feel about what you've done?" I ask.

"Like I said before, marriage is all about compromise. When you're truly in love, you can go to your spouse and say, 'Honey, I need you to come along with me, no questions asked.' If you're in love, you make it work."

Hearing him talk about dragging Josie and the kids into his life on the lam makes something in me snap. I can't take any more of his self-righteous justification—any more delusions that he's a *good* person helping others.

"Parker," I say, "you are crazy."

"No," he says defensively. "I am *not*. It's the world that's gone crazy."

"You rationalize why it's okay for you to conduct yourself outside the bounds of society and its laws," I say, "but you're no better than the criminals you used to put away."

"I *help* people," he growls.

"Tell that to the family of Luisa Ramirez."

This stops him, and for a moment he doesn't speak.

"That was an accident," he says softly. "That wasn't supposed to happen. And the person who made that mistake has paid for it."

"So that's why you killed Harvey?"

He's quiet again.

"That's right," I say. "We found him. I'm looking at his dead body right now. He has a bullet in his face and he's covered in shit. Tell me again how you're not crazy."

Any mirth Parker was feeling earlier is now gone. His voice is so quiet I can hardly hear him.

"You've killed people, Rory."

"Only in self-defense," I say. "Never in cold blood."

"Semantics," Parker says. "Harvey committed murder and had to die."

"And that's the same excuse you used for Jackson Clarke?" I say. "Before you left him rotting in your septic tank?"

"It seemed a fitting place for that psychopath to rot."

"You had to know eventually you'd be found out," I say. "You can't go forever without getting a septic tank pumped."

"That's just the thing," he said. "We *could* go forever. We had to replace the tank back when we bought the house, and the damn county insisted we put in a three-thousand-gallon drum because it's an old farmhouse built for a much bigger family. Building codes go by the number of bedrooms, not how many people actually live there. It was easy to push that murderer into the back of the tank and forget about him. A piece of shit buried in a sea of it."

I open my mouth to tell him that Jackson Clarke was actually innocent, but he cuts me off before I can speak.

"I'm done with this conversation," he says. "You're clearly just a cog in the corrupt machine, and you'll never understand. I wanted to call and say thanks again for saving Leo, and I've done that. I'm sorry that you couldn't catch me. After tomorrow, you'll never hear about me or the XYZ Bandits—or whatever it is you called us— ever again. Goodbye, Rory."

Before he hangs up, I start to shout: "Let Josie and the kids go, Parker. Let them live a normal..."

I trail off because the phone beeps in my ear. He hung up on me.

"Shit," I say to Carlos. "That didn't tell us a goddamn thing."

"Yes, it did."

I raise my eyebrows to him.

"He said, 'After tomorrow, you'll never hear about me or the XYZ Bandits ever again.'"

"So?" I say.

"So," he says, "why did he say 'after tomorrow'? Why not just say 'you'll never hear from us again'?"

I stare at him, trying to figure out what he's getting at.

"They haven't fled Texas yet," he says. "They've got unfinished business. I think they're going to pull one more job."

CHAPTER 46

CARLOS AND I split up. He drives to Josie's mom's house to see if by chance the Longbaughs are there. I start searching the house, looking for any clue to suggest what one last job for the XYZ Bandits might be.

The place is in complete disarray, and I don't even know what I'm looking for.

I first occupy myself in Parker's study, but I can't find anything—no notes about the previous jobs and certainly none about one left unfinished.

Carlos returns, equally empty-handed, and he powers up a desktop computer. A search of its browsing history reveals home-schooling activities and Pinterest ideas for kids' crafts. This must have been Josie's computer, and if Parker had one, he took it with him.

It's almost dawn when we head down in the basement, feeling defeated. Carlos begins digging through the boxes, but he only finds toys and pieces of train set landscapes. I tell him it's pointless.

"It's time to call this in," I say. "We've got two dead bodies up there. If they smell bad now, they're only going to get worse once the sun starts beating down on them."

"I'm not ready to give up," he says, digging through a box of baby clothes the kids would have long since outgrown.

"Look around," I say. "There's nothing here. Parker thought of everything."

He ignores me and opens up another box. It's full of diorama sections from a previous incarnation of Parker's train set. He sets it aside and opens a new box.

"Carlos," I say. "Goddamnit, listen to me."

He keeps searching.

In frustration, I kick the box of diorama parts and the pieces go flying across the concrete floor. Carlos spins around.

"I'm not giving up, Rory!"

But I'm not looking at him. I'm looking at the landscape sections on the floor. They don't have any train tracks on them, just pieces of what look like a stream or a river, with numerous small buildings. One piece contains a model of a recognizable Spanish-style mission.

The Alamo.

I fall to my knees and start grabbing the chunks, trying to put them together like a puzzle.

"What the hell are you doing?" Carlos says.

Now it's my turn to ignore him. I move the pieces around, fitting them together. It might take longer but some of this I can do from memory. I was just there the other day.

I finish what I'm doing and stand up.

At my feet is a large-scale model of the San Antonio River Walk and the surrounding streets—the last place the XYZ Bandits robbed.

"I'll be damned," Carlos says.

Another box is open nearby, full of diorama pieces, and I tip it over and all the sections spill out, chunks of roadway and sections of a river. One glance and I have an idea of what it is—the Brazos River where the armored truck was robbed.

"These were never for the kids," I say, feeling my breath caught in my throat. "These were part of their robbery plans."

Carlos and I look at each other, and then, having the same thought at the same time, our eyes move to the current diorama on top of the plywood.

A model of a train running alongside a river.

"Their next job," I say, my voice barely more than a whisper, "is going to be a train robbery."

CHAPTER 47

WE STUDY THE model train display.

The track doesn't run in an oval shape typical for a model train. Instead, the track runs eight feet across the sheet of plywood, edge to edge. Its route passes underneath a roadway overpass, then runs parallel to a river for at least half the table. The train then crosses the river on a long, angled bridge onto a shoreline road that ends in a T, marked with a crossing gate. A spur road runs down to the river just past the bridge.

A model train stretches at least three quarters of the length of the track. There might be close to one hundred cars on it.

Now that we know what we're looking at, it seems obvious this was never a hobby display meant for kids.

No, this is a scale replica of a real place.

I pull out my phone, look up a number, and call. As it rings, I check my watch. It's before eight o'clock and I hope to God there's someone there to answer. Rays of sunlight pour in through the high basement windows.

"Texas Department of Transportation," a polite voice says on the other end of the line. "How may I direct your call?"

"This is Rory Yates of the Texas Ranger Division," I say. "I need to speak to someone in the Rail Division. It's an emergency."

"Uh, okay," the voice says, sounding flummoxed. "Do you know your party's extension?"

"I need to talk to the most knowledgeable person about the rail lines in this state," I say. "Someone who knows every inch of track in Texas. And make sure somebody's there to answer. I don't want to get voicemail."

She puts me on hold, and I pace the basement floor while Carlos takes pictures of the diorama. I can still smell sewage, as if the stench from the smears on our clothes has attached itself to our skin.

"Alex Lloyd," a man says, coming to the line. "I'm the deputy director here. What can I do for you?"

I tell him who I am and what I want from him.

"Mister, there are over twelve thousand miles of train tracks in Texas," he says. "Twice as much as almost any other state. And you want me to pinpoint a particular place on a map based on your description?"

"Exactly," I say. "If you're not the person for the job, get the right person on the phone." Realizing how demanding I sound, I add, "Please."

"I'm the one you want to talk to," he says with resignation in his voice. "I've been here almost forty years. No one knows these tracks like me."

I describe the scene in the diorama.

"You don't know what river, do you?" he asks.

"I wish."

"Do you know if we're talking passenger cars or freight cars?"

I look at the model. It's hard to know if Parker just used whatever train cars he had available, or if what's in the model is actually an accurate depiction of what they plan to rob. Judging by how intricate the other models were, I assume the latter.

"Freight," I say.

Carlos offers to email the guy some pictures, and a few minutes later Alex Lloyd is opening the photos on his desktop computer while still on the phone with me.

"Hmmm," he says. "There's a branch line out past Odessa that we don't use much anymore. There's a road that goes over the tracks, then crosses over a river. It's hilly country, around where the Pecos River comes in from New Mexico and starts its route down to the Rio Grande. We're talking about the middle of nowhere."

The deputy railroad director asks us to hang on while he pulls up Google Earth.

"I'll be a monkey's uncle," he says.

"What?" I ask.

"See for yourself," he says. "I'm emailing your partner a screen-shot."

Seconds later, Carlos gets an email on his phone. He opens the attached picture. It's a satellite view of a stretch of railroad track running next to a river. One glance and it's clear—the image is identical to Parker's model.

"We need to know when the next train is going through there," I say. "How many and how often? The whole schedule for that line."

"Let me check," he says. "Heck, I think we only use that line once or twice a week."

As he's quiet on the other end, the wait is agonizing. It's all I can do to keep still while Carlos paces.

"Huh," Alex says, surprised. "It looks like one train is using it today."

"What time?"

"It's hard to say when it will be at that exact—"

"Your best guess," I snap.

"Two o'clock," he says. "Give or take ten or fifteen minutes."

I look at my watch. It's fifteen past eight.

"How long will it take us to get there from Snakebite?" I ask.

"In a car?" he says with such surprise that I get the impression he must only ever think about train routes and speeds—not automobiles. "Seven hours at least, I reckon."

"We'll be driving a hundred miles an hour the whole way," I say.

"Um, that's all well and good on the highways," he says, "but you'll be on a lot of backroads out there. Hills. Curves. Winding roads."

"Shit," Carlos mutters next to me. "We'll never make it."

"You want me to reroute the train somewhere else?" Alex asks. "Or stop it?"

Carlos and I look at each other, communicating without speaking.

"Don't stop it," I say. "But can you slow it down?"

CHAPTER 48

CARLOS DRIVES WHILE I ride shotgun.

The truck's flashers are on, sirens wailing. We blow down the highway, passing every car like they're standing still.

We review our options and we're both on the same page. We could call in local law enforcement to converge on that section of track. But any Ranger who's compromised might tip off Parker and Ellis. And if Parker hears a siren or sees any flashing lights or spots anything suspicious at all—any clue that we've figured out his target—he'll be in the wind. Our only chance of catching him is to go it alone.

Which is why we told Alex Lloyd of the Department of Transportation to ask the driver to slow the train down *a little*. Only within his realm of expectation. If it is too delayed, Parker will suspect interference. He'll bolt.

We also decide we don't want the two dead bodies in Parker's yard—Harvey Curry and Jackson Clarke—cooking in the sun all day. So we call the local Snakebite dispatcher and report the bodies. We know it's only a matter of time until word gets back to the Texas Rangers, so we're not surprised when the phone rings with a call from Captain Lightwood.

"Took you long enough," Carlos says into the cab, answering via Bluetooth.

"Where are you?" Lightwood barks. "What the hell is going on?"

"We're following a lead in Dallas," Carlos lies. "I'll fill you in when we know more."

Captain Lightwood starts shouting at Carlos, telling him that he should have called him as soon as we discovered the bodies at Parker Longbaugh's. In fact, he complains, we shouldn't have gone back to the residence without consulting him first.

"I don't like being out of the loop," he snarls. "I don't like the way—"

"You know what I don't like?" Carlos snaps. "Listening to you piss and moan about what you don't like."

I stifle a laugh.

"If you were in charge of this investigation," Carlos says, "those bodies would still be underground, rotting in piss and shit. If you'd actually listened to me from the start, Parker Longbaugh might be in jail instead of making a run for it."

Lightwood is stunned into silence.

"The only words I want to hear out of your mouth," Carlos says, "are an apology. Are you going to apologize for letting a murderer slip through our fingers? Didn't think so," he adds, and he hangs up.

I stare at him in amazement.

"How did that feel?" I ask.

"Awesome," he says, unable to stifle a grin.

"You know you could get in big trouble for that."

He shrugs.

"Doesn't matter," he says. "If we catch Parker Longbaugh, we're heroes. All is forgiven."

"And if we don't?" I ask.

"Our careers are probably over," he says matter-of-factly.

"No pressure," I joke and stare out the windshield as the grassy fields of Central Texas slowly dry up and are replaced by barren stretches of brown land peppered with sagebrush. Pump jacks lever up oil from the ground. The hazy layer of humidity on the horizon dissipates, and the sky grows bluer and bluer.

My body aches from the two-by-four-wielding thugs the other night, and fatigue threatens to pull me into sleep. But I tell myself I can't crash yet. I have to see this through to the end.

Lieutenant Abrams calls me when we're getting close.

"Captain Lightwood just filled me in on the latest," he says solemnly.

I don't say anything, expecting the kind of lecture Carlos just got. But Abrams surprises me.

"Anything I can do to help?"

"Not yet," I say, relieved. "Thanks, Ty."

He tells me that Border Patrol has been notified and all checkpoints into Mexico will be on the lookout for Parker. It's nice to know Carlos and I have a safety net if we fail, but I bet Parker already thought of that and has his own contingency plan.

I just hope no one's tipped him off and—if they have—they leaked the disinformation about us following a lead in Dallas.

When we're getting close, Carlos exits the highway onto a neglected two-lane full of cracks and curves. He's forced to slow down, but he still takes the bends as fast as the terrain will let him.

Far to the right, we can see a freight train—so long its cars stretch out of sight—riding near the top of a canyon. We can't see the river from here, but we can tell the route it takes by the rocky lip of the gorge.

"You ready for this?" Carlos says, holding tight to the wheel with both hands.

Carlos and I have been through some serious situations together. He shouldn't need to ask.

"I'm ready."

"This is different than anything we've done before," he says.

"What are you getting at?" I say as he swerves around a cluster of tumbleweeds blocking part of the road.

"Parker's not going to just put his hands in the air when we show up," he says. "He's going to run. He'll fight back. What happened in San Antonio is proof of that."

"Harvey was the one who shot Luisa Ramirez," I say. "Parker said as much. He made it clear he never wanted to hurt anyone."

"If the only way to avoid spending the rest of his life in prison is shooting a Texas Ranger," Carlos says without taking his eyes off the road, "I don't think he'll hesitate."

I think about this for a minute.

If Parker goes for his gun, will I shoot him down? Can I kill someone I once called a friend?

I'm out of time.

"We're here," Carlos says, as we crest a hill and spot where the road passes over the tracks. "Get your head in the game, Rory."

CHAPTER 49

UP AHEAD, DOWN a gently sloping grade, we see a familiar confluence—just like in Parker's diorama—where the road meets with the Pecos River and the railroad track perched along the canyon's edge. The road crosses over both the tracks and the river via an old iron truss bridge.

There are two men—clad head to toe in black—on top of the bridge, standing next to motorcycles and looking down on the tracks below. As the train barrels toward them, ready to pass underneath their feet, it looks like the two men are getting ready to jump on top of it.

Carlos floors the accelerator, and we roar down the hill toward the bridge. The train, barreling toward the junction, looks like it's going to reach them mere seconds before us.

The motorcyclists turn their heads and spot us. Both men are wearing their helmets, keeping their faces hidden.

One of the figures throws a leg over his motorcycle, kicks the bike to life, and blasts away, heading over the river.

"He's making a run for it," Carlos says.

But the other person doesn't flee. Instead, he climbs over the railing on the bridge and perches himself on the outside. When the train comes roaring beneath him, he lets go and drops.

I hold my breath, unable to see what happens to him.

Carlos slams on the brakes and skids to a halt next to the abandoned motorcycle. We jump out of the truck and run to the edge of the bridge. The train comes into view. The man is rising to his feet on top of one of the freight cars. As the train takes him away, he pulls off his helmet and tosses it over the side of the train, where it clatters down the rocky slope.

Even from this distance, we can tell the figure is Parker. He lifts a hand to us in a mocking wave that seems to say, *Not today, boys*.

"Damnit," Carlos says, his words hardly audible over the noise of the train thundering beneath us. "We're too late."

When we were searching the house, it was Carlos who didn't want to give up. Now it's my turn.

"Go after Ellis," I yell. "I'll get Parker."

He gives me a look that says he can't believe what I'm saying, but he doesn't argue. He runs to the truck and floors it, leaving a cloud of rubber smoke in his wake.

I take a deep breath and hoist a leg over the bridge railing. I hold on and look down at the train racing beneath me. Cowboys in old Westerns make this look so easy—hell, Parker made it look easy—but now that I'm in this position, the idea of jumping onto a moving train is petrifying. The drop to the top of the train is probably only ten feet, but the cars are pounding along at a good forty or fifty miles an hour. And, from up here, the roofs of the freight cars seem impossibly narrow.

I can't do this.

But if I don't, Parker gets away—it's that simple.

I look up the tracks at the train snaking away in the distance. Parker is dozens of cars away now. From where I'm clinging, there's no way of knowing when the end of the train will come.

It's now or never.

I take a deep breath.

And jump.

CHAPTER 50

WHEN MY BOOTS hit the top of the train, my legs are yanked out from under me, like I've tried to stand on a treadmill spinning in reverse. My butt slams onto the freight car's roof, and I roll backward, my head bouncing off the metal with a clang. The momentum of the train rolls me sideways toward the edge. I cling to a riveted joint in the roof as my feet dangle over the side. The train rocks and shakes beneath me, vibrating my whole body.

I feel like I'm riding a ten-thousand-ton jackhammer.

I force myself to my hands and knees and crawl away from the edge. I squint my eyes against the wind as I scan the length of the train to find Parker. He's already spotted me and is facing my way.

I rise unsteadily to my feet. To my left is rolling West Texas desert. If I fall in that direction, I might survive with a broken bone or two. To my right, however, is a steep drop down the canyon. If I fell here, I'd tumble down a hundred feet of rocky cliff slope before smashing into a barricade of boulders on the shoreline.

I lumber forward, like a drunk unable to walk a straight line.

Parker moves toward me, leaping between the cars like an Olympic gymnast. His dexterity gives me confidence, and I pick up speed. When I approach the gap between cars, I don't hesitate. I leap forward and sail over the coupling connecting the cars. My boots skid on the other side, and for a stomach-clenching instant, I think I'm going to slide off the side of the train.

But then I gain my footing and start running again, getting used to the rhythm of the rocking train. The train chuffs and shifts and rumbles beneath me. My boots clang loudly against the metal.

I leap to another car. And then another. Finally, Parker and I meet on the same car—him on one end, me on the other, as if we're dueling gunfighters on Main Street in a dusty western town. Fifty feet separate us. Then twenty feet. Ten.

Parker's pistol is fastened to his hip.

Just like mine.

Parker calls out to me.

"I can't let you take me in, Rory," he says. "I'm not letting you lock me up with the scum I used to put away."

"You called last night to thank me for saving your son's life," I say. "Now you're going to murder me?"

Parker looks stricken. I can tell the warped moral code he operates from is straining to the point of breaking.

"I wish it wasn't you, Rory," he says sadly.

I hold my hands out to my side, away from my SIG Sauer. Parker was always good with a gun—all Texas Rangers are—but he's no match for me. If he goes for his gun, I'll kill him.

I know it.

He must know it, too.

"No hard feelings," he says. "Okay?"

The way he says this, it's as if he's saying goodbye—as if he's offering me forgiveness *before* I shoot him.

"Don't do this, Parker," I say.

"Sorry, old friend," he says, and his hand darts to his holster.

CHAPTER 51

I DON'T GRAB my gun. I keep my arm frozen at my side.

Parker draws fast and aims the gun directly at my chest. I hold my breath and prepare for the inevitable *bang*.

It doesn't come.

Parker simply stands on the train, aiming his pistol at me.

"I knew you couldn't do it," I say, relieved. "I knew there was something left of the Parker I remembered."

"Damn it, Rory," he says.

"No more killing," I say. "It's time to come in."

He looks at the gun like it somehow let him down. Then he hurls it out over the canyon.

I step toward him and tell him to put his hands in the air. I reach for my handcuffs, but when he looks at me, something in his face—a defiance in his eyes—gives me pause.

"I told you," he says, "I'm not going to prison!"

He rushes toward me, and I hardly have time to react. He slams his hands into my chest, giving me a herculean shove that throws me backward. I barely keep my feet, and just as I'm getting my balance back, he throws a jab into my ribs—right where one of the two-by-fours smacked me. I gasp in pain. As quick as a snake, he lashes out with another punch to my gut. I bend over, air whoosh-ing out of my mouth. I take a step back, trying to recover, but he swings a hard uppercut, catching my jaw. My head whips back. I fall onto my back, my head over the edge of the train car's roof. Dazed, I crane my neck and look down at the drop awaiting me—a steep slope of jagged rocks. I experience a wave of vertigo and feel like I'm going to roll right off.

Parker grabs me, hauling me away from the edge.

"I don't want to kill you, Rory," he says. "But if I have to hurt you a little, I will."

I shake my head, trying to orient myself. He's dragging me over to the other side, where the drop might not be deadly.

"No," I say, pushing his hands off. "You're coming with—"

He hits me again in the ribs, and the pain almost buckles my knees. I hobble backward, my arms up in defense. But then I real-ize I'm headed toward the back corner of the train car, running out of space to retreat.

"When you hit the ground," he says, "roll away from the train."

I throw a punch, but he blocks it with his forearm and jabs me in the cheekbone with his other fist. I feel myself reeling, and he hits me with a haymaker that spins me around. I collapse onto my hands and knees, right at the corner of the car. A string of bloody saliva hangs from my mouth, caught in the wind.

"Sorry, Rory," he says. "You might be better than me with a gun, but you ain't got nothing on me when it comes to a good old-fashioned fistfight."

I still have my gun, I realize.

I don't want to kill him. But maybe I can wound him. He doesn't seem to have a problem doing that to me.

I rise, spinning around as I snatch my pistol from its holster. But

I'm too late. He hits me with a side kick—his boot slamming into my ribs like a sledgehammer—and sends me off the edge.

My pistol goes flying.

And my body goes airborne, plummeting toward the ground below.

CHAPTER 52

I THROW OUT my hands and pray that they find something to grab onto. Just as my legs slam against the ground, my right hand snatches a metal bar.

I hold on with all my strength as my legs are dragged behind me in the dirt next to the gleaming metal rail of the train. The giant wheels of the train pump and grind only a few feet away. If I let go, I'll have to roll just right to avoid amputating one or both legs.

I lurch forward with my other hand and grab onto the metal bar. It's the bottom rung of a ladder running along the outside of the train car.

I try to pull myself up to the second rung of the ladder, but I just don't have the strength. Heat emanates from under the train like an open oven door.

From above, Parker calls down to me, and I strain my neck to see him.

"Roll away from the train," he shouts, motioning with his arm.

I say nothing. I can't. It's all I can do to hold on.

Parker looks frustrated. He checks his watch and looks at me with an expression that says, *I can't wait all day. I've got a robbery to finish.*

"Goodbye, Rory," he calls down. "Don't die!"

He disappears.

It's time to give up, I tell myself.

I'm beaten.

But I think of the body of Jackson Clarke, left to rot in a tomb of shit. I think of Luisa Ramirez, shot down in the street in San Antonio. Parker might not have pulled the trigger, but he was the mastermind behind the robbery that killed her.

I growl out in frustration and pain and throw my right arm up to the second rung. My hand grips it and I keep fighting. My other arm grabs the third, and I curl my body and lift my legs off the ground. Hanging only inches from the gravel, I hook my right foot onto the bottom rung and push upward. I grab the next rung and the next, holding on with numb hands. I keep climbing, each step an effort. It feels like the longest ladder in the world, but I finally get to the top and roll onto my back, my lungs heaving, my mouth as dry as the desert dirt.

I examine the damage to my legs.

My pants are shredded, my legs scraped and bleeding. They'll hurt like hell tomorrow, and once they scab up, it will be hard to walk. But for now—my body fueled by adrenaline—I must go on.

I rise to my feet.

Standing atop the racing train, I look for signs of Parker. But from one end to the other, the tops of the train cars are empty.

Parker is gone.

CHAPTER 53

CARLOS TAKES A sharp curve and the tires squeal beneath him. He skids into the gravel shoulder and kicks up a cloud of dust. Then he recovers, stomping on the gas and flying down the bumpy road.

Up ahead, the motorcyclist decelerates around another curve, and Carlos tries to gain ground.

On flat highway, the bike would have lost him already. But here, on this cracked and curvy backcountry road, the motorcycle can't reach its top speeds and Carlos has been able to stick to him.

But he's not sure how long he can keep it up.

Gripping the wheel as hard as he can, he hits the curve, lets off the gas, and yanks the wheel. One tire hits the shoulder, spraying gravel.

The bike zooms over a small hill, disappearing on the other side. Carlos follows, and when he rockets over the crest—his insides lurching with the sudden change in elevation—he feels a disquieting sense of defeat from what he sees ahead. The road straightens out, and already the bike is taking advantage of it. The motorcycle engine whines, and the gap between the two vehicles widens.

Carlos floors the gas pedal, but it's not enough.

But then the road in front of the bike takes a sharp turn.

Through the windshield, Carlos watches as the motorcycle, leaning hard into the curve, slides off the road and into the sagebrush. Bike and rider tumble through the air, kicking up clouds of dust.

Carlos skids to a halt at the curve and runs out of the truck. He leaps over clumps of sagebrush and follows the gouges in the dirt where the bike and rider rolled. He passes the bike first, now a misshapen heap of metal hissing steam and bleeding oil.

Ten feet past that—at least thirty from the road—Carlos finds the rider smashed against a boulder the size of a minivan, his body contorted in unnatural angles. One glance and it's obvious the person is dead. His head—still hidden behind the helmet—is twisted almost behind his back, like an owl rotating its neck two hundred and seventy degrees.

Carlos raises the visor to look at the person's face.

He never met Ellis Kilpatrick, but he'd seen his official military portrait when he was digging into the former Navy man's background. There's no doubt the vacant face looking out from the motorcycle helmet—a trickle of blood running from his nose—is Ellis.

That's two of the XYZ Bandits dead.

Leaving only one left.

As Carlos stares at the dead man, he can hear the distant chugging of the train.

He runs back to his truck, stomps on the gas, and tries to recall from the train model where the road reconnects with the track.

CHAPTER 54

I RUN TOWARD the front of the train, leaping from one car to the next. I look all around, trying to figure out what happened to Parker. Up ahead, the front of the train curves in a wide arc, and I spot, about four carriages back from the engine, an open side door of one of the freight cars. I catch a glimpse of a person inside. Then some kind of object—pale in color and about the size of a ream of paper—comes sailing out from the doorway, falling down into the canyon and hitting a rocky outcropping. Whatever it was explodes into a cloud of gray dust.

Then the train swings back the other way, and I lose sight of Parker.

I mentally mark which car it was and take off running. In the distance, the tracks curve toward a large arch bridge that spans the canyon at a wide point in the river.

I sprint down the cars, ignoring the pain in my limbs. When I get to the correct carriage, I take my boots off before jumping. When I make the leap, I land quietly and sneak over to the side of the train. I peek down. The door is still open. Something sails out of the opening. This close, I have an idea of what it is.

A brick of drugs—cocaine or heroin or meth.

It smashes against the rocks, filling the air with powder.

The engine of the train is almost to the bridge. I find a handhold on the top of the train, take one second to steel myself for what I'm about to do, then swing down, feet first, into the open freight car.

Parker, leaning over a wooden crate, spins around in surprise.

I throw a hard punch into his throat, sending him stumbling backward, gasping for air and clutching at his neck. He throws his other arm into the air to balance himself, and I grab his wrist and give it a twist, using his momentum to drive him down onto the steel floor of the car. If I'm no match for him in a fistfight, then I can't give him a chance to fight back. I bend his arm behind his back, pin him to the floor with my knee, and handcuff his wrist. He squirms beneath me, coughing hard, but I manage to twist his other arm into position and get the teeth of the cuffs around the second wrist.

I stand back and let him squirm around into a sitting position, his arms cuffed behind his back. He takes great wheezing breaths, finally getting enough air into his lungs.

"You son of a bitch," he rasps.

"Now," I say, looking around and taking in the scene, "it's over."

The inside of the freight car is empty except for one crate, four or five feet wide and almost as tall, that was fastened to the wall by compression straps. The straps have been cut and the lid pried open.

Inside, the contents are separated by a wooden partition. One side contains a scattering of drug kilos, what's left of what Parker was tossing out the door.

The other side is full of cash wrapped neatly in stacks.

Lying on the floor is a duffel bag partly filled with money. It's clear that Parker's bag won't hold all of it, but then again, the plan had been for both he and Ellis to be here to load up.

"So you're destroying the drugs and taking the money?" I say to Parker.

He spits blood and says, "Why couldn't you just let me go, Rory?"

"Parker," I say, feeling a strong sense of satisfaction in saying these words, "you're under arrest."

He glances out the open door.

"Sorry, old friend," he says, grinning, "this is my stop."

He jumps to his feet and darts toward the opening. I reach out to stop him, but I'm too slow. He soars out the window, and I race to the opening, expecting to see his body crashing against the rocks.

But we're going over the bridge.

Parker plummets toward the slate-gray water of the Pecos River a hundred feet below. He splashes into the surface and disappears beneath it. The water is choppy with white wavelets, and a moment after he's gone, there's no sign of him whatsoever.

I think he's not going to come up, but finally his head bobs to the surface, and he starts drifting under the bridge with the current.

The train keeps moving, pulling me toward the other side of the canyon.

I have to act fast.

Without thinking, I leap out the door toward the river below.

CHAPTER 55

TERROR GRIPS ME as the water rushes upward toward me. I have time to think that I've made a terrible mistake—that I'm going to die—and then my bootless feet smack painfully against the surface, and my body plunges deep into cold water. I flail my arms, trying to get to the surface.

When my head breaks free, I gasp and tread water. The water churns around me, and I slap my hands against the surface, trying to orient myself. The current drags me under the bridge, which, as I crane my head to look up, seems unbelievably high from here.

I spot Parker, twenty or thirty feet from me, coming out from under the shadow of the bridge and struggling to keep his mouth above water. His head disappears below the surface for a moment, then bobs up again. He spits water and coughs.

The current is strong, the water choppy, and it's all I can do to keep my head above water. But Parker's hands are cuffed behind his back.

He goes under again.

I stroke toward him, but progress is slow. I feel like I'm swimming against a rip current. Parker's head barely surfaces, just his face, and he gurgles out a stream of water before dropping below again. I swim harder than I've ever swum in my life, my arms pumping, my legs kicking. Muscles burning, I arrive to where I think he should be, but I can't find any sign of him.

"Parker!" I shout.

Through the transparent uppermost layer of water, I spot his face, eyes wide in panic, mouth open in what looks like a silent scream. I dive under, grab him around the arms, and pull him to the surface.

He coughs water and gasps and coughs more.

"Hang on," I manage to say, getting one arm around his chest and fighting the current with my other limbs.

There's a rocky beach up ahead that I recognize from Parker's model. The road comes down and it looks like this could be used as the put-in or pullout for rafts and boats.

I head that way, keeping Parker's head above water. He doesn't say anything, just continues to cough.

When I finally make it to shore—my muscles trembling with fatigue—I drag Parker to the point where the water is only waist high. He staggers the rest of the way and collapses onto the rocks, lying on his side, with his arms still fastened behind his back. His chest heaves as he fills his lungs with deep breaths.

I stand over him, beaten up, bloody, and soaking wet.

"Enough of this shit," I yell. "It's *over!*"

But even as the words come out of my mouth, I hear the whine of a motorcycle. A bike rolls down the road, hits the gravel shore, and approaches us slowly. The driver is dressed in black and wearing a helmet, with a submachine gun slung over one shoulder.

The bike stops about fifteen feet from the water. The rider stands upright over it, legs making an inverted V, and aims the gun at me.

Ellis must have lost Carlos and circled back around this way to pick up Parker.

I reach for my gun, but the holster is empty. I lost my SIG Sauer when Parker kicked me off the train.

"Don't," I hear Parker say to his fellow bandit. He hauls himself onto his knees, looking at the rider. "Don't kill him."

The rider lets the gun hang from its shoulder strap, then reaches up and grabs the helmet, pushing it upward. As the helmet comes up, loose strands of silver hair fall down across the rider's shoulder, and my breath catches in my throat when I see who it is.

CHAPTER 56

"JOSIE?" I SAY, barely able to speak.

Parker's wife, her lean body hidden by the black motorcycle clothes so that I assumed the rider was a man, looks at her husband and says, "What choice do we have? He'll never stop looking for us. We have to kill him."

"I don't understand," I mutter, but suddenly I do.

The robberies were always committed by three motorcycle riders. But when we checked the whereabouts of Parker, Ellis, and Harvey, one of them almost always had an alibi. That's because there were never only three robbers. There were four XYZ Bandits. But only three ever worked a robbery at the same time.

When Ellis was at a family reunion in Vermont, Josie took his place. The same for when Harvey was at the bachelor party in Vegas. And when Parker was on the Cub Scout camping trip with his son, securing an airtight alibi, it was Josie who was with Harvey and Ellis robbing the San Antonio River Walk shops.

Josie raises her gun on me again. The strong woman I always admired has a look of cold steel.

"Don't," Parker says again, rising to his knees and stumbling over to Josie. "He saved Leo. He saved *me*."

"I can't believe you two," I say, watching them from ankle-deep water. "I looked up to you. I thought you had it all. I wanted a life just like yours."

"The world is broken," Parker says defensively. "I've done more good breaking the law than I ever did enforcing it."

I stare at him, my disbelief turning to anger.

"Like killing Jackson Clarke?" I say.

"Yes," he says. "The Cereal Killer is not murdering innocent people anymore. Not because I followed the law, but because I broke it."

"That's where you're wrong," I say. "When we reopened the investigation, Lieutenant Abrams made a discovery. The Cereal Killer is a guy named Chase Germaine. He did time and confessed the whole thing to his cellmate. Including details never released to the public. He's still at large—probably still killing people."

Parker stares at me in disbelief. Water dribbles down his face.

"Jackson Clarke wasn't the Cereal Killer," I say. "We know that now."

"That's not true," he says.

"Here's the truth," I say. "*You* murdered an innocent man."

Parker's knees wobble, and Josie reaches out a hand to steady him. The foundation of self-righteous justification that he's built his life on seems to be crumbling beneath him. He might have been able to rationalize killing Harvey because of what he did. And he can excuse his way out of the murder of Luisa Ramirez because he didn't pull the trigger. But faced with the reality that he killed an innocent person, Parker can't take it. His mouth is open in shock, his skin ashen.

"Parker," Josie says with concern, "get on the bike. We have to go."

"If you actually want to do the right thing," I say, "turn yourselves in."

"Shut up, Rory!" Josie yells.

Her brows furrowed in anger, her teeth practically clenched into a snarl, Josie is nearly unrecognizable.

"Are you really going to shoot me, Josie?" I say, trying to appeal to her humanity—if she has any left. "Are you going to join Parker in becoming a murderer?"

She offers me an unfriendly smile that sends cold chills down my back.

"I already did," she says. "I know you saved my son and you saved my husband, just now, but if you don't shut your mouth, I won't hesitate to shoot you just like I did her."

Parker's shocked stare turns from me to his wife.

"You shot that officer in San Antonio?" he says. "It wasn't Harvey?"

"Sorry," she says to him, shrugging. "Harvey offered to take the blame so you wouldn't be mad at me. I didn't know you would kill him for it."

CHAPTER 57

PARKER LOOKS LIKE a smaller, crumpled version of himself. The confident, muscular man has become a hunched-over and hurt little boy. If his hands weren't cuffed behind his back, he might cover his face and begin weeping.

I almost feel sympathy for him—a guy who thought he was helping people only to find out in the span of a few seconds that both he and his wife had murdered innocent people—but then I think about how he brought all of this on himself.

"Why?" Parker says to his wife.

"Why?" Josie repeats, looking at him as if he's stupid. "The same reason you're going to get on the back of this motorcycle: when our children wake up tomorrow morning, they need their mommy and daddy."

Parker looks as if the last thing he wants to do is get on the back of the bike with her.

"Parker, honey," she says, changing to a more supplicating tone. "We can sort all this out later. Okay? But we need to go. Now."

As she says this, I hear another vehicle approaching. We all turn our heads at the same time to see Carlos's F-150 roaring down the road toward us.

"Get on!" Josie screams at Parker, and this time he listens.

I run forward to stop them, but Josie revs the throttle and spins the bike around in a half circle, spraying me with gravel. The bike races toward the ramp just as Carlos comes down it. Josie, riding with one arm and somehow holding her gun with the other, sprays a burst of bullets at the truck. Carlos dives down behind the steering wheel as glass explodes overhead and rounds *thunk* into the metal bed.

"Josie, no!" Parker roars as he tries to cling to the back of the seat with his cuffed hands. "No more killing!"

Josie stops firing and accelerates the bike past the truck.

I sprint over to the truck, terrified that I'll find Carlos filled with holes. But his head pops up behind the shattered driver's-side window.

"You okay?" I say.

"Yeah," he says. "Get in!"

I jump into the truck bed and crawl through the hole where the back windshield was. Carlos spins the truck in a three-sixty, throwing a wave of gravel out into the water, and we tear up the ramp after Josie and Parker.

Josie hits the roadway, fishtailing slightly. Parker wobbles on the back of the bike but he stays on.

"Are *you* okay?" Carlos asks me. "You look like hell."

"I'll live," I say, then add, "I lost my gun."

"Take mine," he says, gripping the steering wheel tightly and shifting his hip in my direction. I pluck his Colt from its holster.

Josie and Parker are about fifty yards ahead of us, but the road is rough, and with Parker perched precariously on the back, the motorcycle is slowly losing ground.

I lean out my window, but then I hesitate. I don't want to shoot them in the back. And if I hit a tire, there's a good chance they'll crash.

"I don't want to kill them," I say, coming back inside the cab.

"I can't keep up with them forever," Carlos says.

The curvy road is straightening out, and the motorcycle is beginning to pull away. We're running between the train tracks and the river now, only a couple hundred yards from the canyon but half a mile or so from the railway. To our right, the train is chugging along, but we're outpacing it, gaining ground.

"I'm going to call for backup," I say, reaching for Carlos's police radio.

"Wait a second," he says. "Look at that."

It takes me a moment to realize what he's talking about. Up ahead, the road splits into a T. Josie leans into the turn and takes the right fork—heading perpendicular to the train tracks now. In the distance, the road crosses the tracks, and Josie guns it, trying to make it before the train does.

Carlos takes the turn, but he's far behind now.

We can only watch.

The motorcycle flies toward the junction. The conductor must see them because the locomotive's horn sounds in a long, panicked blast. The train and its line of cars look enormous compared to the insect of a motorcycle trying to outrace it.

"They're not going to make it," Carlos mutters.

I stare in horror as Josie's bike and the train converge on the same point. I close my eyes at the last second, but the explosive sound of the metal-against-metal collision followed by the long squeal of the train's brakes tells me all I need to know.

EPILOGUE

ONE

TWENTY-FOUR HOURS LATER, I'm standing in front of the door of my house.

I'm a mess.

My legs are covered in painful scabs, the rest of my body full of bruises and welts and scrapes. But it's my mental state that's truly in tatters. Despite what Parker and Josie became—despite the crimes they committed—they were people I cared about. I feel like I'm doubly grieving. I'm grieving their deaths, but I'm also grieving the loss of the friends I thought I knew—mourning the fact that two people I had highly respected turned out to be people I never really knew at all.

Seeing what was left of them—the pieces scattered on both sides of the railroad track, the stain of gore on the front of the loco-motive—was one of the hardest things I've ever done. I kept my emotions together while we were on the scene, dealing with the local authorities and bringing the Rangers up to speed on what happened. And I maintained my professionalism as we found Parker and Josie's kids—hiding out in a hotel in El Paso with Josie's mom—and broke the news to them that their parents were dead.

Now I'm ready to let the dam burst on my emotions. But when I open the front door, my phone buzzes.

Ty Abrams.

Reluctantly, I answer.

"Wanted to check in and see how you're doing," he says.

"I've been better."

He tells me that they've located a stack of files Parker kept with Josie's mom. She thought they were documents for use in case of emergency: insurance policies and the deed to the house and so forth. But the records showed Parker's advance investigative work to the jobs they pulled.

"As far as we can tell," Abrams says, "he wasn't working in cahoots with anyone in law enforcement. It was just good old-fashioned police work that helped him identify his targets."

"Good to know," I say, my mind a fog. "Does it look like Josie's mom was involved at all? Was she an accomplice, too?"

"We're looking into it," he says. "So far, we haven't found anything."

I hope they don't. I'd like to see Leo and Etta live with family rather than go into foster care. That's what Parker and Josie would have wanted, surely.

"How much time you need off?" he asks sympathetically. "A week? Two?"

"I'll let you know," I say, staggering to my front door and fumbling for my keys.

"Take all the time you want," he says. "But then I need you back. We've got a Cereal Killer to catch."

This seems to be his way of saying that I'm forgiven for lying to him. He might be willing to overlook how I went behind his back this time, but it's clear he expects a team approach on the next case. And after what I've been through, I couldn't agree more. Parker went rogue because he lost faith in the Ranger organization.

I might not always agree with my colleagues, but I recognize the value of the Ranger family.

Parker went wrong when he turned his back on the Rangers.

I'll never follow in those footsteps.

I tell Ty I'll be back as soon as I can, and it's true—I just need some time to rest and recover. Right now, I can't imagine strapping on a gun and being any good to any investigation.

Inside my house, I strip out of my clothes, put on a pair of sweatpants and a T-shirt, and crawl into bed. It's still afternoon, with warm sunlight shining in through the windows, but I'm so fatigued I have to lie down.

It turns out I'm too exhausted to sleep.

Too exhausted to cry.

I just stare at the ceiling, listening to the cows and horses in the pasture, and thinking about Parker and Josie. They'd seemed to me to be the model of what two people in love should look like. Somehow their relationship had taken a wrong turn, but they'd never stopped loving each other. That was clear.

I hear a soft knock on my door. I want to ignore it, but whoever it is—my parents, probably—I know they mean well by checking on me. I hobble to the door and open it to find Megan smiling brightly.

"I was in the neighborhood visiting my folks," she says. "I saw your truck."

She's as beautiful as ever, with her dark hair pulled back in a braid and her electric eyes catching the sunlight just right. But as I look at her, I realize I'm disappointed it's her.

She's not the girl I wish was showing up at my door.

I know what I have to do.

"I'm glad you're here," I say. "We need to talk."

TWO

FROM THE AIRPLANE window, I can see the Cumberland River wending its way through Nashville. The landscape is green and lush and beautiful, and I can see why Willow has fallen in love with living here.

After the plane touches down, I buy a bouquet of lilies—Willow's favorite—from an airport gift shop and head outside to order an Uber. I'm wearing jeans with a nice button-down shirt. And my boots and hat, of course. I fit right in here in Music City.

Underneath my clothes, my body is covered in scabs and bruises. And I've never been so sore in my life. But I couldn't wait. I booked the flight as soon as I broke up with Megan.

Willow doesn't know I'm coming.

I don't have much of a plan other than to show up at her door and say, "I'm ready to have that conversation." Then tell her I love her and I want to make things work with her, no matter what.

I wait a few minutes for the Uber, a compact little Hyundai driven by a cheery twenty-something girl with a thick Tennessee drawl. I sit in the back seat and try to calm my nerves as the girl navigates the car to Highway 65 and heads south. Willow used to live in the trendy Five Points area of Nashville back when we were doing long distance, but she's since moved south of the city to

Franklin, where I understand lots of country stars have property. I got her address from Mom, who still sends her a Christmas card every year.

The radio DJ says we're listening to the Big 98, a station I can remember Willow talking about. A song starts up about a girl knowing she's going to get her heart broken, and I think of Megan. She was hurt, of course, but not surprised.

She said deep down she knew it was coming.

I felt bad, but I would have felt worse stringing her along when my heart wasn't in it.

Neither the driver nor I say much. We just listen to the radio as massive oaks and maples roll by. This is beautiful country, with expansive farms and gorgeous woodlands and long driveways leading to huge homes on faraway hills.

"That's Miley Cyrus's house over there," the driver says matter-of-factly. A minute later, she points out the window again. "And that's Tim McGraw and Faith Hill's place. Or maybe they sold it. I'm not sure."

After we're about thirty minutes out of Nashville, she turns down a driveway that leads through rolling hills and groves of trees to an amazing brick home tucked back in a copse of syca-mores. The two-story building must be five thousand square feet, with a steeply pitched roof and ivory columns out front. The drive-way culminates in a circle, with a small fountain in the middle.

"Wow," my driver says. "Is this the house Keith Urban and Nicole Kidman used to own?"

I don't answer.

I'm too in awe. When I see Willow on TV or hear her songs on the radio, it always gives me a surreal feeling. But when she's back in Redbud, visiting my folks or knocking on my door to say hi, it's easy to forget she's a star.

She's just Willow.

But here, stepping into her world and not just glimpsing it from a music video, I feel completely overwhelmed. Suddenly my idea of showing up on her doorstep with a bouquet of airport flowers seems incredibly naive.

But I'm here now, and there's no turning back.

"Can you stick around for a minute?" I ask the driver. "In case she's not here."

"No problem," she says, and even though I never mentioned why I was here, she glances at the flowers and says, "Good luck."

My boots click on the cobblestone walk as I approach the house. Through the window, I can see a massive living room, with high vaulted ceilings. I bet my two-bedroom cottage, which I used to share with Willow, would probably fit in that room with space to spare.

With my mouth dry and my legs like jelly, I step onto the porch. Ignoring the queasy feeling in my stomach, I press the doorbell.

A minute later, the door swings open, and a handsome man stands before me, with a trim beard, a stylish taper-fade haircut, and arms covered with tattoos. One glance and I recognize him from TV, the guy Willow was doing the duet with, "Sincerely, My Broken Heart."

"Can I help you?" Riley Chandler says, glancing at the flowers in my hand.

"I might have the wrong address," I say. "I'm looking for Willow Dawes."

"Somebody here for you," the guy calls over his shoulder.

Two seconds later, Willow pops into view, looking as beautiful as ever in a pair of Lululemon leggings and a white T-shirt tied above her navel. She gasps when she sees me, and her hand goes to her mouth.

"Oh, my God," she says. "Rory, what are you doing here?"

"I promised you we'd finish that conversation," I say.

She lowers her hand and something catches my eye.

There's a large diamond glimmering on her ring finger.

Noticing where my eyes have gone, she holds her hand out so I can see the ring better. With her other hand, she holds onto the man next to her and gives his arm a squeeze.

"This is Riley—my fiancé." Her cheeks flush with embarrassment. "I wanted to tell you before we made it public."

So *that* is the conversation she wanted to have? Not that she was still in love with me. That she had fallen in love with someone else.

The ground beneath me feels as unsteady as the footing atop of the train. It's all I can do to keep my feet planted underneath me and maintain a friendly expression.

I swallow hard.

"Congratulations," I say, handing her the bouquet of flowers.

Then I extend my hand to Riley Chandler. With a confused half-grin on his face, he takes it.

"Word of advice," I say to him. "Don't let her go. You'll regret it."

WATCH YOUR BACK

James Patterson
and **Loren D. Estleman**

PART 1

On Ramp

CHAPTER 1

THE SIGN TOWERED above the horizontal suburb like a pagan shrine: a wide open, baleful eye perched atop a pyramid, reminiscent of the Masonic symbol on the obverse side of the dollar bill.

ASPECTUS read the block letters at the base of the pyramid. Just that, nothing in the legend to explain or justify its existence.

If you didn't know it already, it implied, you weren't worth educating.

Dennis Cooke knew. Aspectus owned a nearly unbroken string of magazines, newspapers, information websites, and TV stations stretching from Lake Michigan to Salt Lake City; local and national were as one in its eye, not so much a global community as a great sprawling ranch ruled by a single patriarch named Todd Plevin.

Cooke coasted into a space near the entrance, cut the ignition, and waited for the motor to chug itself out. It stopped with a clunk and a tragic wheeze, like an old man dropping into an armchair. One day soon, the noise said, the old crate would stay right where it was until someone noticed and came to tow it away.

It made a man feel all used up at the ripe old age of thirty-five.

An arrow directed him to suite 1800, where a young Asian woman sat at a desk working a keyboard. She was slender in a green sheath dress that revealed well-toned biceps, and her hair—a startling cranberry—was cut to the shape of her head.

She looked up, smiling. Confirming his business from a pad, she tipped a switch to tell Mr. Plevin his four o'clock was here. "Go right in, Mr. Cooke."

Todd Plevin stood behind a glass desk, sorting through a stack of glossy sheets: late twenties, athletic build in a cashmere sweater, brushed jeans, and three-hundred-dollar sneakers. His brown hair was tousled after the fashion of dot-com multimillionaires and he had the narrow face and long rectangular jaw that Cooke associated with aggressive types.

He laid down the sheets—photo reproductions, Cooke saw, of airbrushed illustrations—and came around to offer a hand. His grip was light but there was iron in it. Letting go, he tipped the palm toward a scoop chair and cocked a hip onto the desk.

"I see you brought your portfolio." His was a bright tenor; encouragements from third base came in just that tone.

Cooke laid the elephant-folio folder across his lap and began to untie the string. Plevin held up a hand; that seemed to be his chief unit of expression.

"Later. I've seen your website: nice mix of primaries and secondaries, bold, frank images, character in every stroke. A Rockwell for our time."

"That's a polite way of saying I'm old hat."

"People who say that put too much faith in high-tech splash at the expense of tradition. Personally I prefer oils, watercolors, and charcoal sketches to Photoshop; any hack can work a mouse. My walls at home are hung with originals—and they're not all investments, either. I buy what I like."

Cooke felt a warm flush. So far all his interviews—those he'd managed to land—had been with media execs who subscribed to the school of electronic paint-by-numbers. For some time now he'd felt like the last dinosaur.

It was his turn to say something flattering. He indicated the poster board image propped on an easel near the window, a mock-up of the front page of *America Now,* the newspaper Plevin had rescued from bankruptcy and placed in every hotel in the country. "You certainly know composition. That's a front page I'd stop to read even if I were in a hurry."

"That makeover was entirely mine. It was a smudgy mess when I bought it, all gray columns and pictures of guys in suits handing checks to other guys in suits. First thing I did—after replacing the staff—was dump 40 percent of the copy and widen the borders, gutters, and alleys, increase the white space. It's what you leave out that counts."

A cliché, spoken with all the conviction of a revolutionary thought. That, it dawned on him, was at the heart of Plevin's phenomenal hold on the public, his sure grasp of the banal.

He was banal in response. "It certainly invites you in."

Plevin slid off the desk. While he was on it he'd come off as friendly, approachable. Standing, even with his hands in his pockets, he dominated the room. A door had slammed shut on the small talk.

"Unfortunately, we have no openings. I'm cutting staff as it is. Like it or not, Silicon Valley has made it possible to run a leaner, meaner machine. My board of directors knows that, and they answer to the stockholders."

Cooke shrank inside. He'd been negotiating his salary in his head, and now..."Then, why am I—?"

"Here? Assuming it's not a philosophical question, because I wanted to see you in person. When I got your application I checked you out, as I said. I was impressed with your eye for detail;

it suggested the kind of instinct I was looking for. Now that we've met, I'm sure of it. And I think the terms I have to offer will make you very pleased you came."

He smiled, evidently pleased himself. The expression made the boy wonder look younger still, and for some reason slightly sinister.

CHAPTER 2

PLEVIN CIRCLED BACK behind the glass desk and sat. At that point the last of his casual facade slid away. The session took on all the appearances of a formal interview, and Dennis Cooke all the anxiety of a derelict who had offered to work for food.

The first question did nothing to put him back at ease.

"Are you married?"

It was like unexpectedly being asked his name and forgetting what it was. That was the only reason he could think of for the answer he gave.

"Not lately."

The young face registered no surprise at the response; grimness instead.

"If you remarry, make sure you're sure. It's a hell of a thing when a man can't trust his wife."

"To be honest, Mr. Plevin—"

"Please. Todd."

No way was that going to happen. "In my case, I was the one who couldn't be trusted."

Absolute candor: first thing to avoid in job hunting. But then nothing about this session had followed the course of an ordinary interview.

Plevin's expression didn't change. "It's possible I'm off the beam. I haven't a reason to suspect her of anything, but I've gotten this far listening to my gut. I can't shake the feeling she's cheating on me."

Cooke had no response for that. Raw exposure on both sides, five minutes into the conversation.

"Don't think I care so much about being played for a sap," Plevin said. "Anne's my unofficial partner. She hasn't any legal claim to Aspectus apart from the laws protecting marital property, but she is privy to certain details of the operation that if they became general knowledge would destroy it. A wife is just a wife, but a man's livelihood is everything. I'd rather lose the first, pay anything in a settlement, than jeopardize the second." He smacked the desk with a palm. Cooke jumped in his seat.

Plevin turned the hand over, placed a thumb on the underside of his wrist. *Monitoring his pulse,* Cooke thought. Despite the tycoon's youth, he wondered if he had health issues. One of the side effects of rapid success, he supposed. He himself had never had to deal with those.

After a few seconds the man behind the desk sat back. The flush had faded from his cheeks and when he spoke his voice was as calm as when he'd greeted his visitor.

"What's your driving record?"

"I'm sorry?"

Plevin's color rose again. "Traffic tickets? DUIs? License suspensions? Accidents? Damn it, it's a simple question."

"Two years ago I dinged someone's car with my door in a supermarket parking lot. I left a note and when the owner called I sent him a check for the repair. When I was sixteen, I was cited for doing forty in a school zone. I paid the fine and haven't been pulled over since. My record's clean apart from those two things."

"I know. I have contacts in the DMV."

"Then why—?"

"Testing you. As much as I need someone who won't let me down by smashing up or getting arrested, I need someone who won't bullshit me. I don't care if you dipped your pen in the wrong well when you were married. That's a different kind of dishonesty."

"Mr. Plevin, are you asking me to tail your wife?"

He smiled again. "When you put it that way, it sounds sleazy. Anne's leaving for San Francisco day after tomorrow. She's an assistant administrator at St. Jacob's Medical Center and says she's attending a conference on online invoicing; maybe she is. I know there's a conference, because I checked. What I haven't been able to check on is what else she has in mind. I didn't get where I am by ignoring my instincts. There's someone, I'm sure of it. What I need is proof."

"I'm an artist, not a detective."

"That's the point. I can see from your work you're a close observer. It's just what the job calls for. And you need money. That means you won't gouge me by dragging it out, the way a professional might; if I fired him for that, he'd just move on to his next mark and leave me hanging. If you dump airtight leads in his lap, he can finish the job without an excuse to get fancy."

Cooke rose. "Thanks for seeing me. I'm not qualified to peek through keyholes."

"The pay's ten thousand up front. Another ten thousand when the job's done, plus a bonus of ten grand if the evidence is rock-solid either way—who knows, even I can be wrong sometimes. All expenses paid, of course. I can't have someone who represents me slumming it in a Motel Six."

He sat down again. He felt like checking his own pulse.

"I don't know much about these things," he said, "but it seems to me you're spending a lot more to avoid being gouged than you would if you *were* gouged, and to an amateur. Is there something I'm missing?"

Plevin spread his hands. They were the things to watch, not his expression. They spoke five words to his one. "I don't like to give up more information than I have to," he said. "It wastes time and gives ammunition to the enemy. Which is what this is about. I want eyes-on before I hire a professional. It'll be his job to gather proof that will hold up in divorce court. I'm a public figure. I won't risk some motherfucker splashing details of my private life all over the tabloids—my own competitors, for Christ's sake—until I'm sure."

"What airline? And do you have a preference in auto rentals?"

"You'll be driving the whole way. Anne hates flying."

"That's over two thousand miles!"

"Two thousand one hundred and forty-six. I googled it."

The artist shook his head. "My car—"

"It's a piece of shit. I saw you pull up." He leaned back farther, fished in a pants pocket, and tossed a key onto the desk—what they called a key now, a black fob containing a microchip that controlled the ignition. "This year's Corolla—a reliable model, and so popular it's damn near invisible. It's in the parking lot. Go ahead, take it for a spin. If you like it, it's yours. Provided you take the job."

CHAPTER 3

THE TOYOTA MADE his car look like a leaky old rowboat.

It was backed into a space with Todd Plevin's name stenciled on the curb, a machine with the profile of a Stealth fighter jet. The finish was a glistening slate blue, the consumer's color of choice that year, making it practically fade into the scenery along with millions of its sisters.

He got in and was seduced. The cushy black interior, with lumbar support built into the seats, smelled like a swanky luggage shop. The display of dials, gauges, and monitors in the dash made him light-headed. It took him a few minutes to figure out how to start it—with the "key" in his pocket!—and when he slid it into Drive and touched the accelerator, the car leapt forward with a lunge he felt in his testicles.

He'd stepped out Aspectus's door still uncertain whether to accept Plevin's incredible offer; by the time he'd driven around the block his mind was made up.

He had just one reservation, but it was major.

Plevin was waiting on the sidewalk in front of his private space, hands in pockets as before. He stepped up to the car before Cooke could get out, forcing him to slide down the window to ask the question.

"What if I lose her?"

"You won't. Anne made all her hotel reservations on her credit card account. I'll give you a copy."

"What if she changes them?"

The sinister smile crawled back onto the media chief's face. He leaned in through the window and pointed at a square of glass in the crowded dashboard, between the monitors connected to the backup cameras. Unlike them, it was dark. "Push that button."

Actually it was a flat circle. Cooke touched it and the glass lit up, showing a cartoonish car on a stylized highway, poised to drive away from the viewer.

"It's an after-factory option. I had my IT guy whip it up. It's programmed to pick up the homing device he installed in Anne's car, although he doesn't know it's hers. He thinks I'm making a road test. This gizmo feeds you the information in the form of directions, just like GPS. Its range is twenty miles. Japan's ten years behind this technology. I told my guy if it passes the test we'll split the take. It's a cinch for a military grant."

A plucky young intern drove Cooke's old bucket of bolts to his place, parked next to him, waved, and took off at a brisk walk to catch a cab. Cooke sat in the Toyota, looking at the computer printout Plevin had given him. His bank balance was now ten thousand three hundred and sixteen dollars.

He got up several times during the night to peer out the window overlooking the parking lot. Each time he was sure the car wouldn't be there, just his creaky old lemon, and that he'd dreamed the whole thing.

When finally he did dream, it was in abstract: bright colors, earth tones, and pastels; shapes, jagged and curved, working in union and at odds, signifying anything or nothing, and when nothing, saying something about the observer who saw nothing.

Awake finally, Dennis Cooke remembered his attempts at the form; they were early, too early. He wasn't ready. To paint like Picasso and Miró and Pollock, you had first to learn to paint like Rembrandt.

He sat up in his Murphy bed, a fixture of the apartment, an efficiency flat on the top floor of a building that was old enough to be on the Register of Historic Places, but lacked both history and charm. Although the rent was moderate, it posed a challenge some months. He'd taken it over cheaper places for its north light, the artist's best friend.

They were tarring the roof. The *swish-swish* of the push brooms and the slurp of the viscous stuff they were spreading explained his dream. It sounded like brushstrokes.

The workers had finished by the time he got out of the shower. While shaving he tried to bring up the particulars of his dream. There had been a theme of some kind, a concept that might be turned into a painting, but as usual it deteriorated into nonsense when the rest of his brain cells lit up. He thought instead of the job he'd signed on for. It was bizarre—not just because of the circumstances, but because it gave him an eerie sense of déjà vu. By the time he rinsed off and dressed, he had a good idea what it was.

Back in the studio he looked at his latest project, an acrylic of a woman putting on her lipstick in front of a mirror—frankly a rip-off of Edward Hopper he hoped to sell to a publisher specializing in reprints of 1950s detective stories. It would make a striking cover.

That's your problem, Dennis, he thought. *All you can do is retreads. You'll never be an original if you don't learn how to think in the abstract.*

The woman on the canvas was a knockout on the scale of an erotic dream, a trim raven-haired wicked goddess with scarlet lips, wearing only a black silk slip through which the sunlight shone. He'd manufactured her out of his imagination. Even if he could afford to hire a model, he would never find one to match his fantasy.

Yesterday had changed all that.

He took out his wallet and looked at the photo Todd Plevin had given him of his wife, Anne, a full-length color shot of her in a yellow sundress, standing in front of a tree in Lincoln Park: trim figure, glistening black hair, red lips. He felt his ears burn; all his life a telltale sign that his libido was in overdrive. She and his imaginary model might have been twins. Was that an omen, and was it good or bad?

CHAPTER 4

THE HOUSE ON Lake Shore Drive was a Frank Lloyd Wright design—an original, Cooke supposed—that looked like a wooden building block set on top of another, cedar-sided and with a huge picture window. Morning sunlight turned the glass into polished steel, painful to look at.

Anne Plevin's plan was to be on the road by 9 a.m. Cooke had been parked on the street across from the house since eight. Twice a Chicago P.D. blue-and-white had cruised past. Both times he'd slid down in the seat out of sight in case they thought he was casing the neighborhood.

In a way, that's just what he was doing, and it made him feel as guilty as if he were plotting to break in and steal her jewelry. With his stash of snacks for the trip, bottled water, and cash, he was all set for making a getaway.

He started his motor and activated the tracking device as he'd been instructed. The small square screen came to life. A bright-green dot appeared, flashing on and off, just off the left front fender of the tiny car, which represented his own ride. The angle perfectly replicated the position of the garage standing apart from the house in relation to the Toyota. He switched off the monitor and killed the ignition; it was a fairly frosty morning in early spring and he didn't want any telltale exhaust coming from the tailpipe.

At 8:52, a side door opened and the woman from the photo came out, carrying an overnight bag and a train case, a clutch purse under one arm, followed closely by Todd Plevin, lugging a large tan leather suitcase that matched the rest of her baggage. Anne wore a smart, comfortable-looking travel suit with a knee-length skirt and low heels. The suit was a subdued shade of yellow. In person she was even more striking than in her picture, and bore a close enough resemblance to the woman in Cooke's unfinished painting to pass as her sister. She walked with a grace of movement that suited a beautiful woman entering a ballroom in evening dress.

The couple entered the garage through another side door. A minute later, Plevin came out and stood facing the street, characteristically with his hands in his pockets. He made no indication that he saw the Toyota.

Cool customer.

One of the four lift doors slid up and a new Lexus rolled out of the garage, Anne at the wheel. The car had been described to him. Yellow seemed to be her favorite color. Plevin gave Anne an affectionate-looking wave. She didn't wave back. That didn't have to mean anything; she might not have noticed, or been the demonstrative type.

She turned left at the end of the concrete driveway. Cooke started up and activated the tracking device, which was moving ahead of the cartoon car like a blip on a radar screen. He waited until she was several car-lengths ahead, then pulled out into the street. His heart pounded in his ears; he felt a flutter in his stomach. Somehow, until that moment, he didn't believe the thing would happen.

He didn't see if Plevin went back into the house or into the garage to use his own car. He was too busy hoping not to lose sight of his quarry right at the start; the electronic gizmo, as Plevin called it, was experimental after all. It might not perform as promised.

The weather warmed as they headed for the western suburbs. He turned down the heater (he couldn't bring himself to call it "adjusting the climate"), thought of testing the sound system, but reconsidered, at least until they were both on the freeway and he didn't have to concentrate on turns.

As he drove, hearing the light steady reassuring beep of the tracker, his pulse slowed and his stomach settled. Driving had always soothed him, so long as the wheel belonged to a reliable machine. When it did, he often took a break from his easel and his drawing board to tool deep into the countryside. He went where the mood took him, following two-lane blacktops and gravel roads, admiring Wyeth barns, Monet ponds, Grandma Moses fences, and American colonial houses that had inspired artists for two centuries. They cried out for bold acrylics, soft pastels, watercolors, charcoal, brushstrokes either bold and slashing or delicate and patient.

Well, this wasn't rural, but the rowhouses and Victorian fretwork of the residential streets, and Walmarts and mom-and-pop stores in the business sections, had their points. Every now and then a bright mural would come into view, stretching the length of a cinderblock wall, to remind him both that he wasn't the only man left who worked from scratch using traditional tools and that the competition was fierce.

Suddenly he remembered to look at the dashboard. The green dot had stopped moving. How long had that been the case, while he let himself think he was on just another quest for inspiration? He looked up through the windshield, scanned the windows. There was the yellow Lexus, parked at a gas pump belonging to a convenience store. He'd almost passed it. He braked with a chirp. Another set of tires shrieked, a horn blasted. The car behind him filled the rearview mirror, with an angry red face behind the wheel.

Cooke lifted a hand in a sign of apology and swung into the station. Anne wasn't in her car or pumping gas. He pulled into a slot next to the building, got out, and strolled inside. Or tried to stroll. He was sure he looked like a man hobbling on an artificial leg, one not his size.

He opened the door. A chime rang. The building was a sprawl with rows of snacks, refrigerated goods behind glass, car maintenance products, knickknacks, and a line waiting in front of the cash register. She wasn't in it. Cooke wandered the room. There was no sign of her. Panic seized his stomach. Had he missed her outside? She might be in her car and back on the road. A fancy gadget couldn't compensate for stupidity. If he'd managed to lose her three miles from home...

But, no. He looked out the front plate-glass window and saw it was there at the pump, still vacant. Just then a door swung open in a short hallway with a RESTROOMS sign pointing to it and she came out of the women's, a tall slender brunette who turned both male and female heads at the checkout. Quickly he turned away, taking sudden interest in a cat food display, while she passed behind him and outside.

He went out quickly. She was concentrating on filling her tank and didn't glance his way as he got into his car.

In five minutes they were back on the road, separated by two other vehicles, and headed toward I-55. The adventure picked up speed.

PART 2

Merge

CHAPTER 5

SOMETHING MADE A burring noise. A light was glowing on the console. A warning buzz? Of what? He touched the panel. The light went off and the noise stopped.

"How's it going, Ace?"

He swerved onto the shoulder. His tires buzzed on the rumble strips. He yanked the wheel left, bumped back up over the edge of the pavement, overcompensated, fought to stay in his lane, succeeded at last. A set of air brakes hissed, so close he felt the wind up his spine. He could have reached out his window and touched the truck as it thundered past.

Cooke filled his lungs, emptied them slowly as his pulse returned to normal. He'd thought the voice was coming from the back seat, that he'd picked up a stowaway.

Then he looked down at the cockpit array of gauges, monitors, and dials, and realized he had a satellite connection. The voice was Todd Plevin's.

"Um, so far so good." He spoke loudly, like an idiot talking to a foreigner. Did he have to push a button or what?

Plevin chuckled. "Don't yell. It's Bluetooth, not a crank job. How you making out with all the bells and whistles?"

"I might have them down pat by the time I get to San Francisco."

"Tracking okay?"

"Perfect. We're on the freeway. She's five cars ahead."

"Terrific. I'm gonna make my IT guy as rich as me. Just looking in. I won't be butting in all the time. Just say 'Call Plevin' if you need to report." There was an almost inaudible click and Cooke was alone again.

They drove nonstop for thirty miles; apparently Anne had a stronger bladder than his ex-wife's. He opened a bag of chips, more for the salt than anything else, to help retain fluid; if he hit the water bottle too often he might find out just how his plumbing stacked up against hers.

Just as he thought that, her right turn signal came on and she pulled into a rest stop. He did the same.

The building, a low cantilevered structure of steel and concrete, looked new. The asphalt lot was a rich, syrupy black with bright yellow lines separating the spaces and no cracks. He parked a few spaces away from the Lexus, made a quick trip to the men's room, and trotted back out. She emerged minutes later in shirtsleeves. She'd shucked the blazer somewhere along the route.

Reaching for her door handle, she suddenly looked across her car roof, straight at Cooke.

He stiffened, held his breath. Had she recognized the Toyota? If she'd noticed it an hour ago sitting across the street from her house, and spotted it again during the drive, how was she to suspect it was the same one? They'd passed dozens of identical models on the road, several the same color as his. She hadn't had a look at the rear-mounted license plate.

The sun was higher now, shining directly at his window. If the reflection was bright enough she wouldn't be able to see his face. Then again, she might have gotten a better look at him than he'd thought back at the convenience store, and seen him in the rest stop without his knowledge.

All this went through his mind in a half-second. That's as long as she spent looking his way. She slid behind the wheel, backed out, and headed toward the reentry lane, passing behind the Toyota. He couldn't risk pulling out so soon after she did. The wait of a few minutes was agonizing, but the tiny green dot on the dash moved steadily in the same direction it had from the start. Finally he reentered the freeway, tapping his fingers on the wheel until he saw the yellow Lexus half a dozen cars ahead. A car behind him glided into the fast lane and passed: a brand new Toyota Corolla, same color as his. His breathing returned to normal. The camouflage was holding up.

He'd just have to make sure she didn't see him face-to-face.

CHAPTER 6

ILLINOIS WAS A big state; he'd known that in theory, but had never traversed it in a lump. Much of it lay between Cooke, Anne, and the interchange onto I-70 West, which would be their home for most of the route.

He had the designers in Tokyo to thank for removing boredom from the equation of a long drive.

They seemed to have thought of everything: internet access, satellite and analog radio, climate control, Bluetooth (wish he'd known *that* before Plevin's disembodied voice nearly put him in a ditch), a sexy-sounding female on the factory GPS (he immediately named her Lola)—and those were just the features he'd discovered. For all he knew there might be a soft ice cream dispenser and hidden robotic arms to slip him into a superhero suit. He made a mental note to take the owner's manual with him when he checked into Anne's hotel and study up on it.

After a hundred miles, though, he realized that these luxuries could work in the opposite direction and become monotonous. Manually operating a stereo system at least broke up the rhythm, like getting up to change channels on TV as opposed to exercising only his thumb on a remote. Being able to stream thousands of songs from all genres automatically had a soporific effect. He switched to regular AM/FM radio, bobbed his head to jazz, shouted lyrics along with Mick, made snide remarks to blowhard talk-show hosts, listened soberly to national news. In addition, he enjoyed the experience most millennials would never know: passing out of range of one frequency and into another, hearing the broadcast of a Cubs game dissolving into a Royals play-by-play, listening to it grow stronger as he neared the state line. A music station would morph into a PBS panel, country and western into salsa, a live presidential press conference into a hip-hop duet, an old-time radio drama into static.

There was a painting in that; but how to transmute an audio phenomenon into the visual?

Attaboy, Dennis: Keep thinking constructively. Daydreaming could be as bad as texting while driving or falling asleep at the wheel.

"Welcome to Missouri!"

He grinned. "Thanks, Lola." The same greeting sprang up on a sign on the shoulder, along with a silhouette of the state as it appeared on the map. St. Louis's Gateway Arch showed in the upper right corner of his windshield, catching the sun in Day-Glo, and directly ahead of him the dromedary span of the bridge over the Mississippi River. For the space of a few minutes, Dennis Cooke and Anne Plevin were in different states.

His tires sang on the bridge. There were boats on the great waterway, an image he'd seen only in pictures; he'd never been that far west. The sky was a scraped blue, but to the southwest a shelf of blue-black clouds threatened to cross the freeway in an hour or two.

Just for a change of pace—and curiosity—he cleared his throat and said, "Call the Hilton in Kansas City, Missouri."

A woman's voice confirmed his reservation, asked when he expected to arrive.

A mile marker appeared. "About three hours."

"Your room will be ready."

Plevin had said Anne had included all her hotel room numbers on the itinerary she'd given him. She was in the habit of reserving certain rooms, corner suites on the third floor. It was a kind of good-luck totem. He'd arranged for Cooke to occupy suites with connecting doors.

"I don't get it," the artist had replied. "If she's having an affair, why would she give you so much information?"

"It's a blind, a double play. She knows my feelings about professional detectives, so she thinks I won't send anyone to check up on her. It's supposed to reassure me she's faithful. That's what made me suspicious in the first place."

Cooke was conflicted about his opinion of Plevin. He didn't like the man, that was certain. At the same time he admired him for having built an empire from the ground up, while disapproving of his borderline business methods. Stir into that mix Cooke's personal envy for his youthful success, and for the ease with which Plevin was able to think in the abstract.

"I'm sorry," Lola said. "I didn't quite get that."

He flinched and turned her off. He hadn't realized he'd spoken his thoughts aloud. Some detective he was.

CHAPTER 7

THE RAIN CAME bang on schedule, and with a bang. The sky turned black as a cast-iron skillet and even the windshield wipers connected to the miraculous Toyota couldn't keep up with the downpour. An hour east of Columbia, Cooke pulled over onto the shoulder behind a line of cars and trucks whose drivers had already made that move. He sat gripping the wheel tightly while the car rocked on its chassis, whipped by a forty-mile-an-hour gale. At least, he thought, Anne would have been forced to wait it out, too, unless her head start allowed her to outrun the deluge.

"Idiot!" He'd forgotten the little green dot. It had stopped moving. She was as stranded as he was.

Aloud, he asked for information on the storm in Missouri.

Technology complied. In a flash he knew the exact wind velocity, the track of the storm, and National Weather Service warnings, complete with an estimate on when it would clear the area. The entire state was under a tornado watch. So now he had to worry about twisters.

For twenty minutes he listened to weather reports on the radio; they were monotonously pessimistic. Now and then the rain slackened briefly. During those intervals he memorized the bumper and window stickers attached to the pickup parked in front of him, diverted himself by rearranging the letters to form interesting sentences, wondered what kind of person would stick a decal on his back window showing a man peeing on the Chevrolet emblem. Why should the owner care if somewhere in the world someone wasn't driving a Ford?

At last the rain let up enough for the vehicles to resume moving; but electric signs warned everyone to reduce speed, and for once it seemed everyone was in a mood to obey. As an orange sliver of sun appeared beneath the overcast, it became clear that Anne would put in somewhere for the night rather than drive all the way to Kansas City in a state of fatigue.

Well, the green dot continued to keep him informed, even when Anne pulled off at rest stations.

Which made him more acutely aware of the pressure on his bladder that had been mounting since his unscheduled stop.

He drove five miles before one of the blue rest-stop signs appeared, by which time he was hunched over the wheel, as if he could get there faster by pushing the car manually.

At the stop, he saw that he wasn't the only one in distress. He waited ten minutes at the end of a line of men fidgeting restlessly before he got into the bathroom, then in another line waiting for a urinal or a stall to become vacant. A little later he strolled out, practically whistling, but restrained himself at the sight of the longer line at the women's.

It was dark now. He and Anne Plevin had been driving for ten hours. The next time the blinker stopped moving, he was sure she was putting in for the night.

The signal got stronger the closer he got to its source, beeping louder and more rapidly. A sign informed him that there was lodging at the next exit. He took it, and the invention of Todd Plevin's in-house magician led him straight through a complex of hotels and motels to a sprawling, castlelike affair with a copper shield-shaped sign in front embedded in pink mortar. Its name was engraved on the shield: HAWTHORN ARMS. Not a chain he recognized; probably not a chain at all. Bright tulips, immaculately kept, flourished in oval beds lined with painted stones. The impression was one of palatial understatement, if such a combination was possible. How did she find these places, on the spur of the moment?

He turned into the asphalt driveway. Dennis Cooke and Anne Plevin were about to spend their first night under the same roof.

CHAPTER 8

"THE HAWTHORN?" TODD Plevin might have been sitting next to him in the front seat, his voice was that clear. "Yes. She stayed there once before, when she got a late start. Give me five minutes to make your reservation. Treat yourself to room service. You won't need to shadow her too close tonight. Even she's not clever enough to arrange a tryst on such short notice; unless he's local, which is unlikely. Just be sure to get up early and be waiting in your car when she checks out."

He waited ten minutes. He wanted to give her time to finish checking in. There was no solid reason to believe she'd recognize him, but he wasn't about to tempt fate.

He'd circled the lot, spotted her car parked in the valet section, and found a space on the opposite side of the building.

A doorman in a royal blue uniform let him into the lobby with a touch to his visor. It was large, with a vaulted roof, deep leather chairs, spiny dwarf trees in copper pots (hawthorns, he guessed), and a blue carpet that felt like moss under his feet. A tiny blonde in a silk blouse greeted him from behind the desk. His name struck an immediate chord. Smiling, she handed him his key card and asked if he needed help with his luggage. He was carrying only a small overnighter. He didn't want a bellman to overexert himself.

It was a fourth-floor suite; a relief. Despite Plevin's assurances that he needn't be too attentive that night, Cooke was afraid he'd book him on the third—Anne's preferred choice—from force of habit. All he needed to blow the whole deal was to run into her when he stepped off the elevator.

He hadn't mentioned his fears to Plevin. It was just a gut feeling, after all, not enough to risk being fired. His employer had the clout to force him to return his advance and the Corolla.

His suite was as luxurious as the lobby, with bowls of fresh flowers and a bottle of ritzy sparkling water. He sat down to open it and surf through three or four hundred channels on the sixty-inch plasma TV. The cushy suede love seat found every ache in his shoulders and caressed it with the skill of a Swedish masseuse.

After a while the whizzing images made his eyes burn. He turned off the set, put his head back against the cushion, and closed his eyes. When he opened them it was past midnight.

He was hungry as a wolf. He hadn't eaten, really eaten, since breakfast. Snacking on the road didn't count. But the directory on the writing desk told him room service closed at eleven. The bar was open, however, until two. Maybe they served nachos.

But talk about risk! Just because Anne had been driving all day didn't mean she wouldn't have the same idea.

Just then his stomach grumbled loudly. It was saying—no, yelling—*Feed me or I'll keep you awake all night!*

The Hawthorn Lounge, illuminated softly by the lights above the bar and electric candles on the tables, was plush and cozy. It was almost deserted at that hour on a weeknight. He scanned the scattered patrons lingering over their drinks and talking in low voices. No Anne.

A wooden bowl of pretzels beckoned from the bar. He climbed onto a stool and was munching away when the young bartender came over.

"Sorry, sir. Stove's off. No hot food."

He asked for a beer and more pretzels. They arrived simultaneously, the beer in a tall slim schooner.

Sipping, crunching, and watching his reflection in the smoked-glass mirror behind the display of bottles and glassware, he contemplated the strange, strange direction his life had taken, and so suddenly. Two days ago he'd fretted about the rent. Now he could afford to stay in five-star hotels like the Hawthorn on his own.

"Vodka tonic, please. No twist."

He jumped as if he'd been jabbed. Someone had slipped onto the adjoining stool while he was daydreaming.

The voice was a husky purr that made his ears burn at the tips. He'd felt that same sensation recently. Where?

Back home, looking at a picture of a woman posing in a yellow sundress in front of a tree.

He jerked his gaze from the mirror, down to his schooner of beer. *Don't look, Dennis. If you can't see her, maybe she can't see you.* It had worked with monsters under the bed when he was little.

"That's flattering. Girl takes a seat right next to a guy in an empty bar—she could sit anywhere, but she decides to sit here—and he doesn't even give her a glance."

He looked then. Their eyes met in the mirror. At close range and in person, she was even more striking than her double in his painting.

CHAPTER 9

THE BARTENDER BROUGHT her drink and drifted back to the other end of the bar. Cooke turned her way. She continued to look in the mirror. She had a clean profile, straight nose, round firm chin. Her hair was secured behind her ears with combs; still, it caught the muted overhead light and threw it back in blue haloes. Her skin was pale, almost translucent—in the age of sunlamps and weekends on the beach of Lake Michigan—but her most startling features were her eyelashes. They were long enough to cast shadows on her cheeks, and so far as he could tell they were natural.

"You don't have to stare that hard to remember me next time," she told his reflection. "These days everyone has a camera in his pocket."

She wore a pale-yellow top without sleeves, a dark skirt. Her legs were crossed, showing a bare knee. Her calves were smoothly defined. No jewelry showed, and if she had on makeup it wasn't discernible. The scent she wore was barely more noticeable, but it was there. It had an ethereal quality, like mist rising from blossoms alien to this plane.

Bluff it out. What've you got to lose? "I'm sorry if I was rude. You startled me. I didn't hear you come up."

She hadn't touched her drink. She opened the clutch in her lap, took something out and slid it between her lips. He wondered if he was expected to offer her a light, like a character in an old film, before no-smoking laws. Then she drew on it and blew a jet of bluish mist. It was an e-cigarette, feeding nicotine from a cartridge without need of flame. "That was some storm," she said.

"It was. It—" Too late. He'd given away the fact that they'd been traveling in the same direction and had both decided to put in at the same hotel, in the same city, in a gang of competing establishments.

But many motorists had been caught in the downpour; there was nothing suspicious in one or two of them checking into the Hawthorn Arms.

If only he hadn't stopped in midsentence. He'd exposed himself by checking his swing.

She lifted her glass then and sipped, toasting herself on her victory.

"I saw you in the convenience store just before I got on the freeway," she said, "and again at a rest stop. Could've been a coincidence. Not."

"I get that sometimes. I've got one of those faces."

"One of those cars too. It was parked across the street from my house this morning. Also the rest stop and now it's parked outside. It's a mild night. I took a walk." She drew a lungful of fog and let it out through her nostrils. Then she dropped the thing back into her handbag and turned to face him. "Who are you?"

He had nothing to lose by telling the truth. "I'm an artist."

"And I'm Julia Roberts."

He always carried drawing pencils in a pocket protector. He took one out, plucked a cocktail napkin off a stack of them on a saucer, and sketched her profile from memory. He pushed the napkin her way with the pencil.

She picked it up, looked at it. A dimple dented her cheek. "Guess that makes me *Pretty Woman*." She folded it, reopened her clutch, put it inside, and snapped it shut. That surprised him.

She drank again, propping an elbow on the bar. Her eyes when they met his were brushed silver with tiny gold flecks, in the light of the bar at least. "You're good, and I should know. I was Todd's art director before we married." She passed her hand across her body. "Anne Plevin; but I guess you know that."

He took the hand. Her grip was cool and assured. He gave it back. "Dennis Cooke."

"Snooping is a waste of your talent."

Grotesque now to keep playing dumb. Goodbye, bank account. *Sayonara,* Toyota. "So's starving," he said. "Anyone can draw a straight line with a mouse in his hand. I'm like those painters at the turn of the twentieth century, the ones the camera made obsolete. You could say I'm diversifying."

"Those painters found a way around the situation. They went where the shutterbugs couldn't go: Impressionism, Pointillism, Cubism. The only way Man Ray could match *Nude Descending a Staircase* on film would be to build his model out of Legos."

"They had abstract minds. I'm strictly representative."

"You're honest," she said, "I can tell. I see now why Todd hired you. He finally found someone he thinks he can trust. What's he paying you?"

He told her. She nodded, swiveled back toward the bar, rested her forearms on it. She looked down at them. "What if I topped his offer?"

Somehow that surprised him less than what she'd done with his drawing. He took a deep breath, let it out; he hadn't a toy cigarette to make the gesture seem romantic. "That would pose a conundrum. If I accepted, it would mean I'm betraying my boss and that

I'm not honest. You couldn't trust me. So it's just a test. You have no intention of making it good."

"That *is* a conundrum. What you just said proves you're straight as a ruler, but if I were to go by that and go ahead with the offer and you took it, you'd be double-crossing him, and that puts us back to square one."

He sipped his beer, pushed it away. It was warm. "Something like that."

She raised her chin and caught his eye again in the smoked glass behind the bar. "So you *can* think in the abstract."

The bartender cruised back their way. He pointed at the abandoned schooner. "Another, sir? That one's lost its head."

Cooke laughed. He wasn't sure why.

PART 3

Traffic Shift

CHAPTER 10

HE ORDERED ANOTHER beer, not because he wanted it but because the bar was emptying out and he'd spotted the bartender glancing from time to time at the neon advertising clock on the wall; if they weren't going to let him close up and go home, they might as well justify taking up space.

When it came, he went through the motions and took a sip. Surprisingly, the effervescence, crisp heady taste—and of course the alcohol content—lifted his mood. He looked at Anne. "Well, I was looking for a job when I found this one."

"I've never understood that line," she said. She had a fresh vodka tonic in front of her and was inhaling vapor again. He hadn't noticed when she'd taken the e-cigarette back out; and neither, he suspected, had she. It was that artificial twilight hour that took place only in saloons, with everyone in a dream state that had little to do with inebriation. "It sounds like it's supposed to be optimistic, but all it means is you're right back where you started."

"It's just something you say, like it's always darkest before the dawn."

"Not so dark as you think. You haven't failed, you know. In fact, you're closer on the trail than ever. On top of it, practically."

"If you're suggesting I pretend we never made contact and I just keep following you all the way to San Francisco, that's out."

"I'm not going to San Francisco."

She hadn't turned back his way. Her profile really was perfect. He was sorry she'd claimed the sketch he'd made of her; but then he could make a better one back in his room, while the memory was fresh. The unfinished painting in his studio was a lifeless thing now. He'd paint over it or, better yet, dump it. The real-life model he'd found to replace the one from his imagination cried out for virgin canvas.

"If you've changed your mind on my account," he said, "don't. It's none of my business now."

He kept his voice low, but that was just a show of discretion. The young man behind the bar stood at the far end, preoccupied with his cell phone.

"What makes you think I've changed my mind?"

"You said—"

"That paper trail I laid down for Todd was a blind. I've attended that damn conference three years in a row to establish a pattern he wouldn't question. I'm not cheating on him. Not in the way he thinks."

"You know he suspects you?"

"He thinks he's so smooth: Stephen Hawking's brain in Hugh Grant's head." The dimple surfaced again, then vanished. "He can play a wicked hand of poker when it comes to business, but in personal matters he's transparent as glass. Oh, I'm not saying I didn't lead him in that direction; the lunch date with a girlfriend that lasts three hours, saying I'm too tired to talk about it when I get home, whispering on the phone, then hanging up when he enters the room, that sort of bullshit. People buy into clichés. That's how they get to be clichés."

He returned his gaze to the mirror. She was less intimidating in one dimension. "What's the point of making him think you were committing adultery?"

"I read an article once about a man who ran an illegal marijuana-growing operation in his home. The police raided him from time to time, gave him thirty days once for possession. That satisfied them so much they never looked beyond the pot. If they'd lifted the flats of soil where it was planted, pulled up planks from the floor, they'd have found a dozen crates of AK-47s and enough ammunition to fight a war. Their small-time drug dealer had been running guns to the Third World for years."

She drank off the top of her cocktail, set it down, saw the e-cigarette in her hand, put it back in her purse. "He had a stroke and died. His landlord found the guns. Otherwise no one ever would have known except his customers. See, he used a lesser crime to cover up the greater one: an illegal front for an illegal operation."

"If you're confessing to a crime," he said, "I don't want to hear it. I've had my fill of intrigue. All I want to do is go back home and paint."

"If I weren't convinced you're an honest man who won't rat me out, I wouldn't be speaking to you at all. I'm saying I'm letting him think I'm giving him evidence to divorce me in order to give me time to divorce him."

CHAPTER 11

"YOU'RE GOING TO Vegas?"

"Reno. I feel sorry for the old place. It was the divorce capital of the world until the Strip muscled in on its territory. I figured by the time he found out I never got to California I'd have all the papers filed."

"Yes, but a quickie divorce won't get you a settlement. Do you know how much you're giving up?"

"To the penny. I'm a hospital administrator, you know. Half the work is math." She took her glass between her palms and rotated it in its wet circle on the bar, looking down at it as if it were a crystal ball. "I make good money and I've got job security. Getting out of this marriage in a jiffy's worth sacrificing the rest."

"It's that bad?"

"Don't get me wrong. Todd's never abused me in the usual sense of the term. He's a neglecter; *distant* is the usual description. We both put in long hours at work, but I used to take pains to clear space for us as a couple. He never did. It took me seven years to come to the conclusion that I was the only one who was investing in the relationship. Talk about your dot-com bubble! Seven years. Funny, I don't remember breaking any mirrors." The dimple reappeared, but was gone so quickly it might never have been there in the first place.

"Why the cloak-and-dagger?" he said. "Plevin's chief concern is the sleazy publicity where infidelity's involved. It seems to me he'd be relieved it isn't. He'd welcome the quiet way you want to go about it."

"Too chancy. I said he's transparent, not predictable. Otherwise he'd never have made it to the top. Better to push the thing through and dump it in his lap tied up with a bow."

Suddenly she turned her head and looked at him. The gold flecks in her eyes swam in a glistening film. "How old are you?"

"Thirty-five."

"I'm thirty-one; three years older than Todd. That's still time to make a baby."

His ears got hot again.

She laughed, opening her mouth wide and filling the room with the guttural sound. The bartender looked up from his phone, startled.

She paid him no attention. "I didn't mean with *you,* super-stud! I was just curious; you look your age, but you seem younger. I guess that's the wide-eyed artist in you. I was talking about my biological clock. See, I have to deduct the amount of time it'll take to find the right man, convince him he'd make a good father, and get to begettin'. I don't have any of it to waste waiting for you to wake up to what a bad old world this is; no offense, Rembrandt. I was giving myself a pep talk."

He gulped cold beer. He could almost hear his blush hissing when it hit the drink. "I didn't think that was a thing anymore. Medical science and all."

"Spin my eggs on a platter and mix up little Annie or Andy in a test tube? No, thanks. I'm not escaping from one antiseptic lab just to get into another. I'm going to do it the old-fashioned way. I don't even intend to shop online. What kind of story would that make when our friends ask us how we met?"

"Well, good luck."

"Don't be such a grouch. Todd's a great white in the shark tank, but he never goes back on his word. He told you you'd keep the money and the car. You can take that to the bank. Literally."

He raised a smile. "Good luck anyway. I mean that."

"I think you do." She was looking at him with something on her face that might have been surprise. "I wonder why."

"We artists are sensitive types. This is the first time we've been within twenty feet of each other—sometimes it's been almost twenty miles—but it seems like it's been all day, which in a way it has. It's like I know you better than I knew my ex-wife, and we were together three years." Hastily he added, "Don't read anything into that."

"I won't, but I appreciate it. So you're divorced."

"Yes, and before you ask, it was my fault."

"I don't believe that."

"Why, because I'm a nice guy? Sensitive and nice don't always mean the same thing."

"No. Because it's never just one person's fault. I can't blame everything on Todd. He's never once looked at another woman, unless it was to acquire her company. Believe me, he's had opportunities, a fellow with his looks and portfolio. If he has a mistress, it's Aspectus. I could have worked harder to change that, but I was too busy working on my own career. That's one of the reasons I'm not going to pick his pocket."

They finished their drinks in silence. He slid off his stool and put out his hand. "Drive carefully."

She took it; held it. She met his gaze. "What are you going to tell him?"

"That when I got up tomorrow, you'd already left. Maybe you suspected something and took off early. You were more than twenty miles down the road and beyond range of the homing device, and when I got to the Kansas City Hilton I found out you never checked in."

She let go, shaking her head. "I'll text him I'm stopping there early to take a break from driving, which is true. Otherwise I'd have to put in somewhere else tomorrow night, and he'd have to call you and inform you of the change in schedule; less complicated for a newbie like you. Then I'll take 29 North and switch to 80 West to Reno. Why let him think you lost me after one day?"

"I don't know. It seems like I'm taking advantage, finagling another night in a luxury hotel on his dime, and under false pretenses."

"My God. You're not only honest, you're honest to a fault."

"Is that so unusual?"

"Dennis—is it okay if I call you Dennis?"

"I'm surprised it took you this long to ask. Yes."

"Dennis, in my world, it's as rare as lawyers in heaven."

CHAPTER 12

THE MATTRESS WAS just the right combination of firm and soft, and the thread count in the sheets had been calculated as if by Euclid, but he never got under deep enough to dream. When he closed his eyes, Anne Plevin's perfect profile appeared inside the lids, as if projected from a lens inside his head.

At dawn he gave up. He stood a long time under the excellent shower head, dried himself with a plush towel, and shaved slowly and carefully, using the magnifying mirror on its scissors extender and the army of toiletries on the sink. Stretched out on the bed in a terry robe, he watched an inane early-morning talk show on TV, checking his watch every few minutes until seven o'clock, when room service opened. Breakfast was worth the wait; he lingered over it. He wasn't luxuriating in the Hawthorn's appointments so much as giving Anne time to get down the road.

He was ashamed to face her. She'd talked him into entering a conspiracy to defraud his employer; and it hadn't taken much talking. After all that conversation about his trustworthiness, he'd rolled over on his back like a naughty puppy. While trying to sleep he'd told himself he was sympathetic to her situation, that was why, but he hadn't made a convincing case. Over the last of his coffee he made a decision: confess everything to Plevin, take his punishment, and walk away. Let Mr. Aspectus revoke his reward. Cooke hadn't really believed Anne when she said that wouldn't happen. In that moment, he hoped he was right. To return to poverty would be his penance for violating Plevin's trust.

He dressed quickly, eager now to escape that gilded cage. A great burden had lifted from his shoulders, like a miserable fog in the warmth from the sun. When the day clerk at the desk asked him if he'd enjoyed his stay, he said, "Very much," and meant it.

When he started the Toyota and activated the tracking device, the blip did not appear. Only yesterday that would have thrown him into a panic, but now he saw it as confirmation that he'd acted wisely. Anne had risen early as expected and was already more than twenty miles down the road. Reentering the interstate, he accelerated to the speed limit; there was some shred of loyalty in taking steps to retrieve the signal. That's what he'd have done if he were still acting in good faith.

After an hour, signs began to inform him of the dining and accommodations Kansas City had to offer, the Hilton among them; by then the green dot had reappeared, the beep growing stronger and more rapid as he entered the city limits. He took the Hilton exit. The big rectangular building was visible from the ramp. What it lacked in the unique design of the Hawthorn Arms it made up for in the familiar architecture of a major chain with all the creature comforts reassuringly in place.

He circled the building, found the Lexus parked behind it, then continued around to the canopy above the main entrance. In the spacious lobby he waited while another guest finished checking out, then gave his name to the clerk, who found his reservation in the computer. "The room's not ready, yet, sir. Can you wait?"

"Sure. Did Anne Plevin manage to check in?"

He had no reason to ask the question, other than to prove to himself that he didn't care if it got back to Todd.

"We know Mrs. Plevin. She hasn't been in yet."

He'd taken a good look at her car. It was unoccupied. She'd probably assumed it was too early to claim a room and was waiting somewhere.

"Where's your dining room?"

"Just past the elevators, but it doesn't open again until lunch."

"Is there a restaurant nearby? Or a store?"

"Not unless you're up for a hike. There's a Walmart and some fast-food places, but they're all a good ten-minute drive."

Cooke thought of the gift shop. It was unoccupied except for a female clerk behind the counter. He returned to his car and drove back around to the rear of the building. The Lexus was still there. He parked next to it, got out, confirmed the number on the license plate, and leaned against a window with his hands cupped around his eyes. No one was in it. Anne's clutch purse lay on the front passenger's seat. Her leather train case and matching overnight bag were in back.

He went back inside and found the clerk stacking complimentary newspapers on the end of the desk.

"Sorry to bother you again," Cooke said. "Are you sure Anne Plevin hasn't checked in?"

The clerk looked up, frowned. "Sir. Every guest here is entitled to the same courtesy as all the rest. I can't see why this one should attract so much attention."

"What do you mean?"

"Yesterday a guest came to the desk at least five times to ask the same question you did, about the same guest. By the fifth time, we'd received notice from Mrs. Plevin that she was delayed and wouldn't be here until this morning. I told him that, but instead of thanking me he was quite rude. Frankly I was glad when he checked out this morning."

"What was his name?"

"I can't tell you that. It's the policy of Hilton to protect the privacy of our guests."

Cooke chewed the inside of his cheek, in lieu of chewing the clerk's impassive face. "Look at mine."

"Sir?"

He repeated it, and his name. "I included the model of the car I'm driving and the license plate. Look up the number of the Illinois DMV and ask who the car was originally registered to. I'm sure you'll recognize the name—and understand the scope of his influence. I'll wait over there while you make the call." He tilted his head toward an arrangement of deep suede leather chairs in the lobby.

The clerk opened his mouth as if to protest, then shut it and lifted the handset from a console beside his computer. Cooke drew a newspaper off the top of the stack and carried it over to a chair.

It was *America Now,* the paper Plevin had rescued from bankruptcy and placed in every hotel chain in the US. Opening it, he made sure the masthead on the front page was visible to the man behind the desk. He would know who owned it.

Cooke wondered if he'd been had. Anne's story had been convincing, and of course he was predisposed to accept it, given the effect she had on him. Knowing her car contained a homing device, she'd make arrangements for a replacement, probably a rental, abandon the Lexus, and meet up with her lover. That would explain the man's frustration when she'd failed to check in yesterday. The Hilton had been their place of liaison all along, the Reno divorce a blind to put Cooke off his guard. He'd proven a prize ass, unworthy of compensation.

But he could redeem himself by presenting Todd Plevin with his rival's name, giving him ammunition to place in the hands of a professional detective. Anne would get her divorce, whether she wanted it or not.

The clerk spent some minutes murmuring into the receiver. Then he replaced the handset as carefully as if it were made of fine crystal. He turned from the desk, opened a file drawer, and thumbed through the folders. Turning back, he caught Cooke's eye over the top of the newspaper. He had a sheet in his hand.

CHAPTER 13

HE SAT BEHIND the wheel twenty minutes, trying to dredge up the courage to do the only thing that could be done. Finally he called Todd Plevin.

The media titan had not gotten as far as he had without instincts. There was no arrangement in place for his man in surveillance to check in unless something had gone astray. His greeting sounded cautious.

Once again, Cooke had been holding his breath without realizing it. He let it out, and reported Anne's disappearance in the rush of exhalation, with no breaks between the words. It was like a little boy confessing to a broken window in one gust, to get it over with before he lost his nerve.

He said nothing about their meeting in the bar. The story she'd fed him was a blind, to throw him off the trail; there was no use in repeating it, and he was afraid of the reaction if he found out they'd made contact and he'd kept the information to himself. A man in Plevin's position was capable of destroying a disgraced employee just for spite.

Silence on the other end. Drops of sweat prickled along his hairline. But when the response came it was deadly calm.

"What else?"

That part at least was easy. "The desk clerk told me a guest pestered him all last night asking if your wife had checked in. Apparently he was expecting her to arrive on time. He hadn't thought of the storm delay."

"Tell me you got his name."

The paper on which he'd recorded the information from the registration sheet rattled in his hand; it was shaking so badly the writing was a blur. He used his other hand to steady it. "George DeWitt."

"I don't know him. How'd he pay for his room, credit card or cash?"

"Cash."

"What I thought. Nobody does that today unless he doesn't want to be traced. George DeWitt my ass. Anything else?"

"Just his license number." He reported it. It was a California plate.

"Another phony."

"Maybe not. The clerk said the chain's cracking down on nonguests who take advantage of the free parking. Security makes regular rounds, jotting down plate numbers so the personnel can check them against the registration. Any that don't match are towed."

"Well, it's something. I've got contacts in the California Highway Patrol. I'll have them run it."

"Should I wait here?"

Another silence, more brief this time. "No. Chances are they're headed to California. Stick with the plan. Tracking's out, but the farther we get you down the road the better. If it's a wild goose chase—well, that's it."

Cooke was anything but relieved. He'd half-hoped the thing was at an end, even if it meant surrendering the money and the car. "I'm sorry, Mr. Plevin."

"No reason. If I didn't suspect she and her gigolo would hook up so soon, how could you? I'll let you know what I find out." The line went dead.

He sat still five minutes more. He wasn't sure whether he was waiting for his nerves to settle enough to trust his driving or to give Anne and her lover ample time to escape pursuit. Part of him was ready to go into the tank, blow the deal once and for all, and go back home to his unsteady life. Better the devil you know.

He caught his eyes in the rearview mirror. *Stop kidding yourself, Dennis. You won't do that. Not everything she said was a lie. She got your number: honest to a fault.* He touched the starter button. The patented Dynamic Force engine leapt to life with a rumble he felt in the soles of his feet.

"Welcome to Kansas!"

He sent Lola packing with a flick of the finger. She was too perky for his mood.

After a minute he thought about turning her back on. The silence inside the car was oppressive. Its airtight construction sealed out all but the most neglected muffler or heavy truck towing tons of coiled steel. He missed the steady beep of the tracking device; he hadn't realized how much he'd come to depend on its reassuring presence. He powered down the window on the passenger's side, but the sucking noise the wind made lacerated his eardrums. He slid it back up.

Cooke was on his third state. He'd managed to blow his assignment in just two.

Cruise Control locked him in at seventy—seventy on I-70—sparing him the effort of maintaining pressure on the accelerator and allowing him to concentrate on his thoughts.

In retrospect, the Reno story seemed so implausible he wondered if he was just an airheaded paint slinger, unfit for the rugged realities of the world. Or maybe he was just an over-age teenager, letting his hormones make his decisions. A divorced man in his middle years should have experience enough not to put his faith into a husky voice, a bare knee, a spill of glistening black hair, brushed-silver eyes with specks of gold in them. She was an image intended only for canvas, same as a bowl of fruit or a piece of pottery. He'd painted nudes using live models and thought only of making sufficient progress before he lost the light.

The phone made its burring noise.

"Son of a bitch!"

He almost swerved into another lane. The driver of a Greyhound bus that was passing him leaned on his air horn. He'd never heard Plevin raise his voice before; it was as if he'd been reading Cooke's own mind. At that moment they had reached the same conclusion regarding the artist's character. Had his employer discovered that he'd been holding out on him?

"I'm sorry, sir. I—"

"Not you. I just got off the phone with Sacramento. That license plate number belongs to a 2018 Impala registered to Philip Mapes."

"I never—"

"There's no reason you should have. I've been flying solo since before you heard of *me*. The bastard was my business partner."

CHAPTER 14

AS PLEVIN TOLD it, he and Philip Mapes had launched their business from their dorm room at the University of Illinois before they were twenty-one. Two years later, with Aspectus on the Fortune 500 list, Plevin called for a secret audit of the books and discovered that his partner had embezzled almost three quarters of a million dollars from the firm.

"I offered Phil a sweetheart deal," he said. "Return the money, surrender your partnership, and I won't press charges."

"Did he agree?" Cooke had pulled into a rest stop in order to concentrate. The sun was bright and the pavement was dry; no trace remained of last night's rainstorm.

"Depends on your definition of *agree*. Did Sonny Liston *agree* to hand over the heavyweight championship to Ali? But Mapes had no reason to squawk. I even promised to keep our stockholders in the dark. That way if he wanted to climb back into the ring somewhere else there wouldn't be a cloud of suspicion hanging over his head. Generous? Fuckin' A. But I wanted it all dead and gone.

"I got every penny back. That almost never happens. These crooks usually splash it around: ritzy condos, sports cars, women, the track. Guess the asshole thought if he didn't touch it, just let it sit in a safe deposit box for a while, the heat would die down eventually and he could grab it and go. So I was able to cover the shortfall without a whisper of scandal, and saved the couple of million it would've taken to buy him out to boot. Win-win."

"What became of him?"

"Apparently he's fucking my wife."

"Does she know his history?"

"He was out of the picture before I met her. I didn't see any reason to dig it all back up. Now I do. I knew the cocksucker was a crook but I never dreamed he'd sink this low just to get back at me. If I'd told Anne, she wouldn't have given him the time of day. She'd have picked someone else. She may be an adulteress, but she's not cruel."

"Do you want me to keep going?"

"Yes. I'm keeping all your hotel reservations except San Francisco. Mapes is living in LA, or was living there when he registered the Impala. I'll book you in a hotel there and let you know which one. I'll give you his address when you get there."

"What if they go someplace else?"

"Then you're off the hook. Job's done. I'll put a professional on it. I'm still hoping you'll be able to catch them red-handed."

Suddenly Plevin chuckled, a nasty sound. "I thought that last deal I swung with Mapes was the transaction of a lifetime. Wait'll I offer the same to Anne: no settlement, no alimony, and I won't have Lover Boy prosecuted for violation of the Mann Act. Let 'em try to pick up the pieces when he's a registered sex offender and she's Public Slut Number One."

Cooke held his tongue, a near thing. He'd been about to call a multimillionaire who was capable of ruining his life a vindictive son of a bitch. Instead he said, "I don't know what use I'll be. I don't have any experience with peeking through windows of private homes, and I don't intend to gain any."

"Nothing so sleazy. Just seeing them together, going into or out of the house, and I'll tell them there's a witness who can blast her out of divorce court."

Cooke's heart gave a lurch. "You want me to *testify*?"

"It'll never get that far, promise you that. Okay, get back on the road." Plevin rang off.

Putting the car in gear, Cooke wondered what the man would say if he told him what Anne had said, about not wanting any of her husband's fortune if she could get away from the marriage clean. Falsehood that it was, it might wipe that smirk from his voice, if only for a minute.

PART 4

Crossover

CHAPTER 15

A GRIZZLED MOUNTAIN man in buckskins and a beard carrying a big-bore rifle loomed over the freeway on a billboard advertising the Kansas State Historical Society Museum in Topeka. HIS STORY IS OUR STORY, read the legend. Another sign left over from February advertised an annual Indian powwow. Marinas made liberal use of Lewis and Clark to rent canoes. Judging by the evidence, the trade in Native American souvenirs was brisk.

Cooke made a note to stop on the way back home and visit some of these attractions, sketchbook in hand. He was traveling through the kind of history that made the Chicago Fire look like a birthday candle.

Minutes later, traffic began to slow, then ground to a halt. An electric sign warned motorists of an accident up ahead.

An occasional horn made its desultory complaint. A couple in the sedan next to Cooke was having an argument, faces red, gesturing violently. After a while the conflict burned itself out in a gloom of tight-jawed silence.

Whenever there was a letup in the gridlock, it didn't last more than a few seconds, and the pace seldom topped five miles an hour. It took Cooke thirty minutes to travel a mile. He tuned in to a traffic report. Police officers were directing drivers to leave the freeway at the next exit. That ramp, he could see from hundreds of yards back, was jammed bumper-to-bumper. At this rate, Anne and her lover would be across the Colorado state line before Cooke extricated himself from the tangle.

While looking for a break to enter the right lane, he called Plevin, who acknowledged his report without offering a solution. Cooke guessed he was better at navigating the information superhighway than the real thing.

An ambulance streaked past on the left shoulder, whooping and bleating, all its lights in play.

Blue and red lights flashed up ahead, where by craning his neck Cooke saw a tractor-trailer rig lying on its side on the left shoulder, undercarriage exposed like a derailed toy locomotive. The obligatory gawkers slowed the process of escape to lockstep.

The exit was a mixing bowl of intersecting freeways and six-lane highways, both surface and exiting traffic almost at a standstill. Fast-food joints, convenience stores, strip malls, and a mammoth Walmart turned the outskirts of some unidentified suburb into self-contained cities.

An earsplitting chain reaction of honking came his way from up the block, where a stoplight seemed to have taken up permanent residence. An SUV maneuvering to change lanes screeched its brakes, nearly standing on its radiator grille. A pedestrian was racing across three lanes from a combination service station and Subway on that corner, zigzagging between cars: a woman, her black hair flying behind her, placing her hands on fenders for balance as she spun right and left heading straight toward the Toyota, her gaze fixed on that goal.

She was too far away and moving too fast for Dennis Cooke to see the color of her eyes, but he knew instinctively they were brushed silver with gold flecks in them.

CHAPTER 16

SHE GOT TO the car just as the light changed. A hand clawed at the door handle on the passenger's side. Her face bent to the window was drawn tight, the eyes white around the irises. She banged on the glass, working the handle at the same time with the other hand. The action prevented him from unlocking the door electronically from the master switches.

The cars ahead were beginning to move. He gestured frantically for her to stop tugging at the handle. Finally she understood. The lock released with a click. She yanked the door open and threw herself onto the seat.

Then he saw that someone else was just as determined to reach the car.

A thick-built man with sandy crew-cut hair bounded off the sidewalk in front of the service station, paused, bouncing on the balls of his feet to let a car slide past him, then resumed running, following the same serpentine route that Anne had. His face was red with exertion or rage or both. His brown leather windbreaker was unzipped, the sides flapping like wings.

The cars ahead were crossing the intersection at a glacial pace—piecemeal, like a train coupled with rubber bands. Cooke touched the accelerator, then the brake when the car directly in front of him stopped. The traffic light changed from green to yellow.

The sandy-haired man cleared the last hurdle and leapt for the Toyota, reaching for the door handle. Cooke hadn't relocked it. He stabbed at the switch and it clicked just as the man got hold. A wide palm with stubby fingers smacked at the window. Just then the car in front of Cooke crossed the intersection. He stamped on the pedal and followed just as the light turned red. In the rearview mirror, Crew Cut stood straddling the white line between lanes, staring at the Toyota. Then he turned back toward the service station, careful of the traffic now and zipping up his jacket as he went.

But Cooke had seen it spread open when he was running, and the butt of the handgun clipped to his belt.

A series of signs directed Cooke to the next entrance to I-70 West. Anne Plevin was breathing hard, staring straight ahead through the windshield. He thought he could hear her heart thudding; or was it his?

He'd passed two of the signs before he found his voice.

"Who—just who was that?" Although he was sure he knew the answer.

"I don't know. We weren't properly introduced." She took in air between words in great whistling gusts.

"He...kidnapped me...in the parking lot of the Kansas City Hilton. I rode...eighty miles in the trunk of...his car."

He braved a sidelong look. She was dressed as usual in yellow, a plain lemon-colored blouse with three-quarter sleeves, gray tailored slacks, and yellow platform heels. Her clothes were wrinkled and soiled, the shoes scuffed. One half of her shirttail was out. Her makeup was smeared and there were crumbs of grit in her hair.

"Was it an Impala?"

"Right, like I'm a car buff. He pulled up next to me and when I got out of the Lexus he grabbed me and threw me into the trunk. The lid was already open. It was a big trunk, almost kind of roomy. I guess I should be grateful for that."

"If he's driving an Impala his name is Philip Mapes. Todd thinks you were running off with him."

"What do you think?"

"Up until a few minutes ago I thought the same thing. I figured you told me that Reno story to throw me off and that Todd was right when he suspected you of cheating on him."

"And now?"

"I don't know. I just ran a red light to get away from a man with a gun. It put a crimp in my thinking process. Did he say why he kidnapped you?"

"I only heard him speak once, when I was fighting to break his hold. 'Stop squirming. Your hubby's too smart a businessman to pay for a dead pig in a poke.'"

"That sounds like a kidnapping all right."

"He pulled around behind a gas station, took me out of the trunk, and led me to the ladies' room; I guess he didn't want me peeing in his car. There was a window in the room, just big enough for me to squeeze through. I was making my way around to the front to get help when I saw you stopped at that light. That's when I made a break for it. I'm guessing you got hung up in that same traffic snarl that we did."

"This car's the closest thing to a plain brown wrapper on wheels. What made you so sure it was mine?"

"Any old Japanese car in a storm." There was a bitter smile in her voice. It was gone when she spoke again. "How do you know his name and what he's driving?"

"I got his plate number from the clerk at the Hilton," he said. "Plevin had a friend in the police run it. It's registered to Philip

Mapes. He says Mapes was his business partner." He gave her the rest: the embezzlement, the enforced surrender of his piece of Aspectus.

"So Todd thinks I'm shacking up with an old enemy out of spite."

"Maybe not. He says it was before your time and he never told you. So the spite seems to be Mapes's: you steal my half of the business, I steal your wife."

She was silent. He looked at her again. She nodded. "He'd think that, Todd would. That's what Todd would do if the situation were reversed." She drew another deep breath, let it out. But her breathing had returned to normal. "So what now, call the police?"

"No need."

He was looking in the mirror now. He saw the flashing lights first, then heard the siren.

She heard it, too, and turned to look out the back window. "But—"

He slowed down and pulled onto the shoulder.

"I've half-expected it ever since I nicked that light in town. I'm surprised it took them this long to catch up with me. Anyway, it saves us a—"

Two men in uniform approached the Toyota from both sides, drawing their side arms as they came. When they were even with the rear passenger windows, they went into a shooting stance, feet spread wide, pistols in both hands aimed at the pair in the front seat.

"Police! Freeze!"

The response seemed excessive for a mild traffic infraction.

CHAPTER 17

DENNIS COOKE HAD seen the action a thousand times, on *Cops, Law and Order, CSI*—every time, it seemed, he landed on a TV channel—but nothing could compare with being the one taken into custody.

Hands mangled his shoulders, threw him across the hood of the car hard enough to empty his lungs. Feet kicked apart, wrists yanked behind his back, cold steel clamped on wrists, ratcheted tight with a buzz. Hands tore his shirttail from his pants, smacked and groped ribs, hips, groin, thighs, ankles. Through a mist he saw Anne's distended face on the other side of the hood, caught in the same position.

"Wait!" he gasped. "There's some—"

"Shut up!" And in the next second the captives were being read their Miranda rights by both officers in a kind of roundelay. Cooke was conscious of cars slowing as they passed the scene, of curious eyes boring holes in his back.

Next they were manhandled into the rear of the patrol car and left waiting while a voice with no inflection in it spoke over the microphone in the front seat. Cooke could make nothing of the information being passed along. The wait was endless, brutal. He was afraid to look at Anne; if she was as terrified as he was, the sight of it on her face might send him over the edge.

The driver hung the microphone back on its hook and the car began moving, its mammoth engine throbbing. They swung with a sickening lurch into a hole in the congealing traffic, changed lanes suddenly, and slewed into an emergency crossover onto the eastbound, spitting bits of gravel from the median in what seemed unnecessary and dangerous haste. Why should they be in such a hurry after making their captives wait so long?

Some attempt had to be made. Cooke spoke up. "Officers, I want to report a kidnapping. This lady—"

"You can report whatever you like at the post," said the officer on the front passenger's side, without turning his head. "You're under arrest on suspicion of grand theft auto."

The state police post—at least when they were conducted inside—was a place entirely without drama. The wood-laminate floors and taupe-painted walls were clean and ceiling-mounted LEDs shed even light on every surface. Men and women in uniform manipulated computer keyboards with a whispering noise and no sign of interest in the newcomers.

Cooke and Anne were neither fingerprinted nor locked behind bars. They were steered through a maze of L-shaped passages, as in a medical office, where their cuffs were removed. This trooper, not one of the pair who had arrested them, told them to sit in plastic scoop chairs in a small clean room with a square cafeteria-style table bolted to the floor and left them alone.

"What's going on?" Anne said. They were the first words either had spoken since Cooke's exchange with the officer in the car. "Did you—?"

He shook his head. "I told you the truth about the Toyota. The registration's in my name, in the glove compartment. I suppose they'll tow it to an impound or whatever. They're sure to search it, find out the truth, and let us go. It's some mistake."

He spoke low; he had nothing to hide, but on the assumption they were being listened to, he was cautious as anyone whose conversation may not be private.

"Pretty coincidental, I'd say."

"Someone will come in to apologize, and then we can report the kidnapping."

Her smile was tight lipped. For the first time, tiny fissures marred the polished alabaster of her face. "It must be nice to have your confidence."

He had no response for that. To admit otherwise would be to make his fears too real.

An hour—maybe two—passed, and then they were real.

The door opened, startling them. They'd heard no footsteps approaching. Another officer, older than the others with chevrons on his sleeves, stood aside for his companion to enter. To them he said, "This man is a federal agent. He wants to ask you some questions."

The newcomer thanked him, nodded him out, and took a seat between them at a right angle. When he reached inside his brown leather windbreaker, an empty holster showed on his belt. He flipped open a folder, showing a gold shield and an ID card with his picture on it. It was two years old, but Philip Mapes hadn't aged noticeably since it was taken.

CHAPTER 18

ANNE PLEVIN SHRANK from the man, her fingers gripping the edge of the table hard enough to turn the knuckles yellow. Her eyes were open wide and her face had tightened, eradicating the tiny creases. Cooke diverted his gaze. Her terror was too contagious.

"We're not being eavesdropped on. I made sure of that. I checked my piece outside. That's routine during interrogations."

Mapes's tone was quiet, almost humorous. It didn't go with his crew cut or his thick-built military appearance.

Cooke wet his lips. "Just who are you?"

The other pocketed the folder. "What it says. And what Todd Plevin said, but only up to a point. It was my technical knowledge that turned Aspectus into a national concern. Without me, he'd be running a blog somewhere, maybe get a few thousand hits during his time off from some 7-Eleven. When we ended the association, I took my talents to Washington; they assigned me to the California office. I may not look it, but I'm a nerd for Uncle Sam, not a field agent. They don't put that on the credentials."

He turned toward Anne, and his tone changed. "I'm sorry I played rough. You made a monkey out of me, but I don't have a cop's instincts. I almost rooted for you when you left me standing in the middle of the street with my dick in my hand."

"You got my license number," Cooke said. "You knew when you ran it who I'm working for and that I didn't steal the car."

"I'm sorry about that, too," Mapes said, returning his attention to him. "It was the only foolproof way to catch up with you."

Anne's body was still rigid, but she spoke evenly. "When did federal agents start kidnapping private citizens?"

A bitter smile touched his lips, then vanished. "It's been going on longer than you'd think, but we won't go into that." He was still looking at Cooke. "I suppose Todd sang you his song of embezzlement, and how he forced me out in return for not prosecuting me."

Cooke said nothing.

"There was some truth in it. I did siphon off money from the corporate fund, but that was to prevent him from blowing it all on a pipe dream. When the government changed in Venezuela, he wanted to buy up the Communist Party's propaganda machine at a bargain price and expand his media empire into Latin America. I tried to talk him out of it—it was too risky, you never know when a foreign country will reverse itself and leave you—"

"—holding your dick." Anne's voice dripped venom.

"Damn straight. He wouldn't listen, so I transferred seven hundred and fifty grand to my own account.

"The rest you know. Yes, I acted illegally, but it was in the best interest of the firm. Turned out I was right, too. Six months later, the Communists were back in charge and they nationalized all the industries that other American companies had bought during the country's brief fling with capitalism. Had Aspectus been one of them, it would've been as dead as disco by the end of the year. Todd learned from their example and changed tactics, or he wouldn't still be in business. But he never forgave me for going behind his back. I returned the money, which I hadn't touched, and accepted his terms. Otherwise I'd never have been able to recover. For sure, the background check Washington made when I applied there would have turned up any legal action."

Someone knocked on the door. Mapes cast them both an anxious glance, but he called out an invitation. The officer with the chevrons opened up. "Sorry, Agent Mapes. We need the room in a few minutes."

"Give me five."

The other nodded and drew the door shut.

Cooke said, "Well, you landed on your feet. So why grab Plevin's wife and throw her into your trunk?"

Anne said, "You said you wanted Todd to pay to get me back."

Mapes's bottom teeth showed in a shark's grin. "It saved time. You were busy trying to kick me in the nuts." To Cooke: "Leverage, that's why. How do you think Plevin's managed to keep Aspectus afloat without me to guide it in the right direction?"

"You said yourself he changed his tactics."

"Exactly. He abandoned wild speculation for something more solid. Oh, he probably has a twenty-first-century term for how he makes most of his money—say, 'reverse PR professional.' His clients pay him vast sums to keep their names out of the public eye."

"What does that mean?" Cooke said.

"Blackmail. An old established enterprise too big to fail."

PART 5

Exit

CHAPTER 19

MAPES STOOD. FROM that angle, his stocky build showed only a slight layer of fat over muscle. Plainly he didn't spend all his time seated in front of a computer monitor. Cooke could easily picture him wrestling a struggling young woman in athletic condition into the trunk of a car, and he knew from observation that he hadn't exaggerated about the fight she'd put up.

They remained in their chairs. "What now?" she said.

"We go for a ride."

Cooke couldn't resist it. "One way?"

"Round trip. My beef isn't with either of you. You're just security."

Anne sat back, crossing her arms over her chest. "So I'm being kidnapped again, only this time with company."

"Not technically. I've got a couple of John Doe warrants. If you want to complicate things, there's a building full of cops outside who'll throw in with me." He smiled, not unkindly. "'Brothers in blue' is more than just alliteration."

Cooke rose. Anne hesitated, then uncrossed her arms and stood, ignoring the hand he offered.

At the front desk, Mapes accepted his side arm from the officer behind it. It was a blue steel semiautomatic with a checked walnut grip. He holstered it. The officer pushed a rectangle of paper toward Cooke. "Give this to the attendant at the impound, 15th and Madison. He'll have someone bring your car around. No fine."

The man gave no indication of curiosity at what had to have been an unusual turn of events, nor did he show signs of apology for the false arrest. That removed the last shred of doubt from the artist's mind that Mapes was impersonating a federal agent. He might be fooled, but not the pros.

Outside, the sun was resting on the rooftops. The state police post was on a busy street. Even tainted with auto exhaust, the air of freedom smelled sweet.

Semi-freedom, anyway.

An oyster-colored Impala was parked in the red zone reserved for police. Anne was right: the trunk that belonged to the wide-bodied car was big enough for a medium-size human to fit inside without cramping.

Mapes gripped Cooke's upper arm, firmly but not crushingly. "I'll take you to the impound after a little drive. Then it'll be up to you whether you throw in with me or move on. This is the second time I've committed a felony. I won't make it three."

"You already have," Anne said.

"I'm offering you both a lift, that's all. If you don't want it, the impound's a five-minute walk that way." He tipped his head up the block. "I passed it on the way here."

"I don't want it."

"I do," Cooke said.

She stared at him. He shrugged.

"It all sounds too screwy not to be real," he said. "I want to hear the rest. If you'll wait for me at the impound, I'll take you back to Kansas City and you can pick up your car."

"If you're still around to drive me." But she stared at the ground, lips pursed. Finally she looked up again. "You're right. At this point I'm more interested in seeing how this comes out than if I ever make it to Reno."

CHAPTER 20

DENNIS COOKE NEVER did learn the name of the Topeka suburb they were driving through. The string of National Savings and Loans, Midwest Auto Supplies, and Cosmopolitan Cleaners was unenlightening. The country had become so homogeneous you seldom saw a Terre Haute Hardware or a Kokomo Koin Laundry. Had Norman Rockwell lived another forty years, he'd have been at a loss for a homey subject to immortalize on canvas.

Then again, if there were identification signs, Cooke wouldn't have noticed them. He'd started out looking for a simple commission and wound up in a painting so surreal it made Dalí's melting clocks look like business as usual.

Philip Mapes drove casually, steering with one hand on the wheel, an elbow on the armrest. The Impala's motor made inconspicuous use of six cylinders, two more than the Corolla's; there was power in reserve. Cooke sat on the passenger's side in front, Anne in back behind Mapes. From time to time, Cooke turned his head her way. She never broke eye contact with the scenery sliding past her window, no expression evident in her clean profile. Somewhere along the line she'd found time to straighten herself out. She'd had nothing to freshen her makeup, but even so she could walk into any elegant restaurant in town without raising an eyebrow, apart from the admiring kind.

"Your turn, Michelangelo," Mapes said. "When I got your name from your license registration I looked up your site on my cell phone. You're pretty good, with Photoshop, anyway. Hard to tell these days."

"I don't use it. You'll have to take my word for that. I didn't bring along my portfolio."

"Don't get testy. I was just making conversation. If you're working for Plevin, how come you're not standing in front of an easel? Whatever else you can say about him, he doesn't waste talent sending it across country to pick up his dry cleaning."

Cooke told him about his interview in Chicago, the terms of his employment, and the trip as far as Kansas City, where Mapes had entered the—well, the picture. The agent was right; a man who regarded everything inside the composition of a work of art had no business running errands, much less playing Magnum, PI.

The only thing he left out was his talk with Anne in the hotel bar in Missouri. He deliberately avoided looking back at her to see how she was taking it. When he finished, he heard a small gush of air from in back. She'd been holding her breath.

Mapes drove a couple of blocks without speaking. Then: "What else?"

"That's it. You were there for the rest."

"I'm a book juggler, don't forget. I know when something's been left out." He glanced up at the rearview mirror. "You mentioned Reno back there. What was that about?"

"Just thinking out loud," Anne said after a moment. "I don't like the idea of sleeping with a crook. Reno's the remedy for that."

Cooke spoke up, desperate to break the flow of the discussion. "*Your* turn, Mapes. You can't just say Plevin's a blackmailer and leave it at that."

The agent frowned, but nodded. "Fair enough. His information machine is more than state-of-the-art. He digs up dirt on people who can afford to pay to sweep it under the rug and sells them advertising—I'm talking full page in his newspapers and magazines, pop-ups on the Net twenty-four seven, infomercials in prime time—premium stuff for what the traffic will bear, and these clients will bear plenty. He used to have a saying: 'It's what—'"

"'—you leave out that counts,'" Cooke finished. "He told me that in his office. I thought he was talking about white space in *America Now*."

"I suspected it when we were partners, but I had no way of proving it. Thanks to the surveillance equipment I now have at my disposal, I've got a paper trail. But I need more. I need proof: a witness, a second set of books, whatever it takes to swing an indictment for extortion, wire fraud, violation of the RICO law."

"Meaning me," Anne said. "Can't help you."

"Sure?" He smirked at the mirror.

"Positive. He doesn't discuss the money side of his business with former art directors and current wives."

"You know something, all right. You're not attending any medical convention in San Francisco and you're not stepping out on your husband. Lady, I don't care if you want out. If you've found out what he's been up to and can prove it—*then* I care. It'd spare me a lot of time and a hot seat in front of a board of review. Uncle Sam lets us bend the law if it's in his best interest, not for personal revenge on the part of one of his grunts."

"Pull over," she said.

They were passing a strip mall with a dollar store, a Subway, and a nail salon. Mapes turned into the parking lot and pulled into a spot at the far end, where the employees parked.

Something thudded in the rear of the car. Both men turned; Mapes twisted half around, resting his arm across the back of his seat. Anne had tipped up the door handle and thrown all her weight shoulder-first against the door. It was still shut tight. She collapsed against her cushion like a broken kite.

"You've got more spunk than smarts," Mapes said. "You should've known there's only one person in control of the locks in this car."

"You can't blame a girl for trying." She adjusted her position, feet flat on the floor, arms resting at her sides. "Okay."

"Okay what?"

"You can have what you want. That's why you snatched me in the first place, isn't it? To find out what I know and what I can prove."

"Give."

She flicked a glance at Cooke. As always her face was a sphinx. Back at Mapes. "Can't."

"Getting cold feet so soon?"

"No. I can't give you what I don't have. If you weren't in such a hurry back in Kansas City, you'd have given me time to grab my purse. Everything you're after is in a thingamajig no bigger than my little finger."

She looked at Cooke. The sphinx was gone. This was not the icy expression of a femme fatale, but of a woman capable of regret.

"I'm sorry I lied, Dennis, but it was only about the reason I want a divorce. I couldn't trust a stranger with the truth. Well, there aren't any strangers in this car. I can live with a man I don't love, but I draw the line at playing house with a slimy parasite. In any case Reno will have to wait until after we finish up back where we started."

Mapes turned back around and put the Impala in gear. "Kansas City, here we come."

CHAPTER 21

THEY DROVE TO the impound, where the attendant let them in to retrieve Cooke's luggage from the Toyota. Mapes carried the big suitcase. "You might have to pay for the extra storage time," he said.

Cooke looked at him. "You can kidnap a private citizen, but you can't fix a fine?"

"I better not push it. Al Capone bribed thousands of public officials and was responsible for at least fifty murders, but what did they get him for in the end? Tax evasion."

He hesitated before putting his overnighter in the Impala's trunk. The carpet covering the spare tire compartment was buckled, probably from Anne's struggles during her nightmare ride.

Mapes read his mind. To Anne: "Saying I'm sorry doesn't cut it. My bad all the way. I thought you'd have it in a safe deposit box or something: microfilm, CD-ROM, maybe even an old-fashioned ledger. I only took you as far as I did to scare you into giving it up."

She said, "*Now* who's got more spunk than smarts?"

They got back in the car and turned onto the business drive leading to the interstate. "Just what were you planning to do with the evidence?" the agent asked.

"I'm not sure: hold it hostage to keep Todd from raking me over the coals on the divorce, or make him clean up his act, or maybe even do the right thing and turn it over to the authorities. I had more than a thousand miles to sort it out. You can get a lot of thinking done on the road."

Cooke could attest to that.

Traffic was light after dark. There were no accidents this time, and apart from a brief stretch of construction there were no delays. Cooke woke once—surprised to discover he'd drifted off—and looked at Anne in the back seat. Events had worn on them both like forty-eight hours without rest. As the car passed from intervals of darkness to the light shed by the towering pole lamps across the shoulder, her sleeping face stuttered in and out of view. She looked more peaceful than he'd seen in all the time he'd known her.

All the time? How long had it been? Less than a day.

Time enough to fall in love.

The realization shocked him more than the brevity of their relationship. On some level he'd known ever since she'd joined him at the Hawthorn.

After an hour they saw the lights of Kansas City reflecting off the belly of the clouds. Anne was awake now, once again looking through her window at service stations and all-night stores forming light boxes in the dark, stacked rows of parked cars in the employee lots of factories with back-to-back shifts, traffic closing in on the Impala as they penetrated deeper into civilization.

The Hilton was a tall rectangle illuminated by ground-mounted floods. The lot was almost full. A snap-letter sign supported by tall posts—lit also from below—read:

WELCOME COUGARS

Mapes smirked. "Either there's a sports team in for a banquet or it's the annual convention of horny old ladies."

Anne's Lexus was where she'd left it; apparently the hotel's towing policy hadn't kicked in yet. A heavy dew had gathered on its surface in thousands of droplets that sparkled under the parking lot lights as if the car had been dipped in egg and milk and rolled in diamond dust. Cooke entered the image into his memory bank. *Watercolors,* he decided.

They found an open slot two cars down. "Good thing you waited long enough for me to put away my key," Anne said, getting out. She produced a fob from a pocket of her slacks.

Mapes stood sentry and Cooke shielded her from public view while she unlocked the car and leaned across the seat to drag over her purse. It was the clutch she'd had in the bar. She rummaged inside, hesitated—*or did she?*—when she came to a cocktail napkin with her face sketched on it, and took out—

—An e-cigarette. She slid it between her lips, inhaled nicotine mist, and blew it out her nostrils. "God, I needed that!" She looked at Cooke, grinned wide at his expression; he hadn't thought she was capable of showing that much joy. "Todd disapproves, too. He has clean habits."

He couldn't think how to react to that.

"Enough chit-chat," Mapes said. "Is it in there, or are you rehearsing an endorsement for cancer?"

She straightened, faced him—and pulled apart the e-cigarette, showing them what looked like the connection to a computer USB port in the end of the section containing the mouthpiece.

"Great-grandson of the flash drive," she said, "with a kicker: the mist passes through an outer sleeve. It makes no contact with the circuit board, which is tiny enough to lose under your fingernail."

"Plevin's IT genius," Dennis Cooke said.

She glanced quickly at the federal agent. "You didn't hear that from me. You either, Mapes. If things don't fall right, Todd will ruin him."

"You have my word. Who'd back me up anyway? If what you've got there is what you say, I won't need a witness."

"I knew about the homing device," she told Cooke. "He guessed what it was for when Todd had him install it. He'd already stumbled on this—what's in it, I mean." She reconnected the two sections. "Somebody at Aspectus had to have a conscience."

"Why didn't you ditch the homing device?" Mapes said.

"It's hard-wired into the electronics system. I'm not a technician, and I hadn't time. The plan was to get as far away from Todd as I could before he tumbled."

She thrust the small flash drive at Mapes with a flourish. He snatched it up with less grace and examined it. "Whose idea was it, yours or your alleged source?"

"My alleged source. I tell you, if the James Bond movies ever need another Q, they won't have to look beyond him. If Todd suspected I had more on my mind than adultery, he'd search my luggage and purse, might even take a puff on the cigarette." She shook her head. "Thanks to Q, he still thinks I'm a harlot."

"And I'm not wrong. There are all kinds of harlot, Anne."

This was a new voice, but a familiar one. All three turned toward a man standing just outside the glow of the nearest lamppost. A thin shard of light reflected off the barrel of the pistol in his hand.

CHAPTER 22

"TODD?"

It was Mapes who asked the question. Of all three, he'd gone the longest without hearing Todd Plevin's voice, but was the first to recognize it, unless Anne's silence was pure shock. Cooke had been so intent on their exchange, the sudden interruption from the shadows had shattered his faculties of reason.

"Hello, Phil. Put on weight."

Cooke found his voice. "How—?"

The pistol twitched. "One of the advantages of owning a jet and a private airstrip: no security. My pilot thinks I'm here to make an offer for the *Star-Ledger* and KABC-TV." He moved the gun Mapes's way. "Drop the piece, holster and all."

A second crawled past on its belly. They were alone in the lot at that hour. The only sound was the hum of traffic coming from the interstate.

Mapes reached toward the weapon clipped to his belt.

"Uh-uh!" Plevin barked. "It hasn't been so long I forgot you're a lefty."

The agent switched hands, freed the holster gingerly, using the thumb and forefinger of his right, and let it fall. To Cooke's ears, the thud might have belonged to a steel girder smashing to the pavement.

Mapes said, "What are you going to do, shoot us where we stand?"

"No need. All you have to do is fork over the butt." An empty palm slid out of the darkness, alongside the gun in his other hand.

"You're crazy!" Cooke said. "Don't you know this place has security cameras?"

"Not tonight. Your accomplice lost his nerve, Anne. After you pulled your disappearing act, I got suspicious. I figured there was only one reason you abandoned your car: you knew you were being tracked. At first I thought Cooke had tipped you off, but he wouldn't have the guts. The only reason these honest-to-a-fault guys are the way they are is because they don't have the nerve to step over the line."

Cooke flushed; but he couldn't have stirred to protest even if he weren't terrified of being shot. It was just possible the man was right.

"So it had to be the guy who developed the device in the first place," Plevin went on. "Figuring out the rest was easy. I told him I'd press charges against him for industrial espionage. Sharing trade secrets with outsiders is a twenty-year felony. He got off easy, though. All he had to do was disable the security system of the entire Hilton chain; did it all sitting on his can in front of a keyboard. They'll get it worked out by morning. Meanwhile, with the whole shebang off the grid nationally, no one's going to look too hard at this one."

"But you couldn't have him arrested without exposing yourself," Mapes said.

"He folded before he got that far in his thinking." Plevin tilted his empty hand in a gesture Cooke remembered; it was a signal of a man whose bluff was successful. "He's almost as gutless as Cooke. Not like you, Phil. I had to sell the idea of criminal prosecution hard to break through that thick skin of yours. It's no wonder you went into politics."

"I'm a federal agent, not a politician."

"You're all birds of a feather inside the Beltway. You looked good in that puff piece on the New Super Technology in Quantico; I googled you. Caught in your own net, you pinball wizard, you." The hand tilted the other direction. "The butt, darling wife."

"Choke on it, you son of a bitch!" She threw it at him.

Mapes started forward; a movement instantly aborted. Plevin had deftly caught the slim device with his free hand.

Then he stepped into the light. He was dressed casually as before, in a Bulls warmup jacket over a striped V-neck jersey and artfully wrinkled corduroys, pricey running shoes on his feet. The overhead lights made his eyes glow green. The effect was of a wild animal crouching to pounce. Cooke knew him then, this boy wonder of the electronics age, for a madman.

"You've got what you want," Mapes said. "Now go back to Chicago."

"Uh-uh. I can't run a business looking back over my shoulder all the time." Plevin put the flash drive in a slash pocket of the jacket, brought something out, and tossed it at him. Mapes caught it in both hands against his chest. It was a large roll of silver duct tape.

"Do Cooke first," Plevin said, "then Anne. Wrists and ankles. Make it good or when it comes my turn I'll tape you up so tight your hands and feet will turn black and fall off."

"Where are you going to put us?" said Anne.

"The others inside the car. You get the trunk."

Her face went white under the lights. Had Plevin guessed she'd spent most of the morning in a trunk?

"Step it up, Phil. Nights are getting shorter." What he said next froze Cooke to the bone. "Where we go next, we go in the dark."

Mapes started Cooke's way, tearing loose a strip of tape with a nasty sound. Cooke, broken, put out his hands.

"Go Cougars!"

A chorus of shrill voices.

Three people boiled out a door farther down the building: two boys and a girl, teenagers. The girl and one of the boys wore varsity sweaters, each with a big white letter sewn on the front, bordered in gold thread. The girl's sweater hung halfway down her thighs and the sleeves covered her hands. The other boy had on a grubby sweatshirt and his face was painted to look like a big cat's, whiskers and all. They stumbled onto the pavement, giggling. They smelled of beer for yards.

Startled, Plevin swung their direction, clapping the gun to his side.

Mapes's reflexes were faster this time. The tape fell to the asphalt and rolled. He dove for the pistol. But Plevin was already turning back. Anne stepped between them, an act of pure instinct.

Cooke snatched at his own shirt, his fist closing on something and he tore the pocket bringing it out. He swung hard, missed Plevin's arm as the gun came up. He followed through, felt the object in his hand sink deep into soft flesh.

Now it was Plevin's turn to shriek. Mapes got hold of the pistol and wrenched it free. The founder of Aspectus stood with his arms out from his sides, staring at the end of the sharp drawing pencil sticking from the spreading stain under his right arm.

CHAPTER 23

DENNIS COOKE WAS glad to see hotel security come running, both because the terror was over and because he was a lot more comfortable holding a brush than Plevin's nickel-plated semiautomatic pistol, which Mapes had given him after retrieving his own from the ground. Not that it was needed to guard their prisoner. Todd Plevin, held upright only by the wall of the hotel, breathed in sobbing gasps, one hand stalled halfway to the pencil protruding from his armpit, afraid to leave it where it was and just as afraid to pull it out.

It was Anne who addressed the guards first, summarizing what had happened in short, clipped sentences without going into background detail. When the police arrived ten minutes later, Mapes and Cooke told them the rest, each assigned his own officer for separate interrogation. Another interviewed the three Cougars. It amused Cooke to see them answering questions with their hands cupped over their mouths, as if that would staunch the odor of underage drinking.

A young man in uniform dropped the flash drive Mapes had given him into a Ziploc bag and put it in his pocket.

A policewoman trained in emergency medical services removed the pencil from Plevin's arm, tore away his shirtsleeve, and applied disinfectant and gauze while her partner read him his rights. Cooke knew a little something of what was going through the multimillionaire's mind while that was going on.

After a patrol car took him away in cuffs, Mapes, Anne, and Cooke repeated their names for the remaining officers, gave them their addresses, and agreed not to leave the area until further notice.

And then suddenly they were alone in the parking lot.

Anne Plevin stood close. Cooke was struck for the first time by how small she was. There was a lot of powder in that little charge of dynamite.

Mapes smiled at him. "That gives a whole new meaning to the phrase 'quick draw.'"

"I can't take all the credit. It was my best pencil. You're lucky to get a really good one in a whole box. Anyway I wouldn't have done it if I'd had time to think."

Anne smiled up at him. "The excuse made by every hero."

"He wasn't alone," Mapes told her. "You stepped between me and the gun." He stuck out his hand. "I'm sorry again to you both. I couldn't see any other way to handle it. 'Back channel,' they call it in Washington. 'Thirty days' suspension without pay,' they'll call it in the Sacramento office. But I'll get you that ride to Topeka."

"Don't bother." Cooke took the hand. "Let 'em sell the car at a police auction. I'll keep my own rust bucket and be glad to be driving something that won't remind me of this trip." He looked at Anne. "The bad part, anyway."

She smiled up at him inscrutably, as always. He wondered if Leonardo da Vinci had faced the same challenge in his Mona Lisa, and if he was ever satisfied he'd captured it.

"Think you can hold out here for a couple of days?" Mapes said. "I have things to work out with the police here before I go on to

Chicago and start the extradition process—if Uncle Sam doesn't hand the case to someone else. I can give you a lift home then, no matter what the decision."

Anne said, "Let me. I need to clear my things out of the house before the board of directors takes possession. Legally it belongs to Aspectus—Todd's idea, to get around taxes."

"As long as you're twisting my arm." Cooke's ears grew warm, that old familiar sensation.

Mapes shook both their hands and went back to his car.

Walking around to the hotel's front entrance, Cooke's hand brushed Anne's; she didn't shrink away. He started to speak, swallowed, said, "Should we get adjoining rooms or share one? I don't know about you, but I have to start thinking about a budget."

She stopped, looked up at him. "I'm afraid Vernon wouldn't approve of either."

He stared down at her. "Vernon?"

She nodded. "How do you think he knew it was my car Todd had him install that homing device in? He'd ridden in it often enough."

He stepped away. Their hands were no longer touching. Maybe they never had been. He'd only imagined it.

"So that was his name. Vernon. Plevin never said."

She met his gaze. Her eyes were no longer brushed silver. They were allover ice.

"Todd's distant, I told you that. It never occurred to him I didn't have to go all the way to California to have an affair."

He spent the night in a single room, didn't sleep.

At dawn he dressed. The phone rang as he was closing his overnighter. He didn't answer. He knew who it was.

It was early. He shared the lobby with a yawning desk clerk, no one else. The clerk called him a cab. Cooke told the driver to take him to the nearest car rental.

He drove straight through to Chicago, stopping only to relieve himself and gas up. The treasures of heartland history offered no appeal. Cities, counties, states swept past in a white blur. Recent events played across his windshield. So this was what they meant when they said a man's life flashed before his eyes in the moment of drowning. What they didn't say was that only the worst parts showed up.

He smacked the horn button hard. When the driver of the car in front of him made the natural hand gesture, he held up both his hands in apology. His palm continued to sting for miles.

He exited the interstate at first light, rolling through deserted streets, bleak as death; the perfect metaphor for his state of mind.

He parked beside his tired old car in the little lot behind his building. His key made a racket in the back door and again in the door of his apartment, but no one appeared to investigate the noise. He might have been the sole survivor of a nuclear war.

He stretched out fully clothed on his pull-down bed. If he slept at all, it brought no rest. With the sun plowing through the north window, traffic swishing past on the street, he got up, tore the unfinished canvas from his easel, and flung it into a corner, hard enough to splinter the wooden stretcher. He replaced it and painted feverishly, while the memory of his subject was still raw; painted until well past dark, when the gnawing in his gut reminded him he hadn't eaten in three days. He spread peanut butter on a slice of doubtful bread and ate it as he swept his brush in angry slashes with his other hand: back and forth, up and down, southwest to northeast and back. Gouts of red and black and yellow, yellow, yellow flew from the overloaded bristles, streaking his face and clothes like a butcher's apron.

It was finished by midnight, a personal best.

When the paint dried the next day, he sent it to the paperback publisher in a priority box. A sign belonging to a men's clothing store greeted him when he left the post office.

He wore his new suit to two interviews. Waiting for a callback, he finished three projects in a week: a charcoal sketch, an acrylic done entirely in monochrome, and a watercolor he didn't much care for and threw away.

The phone rang. It was the managing editor of the paperback firm. He'd almost forgotten about his submission.

"Mr. Cooke? Thank you for sending such a stunning example of your work. The savage emotion is palpable; our staff was really impressed. Um, we're not looking for abstract expression at this time—"

"I understand. Thanks for calling."

"—but," continued the other, before he could ring off, "as you know, we specialize in reprints: detective stories, Westerns, science fiction from the 1950s, before computers got involved. We're a small enterprise, but I think we can manage a decent salary for an art director, with benefits. Can I interest a talented expressionist in interviewing for the job?"

ABOUT THE AUTHORS

James Patterson is the world's bestselling author. Among his creations are Alex Cross, the Women's Murder Club, Michael Bennett, and Maximum Ride. His #1 bestselling nonfiction includes *Walk in My Combat Boots, Filthy Rich*, and his autobiography, *James Patterson by James Patterson*. He has collaborated on novels with Bill Clinton and Dolly Parton and has won an Edgar Award, nine Emmy Awards, and the National Humanities Medal.

Maxine Paetro is a novelist who has collaborated with James Patterson on the bestselling Women's Murder Club, Private, and Confessions series and on *Woman of God* and other stand-alone novels. She lives with her husband, John, in New York.

Andrew Bourelle is the author of the novel *Heavy Metal* and coauthor with James Patterson of *Texas Ranger*. His short stories have been published widely in literary magazines and fiction anthologies, including *The Best American Mystery Stories*.

Loren D. Estleman is the author of more than eighty novels, including the Amos Walker, Page Murdock, and Peter Macklin series. The winner of four Shamus Awards, five Spur Awards, and three Western Heritage Awards, he lives in Central Michigan with his wife, author Deborah Morgan.

JAMES
PATTERSON
RECOMMENDS

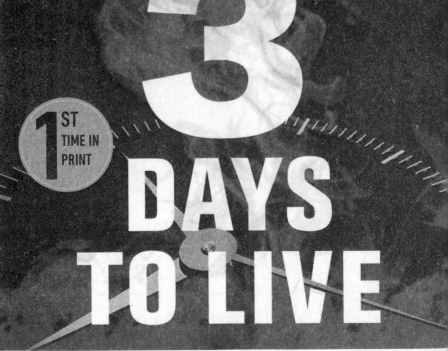

JAMES PATTERSON

3 DAYS TO LIVE

3 DAYS TO LIVE

How chilling is it to think that the closest people to you might be the most dangerous? And when the clock is ticking down, it's absolutely terrifying. Which is why I've brought you these three heart-pounding stories. A CIA-agent bride is on her European honeymoon when she and her husband are poisoned, leaving her seventy-two hours to take revenge. Next, when a deal goes bad on a tech executive in Washington, DC, he turns an order to kill his family into a chance to relive his military glory days. And finally, a Los Angeles doctor trusts her two housekeepers, but when she's murdered in a botched attempt to steal drugs, the pair of grifters vie to control their former employer's estate.

JAMES
PATTERSON

TRIPLE
HOMICIDE

TRIPLE HOMICIDE

I couldn't resist the opportunity to bring together my greatest detectives in three shocking thrillers. Alex Cross receives an anonymous call with a threat to set off deadly bombs in Washington, DC, and has to discover whether it's a cruel hoax or the real deal. But will he find the truth too late? And then, in possibly my most twisted Women's Murder Club mystery yet, Detective Lindsay Boxer investigates a dead lover and a wounded millionaire who was left for dead. Finally, I make things personal for Michael Bennett as someone attacks the Thanksgiving Day Parade directly in front of him and his family. Can he solve the mystery of the "holiday terror"?

PATTERSON

"No one gets this big
without amazing natural
storytelling talent—which
is what James Patterson
has, in spades."
—LEE CHILD

3 NEW
ELECTRIFYING
THRILLERS

THE MOORES
ARE MISSING

THE MOORES ARE MISSING

I've brought you three electrifying thrillers all in one book with this one. First, in "The Moores Are Missing," the Moore family just up and vanishes one day and no one knows why. Where have they gone? And why? Then, in "The Housewife," Maggie Denning jumps to investigate the murder of the woman next door, but she never imagined her own husband would be a suspect. And in "Absolute Zero," Special Forces vet Cody Thurston is framed for the murder of his friends and is on the run, but that won't stop him from completing one last mission: revenge. I'm telling you, you won't want to miss reading these shocking stories.

JAMES PATTERSON

THE HOUSE NEXT DOOR

THE HOUSE NEXT DOOR

The most terrifying danger is the one that lurks in plain sight; the one that is always there, but you don't notice it until it's too late. Here are three bone-chilling stories about exactly that.

In "The House Next Door," Laura Sherman is thrilled to have a new neighbor take an interest in her, but what happens when things go too far and aren't really as they seem? In "The Killer's Wife," six girls have gone missing and Detective McGrath will do anything to find them, even if that means getting too close with the suspect's wife. And finally, "We. Are. Not. Alone." proves that we aren't the only life in the universe, but what we didn't know is that they've been watching us....

JAMES PATTERSON

THE 13-MINUTE MURDER

The perfect murder takes only a few minutes.

THE 13-MINUTE MURDER

I've really turned up the speed with three time-racing thrill-ers in one book. In "Dead Man Running," psychiatrist Randall Beck is working against a ticking clock: he has an inoperable brain tumor. So he'll have to use his remaining time to save as many lives as he can. Then, in "113 Minutes," Molly Rourke's son has been murdered and she's determined to expose his murderer even as the clock ticks down. Never underestimate a mother's love. And finally, in "The 13-Minute Murder," Michael Ryan is offered a rich payout to assassinate a target, but it ends in a horrifying spectacle. And when his wife goes missing, the world's fastest hit man sets out for one last score: revenge. Every minute counts.

THE WORLD'S #1 BESTSELLING WRITER

JAMES PATTERSON

"No one gets
this big without amazing
natural storytelling talent—
which is what James Patterson
has, in spades." —Lee Child

THE FAMILY LAWYER

THE FAMILY LAWYER

The Family Lawyer combines three of my most pulse-pounding novels all in one book. There's Matthew Hovanes, who's living a parent's worst nightmare when his daughter is accused of bullying another girl into suicide. I test all of his attorney experience as he tries to clear his daughter's name and reveal the truth. Then there's Cheryl Mabern, who is one of my most brilliant detectives working for the NYPD. But does that brilliance help her when there's a calculating killer committing random murders? And finally, Dani Lawrence struggles with deciding whether to aid in an investigation that could put away her sister for the murder of her cheating husband. Or she can obstruct it by any means necessary.

For a complete list of books by
JAMES PATTERSON

VISIT
JamesPatterson.com

Follow James Patterson on Facebook
@JamesPatterson

Follow James Patterson on Twitter
@JP_Books

Follow James Patterson on Instagram
@jamespattersonbooks